W9-BZP-951

Praise for the Novels of the Darkyn

Night Lost

"Viehl continues to weave an intricate web of intrigue in this contribution to the amazing series. . . . I became completely engrossed in this compelling story. [She] had me hooked from the first page. . . . Exceptional . . . I definitely recommend this marvelous book."
—*Romance Junkies*

"Fast-paced and fully packed. [Viehl] does an excellent job of world-building and provides characters who continue to be explored book by book. You won't regret spending time in this darkly dangerous and romantic world!"   —*Romantic Times*

"[The] Darkyn tales have been some of the best romantic fantasies [in] recent years. . . . Fans of the series will agree that Lynn Viehl is at the top of her game."   —Harriet Klausner

Dark Need

"Thrilling. . . . What makes the Darkyn novels so compelling is the dichotomy of good and evil. *Dark Need* has a gritty realism and some frightening and creepy characters that will keep you awake late at night. Balancing the darkness is the searing heat and eroticism that is generated between Samantha and Lucan."
—*Vampire Genre*

continued . . .

Private Demon

"Lynn Viehl's vampire saga began spectacularly in *If Angels Burn*, and this second novel in the Darkyn series justifies the great beginning. Indeed, it is as splendid, if not more, than the first one."
                                          —Curled Up with a Good Book

"Strong . . . a tense multifaceted thriller. . . . Fans of Lori Handeland's Moon novels will want to read Lynn Viehl's delightful tale."
                                          —*Midwest Book Review*

If Angels Burn

"Erotic, darker than sin, and better than good chocolate."
                                          —Holly Lisle

"This exciting vampire romance is action-packed. . . . The story line contains terrific characters that make the Darkyn seem like a real species. . . . Lynn Viehl writes a fascinating paranormal tale that readers will appreciate with each bite and look forward to sequels."
                                          —The Best Reviews

EVERMORE

A NOVEL OF THE DARKYN

Lynn Viehl

A SIGNET ECLIPSE BOOK

SIGNET ECLIPSE
Published by New American Library, a division of
Penguin Group (USA) Inc., 375 Hudson Street,
New York, New York 10014, USA
Penguin Group (Canada), 90 Eglinton Avenue East, Suite 700, Toronto,
Ontario M4P 2Y3, Canada (a division of Pearson Penguin Canada Inc.)
Penguin Books Ltd., 80 Strand, London WC2R 0RL, England
Penguin Ireland, 25 St. Stephen's Green, Dublin 2,
Ireland (a division of Penguin Books Ltd.)
Penguin Group (Australia), 250 Camberwell Road, Camberwell, Victoria 3124,
Australia (a division of Pearson Australia Group Pty. Ltd.)
Penguin Books India Pvt. Ltd., 11 Community Centre, Panchsheel Park,
New Delhi - 110 017, India
Penguin Group (NZ), 67 Apollo Drive, Rosedale, North Shore 0632,
New Zealand (a division of Pearson New Zealand Ltd.)
Penguin Books (South Africa) (Pty.) Ltd., 24 Sturdee Avenue,
Rosebank, Johannesburg 2196, South Africa

Penguin Books Ltd., Registered Offices:
80 Strand, London WC2R 0RL, England

First published by Signet Eclipse, an imprint of New American Library,
a division of Penguin Group (USA) Inc.

First Printing, January 2008
10 9 8 7 6 5 4 3 2 1

Copyright © Sheila Kelly, 2008
All rights reserved

SIGNET ECLIPSE and logo are trademarks of Penguin Group (USA) Inc.

Printed in the United States of America

Without limiting the rights under copyright reserved above, no part of this publication
may be reproduced, stored in or introduced into a retrieval system, or transmitted, in
any form, or by any means (electronic, mechanical, photocopying, recording, or
otherwise), without the prior written permission of both the copyright owner and the
above publisher of this book.

PUBLISHER'S NOTE
This is a work of fiction. Names, characters, places, and incidents either are the
product of the author's imagination or are used fictitiously, and any resemblance to
actual persons, living or dead, business establishments, events, or locales is entirely
coincidental.
   The publisher does not have any control over and does not assume any
responsibility for author or third-party Web sites or their content.

If you purchased this book without a cover you should be aware that this book is stolen
property. It was reported as "unsold and destroyed" to the publisher and neither the
author nor the publisher has received any payment for this "stripped book."

The scanning, uploading, and distribution of this book via the Internet or via any other
means without the permission of the publisher is illegal and punishable by law. Please
purchase only authorized electronic editions, and do not participate in or encourage
electronic piracy of copyrighted materials. Your support of the author's rights is
appreciated.

This book is for Thelma Jean,
a girl who once cut off her hair,
dressed as a boy, and
called herself Steve.
She did all of the above
to get a job and feed her family
during the Great Depression.

I am very proud to be Steve's granddaughter.

How are we to live, my lord,
ever together, forever apart?
The night between us poised, a sword,
forged and edged in my cinder heart.
I cannot have you,
however much I long.
I cannot leave you,
this bond too strong.
Thus I go on as I have before,
burning in Eden, with you,
evermore.

—Jayr

Chapter 1

Travis Rayford got a boner watching the kid walk out of the nightclub.

Although the boy tried to hide how puny he was under his metallic brown bomber jacket, his tight leather pants gave it away—long bones with not much meat on them. He wore his hair, blacker than his would-be biker rags, shagged short around big shadowed eyes and full lips. Lips like that, Travis knew, felt like a wet O-ring around whatever they sucked.

Boy toy trying to pass for badass. Travis reached down to adjust his package. "Who is he?"

"I don't know his name, but I seen him around," Glen Garunchek, nicknamed Grunge for his Nirvana love and his laundry hatred, insisted. His left leg jiggled up and down, popping a bony knee in and out of a tear in his dirty jeans. "He works over at that castle place on Forty-six. You know, the one Cheryl makes me take her to allatime."

Thunder, mean and ugly, rumbled overhead.

"You talking about Burger Castle?" In the backseat of Travis's Charger, Dexter Morris looked up from his Nintendo DS to scowl. "Great. All the free fries we can score. Let's jump right on that, Trav."

"I mean the *castle* place," Grunge said, half turning to glare. "Over off I-Four, back in them woods out there by Lost Lake. You know, that place where they dress up, ride around on horses, and play at that King Arthur shit."

Dex swiveled toward the back window to check out the boy coming toward them. Rain plopped and beaded on the glass. "So the dude's some kinda *Lord of the Rings* freak." He flopped around and blew a disgusted breath over his forehead. "Whatever, man."

Travis checked the clock. Three hours until sunrise, and if he didn't score a couple hundred to make good on his back rent, he'd be sleeping on the couch in Dex's trailer for the next month. As much as he was tempted to ride all over the kid's pretty ass, he needed better pickings than a punked-out fembo with a suck-you mouth.

"Dex's right," he said finally. "He ain't gonna have no money on him."

"Gears up like he's loaded, don't he? You know that leather shit ain't cheap. Plus I know he can get more." Grunge sounded more than hopeful. "We only gotta grab him and make him take us in. He's got the fucking keys to the castle, man. Last time I took Cheryl there and we left right before they closed? I seen him locking up the cash office."

"What you gonna say to OPD when they catch us breaking into one of the attractions, pinhead?" Dex lifted his leg and kicked the back of the seat. He changed his voice to a falsetto version of Grunge's. " 'Good evening, Officer. Here are my balls. So how, exactly, would you like me to suck your dick for the next twenty years?' "

The drizzle outside became a steady, hard rain as Travis's neck tightened and his erection subsided. Ever since they'd rolled that swish in Daytona, Dex had been pushing it. He'd just passed the too-far mark.

"Pansy like you already knows how." Grunge forearmed a rim of beer and sweat from his upper lip. "Trav, the castle place is shutting down next week for a whole month. We wanna score, we gotta do him now."

"It's raining, man." Travis drained the last of the Bud from his own bottle. "You sure?"

"C'mon, I don't wanna get soaked for chump change," Dex argued.

Warren Ames snickered. The youngest of the four, he alternated between smoking a cigarette and picking at a wart, his namesake. "I think Dex's scared 'a that nance. 'Fraid he might fall in love."

"Suck my dick, Wart," Dex shot back.

"Y'all shut up—he's coming." Travis watched the tall, skinny boy pass by the Charger, glance back at the nightclub, and then at the watch around his wrist. He didn't look at them or even seem to care that he was getting wet, but Travis was more interested in the watch. He got a good, close look at it, and elbowed Grunge as soon as the kid walked on by. "Fucking-A, man. You see that? He's wearing a Rolex."

"A *got*-damn Rolex," Wart confirmed with a hoot.

"Told you." Grunge grinned. "So whaddaya say we go make friends?"

Stupid or crazy, Travis thought as he edged back into the doorway. No kid in his right mind would be walking alone in the rain in this part of Orlando at three a.m., not without a pit bull on the end of a flimsy chain. But there he was, pretty boy with a ten-thousand-dollar watch, strolling along like he owned downtown. Faggots like him deserved stomping.

And maybe, when they were done, Travis would take him home for the night. Show him what else he was good for.

"Aiight." Travis took his keys from the ignition and pocketed them. "We'll take him over there, by the med building. He's gotta walk between it and the back of the bank to get to the parking lot. Wart, you cut him off in front. Grunge, you and Dex come in from the sides." He pulled on his sparring gloves with quarters inserted in the knuckle pads. "I'll take him down from behind."

"Yeah." Grunge pogoed out of the car.

Travis looked through the rearview mirror at Dex, but waited until Wart climbed out before he asked, "You gonna sit back there and play with yourself all night?"

Dex switched off his DS. "I got a bad feeling about this, man. I know you need the money and all, but shit, you can crash at my place for a while."

The hair on the back of his neck bristled. "Yeah? Why? So you can watch me with your girlfriend?"

His gaze slid to one side. "She'd be okay with you."

"The fuck? You got something to say to me?" Travis reached across the seat and hauled his friend to within an inch of his face. "Pull your dick out of your mouth and fucking *say* it."

"You're losing it again, Trav," Dex shot back, his mouth

tight, his eyes afraid. "Like you did in Daytona. I don't want no more of that shit, man. I don't need it."

Travis saw Wart and Grunge peering in through the rain-spattered windows at them and smiled as he released Dex. "Chill, dawg. It don't have to go down that way."

"Way you are about . . ." Dex shook his head. "I don't want no part this time, Travis. Bad enough I know what you did."

"It ain't happening like that." As Travis did his sincere thing, he imagined both the faggot and Dex facedown on his bedroom floor, wrists and mouths covered with duct tape. "I swear, man, you're getting so paranoid. I'm here for the money; that's all."

Dex wavered. "The money."

"Yeah." Doing the two of them would take a couple of days, but the Charger had a big trunk, and Travis had plenty of time. "C'mon, before he gets away."

Dex got out and, after a long look at Travis, trotted off to get ahead of the kid. Wart and Grunge split off, walking rapidly in opposite directions, shoulders rounded against the rain. That left Travis to take one last look around. He spotted a couple of men walking out of the nightclub: one tall nance and a mother-fucking hulk of a guy in a weird-looking hoodie. Both turned and headed toward the med building.

"Shit." The rain and thunder were getting too loud for him to shout for the guys. Travis thought about jumping back in the Charger and gunning it, but he had to score tonight, or lose his place. He reached in, popped open the glove box and took out the .38, stuffing it down the front of his cargo shorts to keep it dry, and took off.

The kid had already rounded the corner of the med building by the time Travis caught up with his boys. From behind, the kid looked taller and tougher, long muscles playing under the leather pants as he walked. The bomber jacket didn't cover the kid's beautiful little ass, and above the collar the back of his neck gleamed white under a soft fringe of black hair. The rain hadn't washed away the trail of cologne he left behind him; it smelled sweet and spicy, like the funnel-cake-and-corn-dog stands at carnivals.

Travis's cock stiffened under the damp fly of his shorts as he imagined biting into that slim nape and tasting the kid's hot blood. He'd bet it would taste like the little faggot smelled.

He stayed back, far enough to appreciate the guys in action. Dex stepped out in front of the kid, his plastered clothes dripping.

"Hey, homes," Dex called out. "Going somewhere?"

The kid stopped in his tracks but didn't answer. He turned his head, first one way and then the other, as Wart and Grunge came at him from each side.

"Not this way," Wart taunted.

Grunge moved in. "You work at the castle place, right? I seen you there."

The kid turned to find Travis only a few feet behind him. He didn't look surprised, only impatient—or maybe annoyed.

"Hold up, hoss." Travis flexed his fingers before knotting them into fists and planting his feet as best he could on the wet, slippery pavement. Some bums in one of the vacant buildings nearby must have lit a fire, because the air suddenly turned warm and smoky. "You look like you're lost."

"I am fine." The kid had a low, smooth voice that didn't match his raindrop-spangled eyes. The eyes—dark but not black—he could see something in them . . .

"Trav." Dex looked past him. "Somebody's coming."

"Shut it." Travis ignored the approaching footsteps sloshing through the puddles, and the carnival smell of sweet-spicy smoke. "C'mon, kid. You don't have to walk home in the rain. We'll give you a ride."

The kid turned in a circle, checking out the guys before saying to Travis, "I think not." He took something out of his pocket—a black chopstick?—and held it loosely at his side. "Go home, boys. Immediately."

Travis felt a bizarre urge to do just that: turn and run as fast as he could back to the Charger. He saw Dex frown and Wart and Grunge actually take a step back, and then a sudden gust of wind swirled around them, slapping their faces with cold, wet force.

The fresh air cleared the alien fear out of Travis's head, setting a Rottweiler of rage in its place. Be a cold fucking day in hell before Travis Bodeen Rayford turned tail and ran away from a swish.

He pulled out the .38 and leveled it at the kid. "I said, let's go for a ride."

The kid extended his arm, and the black chopstick shot out on both ends, making itself into a pole. "No."

Dex came up behind the kid, his arms open and ready to take hold of him. Only, when Dex grabbed, he got nothing but an armful of air, and skidded on his heels.

The kid disappeared into a streak of dark air.

"Where'd he . . ." Something made Dex's face blur behind a bronze streak.

Metal whip-whistled, water hissed, and what sounded like high-pitched thunder snarled. Dex flew straight up into the air, soaring four feet off the ground before curling over and dropping to the ground with a loud grunt. He tried to push himself up, groaned, and collapsed so hard his clothes farted air and rainwater.

Grunge swore as he ran toward Travis, snatching at the blur of bronze darting between them. Travis blinked, heard the whip of metal again, and thought he saw the kid's long stick slash down. Then Grunge did a perfect backflip into a delivery door, cracking wood as he hit it and slid down into an oil-stained puddle. Wart shrieked and tried to scramble out of the way, his worn sneakers splashing.

The bronze streak solidified into the kid and looked at Travis. "Go home, now."

"Jayr," a deep, pissed-off voice called out.

Travis glanced back, squinting against the rain to see the nance and the hulk cutting him off. He aimed at the ground in front of them and squeezed off two rounds, taking pleasure in the sharp echoes of the shots. "Get the fuck out."

The hulk started forward, but his nance buddy put a hand on his shoulder, as if to hold him back.

"Go on, get." Travis held the gun on them until the nance practically dragged the hulk around the corner. Confident they wouldn't be back, he swung his arm around and aimed at the kid standing between him and Wart. "Drop the rod, faggot."

The kid flipped the stick over the back of his hand, snapping it until, presto-change-o, it shrank back to chopstick length.

"If you shoot at me," he said as he tucked it back into his jacket, "you will only harm your friend."

Travis ran a sleeve across his wet face to clear his eyes before he laughed. "Right." He adjusted his aim for the boy's arm and squeezed the trigger.

A white-and-bronze flash cut the air in front of Travis's face; then what felt like a two-by-four slammed into his gun, knocking it out of his hand. The .38 discharged into the front of the med building, shattering and collapsing a six-by-six-foot glass panel before the gun landed on Grunge's chest.

A tripped security alarm siren began to wail, high and strident against the bass tremors of thunder.

Travis shoved his hand into the blur and caught the kid's jacket, jerking him to a stop. Steam rose from the bronze jacket, and his hold tore open the boy's wet shirt. That was when he saw something that shouldn't have been there. "Shit. You're a—"

Wart came up from behind and pinned the kid between the two of them.

That should have been it, game over, only his feet weren't touching the ground and he was flipping, head over heels. He saw Wart beside him, wheeling his arms and legs, and then the ground rushed up at his face.

They slid together across the storm-soaked ground for what seemed like a mile or better. Travis spit out a mouthful of blood and dirty rainwater, and lifted his head to see two pairs of wet boots stop in front of his nose.

"Young jackals," the nance said in James Bond's voice. "Are there no constables in this city?"

The hulk answered, sounding exactly like that Scottish dude from *Highlander*. "Aye, and they'll be coming."

Pain and fear and movie-star voices couldn't dent Travis's amazement. Not after that kid.

"Ain't right," he told the boots. No one had ever busted him up like this, and surely not . . . "This ain't right."

"The way is clear now, my lord," the kid who wasn't a swish at all said somewhere above him. "We should hurry."

One of the boots drew back, making Travis peer up at the hulk, whose hoodie had fallen back over long bloodred hair and a face full of savage, dark blue tats. "She your bitch, man?"

"Aye." The boot came rushing forward, as unstoppable as the rain. "She's mine."

As Aedan mac Byrne and Robin of Locksley sat in the back of the limousine and discussed the business of suzerains, Byrne's seneschal, Jayr, surreptitiously checked her damp garments for damage. The human had torn the front of her shirt, but her leathers appeared intact. The rain had been a minor godsend.

It had been a ridiculous encounter. She had not anticipated the attack by the four human males outside the nightclub, and as a result had reacted with more speed and force than had been strictly necessary. Still, she had disabled the four and protected her lord and his guest.

The latter, as always, remained her primary duty as Aedan mac Byrne's seneschal.

"Four to one, Jayr. You should have summoned me." Her second, Harlech, tapped the wireless phone headset he wore clipped to his belt. His talent, a form of acute hearing, allowed him to pick up sounds beyond the range of most Kyn and all humans. "Is that not why I wear this contraption when I drive the limousine?"

Since Jayr preferred to keep their human staff to a minimum, she had persuaded Harlech to serve as Byrne's driver. He had no difficulty operating a modern vehicle, but more important, he possessed more battle experience than most of the warriors in the *jardin*. His cool head under pressure and ability to flawlessly assess any threat had proven valuable to Jayr more than once.

She also liked his scent, like that of white carnations, which tinged the air inside the limo without being overpowering.

"It happened too fast." Jayr ran a hand through her wet hair. "They were but children. I should have smelled their approach."

"After a night breathing in this city's stink, and all that rain on top of it?" Harlech sniffed. "I can hardly smell myself."

Jayr had advised against this trip into the city; there re-

mained so much yet to be done in preparation for the annual
tournament that she could hardly spare the time. Byrne had
been determined to escape the Realm, however, and for her to
refuse to go or send another in her place was unthinkable. She
trusted no one to guard Byrne except herself.

Her conscience sullenly corrected her. *More that you would
not risk being usurped from your place at his side.*

Jayr checked the rearview mirror again, this time for her
own gratification. To look upon Byrne strengthened her resolve; she had done her best to serve him well these past six
centuries. Had he wished to discard her in favor of another, he
would have done so long before this night. That she could hold
fast to. That sustained her when nothing else would.

Serving him was all she could have.

As for her feelings, she had fought discontent and longing
until both subsided into a nameless thing that plagued her only
when she was alone. It made her write pages upon pages of
ridiculous poetry that she ended up consigning to the fireplace.
She should have done the same with her sketches, but they were
harder to destroy.

Burning them would be like burning him.

Fortunately she spent most of her hours with or near her
master. Fear of failure refused to abandon her, but it had become a second master, driving her daily to perform her duties
as flawlessly as possible. Perhaps in another seven hundred
years she would at last relax and accept that no one could care
for the master of Knight's Realm as well as she.

Perhaps by then her passion for him would age into something safer and more manageable.

In the mirror Jayr saw her master finish his conversation and
turn to stare at the paling horizon. He did not appear unhappy
or angered by the events of the night, but Byrne rarely put his
emotions on display. Were he displeased, he would not admon-
ish her in front of the men, but would wait until they were alone
to take her to task.

Locksley caught her watching and winked.

Jayr smiled. She liked Robin of Locksley. The suzerain of
the Atlanta *jardin*, he made frequent visits to the Realm that
were enjoyed by everyone, Kyn or mortal. Byrne often

grumbled that there was no tangle that Rob's talent couldn't un-knot for him, but Jayr knew better. Locksley's good humor and sense of fun made him legendary; it was said that even when he was human, the man could coax laughter out of a stone.

When that stone was Jayr's master, all the better. Byrne's melancholy had been particularly noticeable of late. It plagued her that she, who knew all of his dark moods and how best to assuage them, could not fathom the cause.

"If you mean to sit and brood in silence all night, I'll switch on the radio," Harlech warned. "I'm developing an abiding fondness for countrified music."

"Country music," Jayr corrected. "I cannot tolerate it. The bards all sound as if they are drowning in their cups. Or drowning their lovers in their tears."

"That," Harlech told her, "is the best part. You should listen to Faith Hill." He sighed. "I vow, for a human female she looks like a goddess, and sings as an angel fallen to earth would."

"Indeed." Jayr eyed him. "I will have to ask Viviana her opinion."

Her invocation of his wife's name made Harlech shudder. "Well, perhaps not quite so divine. In fact, now that I think on it, she has an odd-shaped nose."

She nodded. "Keep thinking that, my friend. Are the men ready for the tournament?"

"Most are," Harlech replied. "Kirel wishes to challenge Silesia over rights to hunting territory. It seems they cannot am-icably share the parcel you allocated to them."

"I should make them live on bagged blood for the rest of the winter; that would settle the matter." They would have to dur-ing the tournament, as no humans would be permitted inside the Realm. She thought for a minute. "I will speak to Kirel on the morrow."

The warrior nodded. "You might also wish to look in on Rainer. He has been conspicuous in his absence from the lists. I think that arm of his that Beaumaris broke during their last skirmish did not heal soundly."

Jayr often tended to the men's minor injuries, but Rainer hadn't come to her recently for any sort of hurt. "If the bone has mended crooked, his arm will never work properly. Why did Beaumaris break it?"

"You know Rainer. He was throwing daggers blindfolded, showing off for some human. Beau took a blade in the side and came after him. Farlae dragged him off Rain while I saw to the humans." Harlech's mouth curled into a sour twist. "If the arm wants breaking again, I'd be pleased to see to it."

A hand rapped on the window behind them, and Jayr turned, lowering the glass divider between her and Locksley. "My lord?"

"You must be slowing down, Jayr." His long fingers tapped the top of her shoulder. "Your jacket is torn."

Jayr tucked in her chin to inspect the narrow burn mark scoring the bronze leather. "So it is." She reached inside the jacket to check her shoulder, which bore no wound, and felt something caught in a fold of her sodden shirt. She took out and looked at a flattened slug. "The last bullet must have ricocheted."

Byrne turned his head away from the window to eye the slug. His expression remained composed, but the pupils in his eyes contracted to vertical slivers, and the blue-black irises took on a diffused glow, one of candlelight shining through a goblet of burgundy. "You were shot and you dinnae say a word?"

"I am not injured, my lord."

Byrne's flash of displeasure roused something similar in Jayr's own breast, an immense frustration with him that she had no intention of indulging. Byrne had every right to be annoyed with her for nearly leading him and Lord Locksley into an ambush. That she had issued advice against this trip into the city meant nothing. Her duty was to serve, not to chastise.

It would be gratifying, a snide corner of her heart said, *if he would but occasionally listen to me.*

Jayr went to remove the embarrassing jacket, remembered the torn condition of her shirt, and instead pulled up the front zipper. The offending slug she pocketed. "Forgive me. I will change as soon as we return to the Realm."

Byrne looked as if he might say more, then nodded and went back to contemplating the passing streetlights.

"I should not have mentioned it." Locksley sounded rueful

now. "It is only that I have coveted that particular jacket for months, and planned to filch it from your wardrobe. Where did you get it?"

"Farlae, the keeper of the wardrobe, makes all of our garments," Jayr said. "I can have him measure you. He will have a duplicate made by the end of the week."

"What, and further tarnish my dusty reputation?" His amethyst eyes, over which many a maiden had sighed, twinkled. "Never."

The suzerain's jesting did not provoke a response from Byrne as it usually did, another sign of her master's growing discontent. Jayr would have to see to it that the tournament went without incident. Then, too, Byrne had gone many weeks without proper companionship. Although Jayr hated that part of her duties as nothing else, she would procure some human females to entertain him before their staff was sent on leave. Perhaps two or three of the women he liked best would help dispel this strange, bleak mood of his.

Something had to.

Chapter 2

Aedan mac Byrne had lived longer, fought harder, and spilled more blood than a hundred mortal men. He had brawled his way through human life as laird of the mac Byrnes, and then clawed a path from the grave to aid his human liege lord in driving the English out of their homeland for the last time.

"My Highland demon," Robert the Brus had said, smearing blood from one of his wounds across Byrne's brow. "You met this day with honor and bravery."

The king of the Scots would die never knowing that on that glorious day on Bannockburn, when the English were soundly thrashed by an army half the size of their own, the laird mac Byrne had preserved his own worthless hide by destroying the life of an innocent.

Jayr's life, offered to save his own.

That she had given herself to him freely made no difference, Byrne knew. By taking her and changing her from human to Kyn, he had cursed her soul as wholly and completely as he had his own.

Byrne had tried to do penance for the terrible price she had paid for him. From that day forth he had sought a life of peace. Resisting the lure of battle had not been a simple thing, for it was the only trade he had known, and the only place where his affliction had proven of any value. But for Jayr's sake he had resisted, beating it back until the urges dwindled and subsided.

Or so Byrne had believed.

During the *jardin* wars, Richard had made Byrne one of his generals at the front, doubtless hoping to wield him like a club to smash the suzerain who had refused to unite under the high

lord. It had been the first test of Byrne's control over his affliction, and he had won, keeping a level head even in the midst of
the worst fighting.

Many years later, when Byrne left Scotland and the slaugh-
terhouse of memories behind for the promise of a new life in
America, his newfound iron control had persuaded Richard to
raise him above the ranks of the warrior Kyn. As an American
suzerain, Byrne was given rule and responsibility over more
than three thousand of his kind who had already settled in the
colonies. Here, too, he had been obliged to fight occasionally
for what was his, but he had taken up the sword as a man, not a
monster.

His victory over his affliction had seemed complete, but
Byrne knew that what lurked inside his soul would never leave
him. Nothing could destroy the sleeping horror.

Something, however, had reawakened it.

This night he removed his sword belt, tossing it aside as he
basked in the circle of heat from his fireplace. Knight's Realm,
the small kingdom he had made to serve and protect the Kyn,
had all the benefits of modern heating and cooling, but none
reached his rooms. He had ordered his architects to leave his
private chambers as they would have been in his human lifetime: cells of bare, cold stone illuminated only by log fire,
torch, and candlelight.

Not much more than the priest's cell in which he had spent
years praying for mercy from a God gone deaf.

"My lord."

The sweet-spicy scent of tansy accompanied Jayr as she entered his chamber. Her fragrance blended easily with his own,
and chased the tension from his frame.

"Jayr." It had been an hour since they had returned from the
city—too long for her to spend changing her clothing. Had she
forgotten what night this was? "What kept you?"

"I thought I should first see to Lord Locksley's comfort."
She picked up his belt and sword and stowed them on his
weapons rack.

He watched her, noting the dry shirt and the fitted harness of
pistols and blades she wore strapped over it. He could not remember the last time he had seen her unarmed.

No, the God's truth of it was that he could. He simply would not allow himself to think on that day, when fate and all its clever demons had well and truly cursed him.

Byrne watched her work. "Is Rob satisfied with his comforts?"

"He claimed he is, my lord. He talked a great deal about the tournament as well, and these new Kyn coming over from Europe." Jayr went to the corner cabinets and prepared a goblet of bloodwine. "I should not have stayed so long with him. You must be thirsty."

Aye, he was. Would that he were still human and could still drink himself into a stupor. One of the larger annoyances of being an immortal was that the only manner in which he could become intoxicated required him to enrapture and drain a human. The result would keep him trapped and rendered senseless by blood thrall for days, but the Kyn no longer killed mortals.

Yet tonight he had nearly torn four boys to pieces.

"My thanks." As he accepted the goblet Jayr brought to him, he noticed she still wore the oval device on her ear that allowed her to take calls from the telephone and speak to others within the Realm. "Must you have that thing stuck to your head all the night and day?"

"Only during the time of the tournament." Accustomed to his dislike of electronics, she reached up and removed the clip, thumbed a switch on its side, and dropped it into her right hip pocket.

Byrne knew he was being unreasonable—Jayr was in charge of his household, and so had to field all types of communications—but he considered most of the technological advances of humankind little better than the bubonic plague. Those used to make modern weapons slaughtered without discrimination; the industrial revolution had done much to foul the earth. Combustion engines had turned the air to filth; factories had done the same, as well as poisoning the land and water. Even the small electronic devices Jayr relied on seemed insulting to Byrne. It irked him enough that he had to make use of the telephone to speak with other Kyn lords instead of resorting to the couriers and diplomats of old.

Byrne would have nothing to do with these wireless devices, however. If he wished to speak to one of his own men, he would bloody well do it face-to-face, not through some toy that hung from his ear.

"Harlech mentioned that Rainer has been absent from the lists," Jayr said as she wiped down his sword with a lightly oiled rag before returning it to its scabbard.

Byrne recalled the fight he had seen Farlae break up between the man and Beaumaris. "The arm, then?"

She nodded. "I will do what I can, but if the bone has set wrong, I will have to summon a leech from the city."

"Have Farlae help you; Rain will do as he says." Byrne knew his seneschal had a deft touch when it came to most of the minor injuries his men sustained in training, but even her talents were limited. A shame they did not have a Kyn trained in the healing arts, as Cyprien did. Although his leech *sygkenis* had caused more trouble than Byrne thought she was worth, she could be trusted to hold her tongue. Locksley claimed she had even found a potion to reverse the effects of Richard's changeling disease.

A shaft of light from the long, narrow eyelet of his window made Byrne squint. "Dawn already. Wake me an hour before sunset, Jayr. Rob rarely sleeps the day through, and there are matters we should discuss before the others arrive."

"I will." She came to him and knelt between his thighs to remove his boots. "I would apologize for what happened tonight, my lord."

He raised his brows. "For seeing to Rob and listening to him natter on? I should thank you. My ears needed the respite."

"I meant my carelessness in the city." All the softness vanished from her voice. "I allowed myself to become distracted by the weather and did not sense the humans until they surrounded me." Her mouth twisted briefly. "It will not happen again."

Byrne studied her face. Her grave features gave nothing away, but he knew her moods better than his own. He never had to chastise her for a mistake, for she punished herself more harshly than any master could—even when she was not in the wrong.

"We should not have gone there in the first place," he told her. "You were right to advise me against visiting the city at so late an hour."

"I should have anticipated the attack by the humans," she insisted. "I did not pick up their scent in the rain. Even if I had"— she made an uncertain gesture—"I might have dismissed it."

"They thought you a lad alone, with no one to look after you." Byrne could still feel Rob's grip on his shoulder as he had pulled him back out of the alley. Somehow his friend had sensed what had flared inside Byrne, straining and clawing to be released. At least he did not have to explain to Jayr why he had not stepped in to put a stop to the attack. She knew better than anyone how sudden, unexpected violence summoned the thing inside him. "Next time have Harlech or one of the men accompany us."

She stiffened for a moment. "They were but boys, my lord. Well within my abilities to disarm."

"I know that, lass." How prickly she could be, even after all these years. He watched the firelight chase itself through the short strands of her dark hair, threading it with glints of amber and topaz. "Where did you put Rob this time?"

"Lord Locksley requested his usual chamber by the west practice range. I arranged a warm bath and a willing maid to scrub his back." Jayr set his boots to one side, and her gaze shifted to the window. "It is the last night of the full moon, my lord."

Was that resolve in her voice, or resignation?

"I forgot." How quickly he lied to her. Yet he could never tell his seneschal how impatiently he waited for this night each month, counting the weeks and days and, sometimes, the hours. Knowing this was the night of renewal, he had felt his *dents acérées* emerge fully from the moment she had entered his chamber.

Byrne took the hand Jayr offered, feeling the slight weight of the other she placed against his left thigh. Renewing the bond between a Kyn lord and his seneschal required a brief, largely ceremonial exchange of blood once during each moon cycle. Some lords had abandoned the archaic custom altogether, but Byrne would not.

This monthly concord, this communion, this one selfish thing he would have with her.

Byrne brought her hand to his mouth. As ever, the desire to drive his teeth into it pummeled him from the inside. He instead gently scored her palm with only the very tips of his fangs. Her skin, as cool and resilient as his own, parted for him. Only a few drops of her blood escaped before the scratches healed over, but they were enough.

As ever, the slightest taste of her blood made his head spin.

Jayr's voice stirred his hair as she repeated her oath of loyalty to him. "I willingly undergo everything for you, my lord, and will serve as your seneschal for all the days of my life."

Byrne took his mouth from her palm but didn't utter the usual reply or offer her his wrist. He didn't want it to end so quickly this time. This might well be their last exchange.

Until he left, she was his.

Jayr stared up at him. Expanding rings of violet lightened the sienna of her eyes, and the set of her mouth told him that her fangs had extended fully. Before he could see shame in her face, before he could think, he picked her up and set her on his thigh.

Jayr sat rigid in the circle of his arm. "My lord?"

"Stay." Byrne tore at the leather lacing below his collar, opening it. When she didn't accept his offering, he cupped the back of her head with his hand and brought her face to his throat. Her full lips pressed against his flesh, but she still did not use her teeth on him. "Open your mouth."

The soft heat of her breath scalded him as she obeyed, and as soon as he felt the sharp tips of her fangs he pressed her face against him, forcing her to bite into his throat.

"I accept you as my seneschal," he muttered as he held her there, his blood flowing into her mouth, "and give you service, honor, and the protection of my house."

Jayr made a low sound that moved over his skin before she reluctantly sucked at the wounds. The light, exquisite pressure of her feeding inched down his chest and belly, teasing and tightening everything in its path. In that moment, Byrne would have given her every drop of blood in his cursed veins, if only to hold her a little longer.

Fingertips touched his chest; a square palm settled against it. Her scent sharpened and darkened, dragging at him. His chest burned as he fought a swelling, roiling compulsion to claw away her garments and fill his hands with her flesh. As she lifted her mouth from the bite wounds they healed over, and his arms, dull and heavy, dropped away from her.

Jayr eased onto her feet and picked up his boots, carrying them over to the foot of his bed. She remained there, her back to him as she turned down the coverlet and linens.

"Lord Locksley mentioned something about not competing in the archery contest this year." How normal she sounded. "So that others might have a chance at the prize."

"'Tis the only way they will." He saw her rearranging his pillows for his comfort and knew her touch would leave behind the scent of tansy. It had become the only thing that would lull him into the curious sleep of their kind. When she passed within his reach on her way to the woodbox, he almost pulled her back to him. His self-control would not last another minute. "Never mind the fire; I'm warm enough. Go to bed now, lass."

Without him. Alone. Where he should have sent her hours ago.

She started for the door, but halted and regarded him in an uncertain manner. "Forgive me, my lord, but is there something amiss?"

"Here?" Everything. Did she feel nothing when he touched her? "No."

"I meant, has something been troubling you? You seem so"—she searched for the words—"preoccupied of late."

"We have one final performance to give to the humans before several hundred Kyn descend on our household," he reminded her. "Some will be these newcomers from France and Italy. They willnae know how we do things here."

"I will speak to their men." Jayr extinguished the sheep's-tallow candles that she imported from Scotland because Byrne favored their scent. "Good night, my lord."

"Wait." Byrne found that he could not let her go; he was on his feet and catching her shoulder to stop her. "You spoke the truth when you said you were not injured by the human's bullet?"

Jayr reached up and tugged aside the wide collar of her shirt, revealing a slim, unmarked shoulder. "I made a foolish mistake, but I would not lie about such a thing."

As the scent of tansy and heather entwined around them, Byrne stared down at her exposed flesh. His most accomplished fighter, the only Kyn he trusted completely at his back, and all he could think was how like new milk her skin was.

How many times had he wished he could lay his cheek upon that shoulder and feel the smooth touch of her skin against the roughness of his? But there, against the whiteness, two thin, crooked scars gleamed. Unlike the scratches he had inflicted on her palm, the silvery marks were the last wounds Jayr had suffered during her human life. Twin reminders of that which immortality would never heal.

That which he had done to her. The life that he had stolen from her.

"I know you would not." Gently he pulled her shirt back into place. "G'night, lass."

"Sleep well, my lord." She gave him her customary bow before slipping out of the room.

Byrne lifted the hand he had used to straighten her shirt. Three of his fingers burned in the places where they had skimmed over scars. Scars that he had given to her when she had found him in the pit trap at Bannockburn. Scars from the *dents acérées* he had buried in her mortal flesh, tearing at it in his eagerness for her blood.

Damn his soul to hell, but he could still feel the press of her hand on the back of his head, urging him closer instead of pushing him away. She had not been bespelled; his scent had been drowned by the mud of the pit. It had been the sweet warmth of her human blood that had thrown them into the death dream. There his memories ended.

Just as her life had.

To this day, Byrne did not understand why she had done it. Before they had come together at the battlefield, they had never laid eyes on each other. She had worn the garb of a peasant, and had spoken in the tongue of his enemy. Nevertheless, six hundred years ago Jayr had given her human life so that he might live to fight the English. And how had he repaid her? By making her a cursed creature, damned to walk the night forever at his side.

The time it should have ended was long past. He had to do this thing for both of them. His actions tonight made that plain. Someday she would understand why he did it.

Someday, perhaps, she would forgive him.

Michael Cyprien propped his back against a pile of silk-covered pillows and looked down at the naked woman sprawled across his legs.

"You have very good-looking kneecaps," Dr. Alexandra Keller said, tracing the lines of the bones beneath his skin. "Strong, nicely shaped, not too prominent. Pretty elegant for a set of load-bearing joints, pal."

"I could say the same about your feet." He slid his thumb from her heel to the curl of the back of her toes. "Although I believe they are more cute than elegant."

"In France, maybe." She glanced over her shoulder at him. "Do you know that in China I'd be like a supermodel from the ankles down?"

Alexandra's long mane of fiery chestnut curls framed a striking face as stirring to him as the first time he had beheld it. Then she had possessed the gentle, fathomless eyes of a Botticelli Madonna. He had destroyed much of that innocence by inadvertently ending her human life and making her his immortal companion, but now he saw even newer shadows masking the old.

Michael suspected she still dwelled on being abducted by Richard Tremayne, the Darkyn high lord, and what he had subjected her to while holding her captive at his castle in Ireland. It had been a nightmare for him as well.

Distract her from her thoughts.

"I thought you and I might attend Byrne's winter tournament," Michael said carefully.

She considered it. "Byrne was the big redhead with the *Braveheart* tattoos, right? His seneschal looked like he'd never started shaving."

"Byrne's seneschal, Jayr, is a female," he corrected.

"She's a chick? You're kidding." She laughed. "Isn't that against the rules?"

"Jayr is the only female seneschal among the Kyn," Michael admitted. "Little is known or said about her."

Alexandra tucked a pillow under her head. "All because she's a girl, or because she works for Byrne?"

"Her origins are mysterious—there were no female Templars," he reminded her. "I know that Byrne changed her and took her into his service after she saved his life during the battle of Bannockburn."

She gave him an ironic look. "Gee, that sounds so familiar."

"I did not make you my servant," he said, holding up his hand. "You made me yours."

"Yeah, right." She chuffed out some air. "So, how old was the kid when Byrne stuck her with fangs?"

"I cannot say. Obviously rather young."

"Huh." She sat up suddenly. "Hang on. Are there little-kid vampires running around out there?"

He shook his head. "Adolescents, yes, but no child under the age of fourteen has ever risen to walk the night."

She didn't appear convinced. "You're sure about that? In her first book, Anne Rice had this little girl—"

"Anne who?"

"The author I like who writes about vampires," she said. "Or, to be more accurate, she did. Now she's big into the boy Jesus."

"We are not vampires," he told her firmly. "We are *vryko-lakas*. And to my knowledge, Jamys and Jayr are the youngest who rose to walk the night."

"I love how you say that," she told him conversationally. "You make getting infected with a gene-altering, plague-born pathogen sound like the kissy parts in *Phantom of the Opera*."

He arched his brows. "There were kissy parts?"

"I don't remember. I might, if someone hadn't started nibbling on my ear two minutes after I popped in the DVD." She hit him on the arm with the pillow. "So was the transition different for the kids?"

"Neither was considered a child during their human lives," he advised her. "Adulthood in our time began at age twelve."

"You were letting sixth-graders run the world? No wonder it was so screwed up." She nibbled absently at the side of her thumbnail. "It would be pretty interesting to have a look at Jayr's blood, see how it measures up against Jamys's and the adult Kyn samples I've collected."

"Why would her blood be different?"

"She might not have made it through puberty before the change," Alexandra said. "Presenting age has a lot to do with how a disease progresses, and how effective treatment can be. We can now cure eighty-five percent of kids who develop certain types of leukemia, for example, because they're at the developmental stage of life optimum for aggressive treatment of the cancer. Children and adolescents adapt to disease differently than adults do, too. All that means is that I may find something in Jayr's blood that wouldn't be present in yours or mine. Think she'd give me a couple of vials?"

An invisible weight lifted from his shoulders. "You will go to the tournament with me?"

"Sure. It's not like I've suddenly developed agoraphobia." Alexandra traced two fingertips from the inside of his knee to the midpoint of his thigh. "I'm fine. Quit worrying."

"I have you naked, in my bed, with your feet in my hands." He smiled. "There is no male in the world less worried."

"For a vampire, you're a terrible liar." Alexandra kissed his right knee before resting her cheek against it. "I'll let you get dressed and go make arrangements for the trip. You don't have to nibble on my neck and ravish my body forever."

The self-contempt in her voice did not match the strange, stricken set of her features. Michael sensed something beneath the fear—something Alexandra had been keeping from him since he had brought her back from Ireland.

He knew she would not confide in him until she was ready, but he might coax her into it. "Phillipe will make the arrangements. As for me, I can ravish your neck and nibble on your body. Or we can be boring and simply talk."

"You're so easy. I think that's why I fell in love with you." She sighed. "But if I don't let you out of here soon, Phillipe is going to raise the *jardin* and send them in to haul me off you."

"Not if Phillipe values the *jardin*." He rubbed a hand against the back of her head. "Do not concern yourself, *chérie*. You and I have earned this respite. We will take all the time that we need for ourselves."

"You're fine. I'm the one who's screwed up." She wound her arms around his legs. "I don't know what it is, but every time I think about you leaving me alone, I start having a panic attack. It's almost worse than how I felt when I was locked up in Richard's dungeon."

Was this what disturbed her?

"We were kept apart for too long," he told her. "It damaged the bond between us. It needs time to strengthen and heal."

"So I'm still working out my separation anxiety issues? Baby, we both know I can't keep—" The phone rang, interrupting her.

Michael grabbed the receiver and brought it to his ear. "Is the mansion on fire?"

"No, master," Phillipe said. "Forgive the disturbance, but it is Suzerain Byrne. He insists on speaking with you. He says the matter cannot wait."

"Put him through." Michael watched his *sygkenis* bend down to nip the inside of his thigh before rolling away onto her back. He put his hand over the receiver. "It is Byrne. This will take but a moment, *chérie*."

"It's okay." She swung her legs over the edge of the bed. "Take your time."

He caught her hand with his. "We need not go to Florida. I would be very happy to spend eternity here in bed with you."

"Right." The line of her mouth flattened. "Let's hope you don't have to."

As his seneschal transferred the call, Michael watched his lover enter the adjoining bath. Thanks to Alexandra's Kyn blood, her back had healed without scarring, but he imagined he could still see the ghostly remnants of those terrible claw wounds. She had blamed them on an unprovoked attack by Richard, who had been driven to the brink of madness by a massive dose of animal blood.

Michael believed it to be the truth—Alexandra had no reason to lie to him about anything that her captor had done—but when she had told him about Richard's assault, she had sounded almost apologetic. For some reason unknown to him, the incident had left her feeling guilty and frightened.

Had Richard done more than maul her?

"Seigneur." Byrne's voice came over the line, distracting him. "Your man said you were not to be pestered, but this cannae wait." He stopped and then added gruffly, "You and your *sygkenis* are well?"

"We are." He heard water running and breathed in the heady lavender scent from his lover's body, now blending with the herbal bath salts she favored. "I had intended to call you tomorrow. Alexandra and I will be attending your tournament this year."

"We are honored."

"Alexandra should meet more of our kind," Michael said. "My motive is more personal; I will be selecting and reviewing candidates for suzerain. I have named two new *jardin* to accommodate the refugees crossing over from France and Italy, but neither group has clear leadership among them. Now, what has you calling me in the middle of the morning?"

"I meant to invite you and your *sygkenis* to the tournament so that you might choose my successor," Byrne said. "I'll not be suzerain past Christmas."

"Indeed." Michael sat up and reached for his trousers. "Am I to know the reason for this sudden abdication?"

"I'm weary, lad." Byrne exhaled heavily. "I've been suzerain of the Realm for better than two centuries, and I've no stomach for it anymore. It's past time I stepped down."

The prospect of losing one of his best lords did not concern Michael as much as the defeat in his friend's tone. "If you need time away, I will appoint someone to temporarily serve in your place."

"It cannae work, seigneur."

"You may change your mind—"

"Will you bloody listen to me, Michael?" Byrne demanded. "You know what I can do. You've seen it yourself. Six hundred years and better I've controlled it. But tonight I nearly let loose on four bairns, Jayr, and Rob. I'm done."

"Very well." Michael cradled the phone between his cheek and shoulder as he stepped into his pants. "I reserve the right, however, to use whatever means I have to persuade you to remain as lord of the Realm."

"You can try." Byrne uttered a bark of something that distantly resembled a laugh. "I've nae said a word to the lads, and I'd be obliged if you'd keep this between us until you've made your choice."

Michael debated over whether or not to demand more explanation from the man. He valued Byrne as one of the American lords that he could count on implicitly to follow his orders without question. At the same time, he understood the fine line Byrne had walked since becoming Kyn. As a human, he had been a man feared and dreaded by anyone who had encountered him on the battlefield. Even after he had been cursed, his capacity for violence had served the Kyn well.

Those days were no more. Were Byrne to lose control of himself now, in a place crowded with people, as the Realm often was . . .

"Very well, *mon ami*."

After they exchanged farewells, Michael heard water spilling, and got out of bed to go into the bath. The oval tub, its waters fragrant with eucalyptus and mint, sat overflowing onto the floor. Alexandra stood naked before the foggy wall mirror, staring blankly at the blurred reflection of her golden-skinned body.

"*Chérie*, you are starting a flood." He took a moment to turn off the taps before he went to her. She did not move or blink. "Alexandra? What is it? Answer me."

She didn't react to his voice or his touch for a long moment, and then she came out of the trance as if it had never been.

"Why do you love me?" she asked. When Michael tried to embrace her, she stepped back out of his reach. "No. Don't touch me. Just tell me."

He tried to think of something gallant and romantic to say. "I love you because you are the other part of my soul."

"Don't give me pretty poetry." Her face set in remote, chilling lines. "Tell me, Michael."

"I am trying," he said slowly, his mind racing. "I love you because you are always in my head. I cannot go an hour without thinking of you. You have taken the place of my loneliness.

I feel at peace only when you are with me." Her expression didn't change, and his uneasiness plummeted into fear. "*Mon Dieu*, Alexandra, why do you ask me this? You know my feelings for you. After all we have endured and fought through together, you cannot distrust me."

"I trust you," she said. "But *why* do you love me?"

She was toying with him now. "I have just told you."

"No, you didn't," she argued. "*Why* am I always in your head and your heart? *Why* can't you go an hour without thinking of me? *Why* don't you feel lonely anymore? *Why* does being with me give you peace?"

"There is no reason to it. Such things are beyond definition or explanation. There is only you, and me, and our love." He felt appalled. "You do not believe me. I can see it in your eyes."

"No. It's not that." She moved to sit on the edge of the tub and trailed her hand through the steaming water. "It's not you." She let out a long, shuddering breath, and raw emotion quickly filled the terrible blankness in her eyes. "I believe you. I love you. But something . . ." She looked up at him, bewildered now. "Why am I trying to pick a fight with you?" Her breath caught on a sob. "What's wrong with me?"

"It must be an effect of the separation. It will pass." Michael tucked his hand under her hair to cup her neck. "All we need is time together, *chérie*."

She jolted to her feet and hugged him. Against his chest she said, "If being away from you messes me up this bad, you'd better never let anyone kidnap me again."

Chapter 3

"Do you have to leave so soon?"

Robin of Locksley fastened the front of his doublet as he walked to the bed. The human female—what was her name?—lay still tucked between his sheets, her rumpled golden-brown locks forming a soft cloud around her drowsy face. As he stood over her, she breathed in and licked her lips. She had a mouth as full and soft as ripe fruit, and she smelled of the chocolate-covered strawberries he had fed to her.

She was as enchanting as her name . . . which was . . .

Amanda, Rob thought, groping for the memory of it. *Or Miranda.*

To hide his confusion, he bent to put his mouth to hers and kissed her sweet lips with leisurely enjoyment before he lifted his head. "I must, my lady." Out of habit he checked the spot under her ear where he had bitten her, but the small punctures had already begun to scab over. *Tresori* always seemed to heal more quickly than most humans. "Will you be here when I return?"

"I'd love to, but I'm starting my vacation tonight." She checked the slim gold watch still on her wrist and groaned. "My sister's flying in from California, and I've got to pick her up at the airport. She's here for the holidays."

He ran his knuckles along the gentle line of her jaw. "Her gain is my loss."

"Mine, too." She sat up, revealing the tattoo of a black cameo over her left breast. The cameo marked her as a *tresora*, a human trained from birth to serve the Kyn. Details of the cameo's center silhouette would be inked in once she made her oath of service to one Kyn lord; until then she was free to serve whom she pleased. "But who knows, maybe I can convince her to sleep off the jet lag."

It gratified him to see that, unlike other *tresori*, she was not completely resistant to his Kyn talent, which, along with *l'attrait*, allowed him to charm most humans in a matter of seconds.

"Until we meet again, then, my lovely one." Rob pressed his lips to the back of her hand before he picked up his cloak and left the chamber.

Vague guilt walked with him. He enjoyed human females, delighting in their smell and taste and relishing their response to him. He had certainly enjoyed the *tresora* he had just left. Taking her warm, willing body had not done much to exhaust him, but her presence next to him had allowed him a few precious hours of mindlessness. The small taste he had taken of her blood had been sweet and delicious. She had come as close to perfection as a human bed companion could be.

In light of all that, he should have at least remembered her name.

As Rob traveled down the corridor, he exchanged greetings with a few other early risers, all warriors dressed and outfitted for the last battle performance they would give before the Realm closed to human visitors for a month. The spacious rooms Byrne provided for visiting Kyn, located on the opposite side of the castle, provided more luxuries and comforts, but Rob felt more at ease among the men of the *jardin*. Unlike some of the Kyn nobility, the former Templars accepted his presence and treated him as one of their own. They also could not be charmed, as humans were, by his scent.

In truth, Robin of Locksley belonged to neither world. Long ago he had violated his Templar vows to save the human woman he had loved. Before it was over, that one choice had also cost him his family, titles, and lands, and had forced him to become a thief. The outrageous bounty put on his head had done the rest.

Robin had survived, gathering up human criminals and creating an outlaw kingdom in the forests. He trained his men in the ways of stealth and subterfuge, until they became such an accomplished band of thieves that no one and nothing had been safe from them. So his legend had grown over the centuries, until an exasperated Richard had sent an emissary to Sherwood. Not to offer amnesty—the high lord never forgave any crime unless he personally profited from it—but to inform Rob that he was being exiled yet again.

"High Lord Richard Tremayne orders you to leave England this day and never return," the courier had read from the scroll. "If you are ever found on English soil again, you and every human who serves you shall be executed."

Rob did not fear the prospect of his own death—he had been daring it to take him ever since he had lost everything he had ever loved—but he refused to permit his human followers to pay for his sins. His decision had been made for him, however, when Byrne sent a letter informing him that that he and his entire household were leaving Scotland for America. That had decided everything.

So Robin of Locksley had become Robin of America.

There had been Kyn aplenty in the colonies, but no formal *jardin*, and no lords to rule over them. Byrne had somehow intervened with the high lord on his behalf, for less than a month after his arrival Robin of Locksley was elevated from the shame of thieving outcast to the rank of suzerain over the Darkyn in Atlanta.

He would have made his oath to Byrne in Scotland, Rob thought as he walked out to the archer's range, had he not been considered less than vermin by Richard and his cronies. Now all was forgiven, or perhaps Richard had gotten a better understanding of what it was like to be treated like a leper.

He went to the deserted center range, which had been prepared for target practice with earthen butts adorned with circlets of various sizes and colors. Planks for wand shoots lined the edge of the south range, while hanging marks swayed over the north, which was used for clout shooting.

"Lord Locksley." Jayr came to stand beside him, her shadow stretching to match his. "Do you mean to shoot tonight?"

Byrne's seneschal had no idea how much pleasure the sight of her brought to him. He dared not look at her too long, for fear of showing it.

He lived for moments like this with her.

"Not for long," he promised as he tied his mane of black hair back with a lace. "Why are you dressed like that?"

The seneschal looked down at the immaculate white velvet doublet and matching breeches adorning her long body. Her nose wrinkled for a second before she said, "Terence, the boy who usually plays squire for the court processions, telephoned. He has the plague."

"The plague, or *the* plague?"

"Not *the* plague. Something called bronchitis. From the sound of his hacking and wheezing, a very serious case." She eyed her finery again, this time with some resignation. "He offered to come in, but I would rather he not infect the other humans. I will take his place tonight."

Guilt returned, this time a barrel of it.

"Indeed. But squires never wore white to court." Rob glanced down. "Or white with black work boots. Don't you remember the old fashions?" He wagged a finger at her. "And you claim your performances are so historically accurate. That is false advertising and misrepresentation."

She leaned forward and whispered, "If you say nothing, my lord, I daresay the humans will never know the difference."

How easily she made him laugh. "Speaking of our mortal friends, would you tell me the name of that very generous and lovely female who entertained me last night?"

"Cassandra Cooper."

"Damn me." He ran his thumb across his fingertips. "I could not recall it when I left her, and came very near to calling her Miranda."

Jayr shrugged. "She would not have taken offense. She comes from an old *tresoran* family, and understands how we are."

"How I am, you mean." He went to the equipment locker where he had stowed his equipment. "You, at least, remember their names."

From the locker Rob took out the carryall bag he had brought from Atlanta and opened it. He strapped his quiver to his belt in Norman fashion and buckled a bracer to his forearm before taking out his longbow.

Made by his own hands from a single length of Spanish yew,

the stave stretched six feet from end to end, exactly the same height as Robin of Locksley himself. Reviled for centuries as an ignoble and un-Christian device, the longbow had been the decisive weapon that had turned the tide of many great battles during Robin's human life. William the Conqueror may have brought every bastard son of France with him when he invaded England, but it had taken only a single arrow from an anonymous archer's bow to slay King Harold at Hastings.

Not that he had stayed dead for long.

"We installed new lighting since your last visit." She gestured toward the metal poles, topped with oval-shaped bulbs, which had been placed at regular intervals on the edge of the range. "They operate on photocells that cause the light to come on as soon as night falls."

He scoffed. "Kyn eyes need no such thing. A proper archer should be able to shoot anything with his eyes shut."

"It is for our visitors. Many watching the archery contests wished to try their hand at it, so we make it part of the midday performance." She followed him back to the shooting line. "It always surprises them to learn that they have not the muscle to use our weapons."

He eyed the small, rectangular bows segregated to the wall nearest the entry. "I had wondered why you had collected so many plastic toys. I began to think you were running some manner of archer's nursery here."

Rob never trifled with imitations or modern versions of his weapon of choice, but made his own arrows from billets of sound English poplar, planed by hand until they became the proper thirty-two-sided rods ready to be nocked and barbed. During the *jardin* wars he had been obliged to use arrowheads made of copper-coated steel; now he favored solid copper. The days of piercing the impossibly tough hides of Kyn enemies were over, but he didn't believe in using a weapon that could not harm its target. He would stop someday, when he regained his trust in the Kyn, which was to say that he would always carry them.

"You still use robins' feathers," Jayr murmured as he placed a dozen arrows into his quiver. "Harlech will only have goose pinion for his."

"Harlech should use goose wings, for he makes his arrows too heavy. That is why they constantly fall short of his mark." Rob took pride in the lightness and balance of his own. He held out a leather brace. "Take down a bow and shoot with me."

"So that you may shame me more than you did the last time I shot targets with you?" She released a short chuckle. "I thank you, my lord, no."

"You know you are a natural with the bow, and one of the few here who can give me any sport," he said, trying to persuade her. "Come, twelve arrows. I will spot you six, if you like."

"I regret that I cannot. I must go now to see to the performance, else the visitors may sack the castle." She turned as if to go, and then reached out and touched his arm. "I am glad you are here, Lord Locksley. So is my master." She gave him one of her rare half smiles and walked back into the castle.

Glad she was. Glad of his presence. Smiling and laughing with him as a friend. Never knowing, never to know.

Rob turned to raise his bow, pulling the silk string back to his ear and taking aim. He released quickly, maximizing the energy being built up in the still-bending stave, and watching his arrow fly silent and true to bury itself dead center in the smallest of the target circlets. At the same time he plucked another arrow from the quiver and set its nock to the bowstring, drawing and releasing so quickly that the first had not stopped bobbing when the second split it in half.

"Fifty pounds says you cannae do that with your eyes closed," Byrne said from behind him.

Rob had the third arrow already set to his string, and turned to face his friend as he skillfully flipped his longbow and took the shot backward. He didn't have to look to see the result; the sound of the wooden shaft splitting was confirmation enough.

"Fifty pounds, was it?" he inquired politely. "I hope your pockets are deep."

"They will be when you pay me." Byrne pointed at his face. "For you didnae close your eyes."

Rob laughed. "Now who is the thief?"

After he had emptied his quiver and secured his bow and bag, Rob left the archer's range with Byrne and walked down a stone-set path into the castle's formal gardens. A prodigious amount of flowers still bloomed, thanks to the warmth of central Florida's climate, and the pathways were lined with potted poinsettias in honor of the season.

"I spoke with Cyprien. He attends this year," Byrne said in his usual abrupt fashion.

"I would have thought Michael still billing and cooing with his *sygkenis*." Rob halted to pluck a rambling white rose from a cluster at the end of a long, thorny cane nodding in the breeze. It reminded him of Jayr's ridiculous costume. "'Twas said that she suffered some injuries at Richard's hand. She is well enough to make the journey?"

"Apparently so." Byrne looked out at the setting sun. "I had words with Korvel after the thing was done. From his account the lass had a difficult time of it, but kept her head. Even when his scent bespelled her."

"She resisted Korvel's scent? She must be the only woman on earth who has." Impressed, Rob tucked the rose's stem in his pocket. "Cyprien is to be envied." He saw Byrne's expression tighten with distaste. "What is it? Have you some grievance with the seigneur?"

"I'm giving up the Realm, Rob," Byrne said. "I've asked Cyprien to choose my successor during his visit."

Rob stared at his friend. "You have perhaps lost your mind since this morning?"

"More that I seek to preserve my sanity." Garnet-bright hair turned to blood in the last glitter of sunlight as Byrne faced him. "You saw with your own eyes last night. Had you not dragged me back, I would have gone over. I wanted to rip out their young throats and bathe myself in their blood."

"Truly?" Rob folded his arms. He knew how paranoid Byrne was about his affliction, but he saw no reason to coddle him. "You suppose I would have stood aside and allowed it?"

"Their throats, and yours," Byrne continued, as if he hadn't spoken. "And Jayr's."

The Darkyn never made casual threats. Silence filled the air with undreamed nightmares, all of them carved by a flesh-hungry battle-ax. But Locksley knew Byrne's heart, and his strength of conviction. It had not been a simple thing to stand by and watch his friend battle his unseen enemy, but Rob had never once doubted who would come out the victor.

"You were not on your guard," Rob argued, "and you did not lose control of yourself."

"This time. What of the next? What if there is no one to pull me back?" He rubbed a hand over his face. "What if there is no one who can stop me?"

Rob had intimate knowledge of Byrne that few Kyn possessed, and understood the strength it took to carry his terrible burden. "How often are you attacked by stupidly ambitious humans? The Realm protects you." Something occurred to him. "This is why you're giving up the Realm? Because of last night?"

"Centuries it has been locked inside me, seething and waiting," Byrne said flatly. "I live with it. I accept it. But I cannae defeat it, and it will never leave me. For some time I have felt my grip on it slipping. Alone, away from humans and Kyn, I wouldnae fear it as I do now."

"So you would give up your home and your people?" Rob flung out his arm. "This place, these men mean everything to you, Aedan, and you to them. They have served you well—by God, they would go to the cross for you—and now you mean to abandon them? To become a hermit? No, you cannot do it. We shall find another way to deal with this."

The Scot's voice became a growl. "D'ya think I havenae tried? There is nothing more I can do."

"Cyprien's leech found a cure for Richard," Rob pointed out. "You are not so different."

"Richard wasnae an animal in his human life." Twilight made Byrne's tattoos look black. "I was."

"You were a man of our time. Times have changed, and so have you." When Byrne didn't reply, Rob drew back and saw the absolute misery on his friend's face. Friendship and something less noble snarled inside him. "Very well. Whom have you put forth as prospects for your replacement?"

"I will ask Cyprien to select the next lord from those who prevail during the tournament," Byrne said. "My men wouldnae respect anyone less."

"Not even me?" Rob returned his startled look with a placid

smile. "I have great fondness for your domain, your possessions, and your people. If you mean to toss them all away, I would have them for myself."

Byrne regarded the horizon. "One *jardin* is not enough for you?"

"If Cyprien designates me, I will combine yours with mine and bring them all under my rule," he told him. "Jayr can act in my place when I am in Atlanta." And he would put his men in place to watch over her, unless . . . "I presume you are not taking her with you to whatever godforsaken retreat you have planned?"

"'Twould defeat the purpose of the thing if I did." Byrne sounded relieved and, oddly, angry now. "When she learns of Cyprien's choice, she'll stay here and make her oath to the new lord."

"God in heaven, man, you haven't told her?" When he shook his head, Rob's fist clenched. "How could you keep this from her?" He couldn't mask the jealousy in his voice when he added, "She gave herself to you. She *lives* for you."

"She'll know soon enough, and she'll live for herself." The sound of trumpets drew Byrne's attention to the castle. "That's the signal for the end of the last performance. I'm to make an appearance at this feast." He drew from his surcoat a spiked circle of bejeweled gold, which he fit over the top of his head. "Robin—"

"Go play monarch," Rob told him. "I must plan my strategy for winning your kingdom, Your Highness."

Rob waited until his friend had left before he took the white rose from his pocket. He lifted it to his nose, breathing in its sweet scent, and then dropped it to the slate.

I wanted to rip out their young throats and bathe myself in their blood . . . their throats, and yours . . . and Jayr's.

Aedan mac Byrne could deny himself the world to safeguard it, but others would be made to suffer.

That would not do.

Rob brought his heel down upon the delicate bloom and slowly ground it into pulp.

*　　*　　*

Jayr rode in with the procession from the jousting field, playing the role of squire to Harlech's lord. Once they had dismounted, she draped a fur-lined mantle over his shoulders and handed off his lance and sword to a waiting attendant.

"Hey, up here!" A young human female in the stands waved frantically down at Jayr. "Please, up here! Please throw me a rose!"

Harlech heard her call and obliged by tossing up one of the long-stemmed roses that were being handed out to the female guests throughout the performance. The girl caught it and laughed, but again called out to Jayr. What she said was lost in the cries from the other females around her as they, too, begged for flowers.

"You have made a new friend," Harlech teased as they went inside the guards' hall for the last event of the evening, the dinner feast.

"I make many friends," Jayr said dryly. Accustomed as she was to having young human females mistake her for a boy, she barely registered it anymore. "Have you seen the master since sunset?" As the question left her, Byrne entered the guards' room from the garden door. "Never mind, he is here." She changed direction.

Some of the visitors stared at Byrne, but far fewer than in the past. Jayr was very grateful that movies about the war for Scottish independence had become popular; her lord no longer had to conceal the tattoos on his face while among humans in the Realm. Most assumed the dark blue marks were theatrical makeup. Given the rise in popularity of tattooing as well, someday soon Byrne might be able to walk freely among humans in their territory without attracting any attention.

"My lord." Jayr made her bow to him slightly more theatrical for the benefit of the humans watching them. "We are honored."

"Aye." He seemed distracted. "Is this the last of them, then?"

"Yes, my lord." In a louder voice she added, "Will you come to the high table and declare the feast commenced, my king?"

Byrne looked down at her for a long moment. "I am happy to, good squire."

Worried now, Jayr escorted her master to the table reserved

for the Realm's "nobility." Around it sat eleven of their men in various costumes, all of whom rose to their feet as Byrne took his place.

"Hail to thee, my king," Harlech said with a grin. "You look very good in the crown. Rather better than I remember the Brus did. I always thought him too short to cut the proper figure of a monarch." When his master did not reply, he sighed. "*Greith thu* me my grave."

"You seem to be digging it quite well on your own," Beaumaris observed.

As soon as Byrne sat, Jayr filled the ornate chalice beside his plate with bloodwine.

"Glad I am that this is to be the last of it for a time, my lord," Gawain, dressed in the flowing robes of a reeve, said to Byrne. He glanced at the assembled visitors. "Do you know, a pair of humans intercepted me when I came in and tried to hire me to give rides on ponies at their child's birthday party?"

"Send them to me next time; I know a human who would be glad of the business." Jayr clapped her hands together sharply, signaling the waiters to bring in the platters of food prepared for the humans. At the same time, jongleurs emerged, their smooth voices harmonizing as they walked about the hall serenading the guests:

> *I sing of a maiden that is makelees,*
> *king of alle kinges, to her sone she chees.*
> *He cam also stille ther his moder was*
> *As dewe in Aprille that falleth on the gras.*

While the men pretended to eat the food in front of them, Byrne listened to the song and watched the feast with cynical eyes.

"My lord, when does the seigneur arrive?" one of the men asked.

"Tomorrow midnight."

"Cyprien will be attending this year?" When her master nodded, Jayr tried not to groan. "This is sudden news." They had never hosted an American seigneur; until this past year they had never had one. She recalled how much the Frenchman was said to favor gardens. "With your permission, my lord, I will move Lord Savarone and his party to the east tower, so that the seigneur may have the garden chambers."

Byrne made a negligent gesture. "Do as you will with him."

Harlech picked up the joint of meat on his plate and studied it as he might a defective blade. "You know, Jayr, I do not recall in our time ever once sitting down to a meal of roasted turkey parts."

"Or yard greens prettily chopped and adorned with small cubes of bread." Gaillard, the warrior next to him, poked his fork warily into a bowl of the same. "I cannot fathom why they insist on eating weeds in this time. Is there nothing that can be slaughtered and roasted?"

"These mortals don't eat enough to keep a church mouse from starving," Beaumaris said. "Harlech, remember the harvest feast your father held every year after the villeins brought in the crops? Ten pigs, seven cows, and a yearling calf he butchered one year to feed the hands." Gloomily he took a sip of his wine. "I can yet remember the taste of that bacon."

"The meat gone over, the endless boiled cabbage, and the sour, moldy wine; that is what I best remember," Harlech said. "My human mistress insisted all of the food put to the table on high holy days be one color. We did not mind so much the yellow or white meals, but the blue?" He shuddered.

"We must accommodate the needs of the visitors," Jayr replied. "Humans expect more modern foods, and have little experience with hunger or famine. Many do not eat pork now, and the greens are not weeds, Gaillard. Thus prepared they are called 'Caesar salad.' "

"Rip up perfectly good stock fodder, douse it with garlic fish sauce, and call it royal fare?" Harlech grinned at Beaumaris. "Sounds like something a Roman would invent, doesn't it?"

"Excuse me."

Jayr turned to find the human teenager who had called to her from the stands hovering behind her. "I'm sorry, miss, but this table is reserved for staff only."

"Oh, I don't want to sit here. I'm with my girlfriends at the Lancelot table." The girl moved a step closer. "Your name is Jared, right? I'm Stacy."

Some of the men looked down at their plates. Two coughed into their fists to cover other, less kind sounds.

"I am pleased to make your acquaintance, Miss Stacy." Jayr deposited the wine jug on the table and held out her arm. "Allow me escort you back to your table. The tumblers are about to begin their performance, and they should not be missed."

"It's okay; I've seen them about a hundred times already." Blood flushed Stacy's cheeks. "I know I shouldn't be bothering you when you're working, but I sort of need to talk to you?" She sidled close enough to lay a hand on Jayr's arm, and squeezed it. "Wow, you're really toned. Do you work out?"

Beaumaris began having a coughing fit.

"My duties keep me fit." Jayr almost groaned as she saw the adoring warmth in the human's eyes. "I fear I am not—"

"Supposed to talk to the guests, I know. It's okay, really." The girl pressed her fingers against Jayr's lips, and then snatched them away and giggled. "I can't believe how gorgeous you are up close. Like Tom Welling from *Smallville*? Only so much cuter." She glanced at the table before she lowered her voice. "Listen, I don't want to get you in trouble with your boss or anything—"

Harlech joined Beau in his coughing attack.

"—but I just had to talk to you before they closed the castle for the winter." Her eyelids fluttered nervously. "Is there, like, a rule against employees dating customers? Because my friends and I? We are having this Christmas-break party, and I would love for you to hang out with us." She looked hopeful as she added, "As my date."

Gaillard coughed so hard he fell off his chair.

"I am tremendously flattered by your invitation, miss, but I am . . . involved with another." Jayr heard Gawain mutter something suggestive in French, and silently vowed to smack all of the men's heads together at the first private opportunity, but kept her smile pinned in place. "I thank you for asking."

Stacy's pupils expanded. "I love the way you talk. It's so pretty. And the way you ride your horse. I can't stop thinking about you." She seized Jayr's hand. "You're, like, the coolest-looking boy I've ever met."

"Jayr," Harlech said, no longer coughing.

"I know." To Stacy she said, "Please come with me, miss."

Jayr kept hold of the girl's hand and used it to lead her away from the high table and around the corner, where she could deal with her in some privacy. As soon as they were out of sight of the room, and out of range of the humans' noses, Jayr allowed her *dents acérées* to emerge. She did not intend to bite Stacy, but by preparing to hunt she was able to release more of her scent, which would give her more control over the girl.

"Are you having peach cobbler for dessert?" the girl asked. "I love peach cobbler."

Jayr caught the female's chin in her hand. "Look at me, child, and hear what I say."

Now firmly in the grip of *l'attrait*, the teenager swayed. "Yes, Jared."

"I am not the one for you," she said, slowly and deliberately emphasizing each word. "You will stop visiting the Realm. You will forget me and forsake this place. You will go on with your life as it was before you saw me. Do you understand?"

Stacy's cheeks turned bright red. "I will stop. Forget. Go on."

Jayr never liked compelling a human under the influence of *l'attrait*, even when the influence happened accidentally, as it had tonight with Stacy. But if Jayr did not order her to stay away, the girl would keep returning until she was compelled not to.

"You are very lovely and sweet. You will meet another, more suitable boy and be very happy with him." Jayr saw the glitter of tears in the young eyes, and on impulse pressed a kiss to the girl's brow. "Now come. I will take you back to your friends."

She turned to lead the girl back, saw a shadow move across the threshold to the hall, and frowned. Someone must have seen her talking to the girl and turned away to avoid them.

By the time they reached Stacy's young friends, the effects of *l'attrait* had dissipated, and the girl blinked a few times before giving Jayr a strange look.

"Hi," Stacy said, clearly confused. "Is there a problem?"

"Not at all, miss." Jayr smiled at the table of giggling teens. "Enjoy your meal."

"Thanks."

Jayr bowed and returned to the high table to refill the men's goblets. Two of the men left to join the troupe of acrobats who had entered the hall to perform their last act of the season.

"Deftly handled, Jayr." Robin of Locksley came to sit in one of the vacant chairs. "I am supposed to be the Kyn most irresistible to women. I believe I am jealous."

"Too many of us in one room can make such things happen." Jayr glanced at the girl, who seemed engrossed in a conversation with her companions. "I shall have to speak to the maintenance crew about installing a larger exhaust fan."

"Who is this Tom Welling?" Harlech wanted to know.

"A young television actor much admired by adolescent females of this era." Ruefully she ran a hand over her short hair. "It seems I bear a moderate resemblance to him."

"Those brats are a nuisance," Byrne muttered.

Locksley leaned close to whisper, "Someone is jealous because his fierce visage does not attract more pretty girls."

"I could be more careful about how much scent I shed," Jayr admitted. "That is what brings them to me, in truth."

"What about the boys?" The smile Locksley gave her turned mischievous. "A few strapping young males might prove amusing. At least you could get some pleasure out of them."

A chalice slammed down on the table, staining the cloth red with spilled bloodwine. The hot smell of heather grew thick as Byrne lurched to his feet.

"Jayr, with me." He ignored the astonished faces around him and strode out of the hall.

"Harlech, see to the visitors. Forgive me, my lord." Jayr bowed quickly to Locksley and then hurried off after Byrne.

Chapter 4

Jayr waited until she and Byrne were alone in his chamber before she spoke. "Do not be angry with Locksley, my lord. I am sure that he meant no offense."

"Rob's tongue runs away with his wits." Byrne shrugged out of his mantle and surcoat and tossed them over the back of his chair. He looked as if he might throw the faux crown out the window, but at the last moment turned and thrust it at her. "How many children like that girl tonight go about making calf eyes at you?"

"Not very many." She busied herself by shaking out his outer garments and hanging them in the armoire. The offending crown she placed on a lower shelf, out of sight. "It happens once or twice a season."

He didn't like that. "You've nae said a word to me."

"I never thought I should have to, my lord. I've dealt with them as quietly and discreetly as possible." Why was he so upset over the girl's behavior? "I spoke to Stacy while she was bespelled and made the appropriate suggestions. She will not return here again."

"Where were her parents?" he asked. "Why did they not accompany her and keep her in check?"

Byrne's disdain for the modern world often kept him oblivious to the changes in human society. The first time he had seen a human female in trousers, during the American suffragette movement, he had declared that mortal society must be on the brink of collapse.

"Adolescent girls today are permitted to go out without chaperones," Jayr said, trying to keep the irony out of her voice. "There are fewer dangers to them, especially when they go about in groups to public places. Stacy was with her friends."

"Those giggling brats? They were as young and silly as she." He swept the air with his hand. "All of them should be locked up by their fathers until they can be married off."

"You know very well that Americans no longer arrange marriages for their young, my lord." She kept a straight face. "Mothers and fathers both work, often more than one job, to afford a decent living and better education for their children."

"Children who apparently have nothing better to do than toss themselves at you." He gave her a suspicious look. " 'Tis not amusing."

She pressed her lips together carefully. "It seems as if they have too much freedom, but I think they pay for it in loneliness." She remembered the terrible yearning in the teenager's eyes. "They are denied affection and the closeness of family, and so seek to find it from strangers."

"The girl." Byrne braced his hands on either side of one window, looking down at the gardens. "Did you fancy her?"

"Stacy?" She felt bewildered. "No, my lord. I fed earlier, before the performance."

"I saw you kiss her brow."

If he meant . . . But they never spoke of such things, out of respect for each other. "It was to comfort her. I felt sorry for her. I did not fancy taking blood from her."

"I dinnae mean her blood."

Or perhaps all the respect was on her side. "I may look like a boy, my lord," she said stiffly, "but I have never desired other females."

"So you feel no desire at all." He made it a statement.

Jayr supposed when it came to sex that she was more cold-blooded than most Kyn females, but living an abstinent life had not been her choice, only her obligation.

"I feel many things," she defended herself. "I have my predilections and desires, like any Kyn, but little time to indulge them."

"Then why not use these humans who become infatuated with you?" Under the fine linen of his shirt, his broad back muscles tensed. "Their sort would be, as Rob said, a convenience."

"Stacy is a child. I cannot. It is not something that I require anyway." Jayr felt very uncomfortable with the direction of the conversation. "With your permission, my lord, I should go and make sure the last of the visitors have left."

"Wait." His tone brooked no argument. "Tell me of these desires of yours. How do you control them so well?"

Would he force her to recite her every flaw?

"My duties take up much of my time, so I have little to spare for idle pleasures. I have learned to do without human companionship. That is all I meant." That much was true. "In all other ways I am Darkyn."

"I have never known you to take any lover. You wouldnae be so foolish as to trifle with Harlech or the garrison." He turned to face her. "So what do you do when you want fucking, seneschal?"

Jayr knew her master could be crude when it suited him, but he had never used such language with her. As she was thinking of how to respond, her tongue decided the matter for her. "That is not for you to know."

"Isn't it?" He came across the room, looming over her before she could take a breath. "You serve me. You belong to my household. Your choices reflect on me. You'll tell me whatever I wish to know. You'll tell me now."

She ignored the fact that he was shouting in her face and stood her ground. "There is nothing to tell you."

"Is it Locksley, then?" His lips curled back from his *dents acérées*, which were fully extended. "Is that how you *see* to him every time he comes on a visit? Did you think you could conceal such a thing from me?"

Her jaw dropped. He thought she would sleep with a visiting suzerain, an important lord who also happened to be his best friend?

"I do not bed Lord Locksley, nor any of the Kyn," she protested. "Nor do I take humans, male or female."

"You would have me believe you a virgin?"

"You know very well that I am not." She took some satisfaction in seeing him recoil. "When I have need, and the time to attend to it, I see to myself."

"You . . ." As her meaning registered, he stared. "Yourself? Why?"

"Do you never look at me, my lord?" she asked softly, gesturing toward her front. "As I am, no one questions my playacting a squire. I look like one. Were I not so tall, humans would think me a child."

Byrne lifted his hands as if to touch her, and then let them fall away.

"It does not have to be so," he told her, not meeting her eyes. "There are males who find females such as you fetching."

"The only male who would desire this body of mine," she said flatly, "would wish to be with another male, or perhaps very young girls. I would not interest the former, and I would never permit the latter to touch me."

"Not all," he insisted.

For a long moment they stared at each other. Jayr could not tell Byrne her true feelings: that she wanted no other man to touch her but him. She would not further revolt him. She belonged to him already, and that was enough.

It had to be enough.

"As you say, my lord." Heather suffused the air, making Jayr remember her suspicions about the cause of her master's unruly temper. He needed relief. "Forgive me for speaking out of turn. Do you wish some company for the night?"

"I dinnae care." He went to sit in front of the fire and stared at the flames. "Go. See to the Realm."

Jayr stepped out into the hall. Her hands wanted weapons; her chest wanted more air. Suppressed rage made her shoulders rigid and gnarled in her gut, a red-hot viper. Deliberately she made herself relax and see the situation without emotion. Whether her lord wished to admit it or not, he had needs of his own. Her duty was to see to them, and quickly.

The air crackled as she drew on her Kyn talent and dissolved into a blur of motion.

It took her only a few moments to reach the employee lounge, where their human staff spent their breaks and kept their personal belongings. As most were leaving for a full month of paid vacation, the atmosphere was happy and somewhat celebratory.

"Jayr." Sally, one of the kitchen crew, gave her a clumsy hug. She smelled strongly of ale and swayed on her feet. "Come out and have a drink with us. The head cook and all the waiters are going clubbing after work." She frowned down at Jayr's chest. "Your clothes just come out of the dryer?"

"No. I thank you for the invitation, but I cannot go out with you and your friends." Over Sally's head she caught the eye of a sober horse trainer she trusted, who gave her a nod in return. She looked into Sally's foggy eyes. "I would like you to go home with Bill tonight."

"Sure," Sally slurred, and then whispered loudly, "Just don't tell my husband about Bill. He's the jealous type."

"I won't," Jayr promised as she handed her off to the trainer. To him, she said, "Have Eric follow you in Sally's car. Thank you, Bill." She turned to inspect the other women who had not yet left, and made her choices. "Sara, Candace, Ellie, may I speak with you for a moment?"

The women followed her into the connecting meeting room. All three had worked as hostesses at the Realm for many years. Over time, like many of the other females on the staff, they had also become trusted friends and allies who occasionally performed other services for the Kyn.

The women enjoyed their employment, not only for the generous pay and decent working conditions, but because after the Realm closed for the night, they had their pick of the unattached Kyn males. Jayr made it clear to the women who chose to provide pleasure for the men of the Realm that they had the option to refuse anyone they wished at any time. She also did not allow any female on staff to stay more than one or two nights each month. The men of the garrison, who would otherwise have had to go out and hunt for human blood and pleasure, handled the staff females with great care and respect.

"Lord Byrne is restless tonight," she told the women. "Would you be willing to entertain him?"

Candace exchanged a glance with Ellie. "All three of us again?"

Jayr shrugged. "He is quite restless."

Sara, a dark-skinned islander with a beautiful accent, flashed a devilish smile. "Sounds like we'll be putting in some overtime, girls."

Jayr escorted the women back up to Byrne's chamber, and pretended not to hear them as they chatted on how they could best entertain her master. This part of her duties was as necessary as tending to Byrne's weapons or keeping his chamber in order, but she despised it. Had she been a normal woman, she could have seen to all his needs.

Had you been a normal woman, her conscience chided, *he never would have made you his seneschal.*

Jayr let the women into the chamber but remained outside. She had to finalize some travel arrangements for the last of the tourneyers, perform an inspection of the armory, and sort through the ever-present pile of paperwork in the management office. She had not yet found the time to go and see to straightening Rainer's arm. The seigneur would be attending; she would have to call his seneschal, Navarre, and learn what arrangements would best please Cyprien and his *sygkenis*.

Instead, Jayr stood and waited outside while the women entertained her master. It wasn't that she didn't have faith in the women—the three had spent several nights with Byrne—but that she didn't trust his mood.

Or her own. How could she have been so blunt with him?

Jayr knew she had said too much. The ease between them relied on the formality of the traditional relationship between lord and seneschal. She also took great pains to keep him from seeing her as a mere female. Now that Byrne knew she did not take lovers, would he pity her? Did he even suspect how much she wished she could be the one in his bed?

If he knew how often she had imagined it, he would send her away. Or laugh.

Because she was alone and had nothing to do but listen for any indication of Byrne's displeasure, Jayr's imagination began to torture her. Images formed in her mind, tableaus to accompany the faint, soft sounds and voices that were coming through the door.

A big, virile man like Byrne could easily pleasure three human females at the same time. He would strip them bare first and have them pile around him on the bed. He would take the time to arouse them, using not only his scent but his hands and mouth. They would be panting and gasping, drenched in the scent of heather, before he rolled Ellie onto her back and plowed into her. As he impaled her, he would put his mouth to Sara and use his fingers on Candace. Once he had brought them to their pleasure, he might play more with them, having two use their mouths on him while one straddled his face and—

No. Jayr's thoughts became a spear-tipped portcullis and slammed down on the image. *I will not see that.*

She wished she could blame her indecent thoughts solely on her imagination, but she knew exactly how well her master could pleasure a woman.

Jayr had firsthand experience.

It should never have happened. Not there, not with a battle raging only a field away. Not to a girl who had spent most of her life shut away in a convent. Not to the warrior who lay dying in her arms.

Jayr had arrived in the village of Bannockburn in late June, only a day before the army of King Edward II came marching up the old Roman road to mass at the village ford. In the hills a rebel force of Scots only half the size of the English army had already entrenched themselves to the north of the gorge, where the narrow flatlands between the marshes and the hills gave them the advantage. She had tried to walk out, but the Scots had blocked all paths through the forests with barricades of branches and trees as well as cleverly disguised pit traps. An old man in the village told her that neither she nor the English would outflank Robert the Brus.

Even now it seemed impossible that so many men had died in the space of two days. Jayr recalled the long hours she had spent hiding in the root cellar of the inn, listening to the thunderous advance of the English cavalry and the barbaric shouts of the Scots pikemen in their schiltroms, impaling all who came near them on their wall of fifteen-foot spears.

The innkeeper came and went with news from the battle-field. Against an army twice their number, the Scots were holding the line. The English archers had crossed the gorge and fired their arrows too early; they slaughtered hundreds of their own cavalrymen retreating from the advancing Scots in-fantry. When the Scots wavered under the rain of arrows, Keith the Marischal had charged out of his hiding place in the woods, leading five hundred mounted warriors into the field to scatter the bowmen.

Confusion among the English ranks, it was later said, took the day as much as the Scots did.

Now no longer afraid the English would swarm over the village, the innkeeper and his wife had thrown Jayr out, bolt-ing the door against her. She went from door to door, but her English accent failed to gain her new sanctuary. As the Scots advanced in the distance, driving their enemies back toward the gorge, she walked out into the marsh and crossed it, head-ing for the densest part of the forest. There she would have to find a place to hide until the battle was done.

She had to cross one last pasture to reach the trees, and in the center of it she came upon the edge of the pit trap.

Unlike those scattered through the woods, this pit was smaller and deeper, and had been freshly dug. She began to walk around it when she heard a man groan.

"Dinnae leave me alone here, lass."

With hair the color of blood and a face covered with strange blue tattoos, the Scot had looked like a demon leering up from the abyss. But the strange twilight fire in his eyes was fading, and the brutal, torn hand he held up to her shook with pain and exhaustion.

Jayr was not a fool. She could not jump into a pit trap for a dying man three times her size who had just spent two days killing her countrymen.

So, of course, she did.

The door swung away from her back, almost causing Jayr to fall. Heather-scented air poured out of the chamber, and she pivoted to see Sara's dreamy face as she emerged from the chamber.

"Hey, girl." The brunette yawned as she drifted past. "We're done for the night."

"You've finished?" Jayr thought Byrne had settled on the other two—perhaps he was a little tired—but Candace and Ellie followed Sara, and the door closed.

Jayr checked their wrists, but saw punctures only on Ellie and Candace. Sara seemed to be wholly untouched. Evidently none of them had removed their garments; there hadn't been enough time even for that.

"Was my lord displeased with you?" Jayr asked, worried now that Byrne had grown tired of the trio.

"No." Candace, her face still flushed with pleasure, smiled. "He did me without even touching me."

"We're to go home now," Ellie said, her voice taking on the faint burr of Byrne's accent, indicating that she had been told to do so while bespelled. "G'night, Jayr."

The three glided off, still suffused in the pleasures bestowed by her master and *l'attrait*.

He had not taken them. He had pleasured them and then sent them away.

Unreasonable satisfaction scorched through Jayr. Byrne had not surrendered to lust or the means to rid himself of it. Maybe now he meant to do without it, as she did.

Or maybe he had simply tired of the women and wanted new ones.

Feeling elated and wretched all at once, Jayr stared at the door, wondering if she dared go inside and inquire. She knew her master's needs better than anyone. Byrne had never sought to live in celibacy, yet he had not taken a human woman for weeks. By all accounts he should have used the three for the remainder of the night. It made no sense that he would take only a little blood and send them away.

What was wrong with him?

That day on the battlefield came back to her in a rush, his voice from the pit surrounding her, squeezing her from all sides, holding her helpless, suspending time between the past and the present until all that remained were his words, the words that she had imprinted on her mind, on her heart, on her soul.

Dinnae leave me alone here, lass.

Dinnae leave me alone here.

Dinnae leave me alone.

Dinnae leave me.

Dinnae leave.

Dinnae.

And then his hands, and his mouth . . .

Jayr slammed her fist into the wall hard enough to split the skin. She wouldn't go inside or humiliate herself again. She knew her place. She was Aedan mac Byrne's servant and bodyguard, the eyes at his back, his third blade.

Seneschal. And that was all she would ever be.

Jayr knew she would find no rest away from him this night. She turned and pressed her shoulders to the door, sliding down until she sat, her arms resting on her knees. She let her head fall back and gave herself up to the anguish so eager to torment her.

The scent of tansy drew Byrne to the door of his chamber. He pressed a hand against the polished wood, sliding his palm down as he knelt to see a shadow partially blocking the light that filtered through the crack at the bottom. Jayr, sitting on the other side. All that separated him from his seneschal— from her—was three inches of seasoned oak.

Oak, and seven lifetimes of sorrow and regret.

Byrne almost reached for the knob, and then turned, propping his back against the door. He should have taken the humans to bed and rid himself of his lust. The women had been willing, beautiful, and, God knew, talented enough to bring any man, human or Kyn, to his knees.

Byrne appreciated the human women who came to him. True that they were soft and fragile things, requiring gentle handling, but that proved no burden. He had never been a brute in bed with humans.

Under the spell of *l'attrait*, the females Jayr brought to share his nights had always satisfied his thirst and hungers. They tired quickly, so he often used two or three at a time, but he saw to their pleasure first. Taking care with them was natural. To harm them would have been like beating a puppy or choking a kitten.

The problem was with Byrne. He simply couldn't tolerate the touch of human females anymore.

Centuries of slaking his lust on the bespelled had finally taken their toll; each time he lay with a human female his disgust with himself grew until he could not bring himself to do it. Perhaps it was his awareness of this modern era, when women were permitted to make choices about everything that happened in their lives. Perhaps the novelty had finally palled. Whatever the cause, his desire to plow a sweet, yielding body could no longer overcome his utter revulsion for the partners provided to him.

There was only one woman he desired. The one who had saved him in his darkest hour. The one who had sacrificed her life for his.

It had happened so fast. One moment he was riding across an empty field; the next he lay skewered in a stake-lined pit trap, his stallion trampling him in its frantic haste to escape.

Molten agony spread through him, thanks to the copper-tipped stakes upon which he lay impaled. It had taken every ounce of his strength to work himself free of all but one of the deadly spikes. The loss of blood kept his wounds from closing, and as he looked up at the smoke-fogged sky, Byrne suspected his immortal life was rapidly coming to an end.

Then she had appeared, a mop of dark, tangled hair around a pale, frightened face, peering down at him.

Byrne had already accepted his fate, but he didn't want to meet it by himself. *Dinnae leave me alone here, lass.*

She had circled the pit, climbing over the crumbling earthen side and then sliding down to land on top of him, a ragged bundle dressed in nun's black. Her hands went to the bloodied stake that had rammed through his chest, her fingers slipping as she tried to grasp it.

He had covered her fingers with his hand, his voice gone, his certainty that the copper had skewered his heart unshakable. He had only wanted her to hold his cold, heavy hand in hers.

With a muttered prayer she instead wrapped her skirt around the stake and jerked it out of his body. The pain had shifted and changed, and the stink of death became a field of blossoming heather. . . .

Jayr.

Byrne pressed his hand over the phantom pain in his chest, leaned his head back against the door, and closed his eyes.

Chapter 5

"I've been to Disney World," Alex told Michael as Phillipe navigated his way out of the city. "Cinderella's castle was cute, but I can't see actually living in it. Not after the age of twelve."

Michael looked amused. "It is fortunate, then, that my family estates were burned to the ground and the property seized by the Brethren."

"I'm not complaining. Just the air-conditioning bill alone for a castle would put us in the vampire poorhouse." Her mobile rang, and she checked the illuminated screen. "Area code seven-oh-eight, but it's not Val." She eyed him. "You screw around lately with anyone from Chicago?"

He trailed his fingers down the length of her arm. "Besides you?"

"Wiseass." She switched the phone to speaker and answered the call. "Alex Keller."

There was a pause before a man said, "Alexandra, it's John."

"Hey, big brother. You're on speaker, and Michael's here." She gave Cyprien a warning look. "You were also supposed to call me a week ago. Where are you?"

"I'm sorry, I forgot. I'm staying with—" The signal broke up, garbling what he said for a few seconds. ". . . coming to New Orleans."

"You're breaking up, Johnny. We're in Florida right now," she said. "Change the tickets I sent you and fly into Orlando. You can come back home with us when we're done here."

"I told you, I can't," he said, his voice clearer now. "I'm leaving in the morning."

"What?" She stared at the phone. "Where? Why?"

"I can't—" The line went staticky again. Just as Alex was going to hang up and dial back, John's voice came through. ". . . worry, Alex; I'll be all right."

"John, I didn't get any of that. Hang on; let me call you back."

". . . won't be here. Cyprien, look after her." A click sounded as John ended the call.

Alex pressed her fingers against the hammering pain under her left eyebrow. "I can't believe this." She handed the phone to Michael. "Call Val. Tell him to track down my brother and stop him from doing whatever idiot thing he's got planned."

"Do you know exactly where John is?" When she shook her head, he sighed. "Perhaps he does not wish to be found."

"Too bad." She took the phone from him and dialed the number John had called from. A strange voice answered. "Hello? I need to speak to John Keller."

"Don't know any Keller," the man told her.

"He's a big guy with a dark beard," she said. "Looks like Jesus with an attitude problem."

"Lady, this is a pay phone in front of a convenience store," the man told her, "and there ain't no pissed-off Jesus here."

"Sorry." Alex ended the call and thumped her head back against the seat. "Damn him. Why does he keep doing this to me?"

"He said he was leaving tomorrow, and he does not own a car." Michael thought for a moment. "Valentin can check to see if John changed his plane tickets. He can also have the airports and train stations watched."

She shook her head. "John doesn't have a lot of money. He'll probably cash in the airline tickets and take a bus."

"Then I will have Valentin check the bus depots as well," Michael assured her, and kissed the side of her head. "Try not to worry."

"John's pulled another disappearing act while I'm going to be locked up for a month in—hooray—another castle," she snapped. "What's there to worry about?"

"The Realm is not a prison," Michael told her. "Nor is it anything like Dundellan. You will like it; I promise."

Alex was sick of castles, her brother, and the Darkyn, but

she'd agreed to come along with Cyprien for this Scotsman's big party. She'd have to make the best of it. She leaned forward. "Hey, Phil, you ever been to this place?"

"Many times, my lady. Lord Byrne lives as we did during our human lives." The seneschal smiled at her in the rearview mirror. "It should be very learning . . . schooling . . . good for your brain."

Phillipe had been taking a correspondence course to improve his English, Alex had learned when she had returned from Ireland. Sometimes she suspected that it was making his English worse.

"I already know that the way you guys lived back then caused leprosy, tuberculosis, the Black Death, and a whole list of other delightful epidemics. I should go check into a nice, clean Marriott." Or take a flight up to Chicago and track down her brother herself.

"The Realm is clean and comforting, my lady," the seneschal assured her.

She drummed her fingers against the armrest. "That's another thing: What's with this 'my lady' stuff all of a sudden? 'Alex' isn't good enough anymore?"

"I am practicing proper manners with my English," Phillipe said. "It is not correct for a seneschal such as me—such as I— to call you by your . . ." He stopped and asked Cyprien something in French.

"First name," Michael replied.

Phillipe nodded. "Just so."

"Go back to speaking lousy English. I liked it better." She saw the outlines of a building on the other side of a river and nudged Michael. "That it?"

The car came to a halt in front of a private drive barred by a massive wrought-iron gate. Phillipe left the engine running and got out of the car to speak with the guard at the gate, who was dressed in leather and chain mail, and held a nasty-looking spear.

Alex watched as the seneschal and the guard bowed to each other and clasped hands to each other's forearms. "See? I *knew* there was a secret handshake."

The glitter of the moonlight on water drew her gaze to what

she had thought was a river at first. Then she saw the somewhat irregular shape of it.

Her chin dropped. "Is that moat? The guy has a working *moat*?"

"I believe it was once a seasonal lake. Byrne diverts some of the overflow from the St. Johns River to fill it," Michael told her. "There is another, larger lake on the south side of his land. Both help prevent flooding during the rainy season, and the moat provides a more familiar form of defense for the castle."

She couldn't believe she was seeing a castle with a moat in the United States of America. "He couldn't just invest in a decent security system and a couple of Dobermans?"

After speaking with the guard for several minutes, Phillipe got back into the car.

"All is well, master," he told Cyprien. "The Kyn from France and Italy arrive soon." He started the engine as the guard pulled open the gates and walked to what looked like a small podium covered with switches and lights.

Alex couldn't see anything beyond the drive but the twenty-foot-wide moat, which had no bridge across it. "We don't have to jump that, do we?"

Michael gave her an inscrutable smile. "Watch and see."

Alex heard water rushing, and as Phillipe drove down toward the moat she saw the surface of the circular channel churning. Two wide, vertical pilings rose from the moat, revolving and changing shape as they seemed to fold over. Horizontal platforms flattened out and overlapped each other, the edge of the drive, and the edge of the gate road into the castle. Water streamed over the sides in a flood that dwindled to small streams.

"I'll be damned," she said, opening the window so she could stick her head out and look down. "Underwater bridges."

"Submersible bastions," Michael corrected.

"Very nice," Alex said, pulling her head back inside, "but wouldn't it be easier to build the place on dry land?"

"Probably, but water has many advantages over land," Michael said. "Byrne and I share common ancestors, and they regarded lakes and rivers as sacred places. Often they would hurl into the water the gold and treasures they had taken in battle, as offerings to the gods to ensure their next victory."

That made about as much sense as the moat approach to domestic security. "Your ancestors were dumb."

Phillipe drove over the linked bridges toward four towers joined together around the massive gateway entrance. The towers surrounding the gateway soared up at least five stories into the night, illuminating it with dozens of torches blazing in enormous iron sconces. Beneath each torch stood a large man dressed in leather and chain mail and armed with a spear, a sword, and a black shield. Each stood motionless at his post, not looking out over the horizon but watching the progress of the car as they passed over the second drawbridge.

"This would make a great credit-card commercial," Alex muttered. "Or a fortress of darkness."

Phillipe braked just before the gated passage through the four towers that led into the compound. Gears slowly cranked, and the heavy wood-and-metal grate in front of them began to rise. A short distance behind it another, heavier gate also lifted.

"Just what is this guy preparing for?" she asked Michael. "A nuclear attack?"

"A castle was a military and community stronghold in our time," he replied. "We had to be prepared for anything."

"Yeah, but two gates? One wasn't enough?"

"In our time, besiegers force storming the castle could be caught and trapped between two portcullises." As Phillipe drove in, he pointed to openings in the walls and ceiling. "The castle's archers would use these murder holes to shoot the trapped men."

"Charming." Alex silently thanked God once more for not having been born in the Middle Ages. "I suppose they poured vats of boiling oil through them, too."

"Not at all," Michael told her. "Cauldrons of oil were heated and dumped from the battlements onto the soldiers trying to ram the gate or scale the walls."

"How humane of you guys." She shuddered.

"It did not always work," he said. "If they were protected under a movable shed, we would take the rotting bodies of dead livestock and—"

"That's okay," Alex told him, putting her hand over his mouth. "I'm not planning to siege a castle anytime soon. Skip all stories that involve maggots."

Michael nipped her palm, making her laugh.

They passed through four more types of barricades before the passage ended in a cobblestone area that Michael called the outer bailey. In front of the castle stood a giant in a hooded dark cloak and a boy in a white shirt and black trousers. Behind them, three rows of warriors with enormous spears stood in formation.

"Oh, look, honey," Alex said sweetly. "Conan and his barbarian army are here." She checked her watch. "How about we head home? If Phil floors it, we could make it back before the Learjet cools off."

Michael laughed. "There is nothing to fear from Byrne and his men. They are merely showing respect."

"To you, maybe. Me, he doesn't know." She looked up toward the battlements. "It had better not start raining dead cows."

Phillipe parked the car and opened the back door for them. Michael helped her out, put his arm around her waist, and bent down to murmur, "Relax, *chérie*. You will like him, I promise."

"Are you kidding?" Alex surveyed the giant. "I'm going to make him my new best friend."

When they walked up to the waiting Kyn, the suzerain pulled back his hood and stepped forward to meet them. Alex tilted her head to get a better look at Byrne, who had to be one of the largest men, human or Kyn, whom she'd ever encountered. The Scotsman stood half a head taller than Cyprien, who was no shrimp, and had at least seventy pounds on Phillipe, who was built like a tank.

The top of her own head, Alex gauged, almost cleared the top of his belt. Almost.

She'd never seen red hair quite the color of Byrne's, or so much of it on a man. It flowed over his shoulders like dark liquid garnet, turning bloodred wherever the torchlight flickered over it. It echoed the bold red in the clan tartan and kilt he wore, which should have made him look ridiculous but only added to the aura of real danger. The crowning touch, his barbaric-looking facial tattoos, made him look like the walking, scowling embodiment of the Dark Ages.

Someone said their names, and Michael urged Alex forward with one hand. Usually he introduced her to other Kyn lords, but maybe this time the meeting was supposed to be less formal.

"Alexandra Keller," she said to the suzerain, holding out her hand and hoping she'd get it back.

"Aedan mac Byrne, my lady," the giant said, swallowing her hand in his and bowing over it. "We are honored."

Alex controlled a flinch, but Byrne's gentle, careful touch twanged through her, a thrashing, spark-shooting wire. Through the soundless roar of light in her head, Alex glimpsed a different version of his face, one that was masked in gore and blood that paled around eyes of hellfire. She blamed her talent—she could read the thoughts of any killer—but soon realized that the suzerain wasn't hiding any secretive, murderous thoughts. He didn't think about killing at all.

Death on a short leash. Alex felt panic balloon inside her chest. *He's not a killer. He's a weapon.*

"Sorry I didn't get to say hello in Fort Lauderdale before I was kidnapped." He wasn't letting go of her, and, right on cue, she was babbling. "You know how it is when you're hypnotized and being kidnapped by a half-crazed vampire king."

Eyebrows a shade darker than his hair arched. "I cannae say I do."

"Right." She'd better get her act together before she said something to offend him. There, that would work. "Has anyone ever made a list of everything that pisses you off?" she asked. When he frowned, she added, "I'd like a copy. You know. So I can memorize it."

He chuckled, and the menacing grooves of his face became laugh lines. "Whatever you do or say, lass, you're safe with me." He patted her hand before he released it and shifted his gaze to Michael. "Seigneur. Welcome back to the Realm."

"Thank you for having us, my friend." Michael clasped hands with him. "We are looking forward to the tournament."

Only an immortal ex-priest like Michael, Alex thought, trying to feel grumpy again, could look forward to watching a bunch of men beat the hell out of one another. The odd thing was, she didn't feel grumpy. Or angry, or nervous. The loose, scalding panic had vanished, and if anything she now felt content and strangely happy—something she hadn't been since coming back from Ireland. Byrne's scent, she remembered Michael telling her, had a calming effect on both humans and Darkyn. Maybe it acted like Prozac on her.

But what the hell had he done to her before that, when she had seen the vision of his face covered in blood?

"Your presence will inspire the competitors." Byrne turned slightly toward the slim, dark-haired girl standing just to his left. "Lady Alexandra, may I present my seneschal? This is Jayr."

The girl stepped forward and offered her hand instead of bowing. "It is a pleasure, my lady."

"Alex, please. I wasn't a lady even when I was human." Alex breathed in and smothered a groan. Jayr's scent reminded her of the big, warm, icing-slathered cinnamon rolls she used to pig out on at the mall.

"If you are in need of anything during your stay, my lord," Jayr was saying to Michael as she handed him something, "you have but to press two. There is also a radio switch that will summon me directly."

"Thank you," Michael said, pocketing the oval-shaped device she'd given him.

While Jayr introduced Byrne's men to Michael and Phillipe, one of the ceremonial duties performed whenever one Kyn lord came into the territory of another, Alex studied Byrne's seneschal.

Jayr's garments, obviously designed for a teenage boy, made her long frame look even leaner than it was. She held herself differently than a woman would, legs spread farther apart, arms bent slightly, shoulders back. The shorn hair, angular hips, and nearly flat chest reinforced the blurry illusion of an adolescent male, but the big eyes and the full lips were all female.

Is the kid a hermaphrodite? Alex wondered.

Cases of people born with the sex organs of both genders were rare, but not unheard-of, and in Jayr's time there would have been no hormone treatments or sex-reassignment surgery to help her go one way or the other. Other than the deep-set eyes, soft mouth, and long white throat, her body had no noticeable gender characteristics. She could have been a pretty boy or a tough girl.

"My lady?" Jayr gestured toward the archway leading into the keep. "Shall we go in?"

Alex realized she was staring at the girl's chest. "Uh, sure. Lead the way."

The journey to America had been brief but uneasy for one group of Darkyn tourneyers. Driven from Italy by the relentless zealousness of the Brethren, the party could not anticipate how they would be received by their kind in this new world. Completely cut off from any contact with other Kyn for five centuries, they no longer followed the rigid rules of protocol and conduct of the past. Many had never known any Kyn outside their reclusive group. Those among the exiles who had lived under the old ways had discarded much of what they had left behind them so long ago. All knew that this tournament might well prove to be their salvation, or their extermination.

So they came to the Realm quietly, silently, to see how it would be.

The sound coming from below drew one exile to the window. There he stood and looked down upon a good portion of the garrison, armed and assembled for presentation. A subtle aura of power and confidence surrounded a tall, dark-haired male. The deferential positions of the other Kyn marked him as the highest-ranked male. Shadow cloaked him, his woman and the Kyn greeting the visiting dignitary, but as they moved to enter the castle, moonlight revealed what the night had sought to conceal.

Alive.

His gloved hand reached out, clamping onto the stone windowsill as his unblinking gaze followed them. He had watched his enemy fall, and had left England on the assurance that his honor had been restored. But here was proof that the trap had failed. Here was the one thing that made mockery of all he was.

"The blood on my blade," he murmured, deaf to the stone cracking beneath his grip.

Turning away, he saw the walls of the corridor shrink back, shadows swelling like his hatred, taunting him with what would never be his. No castle. No lady on his arm. No title. Nothing to signify his rank. Only the hollow march of time and a meaningless pantomime of existence.

He'd been a fool to believe it over. Now he would have to take again what had been rightfully his from the beginning.

This castle. A lady on his arm. The title to which he had been born.

All of this will be mine.

He went to the window and renewed the vow he had made so long ago. "You will be nothing, as I was. You will be the blood on my blade . . . the blood in my blade . . . the blood of my blade."

It was his bloodright.

Because Byrne and Michael were talking, Alex walked with Jayr and Phillipe. The two seneschals had greeted each other with formal bows but didn't seem especially friendly. Maybe they didn't know each other too well, or were supposed to act that way.

The blood on my blade.

Those five words slammed into Alex's head so hard she could almost feel her eardrums bulge out. A moment later a deep, dark hole opened up in the stone in front of her.

All of this will be mine . . . mine . . . mine.

The toneless voice shrieked from the hole, and she jumped back, colliding with Phillipe.

"My lady?" His big hands cradled her elbows. "Alexandra?"

"That." She turned to him and pointed to the hole in the walkway, but it wasn't there anymore. "What was that?"

Phillipe stared past her. "I see nothing."

"But I . . ." A scream of rage filled her head, and she slapped her hands to her ears while she yelled over the noise, *"Michael."*

He was already there, holding her up between him and his seneschal. "I am here, *chérie*," he said, his voice barely audible over the howling inside her skull. He looked at Phillipe. "She is ill again."

"No. I hear it. I see it." She turned her head and saw a wide black crack run across the stone. "There. It's over there. *Look*, damn it."

You will be as nothing, as I was, blood on my blade the blood in my blade the blood of my blade bloodright bloodright bloodright—

This time the voice deafened her, while the crack in the stone gaped wider and uglier than before and belched out the stink of horses and smoke and death. As if the devil himself were trying to claw his way up from the underworld.

"Alexandra." Michael's lips formed her name, but she couldn't hear him. He shook her. "Speak to me."

"Vengeance. Michael. Here." He didn't understand her because she wasn't speaking English anymore. Why did it sound like English to her when it wasn't? She stared at the widening abyss and felt the stone rumbling under her feet. "Bloodright." As the voice in her head bellowed its rage, she whispered its promise. "It's here, and no one . . . nothing can stop it."

The hole seemed to collapse inward, but a moment later it convulsed and exploded outward, sending a geyser of dismembered body parts, fire, and bloody smoke into the air.

Alex shrieked and covered her head with her arms. But something made her look again, something that glittered like polished bone, something that had not yet come out of the pit—

Whimpering, *Dol an dearg bhàinidh*—

Crying, *The field*—

Shouting, *Burn it down.*

Raging, *Burn it all down.*

"Burn the field." Alex pushed away from the hands holding her, unable to breathe or think as she shouted the words roaring behind her eyes. "Burn the field—"

Alexandra. Come to me.

The new voice seized her, wrapping her in warm velvet ropes. They dragged her to the pit, pushing her over the edge into its suffocating void and what waited at the bottom.

Jayr lunged, catching the smaller woman before she fell over onto the walkway.

"My lady." A moment after Jayr lifted Alexandra into her

arms the seigneur was there, taking her from her. His *sygkenis*'s head lolled against his chest. Jayr saw teeth marks and fresh blood on Alexandra's bottom lip, evidence that she had bitten through it. But why? And why did she not heal at once, as other Kyn did? "My lord, what ails her?"

Cyprien shifted his lady's limp form into a more secure hold. "I don't know. Her talent . . ." He didn't finish the statement, but turned to Byrne. "Is there a place I can take her?"

"Of course." Byrne gestured, and his men dispersed. "Jayr, escort the seigneur to his chambers."

Jayr had seen Kyn display strange talents, but never one that caused them to bite themselves and black out. "My lord, perhaps I should take the seigneur and Dr. Keller to the infirmary."

"Yes," Cyprien said, almost too quickly. "That is preferable."

Byrne frowned but nodded his consent.

Alexandra Keller remained unconscious as Jayr led the seigneur through the back passages to the infirmary. Harlech intercepted them at the threshold but stood back in silence and gave Jayr only a single, narrow look before continuing on his way.

"Does this happen often to her, seigneur?" Jayr asked as she pulled back the linens of one of the gurneys they used to transport men who were injured in the lists.

"Not very often." Cyprien gently lowered the unconscious female to the crisp sheets and brushed her hair back from her pale face. "She will need blood."

Jayr retrieved a bag from the chill room, but was astonished to see that the seigneur had taken an intravenous kit from the supply cabinet and was preparing to insert the copper-tipped needle into a raised vein on the back of Alexandra's hand. No Kyn fed by tube unless they were grievously wounded or unable to swallow.

How to put it diplomatically? Jayr thought. "Should she not drink, my lord?"

"She does not feed as we do." He took the unit of blood from her and swiftly attached the thin plastic tubing that fed its contents directly into Alexandra's vein. He took her other hand in his and watched as the transfusion restored a more natural color to her face.

"There." Jayr relaxed a little. "She looks better. My lord, why does your lady take blood only by tube? Has she no *dents acérées*?"

"My *sygkenis* has an aversion to drinking blood," Cyprien said. "She is a physician, and devoted herself to healing other humans before she changed. She equates feeding to harming them. She has also been influenced by the vampire mythology of this time, which you know is completely ridiculous." He met her gaze, and in his was pure, turquoise-edged steel. "I will not hear her ridiculed for her wishes while we are here."

"No one would be so ill-mannered, my lord." Jayr stepped back from the bed, but felt compelled to add, "You need not be concerned that she will be shunned or rejected by the others. It is common knowledge that your lady has helped many Kyn, and everyone knows that she did not invite the change."

"No, she did not." His lovely mouth thinned. "Byrne must have told you that I forced it on her."

"When you were enthralled," Jayr amended for him, "and she enraptured."

"My *tresora*—Richard's spy in my household—arranged for it to happen to protect the Kyn. She assumed it would kill Alexandra like all the other humans we have tried to change over time." He rubbed his thumb across his *sygkenis*'s narrow knuckles. "Somehow she survived."

"I begin to understand." Without thinking, Jayr placed her hand on Alexandra's forehead. "Poor lady." She abruptly remembered before whom she spoke. "Seigneur, I do not mean to imply that you—"

"She saved me, Jayr. She gave me back my face and my heart and my hope. For that I took away her human life and everything of importance in it. I put her in terrible danger. Then Richard took her from me and . . ." He paused and visibly composed himself. "I want her to rest and enjoy this time here. I want her to see that the Kyn can be as noble as she is."

Jayr nodded. "How may I help, my lord?"

He placed Alexandra's hand by her hip. "I will keep her at

my side as often as I can in the days ahead. I would appreciate it if you could look out for her when I cannot."

Yet another duty, when there were not enough hours in the day to see to the ones already made hers, as well as care for her lord. And this to play nursemaid to a female with whom she likely had as much in common as she did the Queen of England.

But now Jayr knew more about Alexandra Keller, far more than Cyprien or anyone who had not been made Kyn by Kyn would ever know. And perhaps here was someone who could in return understand her as no one ever had.

Jayr bowed. "I am at your service, my lord."

Alexandra stirred, her lips moving as she murmured something. Cyprien bent over, caught the words, and frowned as he straightened.

"What did she say?" Jayr asked.

Cyprien looked at her, his own eyes puzzled. "Something about dragonflies."

Chapter 6

Alex opened her eyes to find herself on her back, staring up at a starry night sky. She lifted her head an inch but didn't see the people she expected to, or familiar surroundings. She was alone in a place she didn't recognize, some sort of wilderness.

But there had been smoke, fire, blood . . . a stone floor cracking, opening up into an endless abyss. . . .

Hadn't there been?

Carefully she pushed herself up to her knees. Nothing hurt, but there wasn't enough light to do a thorough self-exam. Wherever she was, the air felt dry, cold, and dusty. No smoke, fire, or bottomless pits anywhere to be seen, either.

"Hello?" She stood, turning around to get the full view. "Anyone here?"

She'd landed in a desert.

Not the flat, endless sand, Sahara variety of desert; this place was hilly and ugly and had rocks and scraggly little weeds growing here and there. Nothing moved, and she couldn't see anyone around her. The only light came from the crescent moon overhead, and stars so bright and cold that Alex wondered for a second if she had been kicked off Earth and had landed on someone else's planet.

No alien monsters lurking out here. She squinted, making out the silhouette of something small, long-eared, and covered with spines creeping across the dirt. The animal flattened itself and disappeared under a rock. *Wherever here is.*

It would help if she could remember more than being terrified out of her mind, and running from whatever had done that. Her memory felt like a pillow that had been beaten out of shape.

Did I come here on my own? Did I run?

Something seemed to pull her in the direction of one of the bigger hills, and, having nothing better to do, she walked to it. A very earthy-looking snake slithered out from a clump of weeds, froze when it saw her, and coiled back on itself, finally going limp and still.

Great, Alex thought. *I make snakes keel over.*

She had to climb all the way to the top of the hill before she saw what lay below, and then she sat down quickly and hid herself in a patch of weeds.

The valley beneath the hill stretched for miles, and tents filled up half of it. Big tents and little tents—more than a thousand, more than she'd ever seen. They weren't the Boy Scout kind, or the weekend-camper variety. These were the rough, primitive, something-got-skinned homemade jobbers. Except they weren't all pretty and decorated like the ones in movies about Native Americans. Whoever had entrenched here didn't have much beyond some sacks and what looked like skinny pumpkins dangling from at least one of each tent's poles.

Why would I want to come here? Alex rubbed her cold arms and tried to think of whom she had been with before waking up. A tiny dragonfly with glowing purple-blue wings hovered next to her face, making her swat at it. *Maybe I got a helpful push down the rabbit's hole.*

Annoyed, she concentrated, trying to reshape the chaotic images in the back of her mind.

Names were a problem, but she could see the face of one guy with gorgeous turquoise eyes. Very tall, very cute. Another one, scarier and not so cute, but whose yellow-brown eyes made her feel safe. She couldn't quite place either one, but they felt important. She flashed on a third, a red-haired giant with scrolled blue tattoos all over his face. . . .

If they'd dumped her here like this, with her brain a muddle, no supplies, and no way to defend herself, how could they be friends?

A sense that she'd been here before, more than once, made her wonder if she could blame anyone but herself.

She knew this place. Somehow.

The most logical thing would be to climb downhill and see

who occupied the tents; they might shed some light on what had happened. As Alex thought of doing just that, an invisible icy finger traced a slow path down her spine. Suddenly, acutely aware of the sweat that soaked her and her clothes, Alex sat back on her heels and hugged her knees. The little dragonfly brought a friend, and both buzzed around her face.

Don't move from here, something inside her warned. *Not an inch.*

She knew she couldn't sit here all night; she had to get some indication of where she was. The tents had been put up in circles around little campfires, most of which had burned down to glowing coals. A temporary corral set off to one side of the encampment held about three hundred horses and twice as many camels.

Camels?

All right, there were camels. Maybe it was one of those wacky wilderness preserves with emus and ostriches and such. Or maybe she was in Iraq. Whatever the case, there weren't enough animals in the corral. If there was one guy in every tent, two-thirds must have come here on foot. Or maybe they drove, and the parking lot was at the other end of the valley.

Three dragonflies flew in lazy circles in front of her, glowing like purple-blue night-lights.

Alex had a feeling that if she hiked through the hills, she wouldn't see any signs of modern life. No RVs, trailers, cars, or motorcycles. Not a single battery-operated radio, lantern, or camp stove. Whoever was here was here, and didn't have much. If there really was anyone here. Other than the animals and the dragonflies, there were no signs of life, not even guards patrolling the perimeter.

Why would I expect guards? I'm not in the middle of a war zone.

Yet the instant Alex thought that, everything seemed different. During her time in the Peace Corps, she'd seen plenty of tribal and government troops who bivouacked in the rough. They'd kept their encampments just as sparse and tidy as this one so that they could be broken down, packed up, and moved at a moment's notice.

On foot. In a desert. In a place with weird bugs, no electric lights, no parking lots, and stars she didn't recognize.

Alex froze as someone spoke from behind her in a language she didn't understand. She turned her head to see two figures in heavy armor hurrying toward her. One of them was tall, the other blocky, and both were running silent and fast. More dragonflies came, bathing her in their purple-blue light. At the same time, the smell of baking vanilla pound cake filled her head.

Alexandra.

A voice inside her mind. *Well, what else?* At least it was definitely someone she knew, could almost see in her head, although she couldn't think of his name. Someone had taken an eraser to the name portion of her memory for sure; she barely knew her own. Whoever the speaker was, his scent told her that he wasn't far away. She'd go to him. He'd protect her. Somehow she knew that was his job. Somehow she knew him.

The dragonflies, some twenty of them now, formed a straight line that pointed toward the encampment.

I've been waiting for you.

The words sounded gentle and tender, an invitation, not a threat. Whatever he wanted, it was bound to be nicer than whatever the two coming after her intended. She forced herself to her feet and followed the dragonflies as they flew down the hill, almost falling on her face several times before she skidded to a stop at the bottom. She could smell the animals along with his scent now, and saw that the pumpkins hanging from the tent poles were actually decapitated heads. A few were still dripping blood from the raw ends of their severed necks.

All of the heads belonged to women.

Don't look at them. They're not real. The voice came from the biggest tent at the very center of the encampment, one that glowed purple-blue like the dragonflies' wings. *Walk to the light. I am here.*

Alex glanced back over her shoulder. The guys in armor had made it over the hill and were sliding down it. The polished metal of the armor matched the glitter of the long broadswords they carried.

Damned if you do, decapitated if you don't?

Weaving between the smaller tents, Alex made her way

through the camp. The dragonflies flanked her like an official escort. The closer she came to the center tent, the brighter it glowed. By the time she reached it the dark light radiating from it had grown so intense that it almost fried her eyes. Then she saw why.

A million dragonflies covered the tent, their wings still but pulsing with the strange light.

She reached for the tent flap, but a big hand reached out and pulled her through without opening it. The tent was not a tent at all, and for a split second her skin screamed as she passed through a thin layer of scalding, sticky fluid. Before it could burn her alive, she was standing on the other side, inside the tent, shaking all over and staring up at a stern-looking, blond-haired man.

She didn't know him, but he was huge—more than twice her size—and he looked upset.

"Hi." Alex rubbed her arms with her hands. "Uh, nice tent. This a bad time for you? I can come back."

"You stay." He tacked a smile onto the end of that, relaxing the harsh lines of his face and showcasing his snow-white teeth. A face, Alex decided, that would make any woman's insides assume the consistency of pudding. "You came."

"Yeah, I did." It would be great if she knew why, and who he was, but she'd start with the immediate problem. "Where are we?"

"Don't you know?"

Alex glanced around. "Far as I know, I'm with you, inside a tent, in a camp in the desert. Hopefully not a desert outside Baghdad. I left all my rocket launchers and hand grenades at home."

"You're dreaming," he told her, taking a step closer.

"Not really." She felt bemused by the fact that he was built like a professional wrestler but spoke with the elegant English accent of a Cambridge professor. "You would not *believe* what you can buy off eBay these days."

"I meant that this is a dream. One which we are sharing." He opened his arms to her, and then seemed taken aback when she didn't accept his invitation to a hug. "Why are you afraid of me?"

"Knights in shining armor chased me into a camp of headless chicks. Your tent is made out of acid Jell-O. I don't know any British men who could be headliners on *RAW*." She lifted her shoulders. "Makes a girl a little careful about getting into full-body contact."

"You were in danger. I felt your terror. Then you summoned me. I came at once. As I always have." He gestured around them. "This is our sanctuary."

"Uh-huh." His friendliness made her want to jump on him and give him a big, sloppy kiss. Alex didn't often kiss people she liked, much less strangers, so she killed that idea immediately. "How could I call you? I don't have a mobile with me. I don't know who you are."

"I understand. Other things have made you not wish to remember. It is the same every time." His hands settled on her shoulders. "I would not rush you, but God curse me, my patience is not endless."

His touch made a lot of the bad feelings take a hike. Alex wondered why she'd want to forget someone like him. He didn't have turquoise eyes, but who cared? "Waiting is no fun."

"Aye, my lady, and I no better than a lovesick squire since you left." He uttered a short, self-deprecating laugh. "I have not rested since you went away. I begin to wonder if I ever will."

"You're saying that we were together. You and me. In the past." Alex inspected him, but she couldn't recall ever being with an erudite wrestler. Surely she wouldn't have forgotten someone with such a lousy neck tattoo, made to resemble a blurry garrote of green thorns. But the only thing that rang any bells was his scent, like velvety-soft warm vanilla pound cake. "You don't have me mixed up with another lady doctor, do you?"

"Alexandra." He smiled a little as he bent his head. "You are the only lady doctor I know."

Alex didn't expect the kiss, but she didn't kick him in the groin in outrage. The first part felt nice. He put his mouth on hers and used his lips to tug at hers, asking her without words to let him in. Not that she would. This was going to be only a friendly, introductory, hello-again sort of kiss. Something to jolt her brain cells into working a little better, nothing more. He'd probably kissed her a million times.

The kiss didn't ring any bells. Several alarms, however, started clanging, and she went stiff.

He noticed and backed off, although not very far. "I should have taken you when you were bespelled. I could feel your trust, your affection." He ran a big hand over her hair, stroking her curls with rough delight. "You are like no woman I've known."

"That's good," she said, wondering if she could jump back through the tent wall without his help, and if the dragonflies would come after her, "because I still don't know you."

"I am glad you do not. I played the honorable fool." The grooves running from his nose to bracket his mouth deepened. "If I had taken you when I had you in my hands, our bond would have been made complete. You would never have departed."

He was starting to sound like a stalker, not a lover. She'd have to take her chances with the tent.

"Sorry that didn't work out." She braced her hands between them. "How about you let me go?"

"No." He caught the back of her hair in his fist. "I accept that he took you from me. But this is our time, our place. He cannot be here between us. If nothing else, I will have this."

Turquoise eyes. He must have taken her away. She didn't know why or when, but she was supposed to be with him. And not here.

"I gotta go." Tears of frustration burned her eyes as she tried desperately to remember the other man, and how she could get back to him. Her body didn't help matters by ignoring her and rubbing itself up against the blond giant. "I'm not doing this. I can't."

A low hum shivered through the walls of the tent, the purple-blue dragonfly light dimming.

"You will not go to him." He wrapped one arm around her and lifted her off her feet. "He cannot have every moment of your existence. You summoned me. You want me." He put her on his eye level. "You chose me."

He took a couple of steps and dropped down with her into a

pile of robes and blankets and pillows, stretching his body over hers. He pressed her thighs apart with his hands, propping himself in the space he made, on his knees and elbows.

Alex surged up and then swore as the weight and heat of his body made her body clench and ready itself for him.

"This is how it could have been for us that night." He shifted against her, lining up their hips and covering one of her breasts with his hand. His fingers closed and opened over her, kneading the tight mound, rubbing his hard palm against the pucker of her nipple. "All the while I cared for you like a brother, but I wanted more. So did you. With every breath I took I could taste your desire."

"I have a brother," Alex said, feeling a second surge of panic. "You're not him."

"You're so beautiful," he breathed, not hearing her anymore as he played with her breasts. "I've dreamed it would be like this."

Alex twisted, trying simultaneously to avoid his mouth colliding with hers and the thick, wide column of his penis nesting against her crotch. She lost. The man pushed his tongue in her mouth while he settled himself between her legs, and held her there. As he kissed and sucked at her tongue, he fitted the length of his cock against the long notch of her labia, working it over her with small, insistent nudges, only the few layers of clothing between them keeping it all from getting out of hand.

She tried to scream a no, but the word came in instead of out, a rush of excited breath, then an exhaled moan of longing.

"Yes, my lady." He rested his cool cheek against hers. "I know. You need me inside you. I can smell how hot and wet you are. Let me have you. Let me feel you on my cock."

The low, guttural demands almost sent Alex over the edge. She could hear the soft, yearning sounds coming from her throat, and the gnawing ache his erection had created between her legs shrieked to be filled and stroked and sated. If he didn't fuck her, right this second, Alex felt sure she'd go insane.

If she hadn't already.

Hunger, screaming need, and impending psychotic break aside, on some deeper level Alex knew how wrong this was. She loved another man, and that one meant everything to her.

Something else had taken hold of her funhouse and was operating the equipment. She tried to take control, but her body went into full mutiny. She couldn't stop answering the stroke of his hips, the pressure of his sex. She did want him, and she could handle that, but the fact that she didn't love him, didn't know him—

. . . I cared for you like a brother . . .

Naked, facedown on an uncomfortable pallet. A wet cloth wielded by a gentle hand smoothing over her back. Blood and herbs, warmth, safety.

The wanting and the fear slowly drained out of her, leaving behind a limp, distant feeling of déjà vu.

"Water boiled with willow bark and valerian," Alex muttered under his mouth. "Left to cool."

He moved to nuzzle her neck, and then went still. Alex looked down and saw four deep, ugly slashes rip across his chest. "No." He covered the wounds with his hand. "Do not do this, Alexandra. Not again."

Alex studied his face. The light changed from purple-blue to a reddish orange, and created grim shadows around his eyes, nose, and mouth. "Your talent. You wouldn't tell me what it was."

He didn't answer, but rolled away from her, throwing an arm over his face.

She felt grateful rather than relieved. Whoever he was, she liked him. He was a decent guy.

"I can read the minds of killers," she said, turning toward him and propping herself on her elbow. "What can you do?"

"Kyn do not trade tales about talent. Damn you." He swore as he got to his feet and strode around the tent. "I will not relive what has been." He stopped and glared at her. "We can have more than repetitions of what was. We can make a whole new world for ourselves; can't you see that?"

She stared at the top of the tent. "So your talent is worse than mine." Under that very hot, ready-to-do-the-nasty-all-night facade was, Alex suspected, a very nice man. Why else would he be . . .

She sat up. "You helped me. You took care of me. I remember." The memories went as quickly as they'd come to her, and she tilted her head. "You know, when you get pissed off or upset, you smell like vanilla pound cake."

"Larkspur." He came over and knelt before her. "You are not ready for me."

She bit her lip. "That's nice."

"Alexandra." He bent forward and pressed his mouth to her forehead. "Come back. I will be waiting."

Alex nodded, although she was more interested in staring at his mouth. "I have to get out of here now, right?"

"Yes." He kissed her hard on the mouth, and then raised his head and listened. "They will wake you soon. You will be as you were with them."

"I will," she promised. She looked down at herself. "I need some clothes."

He brought a light robe to her and went to stand by the tent flap. He had done the exact same thing before, Alex thought, but this time he watched her dress.

She joined him, startled by how sore she was and how slowly she was moving. "Thank you."

"I am at your service, my lady."

She touched his cheek, took a deep breath, and then pushed herself through the tent wall.

Leaving Cyprien to attend to Alexandra, Jayr went to the men's quarters. Knocking on Rainer's locked chamber door produced no response, so she used her master key to let herself in. The warrior's rooms, which he had painted with stripes of red, orange, and purple, reflected his passion for collecting things. At the moment Rainer was obsessed with traveling shows, and the playbills, costumes, and props he arranged in various artful displays made it seem as if a circus had exploded in his rooms. His lamps stood unlit, and the place seemed unoccupied, but Rainer's scent, like strawberries warmed by the sun, colored the shadows.

"Hiding is pointless," Jayr said. "I can smell you."

"Go away," a muffled voice said from nowhere she could pinpoint. "I am resting."

"You are sulking." Like all Kyn, Jayr could see well in the

dark, but the wounded man's bed lay empty, and none of his furnishings were large enough to hide him. "Where are you?"

A polite cough made her look up.

Rainer hung upside down, his bearlike body suspended from a snare rope bound around his ankles. More rope bound his arms to his sides and secured the end of a black sack, which covered his face.

From beneath the hood he said, "It's not as bad as it looks."

"Christ knows, it never is." Jayr went to the rope where it was anchored, untied it, and lowered the man down until she could grab him with one arm. She stripped off the rope and hood. Dried blood stained Rainer's sea blue tunic and vivid green trousers in patches, but it appeared that his wounds had healed. "Who did you enrage this time?"

"I cannot say. Perhaps God again." He found his feet and turned away from her. "My thanks. You should go, attend to things more important than my misfortunes."

"Your misfortunes are more amusing." Jayr lit one of his lamps and looked around the room, which had been rifled through and left in complete disarray. "Tell me who did this to you."

"Would that I could oblige you. But I went to sleep at dawn, and opened my eyes this evening to find myself in the dark and at the end of my rope." He grinned at his own pun and hobbled over to an armchair draped with a trapeze artist's glittering cape. "I suppose it was Beaumaris," he said as he slowly sat down. "He considered the entire accidental-stabbing incident most humiliating. I don't know why. It wasn't as if it landed in his cods."

"If Beau were still angry with you, he would beat you into a smear on the floor, not hang you like venison to be smoked." Jayr came around him and saw how he was holding his left arm. "Take off your shirt."

"Why, my lady." He attempted a leer. "You should have mentioned that you fancied me long before this."

"Modesty demanded my silence." The lightness of his voice didn't quite disguise the pain beneath it. "Are you going to show me, or am I going to strip you?"

He sighed. "As much as I wish I could display myself for you, I fear it is beyond me."

Jayr brought the lamp over, holding it so that the light illuminated his body. She took in a quick breath when she saw that his left arm appeared bent at right angles, impossibly, in four different places.

"Oh, Rain." She set the lamp aside. "Why did you not call out for help?"

"I have been contriving to release myself. Had I two good arms and a blade within reach, I would have." He tried to lift the twisted limb, failed, and sighed. "My return to the lists must again be postponed. Do you think Beaumaris will miss me?"

"I will tell him and the others not to celebrate too much." Jayr lit two more lamps and made a circuit around the room, but found nothing to indicate who had attacked the warrior. "You truly don't remember anything that happened?"

"Truly, no." He rubbed the back of his neck with his good hand. "I fed, I went to bed alone, and I woke up a bellpull."

The way he refused to look at her, the ceaseless jests, his eagerness to send her away all told Jayr one thing: He was lying. But why?

She crouched by the side of his chair and ripped his sleeve away from the cruelly distorted arm. "Is this all, or were other parts of you broken?"

He answered her through gritted teeth after he hissed a curse. "My dignity is in rather sorry condition. Perhaps I offended this intruder, or he simply happened upon my rooms and disliked my decor."

"No one likes your decor," she assured him. "Does it look as if anything is missing?"

He shook his head. "Everything valuable appears to still be here." He nodded toward a scattering of small red balls. "Even my collection of clown noses."

Jayr studied the new angles injury had made in his limb. It appeared as if all of his arm bones as well as his elbow joint had been broken. "I cannot repair this as it is."

"Never mind it." He patted her shoulder and then hissed. "Harlech will gladly put it to rights."

She carefully felt the bulging flesh over the healed breaks.

"The seigneur and his lady have arrived. When Lady Alexandra is able, I will have her see to it."

Rainer stiffened. "I have no need of a human leech."

"Your arm is badly broken, and she is not human anymore." Jayr watched him avoid her eyes. "Rain, if you're in any sort of trouble, you can confide in me. You know that I will say nothing to our lord or the others." She waited. "Did Farlae do this?"

"Farlae? God, no." He chuckled. "He does not enjoy my brass ooh-gah horns, of course, but I have ceased playing with them in his presence. Would you like to hear them, Jayr? I have them in sixteen different ooh-gahs."

"Rain."

He sighed heavily. "No one likes my ooh-gah horns. Pity." His expression, open and guileless as it was, told her that he was determined to keep from her who had done this to him. Rain was never so winsome and charming as when he was in trouble. "I know how occupied you are with the tournament. Leave me."

"As soon as you agree to permit the lady to repair your bones." When he began to protest she glared. "Or I will see to it that Lord Byrne visits you next."

He sat up quickly, jolted his arm, and winced. "Very well."

Reluctantly she left him, but before she exited the keep she sent two guards back to Rainer's quarters: one to deliver blood, and the other to stand guard.

"Jayr." Harlech trotted out of the stables and caught up with her just outside the smithy. With him came the scent of white carnations, which almost blocked out the smell of manure and horses. "How fares Cyprien's lady?"

"She's resting." Jayr knew Harlech would not have used his talent for hearing voices from a distance to eavesdrop on the seigneur and his *sygkenis*. His expression, however, told her he was extremely agitated about something.

Had Harlech taken out his temper on Rainer? Was that why he was shedding scent like one newly turned? "Where were you earlier tonight?"

"After sending the men to greet the seigneur, I came here to see to the horses being delivered." He gestured toward the stable. "Why?"

"It doesn't matter." Jayr deliberately turned to inspect the jousting field. The colder weather had turned the turf brown, but that could not be helped. She would have to check the soil to assure that the rain had not left it too soft under the dead grass.

That reminded her. "Have the new tilt barriers been painted?"

"They're drying in the barns now." Harlech used a rag from his back pocket to wipe the perspiration from his brow. "Jayr, Beaumaris said that when the seigneur arrived, his lady behaved as if delirious, spoke nonsense, and then collapsed. Is this so?"

"Partly." After the incident with Cyprien and his *sygkenis*, Jayr had expected some gossip to spread, but not this fast. "Lady Alexandra did become ill, and fainted." She remembered Alexandra's muttering. "But I think the nonsense she spoke was in Scots Gaelic."

"What?" Harlech's eyes narrowed. "She is a woman of this century. An American. How . . ."

"The seigneur would not say, and it is the lady's private business." She met Harlech's uneasy gaze. "Instruct Beaumaris to say no more on it. The lady belongs to Cyprien and, like him, is our honored guest."

"An honored guest who is going mad?" He glanced at the keep before lowering his voice. "What if Richard used his talent on her?"

Here was the reason for his agitation, Jayr thought, and it had nothing to do with Rain. When their *jardin* had dwelled in the Scottish Highlands, Richard Tremayne had once visited, and had chastised Harlech for mishandling Lady Elizabeth's trunks. Among other things, Harlech's talent allowed him to hear the voices of humans and Kyn from as far away as a mile, but it also made him acutely vulnerable to the high lord's voice. Richard's rebuke had temporarily deafened him, and the effect had lasted for weeks. Harlech had avoided being in Richard's presence ever since.

"No, it is not that," Jayr said, placing her hand on his arm. "She is as vulnerable to Kyn talent as a human. If he had damaged her mind, she would be like the others—a moving doll."

Jayr saw that she wasn't convincing Harlech. "It matters not. When Cyprien is occupied, I will attend to her personally."

"While you do"—Harlech drew a slim copper blade from his belt and pressed it into her hand—"watch your back."

Chapter 7

Jayr slipped Harlech's dagger into a sheath on her hip, clasped hands with her second, and made her way back to the keep. Only a few hours remained until dawn, and preparations for the annual tournament had reached a critical point. She had yet to see to her master's needs; she would have to do something about Rainer and Harlech, and find a moment to check on Alexandra as well.

She had to move faster.

It could be worse, Jayr thought as she hurried through the corridors to the wardrobe. During her human life, tournaments had included immense feasts that required emptying out the keep's larder and stockyards. Some had lasted for days, even weeks. Fortunately the Kyn's diet limited their choices of nourishment to blood and wine, both of which Jayr had stockpiled for months in anticipation of the demand.

What troubled her was what she could not anticipate. The Kyn driven out of France and Italy had few ties with the American *jardins*, and were likely eager to set up new territories. Most of their lords were men unknown to her or her master. They might use the tournament as a means to acquire new status from Cyprien and eliminate their rivals.

The last time the Kyn had resorted to achieving rank and status through assassinations, they had touched off the *jardin* wars.

Jayr went to the north wing of the Realm, where much of the household work was done. There the keeper of the wardrobe, Farlae, ruled over his small band of tanners, fullers, weavers, and seamstresses.

Most of the garment making took place in two large workrooms. The skilled women of the *jardin* gathered to ply their needles in the busy, friendly confines of the first chamber, while Farlae's sewing machines, forms, and armoires occupied the adjoining room. Anyone could enter the communal sewing chamber, but few dared disturb the wardrobe master while he worked his magic in his private workroom.

"You look as if a leper were paying you court," a soft, amused voice said beside her.

"That might prove more entertaining than this night, Viviana." Jayr turned to see Harlech's wife dressed in a work gown and scarf. In her arms she carried two bolts of cloth, one gray and one so darkly purple that it seemed black. Stains of the same colors spattered her skirts. "I had thought the dye work finished."

"So did I, until a few hours ago." She handed the bolts to one of the seamstresses, who took them to the cutting table. Viviana rubbed her palms together as if ridding them of dirt. "One of the Italians sent his seneschal to Farlae with orders for purple and gray silks."

Jayr frowned. The Kyn held on to few of the old superstitions, but one they did was the custom of retiring the colors of any fallen *jardin*. It showed respect for the dead while neatly avoiding any lingering bad luck they may have left behind.

Purple and gray had enormous misfortune attached to them, for they had once belonged to Sherwood.

"A tribute banner is unlikely," Jayr said to her friend. "Who would want to show them?"

"None save a Judas, I daresay." Viviana tucked a strand of her auburn hair behind her small ear, and for a moment Jayr thought she looked angry. "Unless there are other surprise guests come to bedevil me and my women, all will be finished here by morn." She nodded toward the closed door separating the two chambers. "Farlae will have it no other way."

"My thanks." Jayr thought of Harlech's fear. "You should talk to your husband before night's end. What happened to Cyprien's lady brought back some bad memories for him."

Viviana stared at her, visibly alarmed. "How so?"

"He fears Richard used his voice on her," Jayr said quietly. "I told him that it could not be so, but I don't think he believed me." She hesitated. "Would something like this—something that reminded him of that time in Scotland—cause Harlech to lose his temper?"

The other woman's shoulders slumped before she replied. "No. Unlike Richard, he can control his emotions." Viviana forced a friendly smile on her tight lips. "Do not worry over my husband, Jayr. I will see to him. Better you find out who is trying to honor what should remain in the ground."

Jayr nodded and thought of the lords who had sent word of attending. None had journeyed from Italy. "Where is this Italian now?"

"Gone to town, according to his man. Gildie, wait." Viviana went to the table and stopped one of the women from using her shears. "You must add a measure for the rod sleeve, like so."

Jayr eyed the closed door between the two chambers. Farlae would not welcome the interruption, but she needed more information about this new lord and whether he made flouting custom a regular practice. She picked up one of the completed standards, went to the door, and knocked twice before she slipped inside.

Farlae's machines stood still and silent; the only sound came from the cutting tables, where various widths and lengths of fabrics in violet and white, Byrne's colors, hung from suspended rollers. Silver blades snicked as they sliced across a shivering curtain of priceless amethyst Asian silk.

Jayr waited until the shears finished the cut before she spoke. "Lord Locksley looked with favor on my bronze leather jacket."

"Did he." The words, uttered by a voice so deep that it growled more than it spoke, made the thin silk dance. "That one covets too much."

Farlae stepped out from behind the fabric, folding the cloud of red between his thick hands. Snipped threads clung to his fitted black garments, forming barely perceptible, chaotic patterns. Harsh light from the recessed bulbs overhead whitened his jagged mane and pale flesh, turning him into a specter of himself.

All humans and most Kyn found it difficult to look into Farlae's eyes. The lightness of his right, sea green eye might have been unremarkable if not for the strange, irregular black stain that had eclipsed and paralyzed his left. He had been born thus, and had remained blind in the darkened eye until he had risen to walk the night. Becoming Kyn had given him full vision, but had not removed the hellish mote or allowed the eye to move.

Jayr did not mind the wardrobe keeper's uneven gaze. She knew only too well how it felt to be singled out because of a physical flaw.

Farlae did not order her from the room, but regarded her as he might a sudden infestation of moths. "What do you want?"

Six more hours to a night, the body of a woman grown, and Aedan mac Byrne's love. Disgusted with herself, Jayr held up the standard. "The name of the one who ordered this."

"A newcomer—one with appalling taste in silks and men. His diminutive seneschal did not give me his name." He reduced the bundle of silk to a flatter pile of folds and set it aside. "The little man was in too much of a hurry to perform the usual courtesies."

"Or make a more appropriate choice of colors."

"Not every Darkyn went to the field during the *jardin* wars, and you know what an odd, proud lot the Italians can be. Likely this one thinks he is entitled." Farlae's dark-cast eye narrowed as he consulted a list of figures. "His man did seem to hop with nerves."

"What made him nervous?"

"The prospect of displeasing his lord, delaying his lord, or whatever else terrorizes you seneschal." Farlae reached up and tugged on the edge of twilight-colored damask. "There is but a week left until the ball, and you've not put in a request for a gown. I have some time now to fit you."

"I've no need for one." They had this argument every winter. "When is the Italian's man to return for his order?"

"Tomorrow midnight. Viviana and the women will have the handwork completed by then. Are you sure you don't need a gown? I acquired a bolt of very fetching flame-colored velvet from Peking." His brutal hands moved with uncommon speed and grace as he measured out and marked lines on the damask with a bit of chalk. "I could make it up into something more impressive than those dismal leathers Locksley would filch for himself."

Jayr liked wearing leather for a number of reasons. Yet with all the newcomers expected at this year's tournament, her manner of dress would be more noticeable. "Not a gown."

"A tunic and trousers, then." Farlae's normal eye shifted to the ceiling. "Cut in the usual boring fashion."

She knew her preference for dressing like a male did not sit well with the wardrobe keeper. "It prevents confusion."

"Among other things." Farlae picked up his shears. "I could dress that scarecrow body of yours in something more fetching than squire's rags. With the right amount of boning and padding . . ." He snipped a shape out of the deep purple-blue damask, creating an hourglass-shaped hole. "This could be you."

Jayr gestured toward his face. "While you can use the leftover scraps to fashion an eye patch."

A moment passed before Farlae released a rumbling quake of laughter. "May I never face you on the jousting field. More than my vanity and pride, I suspect, would suffer."

"As would mine." Jayr felt a familiar itch across the back of her neck. "I must go. When the Italian's man returns for his order, summon me at once."

Farlae nodded.

"One more thing." She knew that the women of the *jardin* often shared gossip as they worked, and Farlae heard most if not all of it. "Who do you know besides Beau who has a grievance with Rainer?"

"Our color-blind peacock?" The wardrobe keeper rolled his eyes. "Anyone with taste."

Nottingham watched as his seneschal climbed into the car. As soon as the door closed his driver drove away from the hotel.

"Well?"

"Our contact transferred the last of the money from the accounts in Geneva and London," Skald said. "The authorities have frozen the accounts in Rome and Paris. They are being held as evidence in an unnamed criminal investigation."

"What the Brethren cannot take, they bankrupt." Nottingham watched the humans walking alongside the street and tapped on the glass divider when he saw a lone, youthful-looking female. The driver slowed to park in front of the bus stop and the bench upon which the female sat, a large purse and a plastic bag of groceries beside her.

Skald lowered the window. "Good evening, miss." He held up a folded map and pointed to it. "Could you tell me how close we are to this street?"

The female rose, picked up her bags, and walked to the window, peering at the occupants instead of the map. "What's the name of the street you're looking for?"

Nottingham inspected her. Cheap garments, worn shoes, poorly tinted hair with several inches of dark roots pulled back into a thin tail. But her eyes were a soft sea green, and she had a rather lovely mouth. He nodded to his seneschal.

"It's here," Skald said, holding the map out to her. When she stepped close to take it, he asked, "Would you like a ride to your destination?"

A sudden burst of sharp scent, like spearmint, wafted out of the window into the human's face.

The young woman breathed in the strong, sharp scent, opened her mouth, and then frowned. "What is . . ." The purse and bag slipped from her limp hand and dropped to her feet. "A ride?"

Skald opened the door and helped the female in. She sat across from him, staring at him as if in a fog. "What is your name, miss?"

"Lydia." She swallowed. "I have to go home. My kids are waiting, and my husband will be . . . I have to . . . make . . ." She shook her head.

Nottingham looked into her eyes and saw the confusion fall away into seething, helpless lust. So it seemed that American females would be as easy to control as their Italian counterparts.

And suddenly he despised her for it. "You will do whatever I wish, human."

Lydia's mouth sagged open for a moment. "Whatever you wish."

Skald shifted over to the facing seat to sit beside her and patted her thigh with his hand. "Quiet, now, miss."

The young housewife opened her mouth to speak, frowned, and sat back against the leather cushions.

"Are you certain you wish to go on with this, my lord?" Skald unfastened the front of the girl's trousers and began working them down to her knees.

"I don't mind," Lydia said, as if he were addressing her. "Your breath is really, really fresh, isn't it?" She giggled.

"Your leman has not forgotten; nor has the jester," Skald continued. "They could have proofs that they kept. If they expose you, with him there—"

"They will do nothing." Nottingham was not worried about his former lover, and he had personally seen to the jester. He pulled the pliant human onto her knees before him. "As soon as we arrive, I want my colors hung through the place."

Aniseed blended with spearmint, thickening and heating the air.

Lydia gripped the seat on either side of his thighs and gazed up at Nottingham. "You smell like Halloween candy."

"I must again advise against this," Skald said, gathering the housewife's ponytail in his fist and using it to pull her head back into the proper position. "Seeing your colors will infuriate them."

"Precisely so." Nottingham pushed up the female's chin and put his mouth to the side of her throat. "Do it now."

Skald opened the front of his own trousers and jerked his hips up once, twice, three times. His small hands gripped Lydia's waist as he began a steady rhythm.

"Uh. Oh. Ah." She shuddered, eyes closed, fingernails gouging the leather of the seat. "So sweet. That's so sweet. Deeper. God, *yes.*"

Nottingham drew back, licking the smear of blood from his bottom lip as he watched his seneschal swive the human. "She is noisy." He had to speak over the torrent of praise and encouragement spilling from the female's lips.

"I can cut out her tongue, my lord," Skald said, not missing a beat as he cupped her breasts and squeezed until she whined and quivered. "But that will perhaps make her less amusing."

"Not yet." Nottingham opened the front of his trousers and pulled her head down, stuffing her mouth with his penis. Lydia moaned and sucked awkwardly at him, and that made everything better. "I want you to befriend the lord's seneschal. Find out everything you can about this Realm from him."

Skald playfully slapped the housewife's bare flank. "As you command, my lord."

When Alexandra awoke, Michael thought, she would insist on inspecting the Realm's infirmary. Jayr kept it clean and amply stocked, and Michael had no doubt it served its purpose well. His *sygkenis*'s standards, however, were very high, and she would delight in pointing out every flaw. It occurred to him that he might well keep Alexandra occupied during the tournament by asking her to improve things. Knowing his lover, she would turn the infirmary into a diminutive hospital, and teach Jayr and the men how to repair every sort of human or Kyn injury.

If Alexandra still cared about such things. She had not, he realized, shown any interest in being a doctor since their return from Ireland.

"Master, I think we must leave tonight and take the lady home," Phillipe said. He had arrived at the infirmary shortly after Jayr had left to attend to her master, and now stood brooding at the bedside. The seneschal looked as frustrated and worried as Michael felt. "This is not a good place for her now, when she is . . ." He made a helpless gesture.

"I know her talent can be disturbing to witness." Michael busied himself by changing the bag attached to his lover's IV. "But I cannot lock her away like a mad wife, *mon ami*. She has done nothing to deserve this."

"It is not the lady, but the one who stirred her talent who is the danger." His seneschal adjusted a fold of the sheet. "I spoke with some of the men of the *jardin*. All of the *tresora* and humans who serve here have been sent away."

Michael sat down and held Alexandra's cool hand between his. "Whoever made her ill with their thoughts is Kyn."

His seneschal nodded. "There is no one else."

As the American seigneur, Michael had many serious responsibilities. He had put off all of them in order to care for Alexandra, but Brethren activity in the United States was on the rise, and his suzerain were becoming restless. Then there were the newcomers from Europe, who would trade oaths of loyalty for new territories and grants of formal rule. No one would question Michael for leaving the tournament almost as soon as he had arrived, but it would not enhance his reputation as a leader.

Now it seemed that a Kyn had decided to kill. The tournament provided the perfect opportunity for murder; the weapons and battles they fought were quite real. Occasionally accidents happened. The murderer could cut off a victim's head and blame it on a poorly timed thrust. He owed it to every Kyn attending to discover who intended to inflict such harm—and to stop him before he did.

"Each time Alexandra needs me, I am made to choose between her and the Kyn," he said. "I would give my life for her, and yet somehow the Kyn always manage to come first. I cannot fathom why she stays with me."

"Love," Phillipe said simply.

"That is the worst of it." Michael rubbed his thumb across her slim, fragile-looking fingers. "This love between us is like nothing I know. I fear it will destroy her."

"Or save you both," Phillipe said. "At least, I think that is what Alexandra would say."

"Stop talking about me in French when I'm unconscious," Alexandra murmured, her eyes still closed. "It's rude. Plus I can't understand it. If you have to bitch, do it in English."

Phillipe shared a smile of relief with Michael as he switched to English. "As you will, my lady."

"That's another thing, Phil." She opened one eye. "The 'my lady' thing has gotten beyond annoying. If you don't drop it, I will grab something pointed and copper and stab you where it hurts vampires."

"Very well, *Alexandra*. I will go presently and look at our chambers." Phillipe touched her shoulder briefly before he bowed and left the room.

Michael waited until Alexandra yawned before he permitted the relief to spread through him. "How do you feel, *chérie*?"

"I don't know. Warm. Weird. A bit like I've been having nonstop sex with you." She stretched her arms over her head in a slow, luxurious movement. "You wouldn't do anything carnal and mind-blowing to me without waking me up first, right?"

"I confess, I have secretly become very fond of ravishing you while you are unconscious," he confessed, bending over to brush his mouth over hers. "And I am not finished. Go back to sleep."

"Over my undead body." She froze and then felt with her hand the IV taped to the inside of her elbow. "Hello, there's a needle in my arm." She propped herself up and looked around the room. "This doesn't look like the Marriott. Where am I?"

Michael was tempted to use his talent to remove her memory of the incident, but Alexandra's question indicated that she had already suffered some form of natural memory loss. He decided for the present to say nothing about it.

"You fainted soon after we greeted Byrne and his men," he told her. "This is the keep's infirmary."

"Fainting and memory loss. Okay." She eyed the slowly draining bag of blood hanging above her on the bed's IV pole. "Is that the first or second unit you've given me?"

"The second."

"That would explain the buzz. You're drowning me in the vampire equivalent of liquid cheesecake." With a quick jerk she pulled the IV needle out of her arm and clipped off the supply tube. "I appreciate the thought, sweetheart, but next time? Use plasma."

Michael closed his eyes for a moment, shoving back his impatience with her denial of what they were, and what they had to do to survive. "You have to feed."

"No, what I *have* to do is stay alive and keep my pathogenic mutation from progressing faster than I can track and chart it. Just write it on your day planner somewhere: plasma good, whole blood bad." She dropped the side rail, swung her legs over the edge of the bed, and stood carefully on both feet. "Why did I faint during the meet-and-greet?"

"I don't know," Michael said.

"You get this incredibly sexy look on your face whenever you lie to me; did you know that?" She picked up her jacket and shrugged into it. "I remember meeting Conan and his death squad, and talking to the kid . . . and that's it, until I heard you and Phil arguing about going home." She looked around the room. "The kid. Byrne's seneschal. Jayr, right? She around?"

"It is near dawn, and you are still weak." He caught her in his arms before she could walk away from the bed. "You can speak with Jayr tomorrow night."

"I need to know exactly what happened, and I don't want the edited-by-Michael version." She looked up. "Did my behavior really suck so much that you had to make me forget what I did?"

"I did not remove your memories." He stroked her arms with his hands. "I swear this to you."

"You did it before, when you didn't want me to find out about the changelings." She leaned against him as if she were dizzy. "I'm not mad. I know you only want to protect me from the bad stuff. Just give me back what you took. Now."

"If I wished to break my promise and erase any of your thoughts," he said, "I would use my talent only to make you forget how Richard hurt you."

"Richard? Please." She began to chuckle, and then something made her stop and duck her head. "He knocked me around and clawed up my back; that's all. I've been on worse blind dates. I was out for a little while, and then . . . someone took care of me." A line appeared between her brows. "That was it."

"You can tell me everything." Michael clamped down on his anger and fear and kept his voice gentle. "Don't be afraid, *chérie*. I would never blame you for what Richard did."

Alexandra flinched as if he had slapped her. "He didn't do anything else. I told you everything. Jesus Christ, all that blood you gave me is making my brain do somersaults." She pressed her fingers against her temples. "Do we have to stay here? I make a lousy patient."

"Byrne has given us the best rooms in the Realm." Michael picked her up in his arms. "I can take my rest somewhere else, if you wish to be alone."

"No." She encircled his neck with tight arms and buried her face in his hair. "Don't leave me again."

"Alexandra."

"I only want you," she whispered, her breath ragged against his ear. "Only you."

Byrne sat alone in the guard's hall, which had been decorated with trophies of every war in which the men of the *jardin* had fought, save one. He needed no reminder of the battle of Bannockburn, or what he had done that day.

Still, it came back to him at times like this, when he was alone. Like flesh rot, it twisted inside him, ever ready to eat at his gut and bring him back to the thing he wished most to forget.

The stink of spilled blood and torn bodies had roused the Kyn from the first hour of their rest, preceding the messenger the Brus had sent to summon them back to action. They had been held in reserve, sent out each night to scout and pick off some of Edward's best warriors. Now they were summoned to fight alongside the Brus's troops, for this was to be the last day of the battle. With the aid of his Darkyn, their human prince promised, he would drive the English out of Scotland forever.

"God curses us, the church reviles us, but the Brus calls us brothers," one of Byrne's men called out. "I will follow Robert to hell and back."

Byrne felt the same. Whatever their lot as *vrykolakas*, they were still Scotsmen. There was no question of not going.

Byrne sent most of his men into the forest as the Brus had directed. There they would protect their human allies while the trees protected them from the worst of the sun. On the other side of the river, Locksley had risen to command the English archers, who had no inkling that he would use them to spring the trap the Brus had laid for King Edward.

All that was left for Byrne was to ride out against the cavalry when they tried to flank the Scots, and let loose his personal demon against them. The English had grown soft over the years, and had forgotten the lessons their ancient warrior fathers had taught them.

Byrne was happy to reacquaint them with their history.

The only blessing his affliction bestowed upon him was to wipe away his memory of what he did when he allowed it free reign. And so it was, when the thing was done, he found himself riding alone, his horse and weapons soaked with the blood of the fallen. He would have entered the forest, where his men were surely slaughtering the misled archers, but he spotted his colors left planted but unattended in a pasture. He veered toward them, intending to carry the violet-and-white standard with him as a sign of his own victory.

The summer sun and lack of rain had withered the rich green grass, so he did not notice the patches of dead turf fitted together, or what they covered. His horse had plunged wildly as his forelegs crashed through the pit trap's deceptive roof, and Byrne was thrown over his head to smash down onto stout, sharpened stakes tipped with copper.

Byrne lay impaled and trampled from the horse's efforts to escape. He had already suffered dozens of wounds during the fray with the cavalry that had healed over, but the blood he lost had sapped his strength. Now more blood pumped from these new wounds, which would not heal or stop bleeding until the stakes were pulled out or Byrne died.

He managed to pull through all but the one piercing his chest. That one was stuck fast, and he grew too weak to do more than loosen it.

Byrne knew the pasture lay too far from the battlefield for anyone to spot the pit. His men had a healthy respect for his affliction, and would not search for him until nightfall. Whoever laid the trap knew what he was and how to hurt him; surely they would return to finish the deed.

He was going to die here, alone and forgotten. He accepted that, and listened for the sound of footsteps. He kept one stake curled in his hand. If he were to die, perhaps he could take his killer with him.

Her scent told him she was young, human, and frightened. Not his killer but a girl, perhaps from the village. Her footsteps moved toward the pit, and although he could not see her for the sun in his eyes, he heard her steps change with her direction, and a prayer muttered in, of all things, English.

He called to her in the same tongue: "Dinnae leave me alone here, lass."

A cloud passed over the sun even as the narrow shadow appeared above him. She wore a black dress of poor homespun and no covering over her dark, tangled hair. She had washed recently with strong lye soap, but it could not erase her own scent, like kitchen herbs growing tangled among meadowsweet in the sun.

"I cannot free myself." He held out a hand that shook violently with the effort. "Will you help me?"

He expected nothing. An English girl would not save a dying Scotsman, not after three days of watching his kind slay hers.

She reached down and took his hand, but did not make the mistake of trying to pull him up. Instead she used it to climb down into the pit with him.

Long, silky hair touched his face, tickling his cheek and nose. The girl pulled up her skirts and straddled him, keeping her weight on her knees on either side of him. Now he could see her face, young and stricken, and felt the cautious touch of her hands around the stake protruding from his chest.

"You should be dead, my lord," she said, her gaze moving from his tartan to his face.

"Aye." Byrne saw heaven in her eyes. "Soon, I think." He groaned as she tried to grasp the bloodied shaft, her fingers slipping.

Byrne couldn't feel his limbs anymore, he had grown so cold, and he put his hand over hers. He had no more words, and his heart stilled in his chest as his lungs sighed out his last breath. He would go, if only she would hold his hand.

She did something with her skirt, winding it around the stake and gripping it and his hand tightly. "Father in heaven, too many have died who never had the chance to fight for their lives. I beg you, spare this one man."

Byrne convulsed, his heart roaring in his head as the lass somehow wrenched the stake out of his body. She cried out at the great gush of blood that soaked both of them, now bending low to press her hands against the wound.

Her eyes, dark and filled with tears, were but a whisper from his. "Forgive me, my lord. I have killed you."

"I will live," he murmured, bringing a bloodstained hand to her hair. "What is your name, child?"

"Jayr." She frowned. "I am not a child. I am ten and seven."

"So you are." With the gore and filth all over him, and his severely weakened state, he could not shed enough scent to seduce her into cooperating. Nor did he care to. "Jayr, you must help me again, or I will die."

She reared back. "I will fetch a doctor—"

"There is no time. My enemy could return at any moment, and I am too weak to fight him off. I need you to heal me, lass." He felt his *dents acérées* surge into his mouth, and took no pains to hide them from her. "I must bite you to take some of your lifeblood. It will close my wounds and give me strength. Will you give it to me?"

She went very still, her eyes unblinking as she stared at his mouth. "You are one of those called the Darkyn." When he nodded, she closed her eyes briefly before she fumbled with the top of her bodice and dragged her hair out of the way.

Byrne wondered if he was delirious, for she could not be doing this. "You are not afraid."

"In the convent they say you fought in the Holy Land, and are as fallen angels. That God will richly bless anyone who gives you aid." Her voice trembled as she asked, "But I am a little afraid. Will it hurt?"

"Only for a heartbeat, lass, and then you will forget the pain and the fear," he said, his voice growing thin. "I promise you."

He let her come to him, lying across him as she brought her throat to his mouth. He kissed the sweet, delicate skin there, and on her cheek, and at the corner of her mouth. When he felt her shiver, he put his arms around her and opened his mouth, striking as quickly and mercifully as he could. She flinched, gasping once as her hands fisted in his shirt.

Her blood flowed into him, warm and intoxicating, flooding his veins with unseen sunlight. Byrne drank from her until he felt the edges of his wounds pulling together, and then lifted his mouth to fill his lungs with the taste and smell of her.

Jayr put her hand to the two puncture wounds he had left in her skin, and gazed down to see the wound in his chest closing over. "You are well? You will live now?" When he nodded, she laughed and hugged him, her mouth descending to kiss his with innocent joy.

Byrne caught her face between his hands and brought her

mouth back to his. The taste of her made him forget the killing, the heaps of bodies, and the ugliness of this war. She knew nothing of men, for his tongue in her mouth made her go rigid, but he stroked the inside of her lips and rubbed the softness of her tongue with his own until the tension left her limbs.

A moan humming in her throat, a new dampness coloring her scent, and something inside Byrne fell apart.

He did not think as he lifted her up, shoving her skirts out of his way and then reaching under them, hooking his fingers in the slit crotch slit of her drawers to tear them apart. He only needed the taste of her, and brought her to his mouth so that he might kiss the lips no man had seen or touched. He found her mound bare and fragrant with her arousal, and put his mouth to her there, parting her with his tongue and tasting the barest hint of slickness from her slit. He needed to be inside her, and worked his tongue into her, using it like a cock to penetrate her while she shook between his hands, her voice silenced, her hands digging into his wrists.

The jewel in her tight little purse brushed against his upper lip, a kiss from a fairy's tongue. He brought his mouth up to capture it and suck until she made the sweetest sound he had ever heard from a woman and shuddered uncontrollably in the throes of first pleasure. As she crested, he reached down to yank open his trousers and free his cock.

He could think of nothing but impaling her, and so he did, lifting her again and settling her on the head of his cock. Despite the wetness from his mouth and her pleasure, he could force his way into her tightness only by short, hard inches. Byrne felt her muscles gripping him, drawing him in rather than forcing him back out. Then her maidenhead gave way to him, and one last push lodged him in her to the root.

Byrne looked up and saw that pain and fear had taken her from him, and smashed the hold slavering hunger had over his senses. "Lass."

"It hurts." She drew his face to her throat. "Bite me again. Please," she added when he only kissed her. "Take me there again."

Feeding from her a second time was dangerous, but Byrne could not deny her the ease she would have from his bite or himself another taste of her. He struck a second time, groaning as his fangs punched through her skin and his cock surged deeper. The mists rose inside his head, and he tried to draw back, but they clouded his mind, drawing him down into the bloodrealms, where she was waiting.

Byrne had no memory of what happened after that, but he knew what he had done just the same. He had surrendered to the bloodrealms, where he took her blood and her body, in the most perfect communion of his life.

Where he loved her and was loved by her.

Where he grew strong, and made her weak.

Where he had left her to die.

Chapter 8

Jayr hurried to the guards' hall, where Byrne would be meeting with his captains before retiring for the night, but found her master waiting alone.

Byrne stood by the central fireplace, leaning with one arm on the mantel as he stared down into the flames. It seemed to Jayr as if his eyes glowed as red and hot as the fire. That happened only when his temper grew unmanageable, something every soul within the Realm who knew their lord's affliction feared.

What angers him?

Jayr felt no fear. She could not look at Byrne without feeling his skin against her lips, or tasting him in her mouth. His very presence made itself known on her skin as if she were actually pressed against him. Such unseemly thoughts had never plagued her before, but she now suspected that the bond between them had been affected by their recent blood exchange, reshaped into a new and altogether unwelcome sensitivity.

Perhaps it affected him in the same fashion.

Why had he made her take oath blood from his throat? Before last night he had always made the exchange according to custom, in the proper manner of hand to mouth. What he had done had been too intimate for contact between a lord and his seneschal. He had treated her the way he might a human lover.

What had possessed him to think it necessary? She had never broken her oath to him; he had no reason to demand such a thing. But it was done, and it seemed that both of them would have to suffer the consequences. She had to stop brooding on it. In time it would fade, and everything would be as it had been. She would simply have to remain on her guard until it did.

Jayr shuffled her feet, but Byrne ignored her, evidently as lost in his musings as she had been. "Excuse me, my lord. Should I summon your captains?"

"They have been and gone." His arm tensed, and the knuckles of the hand holding the edge of the mantel bulged. Just as quickly the moment passed, and the frightening cast to his eyes disappeared. "You are late again."

"Someone made mischief with Rainer." She described how she had found the warrior, and the condition of his rooms. "I will question Beau, but I doubt this was his doing. This seems too deliberate."

He nodded. "Cyprien has moved Alexandra from the infirmary to his chambers. Post guards at the access points."

"At once." That part of the keep was already well patrolled, so the request perplexed her. She tried to see his expression. "Is this because of Rainer, or do you or the seigneur expect some new trouble?"

"Rainer likely brought the beating upon himself. Michael's woman is genuinely ill. More than that I cannae say. She is nothing like us." He thrust himself away from the hearth and paced the length of the room. "Cyprien told me that her talent is to read the thoughts of murderers."

Jayr had never heard of such a thing. Kyn talents were unique to the individual, but served chiefly to lure humans or incapacitate them so that they could easily feed. A few exceptionally powerful lords like Lucan and Richard could use their talents on anything living, including other Kyn. Talent was for the hunt, so why would Alexandra need to know the thoughts of murderous humans in order to take their blood?

"Our household staff has left, and none of them would kill," Jayr told him. "Surely there is no one here who could cause her illness."

"She reads the thoughts of humans and Kyn." He stopped under a display of copper-bladed claymores. "Did you hear what she said before she fainted?"

"I did," she said, adding cautiously, "It sounded like the Gaelic you speak sometimes."

"'Twas my native tongue. She spoke like a woman of my clan. No human has done so in centuries." He ran his hand along the length of a blade in the same way he might stroke a woman's arm. He drew back and looked at a long gash on his hand in wonder. "Damn me."

Jayr was beside him before he could bleed, and seized his hand. The sharp edge of the sword had cut through his skin and muscles down to the bone, but instead of healing instantly, the wound remained open. Such a thing could not happen, unless—

"You have not been feeding properly." She felt a sudden appalling urge to strike him. "But you had those women the other night. Why did you not make full use of them?"

"I cannae remember." Byrne seemed bemused rather than concerned by the wound. " 'Tis no matter."

"Your bones sticking out of your wounds might make it difficult to clasp hands with the lords at the tournament," she snapped, examining the gash. Muttering to herself, she added, "This will take hours to heal."

He looked bored. "You make too much of it. Give me a cloth and I will bind it."

Jayr drew the dagger Harlech had given her and slashed her left wrist, pressing the wound to her master's palm. All of this she did too quickly for him to see, much less stop her. By the time he felt her blood pulse over his flesh, they were both healing.

"Dinnae waste yourself on me," he muttered as he pulled his hand away.

"I waste nothing. Be still." She encircled his wrist and brought his palm back to her own shrinking gash, forcing the last of the bleeding into his closing wound. Kyn blood could be used to heal the damaged flesh of another Kyn, but it was done only when the wound proved serious.

He eyed her. "Happy now, lass?"

"No. I don't understand why you've denied yourself like this. Have you tired of human females? Do you wish a new selection?" Part of her wanted to hear him say yes—and no, but not because it would explain his fast.

"I've lost my taste for them." He closed his fingers around her forearm, holding her as tightly as she gripped him. "Do you never weary of humans?"

I weary of playing nursemaid, she thought, but said nothing.

Flames crackled, but not in the fireplace. Jayr looked into her lord's eyes and saw them reflected there. Not the heat of anger or the ashes of melancholy. No, this heat was something entirely new, but part of her recognized it.

So it was true—she was not the only one suffering from useless desires.

"I would offer you different fare if I could, my lord," she said, quickly hiding her own startled pleasure, "but I fear you would not care for the taste of black bear, alligator, or flamingo."

"Aedan."

Her hold on him loosened. "My lord?"

"Aedan. It is my given name," Byrne said, bending until his nose almost bumped hers. "Or have you forgotten it?"

They had shared blood—far more than they ever had at renewal. The bond that tied her to him now tugged at her, as if determined to drag her backward through time, to the day she had first looked into the abyss, and the abyss looked back at her—

Stop this. He is your master, not your lover.

"I have announced your name often enough." She hated the stiffness in her voice, but it could not be helped. For a moment she had thought of him as hers, and that would not do. "You need to hunt, and soon. Master, you cannot afford to have open wounds—"

"Master." He lifted his uninjured hand to her face and ran a fingertip along the curve of her brow. "You've not called me that since we left Scotland."

She had to swallow to find her voice. "When we came here you bade me call you lord."

"I did not want the Americans to think you my slave." As he spoke, his breath caressed her lips. "No." He cupped her jaw and held her when she tried to turn her face. "You still think of me that way? As your master?"

"I am your seneschal." She could not think, could not move. Whatever had seized him and burned in his eyes held her as tightly in its grip. "You have but to say how I am to think. I am sworn to obey."

"Yes." The strange incandescence faded from his eyes. "Of course." He released her and stepped away.

The distance between them helped Jayr reclaim some of her composure. "How is it that Lady Alexandra speaks your language? Could she have somehow drawn it from your thoughts when they arrived?"

"No. My thoughts were not of murdering anyone, and I've made myself think in English since we came to this land." Byrne looked down at his hand, flexing his fingers and then spreading them to flatten his palm.

Jayr saw that his wound had healed over, and made a mental note to double the amount of blood she mixed into his wine for the next few days. "What did Lady Alexandra's words mean?"

"'Twas mostly gibberish." He pulled his sleeve down and straightened the cuff. "One thing I had prayed that I would never hear again." Contempt chilled his features. "The last time I heard it used was when Henry and his armies invaded the land. 'Burn the field.'"

Jayr remembered the old, vile king who had slaughtered anyone who stood in his path during his quest for power. He had certainly deserved to burn for his sins a thousand times over. "What field was burned?"

"All of them." Byrne's eyes dulled. "The English came before harvest that year, as they often did. One of the young farmers incited our villeins to go out and burn their crops where they stood. He had them pledged to see their own children starve before a handful of their grain fattened an English belly." His voice went soft. "Many children did that winter, along with their parents and kin."

Jayr thought of all the scorched fields she had seen on her first and only journey into Scotland. Everyone had blamed the English for them, even the Scots themselves. "I never knew this."

"I tried to find the instigator, but he vanished. Perhaps he starved along with the rest of them. The Brus played the politician; he made sure to blame the bloody English for the burnings, and they were eager to take the credit for it. It enhanced Henry's reputation for cruelty, and martyred those who died of starvation." Byrne's tone turned ironic. "They won, we became merchants, and they wrote the history books. No one could know those words unless they had heard them."

"One of the newcomers must have been there," Jayr suggested. "Given the lady's talent, this could be some sort of warning, a premonition of trouble to come." She took out her radio. "I will alert the men and have them—"

"No." Byrne snatched the device from her and tossed it into the fire.

She had others; it made no difference to her. It was the manner with which he treated her equipment that stirred her ire. Still, this was not the time to protest the waste of resources, even if Byrne would never appreciate them. "My lord, this could be a threat against you, against the Realm. I cannot protect you if you do not allow me—"

"I put the last of my enemies in the ground before I left Scotland," he told her. He stared at his hands for a long moment. "No one will challenge me for what is mine."

Jayr knew he wasn't talking about the Realm now. "At least permit me to investigate further," she said. "We don't know these newcomers. During her spell Lady Alexandra spoke of vengeance. Perhaps she can tell me more about the one from whom these killing thoughts came. I vow I will be discreet."

"You will report only to me," he said finally. "Whatever you learn. Say nothing to Cyprien, Alexandra, or the men."

Did he distrust her? "As always, my lord." She thought of the Italian's ill-chosen colors. "Could this killer be involved in a *jardin* war vendetta?"

"I think not," Byrne said. "After Harold was slain and the six took control of the *jardins*, Richard rounded up and executed all of the traitors."

"Perhaps someone survived." Jayr felt a strange sensation across the back of her neck, almost as if someone behind her were glaring at her. She glanced around the room, but they were alone. "One of the newcomers may be an old enemy."

"I begin to think this tourney cursed." Byrne strode to the door. "It's late, and there is no more we can do this night. Come."

*   *   *

Phillipe woke early that afternoon and, after he dressed, went to check on Cyprien and Alexandra. He found them both still asleep in the adjoining master bedroom. Before her abduction, Alexandra had rarely slept through the day, and did not seem to have the same need for rest as other Kyn. Her ordeal in the hands of the high lord had resulted in making her more restless, and subject to being awakened by the slightest of sounds.

That she was sleeping so deeply here pleased Phillipe. She needed the respite; she had suffered too much these last months.

It would not be difficult for her to rest here at the Realm. A king might have been comfortable in the chambers Byrne had prepared for them, the seneschal thought as he drew the heavy brocade drapes to block out the last rays of the sun. Delicate violet enamel had been applied to the outlines of the white marble stones in the chamber walls, with a stalk of heather cunningly painted in the center of some of the blocks.

A mural of the Scottish Highlands had been painted on the wall facing the east, and the artist must have been Kyn, for Phillipe recognized features of the land that had not existed in centuries. Around the mural were small black circles representing the sun, moon, and human eye, filled with green triskele, which symbolized the land, sea, and sky. Byrne had the motif repeated throughout the castle, and like his ancestors, believed it to invoke balance and harmony.

The enormous bed had been carved from English fir and decorated with different types of spirals, stars, and knots, with several symbols inlaid with gold and garnet to emphasize their importance. Each post on the bed had been worked at the top and bottom to mimic the entwined branches and roots of the tree of life. Whisper-soft white linens draped the bed from all sides, with bejeweled tassels adorning the golden satin drape cords.

A trio of ancient decorated chests lined one wall, each embossed with the intricate knotwork of the Celts, but Phillipe appreciated the more modern addition of white oak cabinetry. As sturdy as the old chests were, modern garments needed to be hung to avoid wrinkling. Bouquets of fresh roses and lavender, bound with silk ribbons tied in lovers' knots, had been placed on the tables and in the wall vases as a quiet tribute to Cyprien and Alexandra.

Phillipe set out clean garments for his master and mistress, and made sure there was enough bagged blood stored in the refrigerated wall unit discreetly hidden behind a painting of a beautiful Highland woman. Seeing his master and mistress entwined together in their bed reassured him as nothing else could. He had witnessed with his own eyes how much the forced separation had hurt both of them, but especially Alexandra, who had never before experienced a testing of the bond between her and his master. Then, too, he thought she had not told Cyprien everything that had happened to her in Ireland. Still, whatever ailed her, Phillipe felt sure his master's love and care would set it to rights.

As he quietly closed the bed curtains, he spotted Alexandra's medical case on her bedside table. He picked it up to move it out of the way, and found a copper-tipped syringe behind it. He held the needle up to the light. It appeared empty, the plunger almost completely depressed, but he could smell her blood on it. He pressed the plunger down, and a drop of blue fluid appeared on the tip of the needle.

Little wonder she slept so soundly. She had given herself a shot of nickel sulfate hexhydrate—what she called "vampire Valium"—a substance lethal to humans, but which rendered the Kyn unconscious for hours.

Phillipe opened her medical case, in which she carried her instruments, and found it filled with dozens of vials of the liquid blue tranquilizer. Alexandra always carried the drug with her, but never in such quantity. He was tempted to remove them, for the thought of his mistress drugging herself to sleep disturbed him, but it was not his place to do so.

If she does so again, I will tell the master, he thought as he took one of the vials and tucked it into his pocket. *He will know what to do.*

For his part, Phillipe could contact an old friend at Dundellan. Richard's men were intensely loyal to him, but Korvel owed Phillipe a blood debt from long ago. The captain would tell him what had been done to Alexandra during her captivity.

Securing the chamber door behind him, Phillipe walked out into the corridor and paused when he smelled another familiar Kyn nearby. "They still sleep, my lord."

"Is that what they're doing?" Robin of Locksley came around the corner with his seneschal. "I had thought that since being made seigneur, Cyprien never closed his eyes."

"Even God rested on the seventh day." Phillipe bowed, and then turned to clasp hands with Scarlet. "I had hoped to meet you in the lists, William. My arm wants loosening before the tournament begins."

"My joints are so rusty that I doubt I will give you much sport." Will's narrow features acquired a long-suffering expression. "Some lords, you see, do not believe in following the old ways."

"Some seneschals dwell too much in the past," Robin replied loftily. "One no longer need ride into battle and swing a sword to acquire power. This era is far more civilized. Raiders confine themselves to acquiring corporations. Hostile takeovers no longer involve holding hostage members of the loser's family. The only decent, wholesale pillaging accomplished these days is on the stock market."

"Do not ask him about the stock market," Will advised Phillipe in a mock stage whisper. "I beg you."

As Cyprien's seneschal, Phillipe was accustomed to Kyn lords treating him and every other seneschal with a sort of distant acknowledgment. Both he and Will had been lowborn peasants; Phillipe's family had served Cyprien's for ten generations. When their noble masters had taken up the cross and joined the Order of the Knights of the Temple of Solomon, their families had persuaded Phillipe and other villeins to take vows as well. The seneschal did not have to be told to sacrifice their lives on the battlefield to protect their masters. Preserving the lives of the highborn was practically second nature.

Robin of Locksley, however, treated every Kyn the same, regardless of the circumstances of his birth. He regarded the humblest member of the garrison as important as Cyprien, and spoke to every man as though he were his equal. This did not sit well with those Kyn who believed in the preservation of rank, but Phillipe often thought Locksley also took some private pleasure in that.

"What are you doing up before sunset?" Locksley wanted to know.

"I must retrieve the rest of the master's luggage," Phillipe told the suzerain. "In the confusion last night I forgot to secure it."

"Jayr likely had the men take it from your car before it was put away," Will said. "She will see to it that it is brought to Cyprien before nightfall."

"If you two are finished fretting over garment bags, I could use some sport," Locksley said as he walked with Phillipe down the corridor that led to the center of the keep. "Will is weary of being soundly beaten on the ranges. What about you, Navarre?"

Phillipe nodded to a passing guard before he replied, "I have no skill with the bow, my lord, and I believe the last time we met I promised your seneschal a thrashing in the lists."

Will snorted. "Go back to sleep, Navarre, for such a thing will happen only in your dreams."

"I can wait for Lord Halkirk, I suppose," Locksley said. "Will, did you find out when he is to arrive?"

"Jayr told me that he took a commercial flight, and it has been delayed," his seneschal said. "He will not arrive until tomorrow, Christ preserve him." He crossed himself.

Like Scarlet and most of the Kyn, Phillipe also disliked flying. It did not seem a natural method of travel for human or Kyn. The private jets Cyprien and the most powerful Kyn used were some of the best in the world, but not all of their kind could afford the luxury of keeping a private aircraft.

Commercial airliners were more dangerous because they enclosed the Kyn in a small, poorly ventilated space with many human passengers. Phillipe had heard darkly comic stories of what happened when dozens of passengers succumbed to Kyn scent simply by close proximity. More troubling were the number of commercial airlines that crashed for one reason or another. Such a disaster might kill every human on board, but unless completely dismembered, Kyn passengers survived. If a flight went down in a remote, unpopulated area or in the deep ocean, it almost guaranteed any surviving Kyn a slow, painful death by starvation.

"I shall have to find Jayr and . . . ask her if . . ." Locksley came to a halt and stared over his head. Hatred flared in his amethyst eyes. "Tell me I am imagining that thing."

Will looked up. "Bloody hell."

Phillipe followed his gaze and saw an overlarge banner of purple and gray silk. It was the Sherwood colors, the likes of which he had not seen since the end of the *jardin* wars.

Sherwood had once belonged to Robin of Locksley. When he had become an outlaw the king had taken it, along with all of his family's holdings, and had bestowed it on Lord Guisbourne, Robin's worst enemy. Like Robin, Guisbourne had also died of plague, only to rise again as Darkyn.

Phillipe did not want to think of what had happened to Sherwood after that. "Perhaps someone's idea of a tasteless joke, my lord."

"Indeed. Someone who should be beaten until their bones are dust." Locksley's voice lost all feeling. "Scarlet, take it down."

"My lord, perhaps I should speak to Jayr about it," Will said slowly. "So that she may—"

Robin of Locksley snapped out an arm, seizing his seneschal by the front of his shirt and dragging him around to face him. His eyes never left the banner. "Take it down," he said, his *dents acérées* gleaming like white daggers, "carry it outside, and burn it."

Will's voice trembled as he said, "At once, my lord."

"I will be on the range. Come to me when it is done." Locksley released him and strode away, leaving both seneschals to stare after him.

"What is this?" Phillipe asked, looking up at the banner. "Guisbourne is dead, Sherwood destroyed. Who could possibly wish to honor their memory?"

"I don't know," Will muttered. "But God save his soul, for if my master finds him it will shortly be leaving his body."

Although a few stragglers had yet to check in, the Kyn attending the tournament had in large part arrived. Jayr sent word to the various *tresori* and seneschal that the first gathering would be an early evening assembly in the guards' hall. As in years past, the lords and their *jardins* would come to exchange greetings and news with one another before the tournament officially began.

It took some diplomacy, of course. The large round tables and seating had to be arranged so that none held a particular advantage over the rest of the room. All of the goblets were filled with the same vintage of bloodwine, and a server was assigned to each table so that no one was kept waiting. Byrne would make an appearance, as he always did, but he would likely do little more than introduce the seigneur and allow him to address the assembly.

Things had changed in the last year, however, and Jayr knew that the American Kyn had become restless. Michael's first decision as seigneur, to allow Richard's chief assassin, Lucan, to create a new *jardin* in the south of Florida, had not been a popular one. Nor was the seigneur's decision to confront Richard in Ireland and take back his *sygkenis* after the high lord had abducted her. Now he had opened their borders to the French and Italian Kyn, and territorial lines would have to be redrawn. Some did not agree with Michael Cyprien's leadership; others were fearful of the future changes he would make to their long-established way of life. The fact that his *sygkenis* was the first human to be turned since the Middle Ages fascinated some, but troubled most.

If they made it through the night without any incident, Jayr thought, it would be a minor miracle.

Once she saw to the guests' needs, Jayr occupied herself by circulating, exchanging greetings with the other seneschal present, and silently observing their masters. The ruling Kyn seemed more secretive this year, guarding their looks and keeping their voices low as they spoke with old friends. What Jayr overheard indicated that the Kyn's main concerns centered around the newcomers, and what lands they would be accorded by the seigneur.

"I petitioned Richard a dozen times to extend my territory into Canada," one suzerain, a ruling lord in the Midwest, complained to his cluster of friends. "I have business interests in the north, and my men desire new hunting grounds. Now I expect the seigneur will give them over to the French."

"Can you blame him?" one of the Irish-born lords asked. "They are his closest blood Kyn."

"I told you to petition the seigneur before the tournament begins," the suzerain's wife said as she plied her fan. "Make it plain to him that you have first claim, or might have, if the high lord had been more generous."

The Irish lord nodded. "'Tis well-known that Cyprien has no more love for Richard. You could work that to your advantage."

"Or petition his *sygkenis* to endorse the claim," the wife put in. "I have heard she is weak. Some say she is still human enough to succumb to talent."

"Do we know anyone who can introduce us?" her husband asked.

Jayr stopped beside the suzerain's wife. "I will be glad to introduce you to Dr. Keller when she joins us, my lord. The seigneur, you see, has charged me with her protection." She rested a hand on the dagger hilt in her right hip sheath. "It is a charge I take most seriously."

The female glowered. "Who are you to—"

"We are much obliged for your advice, seneschal." As the suzerain spoke, he put a restraining hand on his wife's arm. "Women have no head for these matters. I will petition the seigneur directly."

"As you wish, my lord." Jayr bowed and, hiding her satisfaction, moved on.

Chapter 9

It was some time later that a curious hush fell over the guards' room. Heads turned and hands froze in midgesture. Jayr followed the direction of the stares to the side entry doors, where a Kyn lord and his entourage stood as if waiting to be announced or greeted.

Jayr's hands went to her blades before she realized what she was doing and dropped her hands.

The newcomers' lord stood tall and straight in a long black coat and polished boots; long dark hair spilled to curl about his broad shoulders. His face might have been carved by an ambitious hand from pure alabaster, save for a tightly controlled mouth and dark eyes so thickly lashed they seemed bruised. A thin chain of silver relieved the funerary grimness of his garments; on the end of it hung suspended a chunk of crystal striped with uneven bands of green and purple.

Fierce as the new lord appeared, it was not him but his entourage that held the room riveted. A dozen silent, motionless men in flowing black robes and dark blue turbans surrounded him in neat ranks. Each carried a curved sword hung by a scarlet cord from his wide waist sash. Dark beards covered the bottom half of their swarthy faces, while their narrow black eyes beheld the room with decided indifference.

The dark lord had brought with him Saracen guards. Saracens, against whom the Kyn had waged war during their human lives.

"God have mercy on us," Harlech said as he came to stand beside her. "What are those heathens doing here?"

"The suzerain of this castle does not bid welcome to his guests?" the dark lord asked in the silence. He delivered his question in flawless, unaccented English made beautiful by the deep, melodic quality of his voice.

Jolted by the reminder of her duty, Jayr strode forward. "Suzerain Aedan mac Byrne welcomes all Kyn to the Realm, and glad I am to announce your arrival, my lord. If you will but give me your name, I will make you and your men known to our other guests."

The dark lord's face turned toward her. Eyes like soot-scarred crystal flicked a single glance over her before shifting back to gaze upon the room.

He did not know who she was, and obviously would not lower himself to ask.

"I am privileged to serve Suzerain Byrne as seneschal." Jayr stopped a few feet short of the lord and his entourage and offered them a deep, respectful bow. "Jayr, my lord, at your service."

The dark eyes subjected her to a second, longer inspection. Not a single muscle moved in his face, but he gave the impression of affronted displeasure. As Jayr straightened, he looked into her eyes, at her hair, and then at her mouth.

He knows me, Jayr thought, bewildered. Just as she opened her mouth to ask how, the dark lord walked past her without a word.

Gasps, whispers, and more than one smothered chuckle abraded Jayr's ears. She kept her face from reflecting her humiliation, but her heart pounded painfully in her chest. Among the Kyn, refusing to return such a direct greeting as she had offered was the bluntest and most direct of insults. It meant that in the dark lord's eyes, Jayr did not exist. Even the Kyn who disapproved of her serving as Byrne's seneschal had never subjected her to such public censure.

He sees you are female, she told herself, *serving in place of a male. That is what offends him.*

It still stung, no matter how Jayr rationalized it. She wished Byrne would arrive, so she could stand at his side. Being near him was the reassurance she needed now, both of his regard and her place among the Kyn. Whatever the dark lord might think of her, she had earned both.

A shorter, auburn-haired man shouldered his way around the

Saracens. The dull green and poor fit of his garb made him appear shorter and plumper than he was. He strode up to Jayr with a wide smile on his broad face.

"My ill-mannered master is Ganelon of Florence, the Lord Nottingham," he told Jayr, speaking loudly enough for the rest of the Kyn to hear. He sketched an unsteady bow. "I am his seneschal, Skald."

Jayr clasped hands with him and greeted him as an equal, although she kept an eye on his master. "Nottingham is an English name."

"My lord's father hailed from that region," Skald said. "My lord deeply honors his memory."

Nottingham, Jayr recalled, was but forty miles from Sherwood. "We received no notice of your visit, brother."

"I fear the Brethren burned us out," the seneschal told her. "There was no time for anything but immediate, uncomfortable travel. Word of this tournament was sent to us before we left Italy; my lord thought it best we come here." His smile turned rueful. "You cannot tell it by his demeanor, but we have come to beg sanctuary."

"I see." No, she didn't. She had never heard of a Kyn lord named Ganelon, of Nottingham or Florence or any other city, and she doubted the arrogant Italian would stoop to ask for anything, much less haven. Perhaps he served the high lord as a spy. "May I ask your lord's title, so that I might make him known to my master?"

"My lord Nottingham has not yet been granted official rank among the Kyn. We have lived in solitude since rising to walk the night, you see." Skald's gaze bounced from her face to the assembly with uncommon interest. "I hope our lonely state will come to an end here in America, brother. 'Tis said that your seigneur is known for his largesse."

He thought her a male, when it was well-known among the Kyn that she was not. Perhaps what he claimed was true, although Jayr found it hard to believe that the Italian had sequestered himself so completely. Even the most remotely located *jardins* kept in contact by various means, and sent emissaries back to Europe to meet with the high lord on a regular basis.

Odd, too, that an Italian living as a recluse would wish to be addressed as Nottingham to honor an English father. That would draw more attention from the humans around him, not less.

"I wish you well." She eyed the Saracens, all of whom carried copper-plated scimitars. "Your lord has curious taste in bodyguards."

"Ah, yes, the guard." He cast a rolling glance at the ceiling. "Christians were not the only souls cursed on the sands of Jerusalem, you know. The heathens were equally stricken. Most lost their heads, but some escaped to the mountains and lived very well there. They were even worshiped for a time as gods by some of the primitive local tribes."

"Why are they not there still?" Jayr asked.

"They were forced to flee their homeland when the Jews invaded it after the second of the humans' world wars. They found their way to my lord's home and begged to be made useful. Since we were only two, my lord allowed them to make their oath to him." Skald spread his hands in a helpless gesture. "They are quite loyal to my lord, and will cause no trouble. I swear it."

Over Skald's rounded shoulder, Jayr spotted Nottingham going from table to table, nodding and clasping hands with other lords as he apparently introduced himself to his peers. The reception he received seemed lukewarm at best, but none yet chose to give him their shoulder. His guards followed and were completely ignored, but did not appear troubled by that, or the many angry looks being directed at them.

"How many Kyn lived in Florence?" Jayr asked as she signaled for one of the servers.

"Only my lord Nottingham. His mother was the last of an old and honored family," Skald told her. "His wealth and resources remain quite vast. The seigneur could do much worse in choosing a suzerain."

Now it became clear. Nottingham had not come to beg. She instructed the server who came to her to bring in a table and chairs to seat the Italian and his guard. To Skald she said, "You heard a great deal before you fled Florence."

"I serve my lord with all my heart. I fell stricken in Florence, you see, and he brought me to his home and helped me through the change. I would have died in the gutter where they left me." Skald's attempt at modesty fell a little flat; his eyes searched the room with incessant eagerness, and his tense frame almost vibrated with impatience. "Would you do me the honor of making me known to the other seneschal among you?"

Heads turned once more as Byrne entered the guard's hall with Cyprien and Alexandra.

"I fear I cannot, for my lord has arrived with the seigneur." Relieved, Jayr caught Harlech's eye and inclined her head toward Skald. "My second will be pleased to perform introductions. Excuse me, brother."

Before Jayr could take her place beside Byrne, Robin of Locksley strode in from the opposite side of the hall. In both of his fists were wads of torn satin. He walked rapidly toward Byrne and Cyprien, with an anxious-looking Will Scarlet trotting after him.

"Seigneur," Locksley all but shouted. "I would speak with you."

Footsteps echoed in the silence as the suzerain rounded a table of Welsh-born Kyn, and then something happened. Locksley's head turned toward Nottingham and his guards. One of the latter had unfurled a banner and was attaching it to one of the poles on display at the front of the room.

Locksley walked into the back of a chair, beginning to fall over. Scarlet grabbed the back of his tunic just in time to keep him from sprawling face-first onto the stone floor.

"You."

As the word burst from Locksley, he shrugged off his seneschal as if he were nothing more than a mosquito. His face twisted into a snarl as he threw the shredded banners to the floor and drew his sword. When Will stepped in front of him, he knocked the seneschal out of his way.

Jayr recognized the ruined banners at once. They were the purple and gray that Viviana had been working on yesterday.

The sound of Locksley's sword being drawn stirred every male in the room. Chairs scraped back as lords and warriors rose. The men moved silently into position to shield the unarmed women. Every seneschal in the room drew swords and daggers and took position in front of their lords.

Jayr's first impulse was to run at Locksley and disarm him, until she met Byrne's gaze. He lifted a hand in a simple gesture that meant, *Stay where you are.*

Jayr nodded, but remained prepared to move in an instant. She had never seen Locksley angry, and it made her stomach turn over in a sickly manner. Seeing Sherwood's colors displayed so openly must have driven all the sense out of his head.

"Lord Locksley." Michael Cyprien moved with the lethal grace of a great cat, and placed himself between the suzerain and his intended target. "Hold."

"You do not want a part of this, Michael," Locksley said through clenched teeth. He didn't look at the seigneur at all, his gaze fixed on Nottingham. "Be a good fellow and clear the women from the room."

The Kyn males who were still unarmed quickly drew blades. Muttered orders were issued by lords and passed among the warriors. Several of the women also held small bejeweled blades drawn from ankle and thigh straps. Jayr used the distraction to position herself between Byrne and Locksley.

A hundred different scents, released by the Kyn's physical reaction to the threat, blended in a hot, cloying cloud that filled the room. Impending violence, wordless and burgeoning, hung over every head.

"Hey."

Jayr glanced at Alexandra Keller, to whom no one paid attention. The seigneur's *sygkenis* used an empty chair to climb up onto a tabletop, where she put two fingers in her mouth and produced a loud, piercing whistle.

That and her position silenced the room.

"I haven't met everyone yet," Alexandra said, her voice loud and friendly, "but I'm Alex Keller, the boss's girlfriend and the new vampire in town. I just thought I'd mention that this is my first vacation with Michael since I grew fangs. I don't know about you, but I've witnessed enough Kyn bloodbaths to pretty much last me forever. What do you say we just relax, have fun, and not dismember anybody?"

The Kyn didn't quite know what to make of Alexandra's plea. Jayr felt like applauding.

"One more thing: If anyone gets something important chopped off? I'm going to be too busy relaxing on my vacation to stitch it back together for you. So thank you in advance for not hacking one another to pieces. I'm looking forward to meeting you all." Alexandra accepted Michael's hand and climbed back down.

Jayr noted that Cyprien looked pleased, not embarrassed, by his *sygkenis*'s unusual announcement, and her heart melted a little. The talk about Cyprien always pegged him as cold and calculating, and many had thought he went to Ireland to become high lord, not rescue his *sygkenis*. Jayr saw better now, and wondered if Alexandra Keller knew how fortunate she was to have such a lover.

"Never fear, my lady," Locksley said, glaring at the Italian. "It will not be possible to sew back together what I leave on the floor."

"I take it," Nottingham said in his gorgeous voice, "that you are the insolent bastard who tore down my colors."

All around the room came the sound of brittle things snapping and cracking. Jayr saw that the windows were intact, and then her gaze dropped to a nearby goblet. White frost covered the outside of the cup, and the wine inside was covered with a bloom of ice that solidified the surface, as if it had frozen solid.

"You." Locksley's knuckles bulged as he tightened his grip on his sword's hilt. "You do not speak to me." He tried to go past the seigneur, but Michael seized his arm. He looked down in amazement. "You hold me back, and give him leave to bring that filth into the house?"

"He brings ignorance and unhappy memories." Cyprien said something else, too low for Jayr to hear.

Locksley didn't seem impressed. "Exile him, then. Send him back to whatever shithole he occupies."

"Rob." Byrne came to stand beside him and rested a hand on his shoulder. Everyone around them except Locksley seemed to relax. Cyprien left his suzerains and strode over to where Nottingham stood.

Jayr knew Byrne was deliberately shedding his scent to invoke calm and order. Although most of the tension in the room had vanished, it seemed to have no affect on Robin.

"Seigneur." Skald rushed over to Michael, almost skipping in order to take his place beside his master. "May I introduce my lord, Ganelon of Florence, Lord Nottingham?"

Nottingham went down on one knee, moving with the fluid grace of old experience. "Seigneur, it is an honor."

"Nottingham by way of Florence, is it?" Cyprien sounded bored, but anger flashed amber in his turquoise eyes. "You may rise. Who is this woman with you?"

For the first time Jayr saw that the dark lord had brought a human with him. The female huddled between two of the Saracens, almost obscured by the voluminous drape of their robes. She looked pale and dazed. Despite the warmth of the room she trembled, her lips pinched with cold. From her appearance and garments Jayr guessed her to be a young wife, perhaps a mother.

"That?" Nottingham waved a hand in her general direction. "That is food and amusement."

Disgust and dismay made Jayr stiffen. Kyn never removed humans from their ordinary lives as Nottingham had done with this female; it terrorized the humans' families and often resulted in the authorities taking notice.

"There are no humans permitted at the tournament," Michael said. "In this country we do not abduct humans under our influence and force them to serve us. You will return her to her home at once."

"As you will, seigneur." Nottingham spoke to one of his guards in soft, rapid Italian. The guard led the human away from the assembly.

Michael did not appear mollified. "Tell me exactly who you are, and why you have come here."

"We are but refugees, my lord. I would offer titles and ranks, but mine have never been named *jardin* by the high lord; nor have I been given the honor of recognized rule," the dark lord said. Each word from his lips, liquid gold to the ears, rang with dignity and respect. "I am here in hopes of remedying that."

"I have traveled the length of Italy many times," the seigneur pointed out, "but I have never heard your name, nor one mention of your household."

"Brethren threats forced me to become a recluse," Nottingham said smoothly. "My men and I dwelled in the hills of Florence, far from our Kyn, to avoid stirring interest in Rome. We prospered there for hundreds of years before we were betrayed, and the Order sent its assassins. They discovered my holdings, set fire to my house, and slaughtered my human servants. My seneschal and my guards are the only reason I survived."

The sincerity in his voice could not be mistaken, and Jayr felt sure that every word Nottingham spoke was truth. It still did not convince her that he was who he claimed to be. Like a garment, truth could be tailored to fit any expectation. Nottingham might be Italian, but Skald wasn't, and neither were the guards.

"If you were so successful in hiding yourself all these years," Cyprien asked, "how did the Brethren find you?"

"This new Lightkeeper is not content simply to be the leader of the order, as have the others in his position before him. He is using every means he can find to eradicate the Darkyn in Europe, especially Italy and France. He is also a man who knows technology. He tracked us through the moneychangers and suppliers we had used." Nottingham's upper lip curled. "They were also the traitors who led the Brethren to us. Humans of this era will sell their mothers for a few lira."

Cyprien offered no sympathy. "Is that why you employ Saracens, and bear the colors of traitors?"

"I employ Kyn, seigneur." His black-gloved hands turned to display empty palms. "My men once answered the call of their god, Allah, and were cursed just as we were for it." He glanced at the banner. "As for my colors, they belong to my family. They were noblemen, not traitors. I was within my rights to display them within these walls."

Jayr heard Locksley make a low, animal sound in his throat.

Skald appeared by her side. "That one does not seem to like my master's colors."

"No," Jayr said thoughtfully. "He does not." She glanced down at him. "This might have been avoided if you had come to me before hanging your master's colors about the Realm."

He looked surprised. "I was not aware that I should consult with you."

Jayr was beginning to suspect that Skald had little or no proper training as a seneschal. "It is a courtesy when you are in another lord's territory."

"Ah." He bobbed his head. "I will remember that."

"Your unfortunate colors can be debated later, Lord Nottingham." Cyprien studied the impassive faces behind the dark lord. "These men, however, killed many of our Templar brothers during our human lives. Every warrior here has fought them, and watched as they slaughtered our comrades on the field of battle."

"My men have no more religion or country than we do, seigneur. They have made and kept their oaths to me," Nottingham assured him. "They are the reason I do not now rot in a Brethren prison. I will happily vouch for them."

"Very well. You will be responsible for their behavior while you are here." Michael stood and looked at the other assembled Kyn, many of whom looked stunned. To them he said, "The old wars have long been over. Here in America, all who swear their loyalty to me are to be made welcome." He looked at Nottingham. "Just as all who betray that oath will not live long enough to regret it."

"Michael." The tip of Locksley's sword struck the floor as the blade went limp in his hand. "You cannot mean it. You cannot mean to give him leave to stay."

Cyprien didn't blink. "I rule this country, Lord Locksley. You would do well to remember that."

Jayr caught her breath as she saw Locksley's stance change and his sword rise. She knew Robin had good cause to despise any reminder of Sherwood, but his reaction went far beyond displeasure. Killing hatred filled his gentle eyes.

"Robbie," Byrne said gently. " 'Tis not worth it."

Locksley stared at Nottingham for a long moment, his body so still that Jayr did not see him draw breath. Someone coughed, and that seemed to break the spell. The furious suzerain sheathed his sword and silently left the same way he had entered.

No one spoke, and many flinched as Byrne clapped his hands together twice to signal the servers back to their places.

Skald grinned up at Jayr. "Let the games begin."

"That was interesting," Alex said as she and Michael left the guards' hall. Things had been decidedly calmer after Locksley had stalked out, but making the rounds afterward had been awkward. She hadn't made any friends with her little announcement, either. "I thought you told me that the sword fights didn't start until tomorrow."

"They don't." He entwined his fingers with hers. "I'm sorry, *chérie*. I wanted you to see us at our best, and then something like this happens." He guided her away from the hall leading to their chambers.

"Where are we going now?" she asked. "Some Kyn contest where they try to throw one another off the battlements? I meant what I said about being on vacation."

"I believed every word," he said, bringing her hand up to kiss her knuckles. "The moon is full, and Byrne's gardens are beautiful. I thought you might like some fresh air and perhaps some time alone together."

"Alone time is good." Alex herself was in no hurry to go to bed. The only way she could avoid the repeating dream she'd been having was to inject herself with a tranquilizer. Michael hated her experimenting on herself; if he found out she was using the stuff as a personal sleep aid, he'd go ballistic. "Bring on the moonlight."

Alex found that the suzerain's gardens were pristine, beautifully laid out, and held her interest for just over a minute. Someday she would discover just what Cyprien found so fascinating about a bunch of plants and dirt, but for now she had other things on her mind.

Tell him about the dream, one side of her head argued. *He'll know who the blond was.*

Sure, the other half answered. *And when you tell him what you've been doing with the blond, he'll go hunt him down and tear his throat out.*

Alex knew that dreams were not just subconscious self-therapy sessions for the Kyn. Thierry Durand, one of Michael's closest friends, had used his dreams to communicate with Alex while she was awake. Although Thierry's ability was tied up with his talent for being able to enter and influence the dreams of humans, Alex suspected that all Kyn could use them in a similar sense. When Michael had attacked her after she rebuilt his face, his talent had kept her in a dream state.

"Other than when you whistled and climbed on the table," Michael was saying, "you have been very quiet. What is on your mind, *chérie*?"

"Besides dodging a lot of bloodshed and reattachment surgeries, nothing, really." She drew her hand from his and walked toward a bower heavily covered with thick green vines. The white, trumpet-shaped petals of the vine's flowers were unfurling and opening. "I am curious about two things, though."

"What are they?"

"Well, first, why haven't Byrne's facial tattoos ever worn off?" When he gave her a blank look, she added, "The Kyn pathogen heals every kind of wound without scarring. Tattoos are basically ink-injected scars. His body should have absorbed and erased them a long time ago."

"Ah." He nodded. "I asked him this once. Byrne cannot say for certain, but he remembers the woad and other things used to make the ink being prepared in copper kettles."

"That might do it." Alex had already seen Gabriel Seran's permanent green scars, created by burns made by copper-beaded rosaries soaked in water being applied for weeks to his skin by Brethren interrogators. "Okay, second, why *did* Locksley get so ticked off over that purple and gray flag thing?"

"It is complicated. I will try to think of a modern equivalent." He tucked her arm through his. "How do you feel when you see extremists in the Middle East on television rioting and burning the American flag?"

"Like dropping a nuke on their heads," she admitted.

"Kyn feel just as passionately about our colors. Tearing down the Italian's banners was very disrespectful. In a sense, they are the flags of our fathers and our families." Michael led her to one of the stone benches beneath the bower and sat down with her. "During our human lives they symbolized who we were, our bloodlines, and our heritage. Often our place in society as well. Coats of arms among humans became very complicated, so the Kyn used only two colors, and very plain designs, so that we might recognize one another on the battlefield."

Alex chuckled. "Cute trick."

"Our colors also protected the humans who served us as well," he said. "The blue and white—the talon and clouds that were my family's symbols—were known throughout Europe, and held in very high esteem."

Now all the blue-and-white things around Cyprien's mansion made more sense. In reality, the archaic practice didn't seem all that different from what most people did now by hanging sports banners or putting pictures of their kids and relatives on the front of the fridge.

What he was telling her didn't fit with the scene that had played out in the hall, however.

"If these colors are so respected," Alex asked, "then why did Locksley rip down the Italian's purple and gray?"

"Colors also remind us of those whose families fell, often due to their treachery and betrayal." Michael picked one of the white flowers and stroked it across her cheek. "The purple and gray were once Locksley's colors."

"Oh." She frowned. "Nottingham stole them?"

"Robin lost the right to bear them when he was still human. The king branded Rob an outlaw and took everything he and his family owned. Ultimately he bestowed the title of Lord Sherwood on Guy of Guisbourne, a very distant kinsman of the Locksleys. Guy already served the Crown as sheriff, and imposed harsh taxes on behalf of the king. Some said that Sherwood was given to Guy as a reward for his ruthlessness."

Alex let out a stuttering laugh. "Hold on. I thought the names were just coincidence. You're telling me that the hothead waving around the sword tonight is Robin Hood? *The* Robin Hood? The guy Kevin Costner played in the movies?"

"During his human life, Robin was the outlawed noble upon whom the mythology of the Hood was later based." Cyprien seemed amused. "I cannot comment on Mr. Costner or his movie."

"Son of a gun." She recalled the handsome suzerain's face.

He didn't look anything like Kevin Costner, although he had the same casual, lethal charm. "So your pal Robin became a hood, and the king gave his stuff to his cousin, and that's what makes him go nuts when he sees purple and gray." She was going to need footnotes soon. "Is the Italian his cousin?"

"No, he is not, and that is only where it began," Cyprien said. "After he was stripped of his title and lands, Robin left England to join the Templars. Guy, of course, stayed behind to rule Sherwood and serve the Crown. Both were cursed by God and rose to walk the night as Kyn, Robin for fighting in the Holy Land, and Guy for his treatment of the poor."

"They were both infected with the pathogen," she corrected him. "God had nothing to do with it. So what happened? Did they get back together as Kyn and try to duke it out?"

"In a sense, yes. Our high lord at the time was Harold, and he believed in diplomacy over battle." Cyprien put his arm around her shoulders. "The Brethren, of course, had already formed their secret order, and were using the Inquisition to interrogate our human families and servants. They pretended it was to expose them as heretics, but they were interested only in compelling them to betray us."

"You guys are responsible for the Inquisition, too?" Alex snorted. "Jesus, you have a completely fucked-up history. Next you'll be telling me you touched off World War Two."

"Hitler discovered our existence before he came to power," Cyprien said, grinning as he watched her face, "but that is a story for another time. During Harold's reign, the horrors wrought by the Inquisition convinced many Kyn that it was time to form an army and declare war on the Brethren. Fight them the same way we had the heretics in Jerusalem. There was even some talk of marching on the Vatican, to be sure that the order was completely wiped out."

"Shame you didn't. That might have saved my getting slapped in the face by the bishop," Alex said absently. She saw him frown and added, "Something evil the Church does to teenagers when they get confirmed. Doesn't matter. What happened next?"

"Harold did not agree with the proposal. He felt that the Kyn should not challenge the order, but strike a truce with them. He did not recognize the wrath so many Kyn felt over those of our kind who had been tortured and died terrible deaths at the hands of the Brethren. His decision set off a power struggle for control of the Kyn. First came the assassination attempts on Harold and the suzerain loyal to him. That led to the insurrection—what you hear us sometimes refer to as the *jardin* wars."

Michael told her that after the assassinations failed, several *jardins* banded together, gathering and training as a secret army intent on staging a coup against Harold and his loyalists. The traitors had been led by Guy of Guisbourne, now the suzerain of Sherwood.

Cyprien stopped there, and was silent for a long time after that.

"Listen," Alex said. "You don't have to go into any more detail. I can imagine how awful it was."

"I have fought in many wars," Michael admitted. "None was as terrible as going into battle against soldiers whom I had called friends and allies for centuries." He shook his head. "The greatest treachery came the night before the final battle in France. A wounded herald came riding into camp. He had barely escaped England with his life. He told us that months before, Sherwood had secretly sent some of his warriors across the Channel with orders to invade and destroy the households of those loyal to Harold. While we were off fighting they butchered the women, *tresori*, and human servants who had been left behind. So confident was Guisbourne of victory that he instructed the assassins to take possession of the properties once they had killed the families."

Alex felt nauseated. "Please tell me Guisbourne and his thugs lost."

"They lost."

"There is a God." Bracing her back against the curving lattice, Alex watched the moon make a shimmery circle on the surface of the pool. "So who is this Italian? A leftover from Sherwood?"

"I doubt it. When Richard succeeded Harold, he had every member of the Sherwood *jardin* brought to him in London, and had his men verify their identities. Their names were checked against the bloodscroll—a kind of membership list that is created when the *jardin* is formed and maintained. He assembled the loyalists whose families had been murdered, turned the men of Sherwood over to them, and had them perform the executions. Guy of Guisbourne he saved for last."

"Wait." Alex closed her eyes. "I don't want to know how he died."

"No, you don't." He shifted closer and put his hands on her waist. "The Sherwood *jardin* was the only blood family Robin had left, but he had wisely chosen to fight under Richard as a loyalist. When judgment was passed, Rob was pardoned but made to watch the executions, and later bury the bits of them that were left."

"No wonder he was so upset." She looked up at him. "You're not going to let Nottingham use those colors again, are you? Robin doesn't need this shit in his face."

"If Nottingham wishes to join us, he will abandon them." He pulled her to him and plucked the combs from her hair. "Do you know the moonlight makes you a goddess?"

Alex nestled closer, expecting her fangs to punch out into her mouth and her body to go into overdrive. But when Michael began kissing her, a shriveled, miserable lump formed in the back of her throat. She gripped his jacket, tearing the fabric as she held on and made herself return the kiss.

Michael eased away. "*Chérie*, I think you are tired."

"No." She grabbed him by the hair and jerked his mouth back to hers, slicing open her bottom lip on the tips of his fangs. "Damn it." She pressed her fingers to her mouth and got up, stumbling away from the bench. Her entire body shook. "I'm sorry."

Michael came after her and turned her to face him. "Are there more killing thoughts?"

"No. It's okay." She was scaring him again. Was that all she was good for anymore? Giving him more to worry about? "I'm being a klutz; that's all."

He put his arm around her and steered her back toward the castle. "Can you remember the killer's thoughts from the first time, when we arrived?"

"Bits and pieces. It's very fuzzy." She wiped the blood from her mouth with the back of her hand. "Whoever it is, he's Kyn, and I think he's English. He didn't think of killing until he came here; that's why it was so sudden and violent. It's someone he tried to kill before, too, maybe a long time ago. He's going to use the tournament to do it. Does that sound like anyone you know?"

"Most of the Kyn attending the tournament are English-born," he said, disappointing her.

"At least it's not the Italian." Not wanting to face another injection, Alex dawdled. "Maybe I picked up the wrong idea from this guy. I mean, look at how the men circled the wagons around the women tonight. Maybe it was someone indulging a little fantasy." Alex thought for a moment. "You know, Jayr was closer to Locksley than anyone, and nobody stepped up to protect her."

"Jayr is hardly defenseless."

"Neither am I, but you and Phil had me shoved behind you in two seconds, regardless." Alex remembered the look on the Scotsman's face when he saw Locksley draw his sword and Jayr move in. "I did think Byrne might do something reckless and heroic. He never took his eyes off her the entire time."

"Likely he was signaling her on how to proceed," Michael said.

She smiled at the moon. "If you say so."

"What is your point, Alexandra?"

Her gaze shifted to someone walking out of the keep. "I thought it was an interesting situation; that's all." She gestured toward the long, lanky form approaching them. "Speak of the seneschal."

Watching Jayr, Alex felt envy settle into her heart and decorate it top to bottom with virulent green. Jayr had the tall, long-limbed body she had always coveted, and even clothes designed for a man couldn't disguise that spare, clean beauty.

"How could anyone think she was a guy?" Alex murmured. "I mean, look at her. Put high heels and a little makeup on her, and she could stroll down any runway in the fashion world."

"I cannot envision Jayr in couture."

"That's because you're not interested in anything outside Armani's suit line." Alex sighed. "She's got great moves, legs that go on forever, and that fuck-you look in her eye. She never smiles; have you noticed that?"

Michael shrugged. "Jayr takes her duties very seriously."

"Or something," Alex said as the seneschal reached them. "Hi, there."

"Good evening, my lady." Jayr performed a hasty bow before addressing Cyprien. "Seigneur, your seneschal asked me to relay a message from Ireland. The high lord wishes you to contact him before sunrise." She breathed in and her dark eyes focused on Alex's face. "You are bleeding, my lady?"

"A little accident." She patted Michael's chest. "I kissed him too hard. Fangs got in the way. No big deal."

"You do not heal as quickly as we do," Jayr said, and then ducked her head. "Not that I should remark on such a thing. Forgive me."

Alex felt a little impatient with the girl's constant scraping and bowing. "I heal much slower than the Kyn. Michael's probably already told you that Kyn talent also still affects me."

"He did, my lady," the seneschal said, exchanging a look with Michael. "I will see to it that you are not subjected to any unwelcome influences."

Alex nudged Michael. "Better late than never."

"My master also wishes you to know that the infirmary is at your disposal, should you wish to make use of it," Jayr continued. "I will leave the keys to it with Navarre." She looked over her shoulder, and one of her hands clenched. "If you will excuse me, I must attend to my master now. Good night, my lord, my lady." Jayr bowed a second time before she sauntered off into the castle.

"That girl works like a slave," Alex muttered. "I guess it's better that the guys around here treat her like an equal instead of a woman. Otherwise she'd be down by the river, scrubbing Byrne's clothes on a washboard."

"What Jayr does for Byrne is no different from what Phillipe does for me," Michael reminded her.

"I know, it's just . . . " She blew out a breath. "Odd. Really odd. When I first saw her and Conan together, they seemed more like a couple than boss and underling."

"It is likely because Jayr has served Aedan since the Kyn

first rose." Michael plucked a leaf from her hair. "They have been together for a very long time and know each other well. Like Phillipe and me."

"I guess." Alex looked up as a window four stories above them opened, and saw Jayr outlined in it for a moment. "Whoa. How the hell did she get up there so fast?"

"She does not dawdle as you do." Michael ushered her inside.

"What were you bloody thinking, Aedan?"

Byrne looked up as the door to his chamber slammed into the wall and Locksley appeared. "That I should invest in copper locks comes to mind now."

"Do not jest with me. Not about this."

He closed the Dumas novel he had been reading and set it aside. "What should I have done, lad? Let you cut down the man in front of everyone? Watch his heathens do the same to you? 'Twould have made a memorable opening to the tournament, I suppose."

"It would have for me." Locksley walked to the fireplace and picked up a length of wood, snapping it into pieces, which he tossed into the flames. "Who is he?"

"An arrogant prick pecking at old wounds, or an ignorant fool interested in making new ones." Byrne went to his cabinet and took out a bottle of whiskey blended with blood. "Come and have a drink."

He made an impatient gesture. "I can't stomach that stuff."

"Every man cannae be a Scot, more's the pity." Byrne poured a small measure into two glasses and brought one to his friend. "Cyprien has a head for intrigue, and rules over us all. He'll sort out this Italian, prohibit the old colors, and set it to rights."

"I'll drink to that." Rob drank, nearly choked, and dragged in air. "Or not. How do you swallow this swill?"

"Quickly." Byrne took a sip from his own. "Did you recognize him? The Italian?" Robin shook his head. "I thought he might be a bastard of Guisbourne's. He doesnae have Guy's curls or his height, but those snake eyes remind me of him."

Robin's mouth twisted. "My dear cousin never left England,

and before he filched my lands and wealth he eliminated any other potential heirs. Every male in the family died young, either in battles fighting for the king or from illnesses that fell upon them overnight."

"Poisoned," Byrne said, nodding. "His mother was accused of killing his father with her herbs." The old woman had been a recluse, living in the deepest level of Guisbourne's castle. Some said it was to hide an advanced state of skin rot; others claimed she craved concealment in order to freely practice the dark arts. "Would she have taught Guy her witchery?"

"She doted on him, the hulking bastard. Perhaps she gave him a spell to cheat death."

Byrne felt skeptical. "One that made him six inches shorter, prettied his face, and blackened his hair?"

"Alexandra gave Cyprien a new face," Locksley said, sounding defensive. "His nose was never that straight, nor his chin so square."

"Guisbourne is dead," Byrne assured him. "Of that I am certain. I stood by you and watched him die at Richard's hands."

"I know it. Damn his soul." Robin stared into his glass. "It cannot be him."

Byrne hesitated before he pressed the issue of an heir. "If Guy had sired a bastard son during his human life—a child whose mother might have fled the country to protect them—and this Italian is a descendant—"

A snarl erupted from Robin, who threw the glass across the room. "No."

Jayr appeared out of nowhere and caught the glass before it smashed into the wall. "Lord Locksley, may I bring you some wine? I fear few acquire a taste for my master's whiskey."

The wrath drained from Robin's features. "My temper escapes me. I beg your pardon, Jayr." He bowed and turned to Byrne. "For the sake of our friendship I will leave it to Michael. But tell this pretender to stay out my path." With one final look at Jayr, he departed.

"Close the door, lass," Byrne said quietly, and went back to his chair. He had no desire to reimmerse himself in the righteous vengeance of Edmond Dantès, but instead watched Jayr as she went about her work in the chamber. Her movements, which he had seen thousands of times, soothed him as much as her scent.

He spotted fine yellow dust on the yoke of her tunic. "You went to the gardens."

"I did. I saw the seigneur and his lady walking there, and went to assure that all was well with them." She rearranged his bed pillows, piling them in a small heap as he preferred, before drawing the curtains on the window side. "The lady is very forthright, isn't she?"

"That's a pretty word for it." Byrne imagined having to deal with a woman such as Alexandra Keller. "I thank Christ that she belongs to Cyprien. A man would have to possess an endless well of patience to put up with such antics."

"Such are modern women," Jayr said. "I do admire her wit. She never seems at a loss for words." She grimaced as she came to kneel before him. "I should have had those banners taken down before Lord Locksley saw them."

"Bollocks. No, let me do it." Byrne leaned forward to remove his boots. "Taking them down would have been an insult to the Italian, if that's what he is."

Jayr sat back on her heels. "He doesn't seem right to me, either. His voice is persuasive and beautiful, but too practiced. His talent may be even more dangerous." She told him about the wine being frozen in every goblet. "If that was caused by him, of course." She rose and took his boots.

"I've not heard of a Kyn with the talent to steal warmth." Byrne followed her over to the cabinet. "What else did you notice about him?"

"That he trusts his back to Saracens is worrisome. I think he must never have taken vows." She shook her head a little as she placed his boots in the cabinet. "He speaks English without an accent, and has courtly manners, but he would not acknowledge my greeting and offer to introduce him. He seemed most interested in meeting—"

"He ignored you?" Byrne took her arm and turned her toward him. "In front of the guests?"

"Many Kyn do not approve of me, my lord," she said, her voice low, her eyes shuttered. "It matters not. I do not serve them."

"He deliberately insulted you." Alternating surges of cold and hot fury rose inside him. "Yet you said nothing to me."

"My lord, it *is* nothing." Jayr looked up at him. "I do not require Lord Nottingham's attention or approval. I merely sought to be of assistance. That he refused it is his loss, not mine."

"It is something, and I should have let Rob ventilate his jacket." Putting his arms around her eased some of the tightness in his chest, but it would not remove the humiliation she had suffered. "I'm sorry, lass."

Jayr stood quietly in his embrace, saying nothing. Byrne gave in to the temptation to spread his hand over her long, narrow back, stroking it with gentle circles of his palm.

"I did feel mortified at first," she finally confessed, lightly resting her cheek against his chest. "No one has ever turned his back on me like that. It made me wonder how many other Kyn feel the same as he, but mind their manners out of deference to you."

"I will let Rob skewer him tomorrow," Byrne decided. "As an opening for the tournament. While we both watch."

Jayr chuckled. "Only if I am permitted to take photographs to mark the occasion." Her chin lifted as she met his gaze. Her lips, always so tight and flat with control, looked full and soft. "Thank you, Ae . . . my lord."

"Aedan," he prompted, watching her mouth, wanting to see it frame his name as no other could.

Her voice dwindled to a whisper. "Aedan." Her *dents acérées* flashed, sharp and white, changing her speech. "Thank you, Aedan."

As her scent darkened, Byrne shuddered and closed his arm tighter around her slim waist. His hand had drifted down the length of her back and now rested on the slight flare above her narrow hips. He imagined pressing her forward, guiding her up against him so he could feel the soft plane of her belly. Or moving his hand around to cup her and rub his fingers against her. His cock strained, eager to do what his hand would not.

Something between them gave off an electronic chime, and Jayr's eyes widened as she pulled away and fumbled in one of her pockets. She brought out yet another of her countless devices and consulted its tiny, illuminated screen. "Excuse me, my lord; I am needed. Thank you for your kindness. I must go and . . . I must go." She spun on her heel and disappeared in a blur.

Byrne stood, bathed in her perfume, surrounded by empty air. "No, lass. I must."

Chapter 10

Alex had spent most of the day lying beside Michael and watching him as he rested in the curious, trancelike state that passed as sleep for the Kyn. Although she was tired, she had little interest in doing the same. Someone—Phillipe, probably—had swiped a vial of vamp tranquilizer out of her bag. She could endure a couple of sleepless days to keep the peace between her and Michael. She'd have to tell him about the dreams eventually. She just wasn't sure she wanted to know why she was having them.

Michael would know why.

Once the sun had dropped to the midafternoon position in the sky, Alex eased out of bed, dressed, and decided to stash her supply of tranquilizer where she could get to it without Phillipe or Michael being the wiser.

After pocketing the keys to the infirmary that Phillipe had given her, Alex grabbed her medical case, walked out, and tried to retrace her path to the guards' hall. The empty corridors indicated that none of the Kyn were early risers, although she spotted a number of security cameras set up in discreet corners, and what appeared to be motion sensors set into the door frames of some of the chambers.

Setting off an alarm wouldn't make her a popular girl, so when Alex found the guards' hall she took the right turn she remembered and followed another hall to the castle infirmary.

Over time Alex had discovered that, unlike Michael, the majority of the Kyn had little use for doctors or medical treatment. Part of it was due to the barbaric state that medicine had been in during their human lives in the Middle Ages. A doctor might be the village barber, a crazy old woman, or whatever quack

decided he understood the healing arts. After Michael had described some of the standard treatments of the day for open
wounds—irrigating them with urine, packing them with poultices made of dried grass and manure, or adding third-degree
burns to them with a heated poker—Alex didn't blame them.

The other factor was the Kyn's ability to heal spontaneously.
If a *vrykolakas* were healthy and well fed, any wound someone
managed to make in them would close over in a matter of seconds and disappear. The pathogen infecting them had completely replaced their immune system, attacking and destroying
any benign or hostile organism that entered the body, which
meant they never fell ill. The Kyn were difficult to hurt, and almost impossible to kill.

Despite the prejudice against medicine, Byrne had a fairly
decent setup in his infirmary. Alex saw that copper, the only
substance that could pierce a healthy Kyn's flesh, coated all the
instruments. Suture kits with dissolving thread were stacked
neatly next to various splints and bandages. Alex opened one
heavy steel door and found a refrigerated walk-in, its shelves
filled with several thousand bags of whole blood, plasma, and
saline.

"Good God Almighty." Alex left her medical case on one of
the counters and went inside the chilly room. She began checking labels; according to the dates not one of the bags was more
than a few weeks old. "Somebody knock over a hematology research lab?"

"They were given to us freely," Jayr said from behind her.
"Good afternoon to you, my lady."

"Freely, huh." Alex eyed the seneschal and the towering hulk
standing next to her. His size should have made him intimidat-
ing, but his pink vest, red trousers, and the yellow jacket draped
over his shoulders spoiled the effect. "Who's your friend?"

"This is Rainer, my lady."

The man bowed. "Delighted to make your acquaintance, my
lady. I will not interrupt your reverie—"

"Sit down," Jayr ordered. To Alex she said, "Rainer's arm
was broken last night and has healed wrong. I was hoping you
could advise me on how to properly set it."

Alex waved toward a gurney. "Have a seat." She sucked in a

breath when Jayr removed the man's jacket. "Jesus Christ." She glared at Rainer. "You let it heal like this? Why didn't you get help when it happened?"

"I was tied up," he told her.

Alex went to work, with Jayr assisting. An hour later, she finished wrapping Rain's arm and tucked it in a sling.

"That should do the trick, but keep the arm out of commission for at least a week," she told him. "Come find me in a couple of days so we can do a follow-up. Or I'll find you."

"You cannot miss me." He grinned at her. "You have but to look for the most stylish fellow in the Realm."

"Break that arm again," she warned, "and next time I'll put your butt in a sling."

Rainer left, but Jayr stayed behind to help Alex tidy up. "I thank you, my lady. Rain is very dear to us."

Alex nodded. "Then why did someone do that to him? Don't bother repeating his story about slipping and falling. He'd have to fall down sixty flights of stairs to sustain that many breaks, and they wouldn't all be on the same arm. Someone tortured that man."

"I am of the same opinion." Jayr grimaced. "But he will not tell me who did it."

"Look for a real sadist." Alex went back into the refrigerated room to retrieve some plasma. "There are labels here from a dozen different hospitals and blood donation centers. You in big with the AMA?"

"Blood donated by humans to their hospitals and collection centers is tested before it is entered into inventory and used for patients," Jayr said as she joined her. "If the blood is found to be diseased, it is removed and destroyed as a biohazard."

"Which is why this stash of yours is really bugging me," Alex said. "Getting people to voluntarily donate blood is like asking them to pull out their own teeth. There's enough blood here to supply a major surgical hospital for a couple of months."

"I must disagree on that point, my lady." Jayr nodded toward the shelves. "All of the blood we store has been discarded. It was tested and found to be diseased and unusable."

"By anyone but Kyn," Alex said slowly, "because we're immune to human diseases."

"Yes. Our supply comes from three different hazardous-waste collection companies that serve most of the medical facilities in Florida and several surrounding states. They deliver the blood to another company, one we own, which is contracted to incinerate it. Instead the company delivers the blood here." Jayr tried to look modest. "We also take a share of the disposal fee."

"Good-bye, biohazard. Hello, breakfast." Alex picked up one of the bags. A second label on the back indicated that it had been found to be contaminated with hepatitis B. "Recycling bad blood. I'd never have thought of it. It's brilliant."

"I like to think that we help humans in a small way by doing so." Jayr leaned against the doorway. "This cache, combined with the millions of human visitors who come to vacation here each year, keeps us well supplied."

Alex frowned. "You have all this and still hit up the living?"

"We hunt," she corrected, "because as plentiful as the bagged blood is, it provides only nourishment. Humans provide warmth and life."

"And lots of sex."

Jayr shrugged.

"Don't look so innocent. You drug them with *l'attrait*, which makes Rohypnol look like a vitamin pill, and then you can have your orgasm and eat it, too. Pardon me if I don't shake my pom-poms." Miffed all over again, Alex came out of the refrigerated room and slammed the door. "I assume that you're like the rest of them, and are okay with this?"

"Blood banks came into existence only in the last century." Jayr didn't seem offended. "To survive we must have blood from humans."

"Sex, on the other hand, is optional," Alex pointed out. "You don't have to give me the speech about how few girl vampires there are, and how the guys all renounced their vows of celibacy long ago. I've heard it a million times." She thought of all the large, muscular men she'd seen around Byrne. "Bet you never have to beg for a date, though."

Jayr looked pained. "I do not . . . date . . . humans."

Alex thought of the rows of warriors who had stood around Byrne. "I guess with the way the guys around here look, it would be slumming."

"Nor the men of the Realm."

"You're kidding. Are you blind?" Alex demanded. "Or gay?"

"Neither." The seneschal looked uneasy. "I am celibate."

"Oh, so you're insane." Alex laughed as she rigged the bag she'd brought out for transfusion. "You're a better woman than I am, Jayr. If I lived here and were single, I'd make sex my personal hobby."

"The men look to me for leadership, not relief. I cannot be a seneschal and a leman." She checked her watch. "My master will be waking soon. My lady—"

"Please. After last night, no one is going to call me a lady. Make it Alex, or Dr. Keller."

"Dr. Keller." Jayr seemed anxious now. "I have already taken advantage of your kindness, and I must go, but tomorrow would you be willing to examine one more Kyn?"

"Sure, who?"

"Me."

"Why did you not come to the hall last night?" Farlae asked as Viviana finished tidying the workroom. "You missed quite a show between Locksley and this Nottingham of Florence."

Viviana had gone to the assembly with Harlech, but had slipped out as soon as Nottingham had arrived.

"I felt weary," she lied. "You have been using us like deck slaves."

"Aye, I have." Farlae's black eye seemed to pierce through her head. "Yet here you are, hard at work with the sun still in the sky."

She gathered the cording for the lord's new bed curtains and sat down well away from the window to work on it. "The work will not do itself."

"Vivi."

"Don't." She did not look up. "I have never asked why you and Rain always go to town on the same night, or come back smelling of each other, have I?"

"If you think to shame me into abandoning my regard for you," the wardrobe keeper advised her, "you will have to work harder than that. Everyone knows about me and Rain. We've been together since the British invaded for the last time."

"Forgive me." She put down the cording and rubbed her irritated eyes. "There is much I have done in my life, before I came here, that I regret. I was reminded of that last night. That is all."

"No, it is not," he said, giving her a wry smile, "but very well. You know where my ears and my shoulder are." He picked up a stack of newly hemmed table coverings and left.

Sewing had always been a mindless, soothing occupation for Viviana, but today the familiar play of needle and fabric gave her little relief from her thoughts. Her mind had become a snarled nest of fear and anger, bound tightly with despair.

Now that he is come, all will be revealed.

She had not wished to keep this secret. Indeed, she had tried to confide in Harlech a thousand times, but the right moment had never presented itself. No, to be brutally honest, she had made excuses so as to keep her husband in ignorance. Harlech would never expose her, but she had feared that the truth would drive him away from her. Surely after all that had happened, after all that she had lost, she deserved some happiness?

The answer to that came from behind her, in a voice that seemed too lovely to belong to a man. "How delightful it is to see a woman at such gentle work."

The hot, heavy scent of aniseed closed around her like a black wool cloak.

She bundled up the satin cord, tangling some of the shining strands she had been wrapping as she went to put the pile into her work basket.

"Ana." A black-gloved hand stopped her, trapping her fingers between the cord and the soft leather. "Are you not happy to see me?"

She faced him. "What would you know of happiness?"

"Not the welcome I expected, but it will do." He straightened. "It is astonishing how well you look. Your pretty face is the same as it was the day that my mother gave you to me."

"I am no longer an ignorant child desperate to feed my family. The family your mother let starve." She lifted her left hand, showing him the plain gold band that Harlech had placed on it. "I have protection now."

"My seneschal told me that you had taken a husband. Interesting news, I thought, considering your past . . . and mine." He walked around her, inspecting her as he might a horse. "I feared that time would somehow ravage your beauty, but you truly are as you ever were: a flame among ashes."

"The past is dead, and I belong to another." She felt his hand tug at her headrail, and she grabbed it, outraged. "You will not trifle with me. Not if you wish to continue this obscene charade."

"Why, Ana, was that a threat? You have grown up." He smiled. "I confess, I was shocked that you ran from the room as soon as you laid eyes on me. I expected the charade to end then and there, for you have been made an honest woman. You did tell this husband about me, did you not?" He bent close. "Oh, my. You kept your secrets from him. What a pity."

"Harlech did not know me until after the *jardin* wars were over. We have never discussed what happened to us before we met. It was not important." She refused to cower. "What do you want?"

"Power. Pleasure. Many things." He took a tendril of her hair that had escaped her headrail and tickled the side of her jaw with its ends. "We have so much to talk about, you and I. You will come to my chamber tonight, after your husband retires." His other glove traced the arc of her breast. "I look forward to how we will become reacquainted."

"No."

"That was not a request." He jerked off her hair covering, seized her hair in his fist, and used it to drag her up against him. "You will come to me, Ana, and you will do exactly as I say. Otherwise, your husband will have to be made aware of many things." His hand closed cruel and tight over her breast. "I think I will start with from where you come."

Viviana drew her dagger and pressed it against his ribs. "If you wish me to keep my silence, you stay away from me and mine."

"Or what?" The tip of her blade pierced his tunic and

pricked his flesh, but he didn't flinch. "You will expose me? You cannot do that, my love. Not if you wish to go on living. Old memories being what they are."

She knew that if she gave in to his demands, he would take everything from her anyway. "Test me and find out, my lord."

He put his mouth on her cheek, cupped her hand with his, and pushed it against his body, inhaling deeply as the tip of the copper cut through his side. "There, the angle is better. One thrust and you will have my heart. You did covet it once, I think." He held her in place as she jerked. "Don't be timid, Ana," he whispered, his cool breath caressing her ear. "You've held my fate in your hands before this. You've always done the right thing."

Her hand went numb, and distantly she heard her dagger clatter on the stone floor.

Nottingham lowered his head, kissing her stiff lips before he smiled against them and stepped back. "Tonight, in my chambers." He replaced her headrail and arranged the veils around her face. "Wear your hair down for me."

Viviana closed her eyes, and kept them shut until she heard the latch fall. She looked at the cording, which during the struggle had fallen to the floor. Her hands had torn and shredded it beyond repair.

Chapter 11

Jayr rose early and met Alexandra Keller in the infirmary the next afternoon for her examination. The doctor watched without comment as Jayr lowered the blinds and secured the door.

Jayr faced her. "What should I do first, my lady?"

"Stop calling me 'my lady.'" Alexandra smiled. "It's Alex. So, why am I giving you a physical? Something bothering you?"

"My body is not as it should be."

The doctor nodded. "Right. When did you begin identifying as a male?"

Jayr gave her a perplexed look. "I do not know what you mean. I am a female. I cannot identify as anything else."

"Oops. Language blip. Sorry." Alex thought for a minute. "Let me take a stab at this. You don't look very female. You want to know why, and if I can do anything to . . . make you look more feminine?"

"Yes." Jayr felt relieved. "Exactly." Her gaze skittered to Alex's medical case. "I have never been examined by a modern physician."

"It's much nicer now," Alexandra promised. "We don't cut open veins to let the bad blood drip out or dose you with cow urine. And there is absolutely, positively no application of poultices made with manure on any part of your body. I do charge a fee, though."

Jayr frowned. "You wish me to pay you?"

"I'm working up a database of hematological profiles on the Darkyn," Alexandra said. "My fee for the physical will be a couple of vials of your blood."

That seemed reasonable to Jayr. "Why are you creating this database?"

"Once I have enough samples, I can start working toward a cure for us," the doctor told her. "With a lot of work and luck, I think I may be able to reverse the condition that caused and sustains the Kyn mutation."

"Indeed." The possibility of becoming human again intrigued Jayr, although she doubted most Kyn would feel the same. "If I were turned back to human, would I begin aging?"

"I won't know until I actually find a cure, but since all humans except Cher age, that's pretty much a given." Alex picked up a blank chart. "Why don't you sit down, and I'll start asking you some terribly personal questions?"

Jayr gingerly lowered herself into the chair Alex indicated.

"We'll kick off things with the family history first," the doctor said. "Where and when were you born?"

"I was born in Scotland sometime during the year of our Lord twelve ninety-seven," Jayr said. "My parents abandoned me in a church when I was but an infant. My benefactor sent me from there to a convent in London."

"Your benefactor?"

"A local squire or lord, I presume. He paid for the sisters to take me in and educate me. I was never told his name." She felt wistful. "I tried once to find out, but there were no records."

Alex began writing on the top page of the chart. "So much for family medical history."

"I do have this." Jayr removed the worn gold ring from her hand and held it out. "It was left with me."

Alexandra turned it over and held it up to the light to look at the inside. "J . . . A . . . Y . . . ryan."

"It is a betrothal ring," Jayr told her. "The sisters used the first four letters to name me."

"Very pretty." She handed the ring back to her. "You think your family name could be Ryan?"

"I had hoped it was my father's name."

Alex nodded. "So you grew up in a convent. That must have been a barrel of laughs." When Jayr didn't know how to respond, she added, "Sorry. I went to Catholic school. I'm still recovering from ruler phobia. How did you like hanging out with the sisterhood?"

"We had a hard life, but a good one. So many people with families died of plague and famine anyway. As an orphan, I was incredibly fortunate to have a place and the power of the church to protect me." Jayr shrugged. "I did not appreciate it then, I fear. Our abbess wished me to take vows and join the order, but I felt no calling. When she pressed the issue, I ran away and went back to Scotland to search for my family."

"When did you become infected?" At her blank look, Alex added, "Uh, cursed?"

"Thirteen fourteen. The year I ran away."

"You've been around for a while." Alex noted something else on the chart. "Was Aedan the one who turned you?"

Jayr nodded.

Alex propped her hip against the edge of a gurney. "Tell me how it happened."

"We were at Bannockburn. I came upon him after he had fallen into a pit trap. I was too small and weak to pull him out. I climbed in and tried to help him out, but he was dying." She paused, her brows drawing together as she thought. "What happened after that is not clear in my memory, but I believe that was when I gave him my blood."

Alex gave her a sharp look. "Voluntarily?"

"It was not because of *l'attrait*," she told her dryly. "My lord Byrne lay covered in mud and muck, impaled on a wooden stake through his chest, and partially trampled by his horse. He hardly had the strength to lift his head."

"No pheromone inducement, check." Alex eyed Jayr's torso. "How old were you at the time of transition?"

"Seventeen." She saw Alex's reaction. "I am not lying."

"I didn't say that you were, although your body is telling me a different story." Alex got off the gurney and pulled on a pair of latex gloves. "Now you get to take off your clothes and let me see you naked; then you'll lie down and let me do the really embarrassing stuff."

Jayr stripped and stood motionless and naked as Alex circled around her and made notes. Rarely had she felt so uncomfortable or vulnerable, but if the doctor could help her, then it would be worth it.

"Were you born with this?" Alexandra said, tapping the patch of puffy purple skin six inches above the flat circle of her left nipple.

"Yes." Jayr covered it with her hand briefly. "I should have mentioned it. I know it is unsightly."

"Port-wine birthmarks are attention getters." The doctor used the flat of her fingertips to push at the edges. "It looks like a dented heart. Kind of cute. Any bleeding or inflammation here?"

"None, ever."

"Good. They can be a problem sometimes. So, no breast development, low body weight, narrow hips, no pubic or underarm hair—you don't shave it off, do you?" When Jayr shook her head, Alexandra took out a slim pen that, when she clicked its handle, shone a narrow beam of light. "Open your mouth nice and wide." She directed the light inside Jayr's mouth and peered in. "Unlike your fangs, your wisdom teeth never erupted." She stepped back, sniffed, then leaned in and sniffed a second time. "Do you use tobacco?"

She should have bathed before coming. "No, Doctor."

"Your hair smells singed. Must be from lighting the fireplaces." She pointed behind her. "Hop on the gurney and lie down."

Jayr remained quiescent as Alex measured the length of her arms and legs and used a device she said would determine Jayr's muscle mass. "Why do you wear gloves?"

"Leftover human habit. It intimidates some of the more pigheaded Kyn, too." She straightened. "I need to perform a pelvic and an ultrasound to confirm it—if you can requisition some gynecological supplies and an ultrasound machine from someone, I can do that later—but my educated guess is that you never acquired secondary sexual characteristics when you were human."

The long words made her head spin. "What does that mean?"

"You didn't go through puberty, Jayr. At least, not all the way." Alex handed her clothes to her. "Every human makes a physical and emotional transition from childhood to adolescence. It's triggered by the pituitary gland secreting hormones called gonadotropins, which stimulate the sex organs to mature. In girls, the ovaries are stimulated, in boys, the testes." She frowned as she watched Jayr dress. "You've got a slight bowing to your calves."

Jayr eyed her own legs as she pulled on her trousers. "They have always been shaped so."

"It's usually a sign of malnutrition," the doctor told her. "Did you have to go without food a lot when you were human?"

"Many times. The convent where I was brought up was very poor, and food was often scarce." She glanced down at her flat chest. "One of the sisters said hunger was a good thing. It kept me from having my moon time."

"Body weight is definitely a contributing factor in the onset of puberty," Alexandra said. "It's the reason so many overweight kids today go through puberty much younger than they should. Starvation, on the other hand, has a way of postponing things. After you made the transition to Kyn, did your body mature in any way?"

"No. I remain exactly as I was on the last day of my human life." She glanced down at her boyish chest and felt the usual bleak wash of depression. "I have lived in this body for six hundred years and better, so I have accepted my fate. Still, if there is something that could be done to make me like other women . . ."

"I don't want to give you any false hopes," Alexandra said firmly. "If you were human, we could try medication, maybe some artificial implants, but your Kyn metabolism would automatically reject them. You have almost no body fat, which is the only thing I could possibly transplant to build up your breasts. About the only thing surgically I can do for you is get rid of that birthmark, if you want."

Disappointment made Jayr retreat into herself. "I thank you, but no, I am used to it."

"Well, maybe we can try some other things," Alex said. "First, though, I'd like to do a gynecological exam and perform that ultrasound, so I can be sure there's no internal trouble contributing to the problem. Do you have a decent medical vendor?"

"An excellent one. I will see to it that the equipment and supplies you need are delivered before the week's end," Jayr promised. "What could be inside me that would cause this?"

"Some parts that don't belong there." Alex gestured toward her abdomen. "Nature can't always make up its mind whether it wants a girl or a boy, you know. In very rare cases there are people born with extra reproductive organs. You might have ovaries *and* testes." She took out a copper-tipped syringe. "Time to pay the bill. Slide up your sleeve, please."

Jayr watched Alex draw two vials of blood. "What do these people born with too many parts do about it?"

"In your time they had to live with it, if they were allowed to live at all. A lot of hermaphrodites—that's the common term for people with the condition—were killed at birth if they showed visible characteristics of their dual gender."

"Characteristics?" Jayr said faintly.

"Being born with a vagina and an oversize, elongated clitoris. There's been a lot of debate over the last fifty years as to whether or not the clit is just an underdeveloped penis. Some can be hidden from view by the labia, and evident only when engorged or displayed." Alex gave her a guileless look. "Got anything tucked away down there that I should know about?"

"Ah, no." Jayr felt mortified, but added, "I have attended to some visiting Kyn females in their bath, and I confess I used a mirror to look upon myself and see if I was made the same. I have no body hair, but I am as they are fashioned."

"Good to know—and there's nothing wrong with being curious about your body." The doctor stripped off her gloves and discarded them. "One more question, and then we're done. You've been this way ever since you became Kyn, so why do you want to change it now?"

"I do not despise how I am made," Jayr said slowly. "For many reasons, not least of which is my position in this household, it is better that I do not look much like other females."

"I would cheerfully switch bodies with you, you know," Alexandra advised her. "And you didn't answer my question."

She met Alex's gaze squarely. "I am a woman. I never

wished to become a nun or live as a celibate. I would like the same chance to enjoy what other females have. With my body as it is, I cannot."

"Some men really love the skinny-supermodel look, you know." Alexandra's gaze turned shrewd. "Oh, I get it. You've already got your eye on someone, and he likes his ladies fully loaded."

Jayr cringed a little. "Something like that, yes."

"At least some of your hormones are in good working order." Alexandra chuckled, and then grew thoughtful. "There was another girl I met in Chicago—Jema Shaw—who made the change from human to Kyn. She was first infected with Kyn blood when she was a baby, and kept in a partial state of prepuberty for years by a nutcase."

"No nutcase has done this to me, Doctor," Jayr assured her.

"I know." She smiled absently. "It's just that by suppressing the development of Jema's pituitary gland, her nutcase doc was able to keep her human for thirty years. I'll need some very specific drugs, but I think that if I reverse his formula, I might stimulate your body to finish growing by itself."

Jayr allowed herself to feel a twinge of excitement. "Then I would be as I should have been. We have friends in the city who can obtain whatever drugs and equipment you require."

"I can't guarantee it will work, kiddo. There are enormous difficulties involved in using synthetic hormones on Kyn. Encouraging hormone production is going to be a lot harder than suppressing it." Alexandra picked up a notepad. "I won't promise you a miracle, but with some luck, maybe we can jump-start the natural maturation process."

"I would be grateful for anything you can do." Jayr held out her hand and clasped Alex's forearm as she would an equal. "My thanks, Doctor."

"You're welcome." She began writing. "Now let's put together a shopping list."

The beginning bouts of the tournament filled the next several days at the Realm with activity. When no further incidents occurred between Locksley and Nottingham, who seemed to be taking pains to avoid each other, Phillipe began to relax and enjoy himself. With Cyprien occupied in talks with his suzerain, and Alexandra content to work on her medical research in the infirmary, Phillipe took some time for himself each evening to go down to the lists, where the seneschal preferred to gather to talk and train.

Among the serving class of the Darkyn were men of myriad backgrounds and lineage. Once they would have formed subclasses, with the younger sons of nobles and wealthy merchants at the top of the pecking order, and former villeins and common laborers like Phillipe at the bottom. That had been part of their human lives, however, and the common bond they all shared as Kyn had, for the most part, erased those distinctions.

"Navarre, are you rested?" Will Scarlet called out from atop the Belgian he had wrestled to the ground. He spoke, as they all did, in the archaic French they had used during their human lives. "I fear the bones of my sword arm have grown thin as I waited for you."

"Bring them here when you are finished with your sweetheart," Phillipe told him as he belted his scabbard and pulled on his gauntlets. "My sword wants polishing."

Several men around them snickered at the blatant innuendo.

Scarlet cuffed the Belgian across the head, stunning him momentarily. He flipped him over and pinned his shoulders for a ten count to end the bout.

"Better, Eustace," he said as he helped his opponent to his feet. "I barely broke that spleen-wrenching hold of yours this time. You but tarried too long powdering my face with the dust."

"On the morrow," Eustace promised, rubbing the grit Will had tossed in his eyes, "I will persuade you to dine on it."

Scarlet laughed, slapped his shoulder, and shook himself off before joining Phillipe outside a dueling circle. "What is this I see, no armor, no braces? Am I to spar with you or a damsel? Not that I think the difference would be greatly noticeable."

"I trust you will not steal the heart from my chest." Phillipe removed his jacket and rolled up his sleeves. "After all, it is not Italian."

"Lucky for you," Scarlet said, more soberly.

"A poor jest, Will." Phillipe tied his hair back with a strip of leather. "How fares your master?"

"My lord Robin has removed himself to the range." The seneschal sighed as he pulled on his belt and buckled it. "Permanently, it would seem. All should be well, as long as he does not run out of arrows."

Phillipe scanned the long, barricaded corridor of the lists, but saw no unfamiliar faces. "The Saracens do not train, then."

"They are heathens, not idiots." Scarlet waited until Phillipe stood ready, and then stepped into the circle and drew his sword, bringing it up before his face in a formal salute. "On your guard, Navarre."

Phillipe so often trained with Cyprien, who favored fighting with two swords, that it took him one round to adjust his balance and blocks. Some of the other men gathered around in a loose circle to observe and shout their encouragement, mostly for Scarlet.

"Am I the underdog, then?" Will asked as he thrust his blade at Phillipe's ribs. Steel clanged as their swords clashed together and Phillipe forced him back a step. "It must be your pretty face that bespells them, my friend, for it cannot be these ham-handed techniques."

"Step outside the circle by one hair's width," Phillipe told him, "and their opinion of you will not be in vain."

Dueling had its rhythms and levels, as did a familiar opponent. Scarlet tended to disdain the customary practice of circling left and attacking to the right, but he would switch directions without warning and liked to follow a feint with a lethally swift thrust. Phillipe knew he was a fraction slower than Locksley's seneschal, but he had more patience, and watched for opportunities instead of trying to make them. Had they been human, he could have simply exhausted Scarlet, but Kyn blood gave them a hundred times more strength and endurance. Legitimate duels between well-matched Kyn could last for five or six hours.

"If you intend to lurk instead of fight," Scarlet said testily, "I have bows to string and arrows to fletch."

Phillipe started to reply, and then jerked his head to one side to avoid losing an ear. His counterthrust came more from instinct than intention, and his sword pierced Scarlet's wrist, the steel tip exiting his forearm halfway to his elbow.

"Damn me." Phillipe yanked his blade out of the other man's flesh and signaled a draw by planting the sword in the dirt. With a grimace, Scarlet did the same. "Did I crack the bone?"

"No, but your steel bestowed a cold kiss upon it." Scarlet stepped out of the circle and accepted a length of white linen from one of the men watching. "Your responses are twice as fast as they were the last time we danced. Cyprien must be hauling you into the circle regularly."

"Four or five nights a week since summer," Phillipe admitted. "At first in preparation to face the high lord, but now . . . now I think he battles more inner demons."

"A familiar ailment." Scarlet mopped up the blood from his arm. "I must convince the seigneur to spar with me. Perhaps he can show me how I may fend off those plaguing my master."

Reassured that he had not seriously harmed his friend, Phillipe accompanied him to the benches. By the time they sat down, the wounds had closed and Scarlet was gingerly flexing his fingers. For a while they watched the other seneschal duel, wrestle, and fight bare-handed.

Scarlet hooted as an Irishman disarmed two Spaniards with one sweep of his blade. "God's teeth, but that was handy."

"I've fought him. He's clever but reckless," Phillipe said. As if to confirm his statement, the next challenger quickly defeated the Irishman. "Who do you see taking first in the *pas d'armes* with the blade?"

"If I do not take on all comers?" Scarlet grinned. "Jayr."

Phillipe tried to remember seeing Byrne's seneschal in single combat. "She never competes in anything but the joust."

"We could goad her into it," Scarlet suggested. "When I see her next I will challenge her. When she refuses, I will mention that her back has turned a lovely shade of yellow, and you may remark that it conceals her lack of spine."

Phillipe knew that his friend did not speak seriously, and was as fond of Jayr as was his master, Locksley. It did not keep Phillipe from teasing him. "I thought you did not wish to spar with damsels."

Scarlet scoffed out some air. "Jayr eats damsels for breakfast." He stretched out his sword arm and sighed. "She also keeps the Realm running as tight as a Prussian's timepiece. Cyprien would do well to consider one day giving her a *jardin* of her own."

The thought of a woman serving as suzerain seemed a bit ludicrous to Phillipe. "No one would accept her rule."

"You've seen her wield a blade." When Phillipe shrugged, Scarlet added, "You've never sparred with her, have you? You should. It is an education in humility."

"I do not spar with females," Phillipe said.

"Nor does she, but for you I think she would make an exception." Scarlet jerked his chin toward a cluster of Byrne's men. "She trains daily with them, you know. They have great respect for her blade."

"Their lord's temper might have something to do with it," Phillipe said.

Scarlet laughed. "She will come soon. Why don't you challenge her and find out for yourself?"

Uneasy at the thought of fighting a female, Phillipe changed the subject, but a short time later Jayr entered the lists, followed by three of the men. Phillipe was surprised to see that despite the clear sky and fair weather, her hair was wet and her garments dripping.

Scarlet nudged him. "Here is your chance at thorough mortification."

"I would not disgrace her so," Phillipe said.

"Of course you wouldn't." Scarlet sniffed. "The mortification I spoke of would be yours."

Phillipe shrugged. "Perhaps. Why is she all wet?"

"She always trains so." Will watched her go to the armor hooks, where she took down and strapped on a chest protector. "So she will not set herself on fire." He saw Phillipe's face and laughed. "Watch, *mon ami.* You will see why."

Jayr strapped on two scabbards and stepped into the circle with a warrior a foot taller than she was and three times her weight. Phillipe thought the bout would be over quickly, and it was. Jayr ducked under her opponent's initial attack, knocked his sword from his grasp, and hooked one of her feet behind his knee. She slammed the pommel of her sword into the center of his chest, and he went reeling out of the circle.

All this had taken place in a matter of ten or fifteen seconds.

Scarlet eyed him. "I can read your thoughts like a sorrily scraped palimpsest. You didn't see her pivot around him, did you?"

He focused as another opponent stepped into Jayr's ring. "I will this time."

Watching carefully, Phillipe saw Jayr offer the traditional salute, shift to a responsive rather than aggressive stance, and wait for the opponent to attack. He lunged, she parried, he lunged a second time, she parried again. Although the male was attacking, Jayr was actually gaining ground each time she countered, inching him backward.

Phillipe thought she was being foolhardy, neglecting her cover inside and out while she depended entirely on her parrying. Still, the blade never came within a foot of her body, even when she left a tantalizing opening for him to pierce.

"She is taunting him," he muttered.

Scarlet nodded. "That is the defender's advantage."

"She is not defending herself," Phillipe insisted. "She is attacking by luring him in with false openings. A moment before he attacks the opening closes, and she uses a parry like a hammer to drive him back. And the way she moves . . ." He frowned. "How does she do it?"

"That I have asked frequently." Scarlet scowled. "She says it is nothing, only her style of fighting. The speed is her talent. No one is faster."

"I have never seen anything so deliberate," Phillipe said, seeing now the faint blurs where there should have been discernible motion. Jayr moved swifter than the eye could follow. "Nor so devious."

"Neither have I. I fought her once, you know. Our men still joke about my defeat." Scarlet straightened. "Look, here is that Italian's pet dwarf."

Phillipe followed his gaze and saw Nottingham's short, red-haired seneschal stride into the lists. "What is his name?"

"Scarf, Scruff." His friend made a dismissive gesture. "Who cares?"

"Brother!" The Italian's seneschal made a beeline for Jayr's sparring circle, stopping at the edge. Ignoring the common courtesy of not addressing someone inside the sparring ring, he cried, "Why did you not send word that you are all training? I would have been among the first here."

Jayr did not spare him a glance, but several men of the Realm gave him filthy looks. To speak to someone engaged in a bout was a distraction tactic, and considered by all to be beyond rude.

Phillipe felt puzzled. He didn't know how things were done in Florence, but seneschal always trained as soon as the sun set, to take advantage of the twilight hour before their masters rose.

"He calls her brother," Scarlet mused. "This could prove amusing."

"I am Skald, seneschal of Lord Nottingham." He grinned as if blind to the scowls being directed at him. He drew an épée that looked more like a riding crop than a weapon and brandished it, swiping at the air with theatrical zeal. "I am known as the finest swordsman in Florence."

A short silence descended over the men.

"The finest, or the smallest?" someone drawled.

Another spit on the ground. "The loudest."

"I will be next in the circle," Skald announced, apparently also deaf to his critics. He shrugged out of his velvet jacket, revealing an ornate leather-and-brass chest protector that had been joined at the bottom with a large codpiece, also made of brass that had been styled to resemble a wide, erect phallus.

Phillipe felt a twinge of pity as laughter rang out, and Skald joined in, unaware that he was the object of the amused scorn.

"Tell me," Scarlet asked in a very grave tone, "do my eyes deceive me, or is this peahen sporting more steel in his crotch than in his fist?"

"Your eyes are painfully honest." Phillipe rose as he watched Skald still whipping his blade, now dangerously close to crossing into the circle. The vain seneschal seemed unaware that he was intruding on an ongoing bout, something considered unforgivable in the lists. "Will."

"I see him, the damned fool." Scarlet was on his feet and moving.

Before they could reach Skald, Jayr's opponent released a shout of fury. Phillipe saw a long line of red appear across the man's upper back, and his sword arm go limp. Skald had cut through several muscles.

"Oh, dear. Excuse my interference, brother." Skald retreated up several steps, lowered his bloodstained épée, and took out a handkerchief to wipe the blade. He pulled a face as the wounded man conceded to Jayr. "I did not mean it, you know. I fear my eagerness would precede me into battle."

Before Skald could cross over into the circle, Scarlet stepped in front of him and folded his arms. "Have it precede you into the keep, little one."

"I cannot, brother, for I have issued a challenge. Jayr is to fight me," Skald insisted, hopping up as he tried to see over Scarlet's shoulder. "You will engage me, will you not?"

Jayr did not answer, but turned her back on Skald and asked her wounded opponent if he required her assistance. He refused and withdrew, giving Skald a wide berth as he left the lists.

"I don't understand," the short seneschal said. "What is wrong? Is it something I said?"

A flare of purple glittered in Jayr's gaze before it subsided. "Navarre, can I interest you in a match?"

He eyed her men, who had formed a living, motionless wall between Skald and the circle where he and Jayr stood. "You can."

"When you are ready, sir." She moved to the inner edge of the circle, and correspondingly her men moved out, widening their ring of protection so that they were out of blade range.

Phillipe heard Skald's emphatic protests as he drew his sword, rotated his wrist to ease the tension in his arm, and stepped into the ring. "On your guard, mademoiselle."

Their blades met in the center of the circle, locking at the hilts. Phillipe felt the strength in her arm coiling to overpower his before they broke apart. He kept his gaze steady as he parried and thrust, standing almost completely still, the gap between them barely reaching the measure of a blade and a half.

"First blood," Jayr said after she feinted right.

Phillipe felt the burn of copper across the top of his shoulder and blinked. Her arm had been a blur; he hadn't seen the hit before she had struck. "How do you move so?"

Her mouth hitched. "I have excellent motivation."

He used a series of short, brutal thrusts to chase her in a half circle; she turned it around and beat him back in the other direction. Just as Phillipe began to wonder if he had any real chance of prevailing over her, the air turned chilly and a man's voice called out, "Halt!"

Jayr nodded to him and they drew back to opposite sides of the circle, planting the tips of their swords in the ground. Phillipe saw the air around her shimmer briefly, as it did above the roadway on a hot day. She made a quick gesture, and the men encircling them parted, affording them a view of what was happening.

In another circle, Will Scarlet looked down the length of his sword at Skald, who lay dazed and bleeding on the ground.

Nottingham came to stand at the edge of the circle.

"This match is over," the Italian said, bending down to grab the back of his seneschal's collar and using it to drag him to his feet. "You will attend me now."

"Yes, master." Skald bobbed an awkward bow and tried to sheath his épée. Blood from the closing cuts on his hands made them slippery, and he dropped the sword twice.

Nottingham seized the blade and flung it away.

Phillipe saw a smear of movement dart around him and stream across the lists. Jayr appeared in front of the Belgian Will had fought earlier, who had his back toward Nottingham, and snatched the hurtling épée a moment before it would have run him through. She rammed the weapon into the ground as smoke rose in wisps from her shoulders and legs.

Nottingham said something succinct and contemptuous in Italian before turning on his heel and returning to the keep. Skald babbled excuses as he hobbled after him.

"Seneschal," someone called out. "Your hair."

Jayr put a hand to her head and disappeared in another streak, reappearing beside the water barrel. As her hair burst into flames, she dunked her head inside, extinguishing them. The sizzle echoed around the lists.

"*Mon Dieu.*" Phillipe hurried over to her.

Jayr straightened and shook her head, wiping the water from her face. She saw Phillipe and offered him a wry look. "I think I must concede to you, Navarre."

The burned straps of her chest protector chose that moment to snap. She caught the armor before it fell to the ground.

Phillipe gaped.

"I thank you for the match," she said, as if nothing unusual had happened, and bowed. "You are an interesting opponent."

He stared at the scorched straps. "As are you, mademoiselle."

She gave him a half smile, passed the ruined chest protector to one of her men, and retreated to the keep.

Will came to stand beside him. "That was nicely done. Congratulations. You've just become a legend around here."

"It was pure charity on her part." Phillipe seriously doubted he could have beaten Byrne's seneschal. He recalled the shimmer around her when they had stopped fighting. "She creates heat when she moves so quickly. If she does so too long, the heat burns her. That is why her hair caught on fire."

Will consulted the clouds overhead. "The light, it finally dawns."

Phillipe grew thoughtful. "She cannot use her talent while she is riding. That is why she enters only the joust during the tournaments. No one could prevail over someone who can move faster than the eye can see."

"Jayr thinks it an unfair advantage in a real contest," Scarlet assured him. "She is like my master that way."

Phillipe suspected that much of what Jayr did was not what it seemed. "She will have to use it if she is to keep Skald from decorating someone's steel. He delights in spreading mischief like the pox."

"Aye." Scarlet stroked his chin. "Almost as if he were ordered to."

Chapter 12

"Relax." Alexandra sat down next to the exam table and switched on the blocky machine. "This will be a lot easier on you than the pelvic was. After this I'll administer the first shot, and then we'll see what happens."

Jayr glanced at the monitor atop the machine, and then stiffened as the doctor plugged in the cord attached to an odd-shaped device. "Does that thing go inside me?"

"Not unless you're pregnant, which I think we can check off as a permanent no on your chart." Alexandra picked up a tube and pulled back the drape over Jayr's lower abdomen. "I'm going to rub the end of it against your tummy. But first I get to smear you with some cold, icky gel."

She had not specified where the gel would go.

"Perhaps we could do this another time." Jayr tried to sit up. "My master must be wondering where I am."

"The gel stays on the outside this time, I promise." Alexandra gave her a pointed look. "Quit being so uptight and medieval. Modern women have these exams twice a year."

"They do?" Remembering the horrors of the speculum, she lay back against the pillows and closed her eyes. "I am ready." She clenched her fists at her sides.

Alexandra muttered something under her breath before she applied the gel, which was cold. "Don't tense up now. Think about something else. Tell me about your job; Phil never talks about it."

"I am my lord Byrne's seneschal," Jayr answered. "His third blade, the eyes at his back."

"You're reminding me of a really creepy Stephen King story

I read once," Alexandra said. "But so much for the job title. What do you guys do?"

"A seneschal must be prudent and faithful and profitable," Jayr said, remembering the charges laid out in the *Seneschaucie*, which she had studied more faithfully than she had the Holy Scriptures. "We are to know the law of the land, to protect our lord's business interests, and to instruct the household on how to adhere to their restrictions. We oversee the rents, services, and customs, deal with the merchants, issue franchises, collect tithes, and distribute endowments." She sucked in a breath as she felt the bumpy end of the device touch her stomach. "Are you certain we cannot do this next week?"

"Keep talking. Don't tense up like that."

"We—we deal with humans who cannot be avoided, so that our lord need not." Jayr felt a faint hum spread over her stomach and forced her muscles to go lax. "We enforce Kyn law, and the rule of privacy among the *jardin*. We train *tresori* as well as the lord's personal guard and garrison. We escort our lord and shield him from harm. We attend to his needs and the needs of his guests." She heard Alexandra make a strange sound and opened her eyes. "What is it, my lady? Is there something wrong with me?"

"Yeah. If you could cook, you'd be every man's wet-dream wife." She moved the device down to Jayr's right hip, spreading the gel with it. "Does Phil do all that stuff for Michael?"

"I would assume so. Navarre is known as an exemplary seneschal," Jayr said. "Often I have heard other seneschal say that they have consulted with him on matters of estate, and his advice has greatly aided them." She thought of how well he had conducted himself in the lists. "He is a very good fighter."

"He can arrange a mean vase of flowers, too." Alexandra fiddled with one of the machine's dials. "So when you're not running this place, and obsessing over making every aspect of Byrne's life perfect, what do you do for fun?"

"Fun." Jayr tried to think.

"You know, something for your own enjoyment," she said, adding another dollop of the cold gel to Jayr's skin. "Something you like. Something that doesn't involve your lord and master."

Cyprien's *sygkenis* still thought like a human. "My duties give me great satisfaction."

"But you've got to have a hobby or something. You can't devote every waking minute to handling stuff for Byrne." Alex pushed the end of the device harder against Jayr's left hip. "Do you ever go shopping, or hang out at the beach, or see a movie?"

"Our merchants deliver. The beaches are dangerous places at night. I do not care to watch moving pictures." Jayr thought of something. "When my lord has no need of me, I will take a long bath and read. I am very fond of Sara Donati's Wilderness novels." She hesitated. "Sometimes I sketch; other times I attempt to compose poetry. That pleases me, I suppose. When it does not bedevil me."

"I'd like to hear some poetry," Alexandra said. "Can you recite it off the top of your head?"

"It is not very good," Jayr warned her. "Most of it does not rhyme."

"Like I'm a critic." Alex moved the device down to a spot just above her mound. "Come on, kid, hit me with a dirty limerick or something."

Jayr recalled a short piece she had written at the beginning of the winter, and repeated it out loud:

> *"We live in darkness, cold and dead,*
> *and wish for the light, warm and alive*
> *but from darkness came the heavens*
> *as the night bears the day*
> *and winter frost the summer bounty.*
> *What will come from the Darkyn*
> *will be tender and new, a light*
> *more radiant and giving than the sun,*
> *and the souls against whom we sinned*
> *will at last bless our name."*

Alexandra was silent for a long time. "That's really pretty. Simple, but powerful." She looked as if she might say something else, then shook her head as though disagreeing with herself. "Right, I've got to do one more pass and we'll finish up with the injection." She turned the machine sideways. "Want to see what your plumbing looks like?"

Jayr observed the odd black-and-white images appearing as Alexandra continued the exam. "It looks as if I've swallowed a handful of truffles whole."

"Good analogy. Your uterus and stomach are about the same size as walnuts." Alex paused, regarding the screen thoughtfully. "I think I've found out why you never menstruated while you were human, too. The good news is, you don't have any male sexual organs, so you're not a hermaphrodite. The bad news is that your ovaries"—she tapped the screen in two places—"are raisins."

Jayr looked at the tiny spots the doctor pointed to. "Is that not how they should be?"

"In Kyn females they should be about five times larger, the size of prunes. My guess is your ovaries were diseased or deformed from birth." She shifted the device. "Can I ask you something that's probably going to offend you?" When Jayr nodded, she said, "You're not a virgin, so why aren't you sexually active now?"

Jayr felt appalled and stared at the monitor. "You can see that as well?"

"Not on here. I noticed that your hymen had been ruptured when I performed the pelvic," Alex told her. "Was the first time painful? Is that why you're still living like a nun?"

"Yes and no."

Alex sighed. "Kid, stop. You're drowning me with all this unnecessary information."

Jayr shifted her gaze to the lights above the table and tried to think of how to explain. "My first time was not terribly painful. It was the only time. I am celibate because I do not feel strong needs." That, at least, was partly true. She did not have to mention the endless, gnawing need she still had for Byrne.

"Well, missing out on puberty left you with an underdeveloped body *and* a dormant libido." Alex set aside the device, shut down the monitor, and wiped off the gel from Jayr's stomach. "Once we start this therapy, that may change. You could start having all kinds of inconvenient feelings. Are you okay with that?"

"Of course." Jayr looked at the liquid-filled needle Alexandra prepared. "I do want to be like you and other females, Doctor. However long it takes."

"We're about to find out. Hold still now; this will pinch." She plunged the tip of the syringe into the side of Jayr's neck. "I talked to Jema, and she said the injections always made her feel better. I'm hoping reversing the formula won't cause an opposite reaction."

"I can feel nothing but the sting of the wound," Jayr said honestly.

"Good." Alexandra removed the needle. "The synthetic gonadotropin probably won't start working immediately; your pituitary has been dormant for a long time, and I'm sure that the pathogen will run interference until it decides to accept the new hormones. I may have to add more plasma into the mix to tempt it to cooperate, too. But that's it; you can get dressed."

While Jayr changed into her clothes, the doctor printed out several of the images the ultrasound machine had stored and clipped them into a chart. She checked her watch and swore.

"I promised Michael I'd go with him to this big dance tonight," Alexandra explained. "That means closing up shop and going and making myself look pretty. Cyprien bought me this gown with a million little hooks up the back. It's gorgeous, but he'd better be in our room to help me get it on or I'm going in jeans. What are you wearing tonight?"

"Our wardrobe keeper made a new tunic and trousers for me." Jayr grimaced. "I wanted leathers, but he favors velvet."

"You're off duty, aren't you?" Alex asked. "Why don't you wear a dress?"

"Because I do not own any."

She made a *tsk*ing sound. "If you're going to have a woman's body, kiddo, you should clean out the closet and go shopping. Wearing women's clothes will make any changes that pop out less startling to guys around here. You might look into getting some bras, too."

"Bras."

Alex nodded. "They're the modern version of corsets. Just avoid the ones with underwires, that are made entirely of lace, or that are labeled 'push-up.' They're actually instruments of torture disguised as underwear."

Jayr dreaded the prospect—she had not coped with the restrictions of skirts and bodices since her human life—but added them to the cost of what she would gain. "Thank you, Doctor. I must go and dress my lord for the ball. I will see you tonight."

As Jayr left, she heard Alex mutter something that sounded like, "What, he can't even *dress* himself?"

"You've had time to conduct your meetings and turn them over in your head a thousand times," Byrne said as he handed Cyprien a glass of bloodwine and joined him by the fire. "Have you made your final selections?"

"I have." Michael cradled the glass in his long fingers. "You will not reconsider your decision?"

"Replaced or not, I am leaving," Byrne told him, "the first of the year."

The seigneur inclined his head. "I have finalized the candidate list to five names. I will choose among them after the joust."

"Who are they?"

"I did not expect you would care." Cyprien's mouth curled. "Adolfo, Daven, Halkirk, Locksley, and Nottingham."

Byrne couldn't imagine the cold Italian as master of the Realm. "Why would you think Nottingham a suitable candidate?"

"He interests me in the same way Lucan once did," Cyprien said. "One should make allies of those who would otherwise be enemies."

Byrne put a hand to his ear. "Is that Richard's voice I hear coming out of your lips?"

The seigneur's mouth hitched. "Tell me what you really think."

"You've an interesting quintuplet." Byrne sat forward as he began picking apart the list with relish. "Adolfo has little love for humans; he couldnae tolerate our tourist trade."

"He need not keep the Realm open to human visitors," Cyprien said.

"He had better play the stock market as Rob does, then,"

Byrne suggested, "as the profits from the tourist trade are what finance the *jardin*."

"Strike Adolfo. What about the others?"

"Daven is an incessant womanizer. He would turn the place into a brothel or end up losing his head to a Kyn he carelessly cuckolds." Byrne stretched his arms until the joints popped before settling back. "Halkirk seems a decent sort, but he cannae deny his *sygkenis* anything, and you know how expensive her tastes are. The two of them would empty my coffers in a fortnight."

"True," Cyprien said, "but they will not be your coffers after you go. Do not glower at me like that. I am of the same opinion. What do you think of this Nottingham? He may have offended Locksley, but he readily agreed to surrender his colors, and seems willing to adapt to our customs."

"He employs heathens, and his seneschal is a caltrop with a mouth, arms, and legs." Byrne brooded for a moment. "He seems cool and polished enough, but he is hiding something. I cannae say what or why, Michael, but I dinnae trust him."

"Very well." Cyprien folded his arms. "That leaves only your friend Locksley."

Friend? He hardly knew anymore. "Aye, Rob."

"His petition surprised me, but he expressed a wish to join his holdings with yours and make them a single suzerainty. I can see some advantage to that. He knows the Realm as well as you, and your men favor him, although something tells me that your friendship is strained." Glass snapped, and he looked down at the pieces of crystal in Byrne's hand. "The wine spilling down the front of your doublet, perhaps."

"You always had a gift for stating the obvious, lad." Byrne rose and discarded the shattered glass, pulling off his soaked tunic on his way to the corner basin, where he washed the sticky dregs of the wine from his skin. He retrieved fresh garments from his armoire and began dressing as he tried to think of how to word his opinion. "I cannae deny that Rob is the best candidate any more than I can hide my discomfort with his bid."

Cyprien's brows rose. "What unsettles you about it?"

"I told him the day after I spoke with you. I dinnae know why; maybe I craved him to say my decision was wise." Byrne loosened the laces at the front of his shirt. "That he instead leaped at the chance to rule the Realm himself troubled me. Made me wonder if he ever was my friend."

"*Did* you make the right choice?" Cyprien asked.

"For the good of the men and the Realm, aye, I did." Byrne threaded his belt through his scabbard and buckled it over his hips. "You must choose as you will, Michael. My opinion matters not. Whoever replaces me will be your man, not mine."

A quick knock sounded at the chamber door before it opened and Jayr entered.

"Good evening, seigneur." She bowed to him. "Your lady would appreciate your presence in your chambers. She asked me to say that she needs your assistance with the hooks on her ball gown."

"She has not yet discarded it for faded denims and a Disney T-shirt? Incredible. Byrne, I will see you at the reception. My thanks, Jayr." Cyprien smiled at her and left.

Jayr glanced at the wine-soaked tunic on the floor before turning to him. "I see you are already dressed." She sounded slightly disappointed. "All is well, my lord?"

Byrne nodded and ran a hand through his thick hair. She had washed it for him last night, but he had neglected to brush it out. "Will you do something with this owl's nest, lass?" He picked up a stool and brought it over to the old mirror. His image scowled at him. "I should shave my head. I vow my hair grew another foot last night."

"It always grows thus during the waning moon." Jayr retrieved a comb, brush, and shears, and took a position behind his stool. "It is too beautiful to shave off, my lord. You would break the heart of every woman in the Realm."

"Our family priest disliked women, and made the first Bible story I memorized that of Samson and Delilah. I promised myself that I wouldnae cut my hair lest I lose my strength. I was so adamant that my mother took to trimming it while I slept." He stared at the reflection of his broad, tattooed face. "I dinnae know what you see, Jayr. No one could call me a beauty."

"No, for you are too fierce and manly," Jayr said as she draped a hand towel over his wide shoulders. "That is why God gifted you with this glorious mane."

Byrne sat still as she combed out the tangles that a restless sleep had tied in his hair. She then plied the shears, cautiously snipping away to restore his hair to its former length. She stepped back to view the cut and then brushed the trimmings from his shoulders before taking up the comb and the small ties she used to secure the ends of his braids.

Jayr remained silent, but Byrne could almost feel her pleasure as she wove his braids. She took prodigious interest and time in grooming him, a rather feminine penchant for a seneschal, but he enjoyed the attention and always sat in front of the glass so that he could watch her work. Had she not cut her hair so close to the scalp, he would have done the same for her.

She had not always worn her hair shorn short, Byrne remembered. The day she had saved him, her hair had twined around him as soft and binding as snares of midnight silk. His memories of that encounter were blurred, but he had the distinct impression that he had played with her hair. . . .

"My lord?" Her gaze met his in the mirror. "Are you not pleased with the braiding?"

"No, 'tis cleverly done." He had never cared what she did, only that she did it. "Come around me, here." He guided her in front of him.

Jayr mistook his intent and knelt down. "Do you wish me to change your boots, my lord?"

"No." He worked his fingers through her short, dark locks, lifting them away from her head, searching for the memory of what he had done with it all those centuries before. It seemed shorter now than it had earlier in the day. "Why do you cut your hair so?"

"I do not . . . I mean, I have always kept it so."

"No, when you came to me you had hair down to your hips." As he sifted the dark strands through his fingertips they shimmered with tangerine light. "The first part of you that touched me was your hair, wasn't it? I mistook it for satin ribbons from your gown."

"I owned nothing made of satin, I assure you." Jayr's face lowered, hiding her expression. "The nuns intended to shear me and make me take my vows. My vanity gave me another reason to run away."

"I cannae criticize them, for they drove you to save me." Byrne slid his hand over the back of her neck to feel the fine, tiny hairs that grew there. "It still feels like satin, only a fringe instead of a ribbon." He tilted her chin up. "What happened to this defiant vanity, then?"

"It became besotted with another head of hair. One far more beautiful than its own." Her hand lifted and adjusted one of the narrow braids near his temple. "You look magnificent, my lord."

"Your hands work magic." Byrne smiled and bent to breathe in her scent. When she stiffened and tried to stand, he put his hands on her shoulders. "Let your hair grow long again, Jayr, and I will braid it for you."

Confusion chased the dismay in her eyes. "My lord, I cannot."

"Why?" He cupped her cheek with his hand. "Do you still fear your vanity?"

"The inconvenience. It would get in my way." Her throat moved as she swallowed. "I should go and change now if we are not to be late." She slipped out from under his hands and stood. "I will return shortly."

Byrne watched her flee from him, and almost gave chase. He didn't understand this new, primal hunger he felt, or why it clawed ferociously at his insides, but he wanted to run her down and drag her back to his chamber. He would bar the door, bind her wrists, whatever it took to keep her with him. Then . . . then . . . he would give her what she denied herself and him.

What saved him from abandoning himself to the madness and the pleasures it promised was how much it resembled his affliction. Who was to say it was any different?

"I am a thinking man," he bit out, almost doubling over as he fought for control. "Not . . . a raging . . . beast."

Her scent followed him as he escaped his chamber.

Jayr bolted the door and leaned back against it, her heart leaping beneath her breast. Her face burned hot and cold; invisible sand filled her mouth. Her chest wanted to collapse in on itself.

"Nothing is amiss," she said, unaware that she was speaking out loud as she pushed herself away from the door and went to retrieve her outfit for the ball. "It is the injection. The doctor said it might make me feel such things."

Only not so soon, or so she had assumed.

Jayr tore out of her damp tunic and trousers and went to her basin, filling it with warm water and sluicing off the sweat and the smell of heather from her skin. The water felt acutely wet and slick against her flesh; the towel she dried herself with created an almost pleasant abrasion. Between her legs a sluggish, glowing warmth intensified, but when she pressed the washcloth against it, an unseen lance of emptiness impaled her from her crotch to her throat.

Go back to him, the void whispered, snaking back and forth inside her. *Let him put his hands on you. His mouth. His tongue.*

"Sweet Christ." She nearly jumped out of her skin and flung the cloth away. "What has she done to me?"

Jayr yanked on the new garments, ignoring the sensual way the velvet slid over her limbs and taking pains to avoid touching the place between her legs. As soon as the ball was over she would see Alexandra Keller and have her stop the treatment. The formula given to Jema Shaw would serve as a counteragent.

It had to. She could not be like this. Not around him.

By the time Jayr felt composed enough to return to Byrne's chamber, the sensations had for the most part subsided. She would be herself again, and he would be none the wiser. She felt the ache in her chest return when she saw his door left open and his rooms empty. From the scent of heather still lingering on the air, she knew he had left only a few minutes ago.

She had disgusted him. That was why he had not waited for her return.

A hand fell on her shoulder. "You look like a sprite of autumn."

Jayr spun around, her hand on her rondele, to stare into the astonished amethyst eyes of Robin of Locksley. "My lord."

"Jayr." His gaze fell to her hand. "Should I rethink my compliment?"

"Yes. No. I thank you." She jerked her hand from the hilt of her blade. "I beg your pardon, but you startled me." She looked down both sides of the hall, but didn't see her master. "Will you accompany me to the ball?"

"It would be my honor." Locksley took her arm and linked it with his. "I know you will not dance, so I am depending on you to applaud my efforts with the ladies."

"My clapping shall be the loudest." A trace of bergamot cleared her head. "Have you seen my lord?"

"I have not." He peered down at her. "Is this paint I see on your face?"

"No."

"You are terribly flushed." He pressed the back of his hand against her cheek and pulled it away to rest his palm against her brow. "God's bones, girl, you're burning hot." He checked her other cheek and the side of her throat. "What has done this to you? Are you ill?"

What would he believe? "Feeding," she blurted. "It always makes me grow very warm. It will soon subside."

"Chilled blood cannot warm you like this," he said, looking suspicious, "and there are no humans here to heat your veins."

"I went to town earlier," she lied. "I tire of bagged blood sometimes. Who do you favor to win at the ranges this season?"

Locksley seemed satisfied with her excuse, and began talking about the strengths and weaknesses of the different archers in the competition. Jayr listened and made the appropriate comments along the way, but found that most of her brain was preoccupied with tracking her master's scent. The closer they drew to the ball the more it thinned, until it seemed to vanish completely.

At the same time, the strangeness that had racked her also disappeared, leaving her as calm and collected as ever.

Before they entered the hall, Jayr saw Will Scarlet waiting, and drew her arm from Locksley's. "This is where we must part ways, my lord. Expect to hear my applause above that of your many admirers." She bowed and went through the doors before he could respond.

"Jayr." Harlech came to her side. "You are later than I expected. Have you seen Viviana?"

"Not yet." She scanned the crowd, looking for Byrne, and taking a sharp breath as the bizarre, heated ache returned and simmered just under her skin. "Where is our lord?"

"I had thought he would be with you. Excuse me; I must find my wife." Harlech turned and hurried after one of Viviana's maids.

Jayr wandered among the guests, nodding to those who greeted her but feeling too distracted to converse. Suzerain von Lichtenstein, a strapping Prussian in a red tunic embroidered with the figure of Aphrodite, asked her if she would deliver a note to the Lady Alexandra for him. Jayr accepted it, knowing the letter would contain a badly written poem, and that the suzerain would later call her and request she destroy it. They had played this game of unrequited courtly love and courier with other females many times over the years.

She found an empty table on the other side of the room and sat down to watch the dancers.

Dressed in their finest, the Kyn filled the large dance floor with the men in elegant black tie and the women in the Garden of Eden of gowns. The first of the dances had begun, with the lively music for it provided by an ensemble of Kyn musicians playing in the balcony above the floor.

Nowhere, however, could she see Byrne.

Chapter 13

Harlech had never hunted his own wife, but exasperation and her continued absence left him no alternative. He searched the ballroom until he picked up her scent and then followed its trail through the halls and into the guest wing. From there he used his talent for sound to search for her voice.

She did not often come here, but likely she had accompanied one of her friends to mend a torn hem or sleeve. Women always viewed such things as disasters during a dance.

The trail of her scent ended at the door of Nottingham's chambers, but even that did not alarm Harlech. The dark lord's manner and dress marked him as a fop; he must have drafted poor Vivi into refitting something of his. He lifted his hand to knock, then stopped as he heard the Italian's voice.

"It is not enough, Ana. I will have my due."

Ana? Harlech had never heard anyone call her by that name.

His wife replied in a voice so bitter and cold Harlech almost thought it was another woman speaking. "Who do you think I am here? The lady? I am but a seamstress. I have told you what I know. I have done what I can do. Release me."

Nottingham made a sound that might have been a laugh. "Your prison is of your own forging."

"As is yours. Forget him and this thing before you destroy yourself."

The despair in her voice made Harlech step back. He moved around the wall and into the alcove beneath a window where he could not be seen. Soon afterward Viviana came into the hall, her skirts flaring as she was caught from behind and spun. Nottingham laughed as Viviana struck at his chest with her small fist.

Harlech pulled the dagger from his belt and took a step out, intending to gut the Italian where he stood, only to freeze as Nottingham spoke.

"My blood runs through your veins, Ana. My mother may have been your mistress, but I created you as surely as God did Eve." He caught her fist before it connected with his face, and took her into his arms. The hot licorice smell of aniseed, dark and pervasive, spread throughout the hall. "You owe me your life."

"My debt to you was paid the night I helped you leave England, my lord. You have no claim on me."

"Do I not?" Nottingham touched her mouth with one gloved fingertip. "Have you forgotten all the nights we shared? How sweetly you gave yourself to me? How I made you scream with pleasure?"

"I was a maiden." She slapped him. "I will *never* forget how you used me."

"Not even for Harlech's sake?"

Viviana sagged, her breath catching on a sob. "Please, for the love of God, release me. I honor my husband. I am faithful to him. I love—"

Nottingham stopped her words with his mouth.

Harlech watched with a distant, icy wonder as his wife withstood the kiss, and then slid her hands around the Italian's waist.

"You see, Ana," Nottingham whispered as he kissed a path down the side of her neck. "You do remember." He lifted his head and set her back at arm's length. "We will finish this later. Come to me when he sleeps."

Viviana wiped her mouth with the back of her hand. "If I come to you again, it will be when *you* sleep, and the next caress I give you will be with my blade."

Nottingham smiled. "I am all anticipation."

Harlech watched his wife stalk away, as did Nottingham. The only thing that kept him from stabbing the Italian in the back was the pain Harlech saw on his face when he turned back to walk into his rooms. Pain not unlike a man who had been thrown from his horse or kicked in the groin.

Harlech left the guest wing and returned to the ball. He said nothing to Viviana when she came to him, and accepted her excuse of being delayed by a guest in need of her services.

"All these last-minute alterations are a bother," Viviana said as he led her out onto the floor and took her into his arms. "I am sorry to make you wait, but Farlae has no patience for the fine work."

"I would forgive you anything," he told her, seeing her differently. How many times had she gone to Nottingham and done his bidding to protect him? "You are my wife."

"That I am." Her complacent smile faltered as she looked up into his eyes. "Harlech? What is the matter?"

"He will never leave you alone," he heard himself say. "You must know that."

She stumbled over her feet, but he lifted and turned her, smoothly covering the mistake.

"I beg your pardon." She tried to smile up at him. "Never worry about Farlae. I will tell him that Helvise can see to the guests."

"What of Nottingham?" he asked politely. "Will she go to him tonight in your place?"

She paled. "Harlech, what are you saying? Who has told you these lies?"

He spun her to the edge of the dance floor, where he kissed her brow and then looked into her fearful face. "I saw you tonight, outside his rooms, in his arms. I saw how he looked at you. You are in his heart."

"You are wrong." She shook her head. "He never loved me. He only took my life and made me Kyn."

That explained the hold Nottingham had over her. Viviana never spoke of her past, and Harlech had always assumed that, like so many Kyn females, the curse had been passed onto her from a member of her family who had served as a Templar.

Instead, Nottingham had forced immortal life upon her by draining the blood from her body and compelling her to drink his own. Changing humans to Darkyn in such fashion had been possible during the hundred years after the first Kyn had risen to walk the night. Kyn lords created entire households of warriors, servants, and leman to serve them for eternity. Then God had punished the *vrykolakas* for their arrogance by striking down any human who drank Kyn blood. Before the process of the change could even begin, they all died.

Few things were more durable than the bond between a Darkyn and a human he had turned. Then there was the possibility that a deeper bond had formed between Nottingham and Viviana: that of a lord and his *sygkenis*. It happened when the change created an emotional and physical dependence between the two. Often only death could sever the ties shared between a Kyn male and his life companion.

Either bond would still affect Viviana, but if she had once been Nottingham's *sygkenis*, and the Italian had somehow reawakened those feelings, she would be unable to deny him anything.

"Have you given yourself to him since he came here?" When she opened her mouth, he shook her once. "Tell me the truth."

"No." She swallowed and looked down at the floor. "Not yet."

"Then I cannot kill him." He dropped his arms. "Not yet."

"Harlech." Her hands seized his. "We will go away. Somewhere he cannot find us. We will go away and be happy together, as we have always been. Tonight." She gave him a brilliant smile and tugged at his hands. "Come; I will pack our things. We can be gone before the moon rises."

"This is my home. I am not leaving." He took his hands from hers. "You must decide between us now, Vivi. Stay with me, and I will protect you from him. But if you go to him tonight you need not bother returning to me."

She flinched. "You do not know what you ask."

"I ask that you choose to be my wife," he said gently. "Not his lover."

Tears streaked down her face as she gathered up her skirts and fled.

"I take back all the stuff I've said about the Kyn being dull," Alexandra said as Michael led her from the dance floor. The skirts of her ivory gown brushed against his trousers as she twisted, making them whirl. "You guys really know how to party."

"We should." He rested his hand against the small of her back. "We invented the party."

She laughed. "Is there anything the Darkyn *haven't* done?"

He gave the question serious thought. "Mastering the Macarena. It does not strike us as a particularly attractive dance." After nodding to Lord de Troyes, whose face fell as he saw that they weren't returning to the floor, he sat down with Alexandra at their table and asked, "Were you working in the infirmary all afternoon?"

"Only a couple of hours. I couldn't sleep." She picked up one of the place cards and used it to fan herself. "Jayr let me set up a minilab so I could update the database and take a peek at her blood."

Michael recalled how interested Alexandra had been in testing the seneschal's blood. "Have you come to any conclusions about her?"

"Working on it." She smothered a yawn. "Thanks for talking Byrne into giving me that sample. It'll help with identifying the shared pathogen factors in Jayr's blood."

He smiled. "Every female here delights in jewels and gowns and attention, and devote themselves to acquiring more. Yet all it takes to give you equal pleasure are vials and microscopes."

"Costs about the same." Alexandra glanced up as the musicians ended the set. "Is that Scarlet up there? What does he play?"

"Will favors the lute, and plays it very well, but I think he means to sing."

Locksley's seneschal stood at the balcony railing and propped his foot up, placing one hand against his chest. "When I see Kyn appear beside each other unarmed, exchanging the kiss of peace and being gentle with one another, I know no finer joy." He cast a jaundiced eye down on the crowd. "I also know that, like the chastity of a rich merchant's daughter, it cannot last."

Laughter swept around the room, and the dancers left the floor to refresh themselves and listen.

Scarlet nodded to the musicians, who began to play a soft, sweet tune to accompany his song.

"Bryd one brere, brid, brid one brere,
Kynd is come of love, love to crave
Blythful biryd, on me thu rewe
Or greyth, lef, greith thu me my grave.

Hic am so blithe, so bryhit, brid on brere,
Quan I se that hende in halle:
Yhe is whit of lime, loveli, trewe
Yhe is fayr and flur of alle.

Mikte ic hire at wille haven,
Stedefast of love, loveli, trewe,
Of mi sorwe yhe may me saven
Ioye and blisse were me newe."

Scarlet bowed to the applause, and then sang the song again in English.

"Bird on a briar, bird on a briar,
mankind is come of love, love thus craves.
Blissful bird, have pity on me,
Or dig, love, dig thou for me my grave."

From the garland around the railing, Scarlet plucked a flower and tossed it down to Alexandra, who caught it with a look of shocked pleasure.

"I am so blithe, so bright, bird on a briar,
When I see that handmaid in the hall:
She is white of limb, lovely, true,
She is fair and flower of all.

Might I her at my will have,
Steadfast of love, lovely, true,
From my sorrow she may me save
Joy and bliss would wear me new."

Scarlet bowed to Alexandra and Michael, then picked up a lute, strumming it before he joined the ensemble in playing a quick, lighthearted tune.

"That is a planxty," Michael told her. "They rarely have lyrics set to them, but were written by jongleurs for traveling minstrels, or to honor their patrons."

Alexandra twirled Scarlet's flower between her fingers. "I get the feeling you put him up to this."

She never accepted anything at face value, Michael thought, and then wondered why that bothered him so much. "That song was written and performed long before America was even discovered."

She reached over and hooked her hand around his neck. "Thank you," she said, and kissed him.

"Enough of that." Locksley stood over them, grinning. "When my seneschal stops playing the fool, will you dance with me, my lady?"

Alexandra glanced at Michael. "Am I allowed to, or are predance diplomatic talks required?"

Before he could answer, a squabble broke out between two Kyn women at the next table. Michael had seen them at various assemblies but didn't recall their names. A furious brunette in a red-and-blue gown hissed an old curse in Anglo-Saxon, reached over, and slapped a sneering blonde in a glittering black sheath. The blonde answered with a vile threat in archaic French. Jewel-encrusted copper daggers appeared and the Norman struck first, stabbing the brunette in the upper arm. The brunette snapped her wrist and slashed the blonde's right cheek. Alexandra saw the blood and started to rise, but sat down as the wounds healed over and the brunette hit the blonde again, this time in the nose with her fist. They lunged at each other and toppled to the floor.

Michael signaled two guards, who separated the writhing women and marched them out of the hall. Low laughter from the guests followed them.

Alexandra watched them go. "What was that all about?"

"A recent feud, I imagine," Michael said.

"Rather an old one," Robin corrected. "Lady Helvise, the brunette, is Saxon. Lady Desora, the blonde, is Norman."

Michael shook his head. "They should not have been seated together."

"Why not?" Alexandra asked.

"Normans are conceited and obsessed with courtly behavior," Robin said. "They believe in using utensils, napkins, and having their meals served in separate courses. Saxons are aggressive and boisterous. Their manner of dining is to get drunk, gather around a spit, and rip half-cooked chunks from whatever is roasting. Oftimes, after William the Bastard invaded England, it was a stray Norman. That is why one never sits a Saxon next to a Norman."

"I didn't think nationalities mattered to you guys," Alexandra said. "Who cares what you were during the Middle Ages?"

"Spoken like a true American," Robin said. "Every nationality, however, has their sins. The English are cold and indifferent, the Germans lewd and brutal, the Spaniards fickle and faithless, the Irish self-indulgent and superior."

"Really." Alexandra nodded toward Michael. "How about the French?"

"They're the worst." Robin leaned forward and lowered his voice to a whisper. "Arrogant, opinioned snobs, the lot of them."

She laughed. "That sounds about right. You ever go shopping with this guy when he's looking for a new suit?"

Robin nodded. "It did not take that long to fight the Hundred Years War."

"I am sitting right here," Michael said plainly. "I have not gone deaf."

As they laughed together, calls for another song were shouted from the floor to Will Scarlet. At the same time, Nottingham and his Saracens made their entrance.

Locksley stopped laughing, his face turning to stone.

Scarlet stood and this time brought his lute with him, strumming it as the other musicians and the guests fell silent. He saluted his master, who Michael saw was too busy staring at Nottingham and his entourage to notice. Will's voice softened with melancholy as he began to sing:

> *"The woodwele sings, and will not cease*
> *For song is vanity,*
> *but lo, I'll tell ye of the Hood*
> *and how he came to be.*
> *A poor but noble knight was Robin,*
> *the last of Sherwood's sons,*
> *his love was Maiden Marian*
> *an heiress raised by nuns*
> *Rob offered for her without guise*
> *but Marian was sold*
> *by her sire to the Prince of Lies*
> *for treachery and gold.*
> *The maiden fayre did fly to Robin*
> *afraid of her betrothed*
> *for Guy of Guisbourne wore his sin*
> *like other men their clothes."*

Michael heard a number of Kyn mutter under their breath and watched a few cross themselves. Too many had lost blood Kyn to Guisbourne's treachery, and even the mention of his name filled them with hatred.

"Excuse me, my lady," Locksley said, bowing to Alexandra before he walked away.

Michael watched Robin, but Nottingham seemed oblivious to Locksley. From where he sat with his men, the dark lord stared at the singing seneschal without blinking.

> *"Maid Marian entreated Rob*
> *to help her flee the louse,*
> *and take her to the house of God*
> *where she might take her vows.*
> *They donned the hood and rode away,*
> *the hero and his maid,*
> *but Guy did track them night and day*
> *and many traps he laid.*
> *When last the maiden safety found*
> *good Robin took his blade*
> *and went to fight on holy ground*
> *not knowing what he saved."*

Alexandra tugged at his sleeve, and he bent over to hear her whisper, "Is that true? Robin dumped Marian somewhere and left to go crusading?"

Michael felt a change in the air and frowned. "There is more to it than that, *chérie.*"

> *"The king gave Guy in lieu of bride*
> *the lands of Robin Hood*
> *but Guy was never satisfied*
> *and so brought down Sherwood.*
> *Robin fought the heathen*
> *and marked the sands in blood,*
> *came back to claim Maid Marian*
> *but she lay in her shroud."*

Michael saw Alexandra shiver, and something moved across the surface of the water in her goblet. He picked up the glass, which was colder than ice, and saw crystals forming around the sides.

The temperature of the room had not changed, but a quick glance told him the liquid in every cup was turning into solid ice.

He looked at Nottingham, who had stopped glaring at Scarlet and was now staring across the assembly. At the other end of his gaze was Locksley, standing now and leaning against a post, looking as if he might draw his sword and start across the room.

"Michael."

He looked down at his *sygkenis*, who had wrapped her arms around herself and was shivering violently. He was appalled to see that ice crystals had formed on her eyelashes.

"I can't," Alexandra said through chattering teeth, "feel my feet or my hands."

> *"An outlaw scorned by stupid men,*
> *the Hood became a brother,*
> *for love of Lady Marian,*
> *he never loved another.*
> *Take heed, my patient, kindly friends,*
> *walk not where Rob had gone.*

Love's lost path never ends,
and now my song is done."

Michael removed his jacket and wrapped it around her before striding over to Nottingham and his men. A thick sheet of
ice covered their table, and frost whitened the Saracens' blades.

"Lord Nottingham." Michael had to repeat his name twice
more before the Italian gave him his attention. "Your talent is
causing discomfort here. You should retire for the evening."

"Is this your idea of entertainment, seigneur?" Nottingham
inquired remotely. "Listening to common criminals sing lies to
glorify the craven acts of a thief and a murderer?"

"Do you wish to sing a different song?" Locksley said as he
came to stand beside Michael. "I would be glad to hear it."

Nottingham's Saracens rose as one to their feet, but the dark
lord lifted one white-gloved hand. At the same time his gaze
shifted to Jayr, who was striding toward them. His lips peeled
back from his *dents acérées* in a silent snarl.

Michael looked from the Italian to Jayr, who had come to a
stop several feet away and was staring back at Nottingham, her
face strained with distress and confusion.

"Another time, perhaps." Nottingham rose and bowed only
to Cyprien before retreating.

Jayr turned and strode away as quickly as she had come.

Michael glanced at Locksley. "Do you know him?"

"No. I have never before laid eyes on him, and I would tell
you if I had." The suzerain stared at the dark lord's back. "I can
tell you this." He turned to face him. "He stinks of Sherwood."

Hours passed unnoticed. Jayr watched the couples dancing
the branle, but heard the ensemble's music only as if she sat
somewhere far removed from the ball. The events of the
evening seemed to please the guests of the Realm, something
that should have gratified her. It was her duty to attend to them
and the thousand unseen details that ensured their pleasure. Yet
here she sat, doing nothing at all. This unwelcome awareness
had made her as useless as a moonstruck girl, caught between
the two cruelest of heart torments, doubt and hope.

It mattered not. Soon, Jayr knew, her wits would return and

drag her back to her senses. Soon she would shrug off this appalling paralysis and get on with seeing to her master's guests. Soon—

Byrne's hand came to rest on her shoulder, half on the velvet yoke of her tunic, half on the bare curve of her throat. He leaned over to murmur, "Rob fancies himself a danseur this night."

Locksley might have been performing a string of triple *tours en l'air* and Jayr would have missed them, so absorbed was she by the weight and feel of her master's touch. His soft breath set fire to her cheek; the warmth of his nearness reduced her to ashes. The world dwindled to nothing but Byrne. She felt the length of his arm pressing across her back, and could it be . . . yes, there, the absent stroke of his thumb against her neck. He was petting her.

An idle caress. It means nothing.

Jayr smelled tansy entwined with heather and swallowed against the ache at the back of her throat. Locksley. Byrne had said something about his dancing. "The suzerain has much skill on the floor."

"How can you tell?" He shifted his palm, causing his calluses to delicately chafe the edge of her collarbone. "Have you danced with him?"

"No, my lord. I have not had that privilege." Thank Christ, the ensemble had nearly finished the set. As the branle came to its elegant end, Jayr forced herself from her seat. "I should check on the bloodwine."

Byrne stood, catching her around the waist and turning her toward the politely applauding couples. She expected him to point out some flaw, some error to be corrected, but his hand urged her forward, through the spiral of tables and to the very edge of the dance floor.

Jayr heard muttered Arabic and low snickering, and felt Nottingham's Saracens staring at her. Ridicule's whip straightened her shoulders and kept panic at bay, even when her master drew her toward him. He stepped back, and then something happened that froze her in place again.

Aedan mac Byrne made a brief but perfect *révérence* to her. It had to be a mistake. The suzerain of the Realm never showed such regard to his seneschal, his third blade, the eyes at his back. Such a man made *révérence* only to his lady, whose silk and lace swathed her soft limbs, and whose long, perfumed curls framed her delicate features.

Jayr could not be seen as a lady. She was not even wearing a gown.

"My lord?" Perhaps he made a clever jest. A moment of mockery to amuse the assembly. That had to be it. No wonder the heathens were entertained.

A lord paramount never bowed to his lowly servant.

Byrne said nothing, only taking up her hands in his. He arranged her arms in counterpoint to his before nodding to the leader of the ensemble. They began to play one of Strauss's pieces, one Jayr should have been able to name, had her voice and her brains still functioned. Her master turned her again as he guided her out among the whirling couples and into what had long ago been a vigorous and rather silly provincial dance.

He was dancing with her—waltzing with her.

Jayr could not ask her master if he had gone mad. Moving her feet in the whirling patterns of the dance demanded much of her concentration, and the rest seemed fixed on the lacing at the neck of his shirt. She also suspected that if anyone might lose their wits on this night, it would be her.

"My lord," she finally forced out, "I am honored, but perhaps you could exchange me for a more appropriate partner. Lord de Troyes seems rather ill matched with his lady, and I would—"

"Jayr?" He spun her down the length of his arm and back to his body.

She braced herself against his chest to keep a respectful space between them. "My lord?"

Byrne seized one of her errant hands and worked his fingers through hers, locking them together. His arm pulled her in until their bodies brushed. "Shut up and dance with me."

"Yes, my lord."

Jayr found no comfort in silence or the waltz. She busied herself with counting steps and avoiding eyes. It seemed as if every lord and lady on the floor was gaping at them. And why should they not? The suzerain of the Realm held his seneschal in his arms. Among the Kyn, such a thing had never happened.

Jayr cursed herself for not listening to Alexandra and donning more feminine attire. She might have looked less the skinny boy in a gown, and the skirts would have enforced a respectable boundary between their bodies. As it was, his person met hers in the most unseemly places: the flat of her belly, the small of her back, the front of her thighs. Little wonder that the waltz had often been condemned in the past as insidious and improper. The intimacy of it, the constant press of his body to hers, quickly became unbearably erotic.

Behind the torture, a very small part of Jayr hoped that the waltz would never end.

As the music swelled to a giddy madness, Jayr glanced up to see her master's face darken, and followed his gaze. Alexandra, resplendent in an ivory lace gown, laughed as Cyprien lifted her off her feet and kissed her while they still twirled among the other couples.

What would it be like, Jayr thought, to have such love that you did not care who saw you express it? "The seigneur seems blessed in his choice of women," she said before she remembered that she was supposed to be holding her tongue.

Byrne changed direction, leading her through a tangle of couples and toward the shadowy end of the floor, far from the sharp ears of those watching from the tables. When a burst of laughter drew the attention of the assembly, Jayr found herself being marched from the floor and around the corner to the empty corridor that led outside to the gardens and herbarium.

"I thank you for the dance, my lord." Jayr stepped out of his hold and straightened her sleeves. "It was most pleasant."

Byrne's broad back blocked out the moonlight streaming through the long, narrow panes of pale blue glass. His scent changed, growing heated and dark. When he put his hand to her throat, Jayr flinched.

"Pleasant, you say?" he asked, his voice dangerously soft.

"I meant enjoyable," she quickly added, feeling his fingers tighten. "Quite enjoyable. You are most accomplished, my lord."

"Pleasant." He walked her backward. "Enjoyable."

She felt cold stone against her shoulders. "I regret that I am not more adept myself. I rarely dance." He had her pinned now, body to body. She averted her face. "My lord, I should return and see to your guests."

"And Rob?" Byrne thrust his hand into her hair, his fingers curling against her scalp. "You will see to him? You will dance with him?"

She glanced up, confused. "Of course. I am happy to see to Suzerain Locksley's desires."

"He makes you happy. Unlike me."

Byrne's scent had fogged her thoughts; surely she had not heard him correctly. "My lord, it is not for you to make me happy."

"Is it not?" He lifted her in the same way Cyprien had Alexandra, sliding her up the stone wall until their eyes were level. "Did I not make you, Jayr?" His gaze moved from her eyes to her mouth. "Did you not swear your oath to me? Do you not belong to me, body and blood?"

Jayr felt drunk on his scent and touch, so much that she lost the last shred of her composure and shuddered uncontrollably against him as she told him the truth: "I am yours, my lord. Do with me what you will."

Byrne bent his head to hers, his long garnet hair spilling against her cheek as his lips touched hers. The contact made her jerk with shock, but he held her in place, his mouth slanting over hers as he deepened the kiss with his teeth and tongue.

Jayr had dreamed of this moment and what she might feel, but those paltry fantasies had not prepared her for how Byrne would take her mouth. He took and bit and thrust, reveling in the claiming, allowing her no retreat. The heat and scent of his passion smashed over her, reducing her to a clinging, moaning wreck writhing between his arms. In desperation she seized his shoulders, clutching at them as she fought her body's shameful response. His body became an oak, still and unmovable, to which she had been chained. And there, pressing hard between her thighs—thrusting against her crotch—the heavy, stunning weight of his erection.

The ferocious hunger of his mouth eased away. "Mother of God." Byrne sounded as astonished as she felt. "What am I doing to you?" He carefully lowered her until she stood on her own again.

"You kissed me." She saw the pain and regret in his eyes, and cold, clammy horror crawled along her spine. She made her bruised mouth form a smile. "Needs are like cherished guests, my lord. At times they may be inconvenient, but one should never allow them to go unattended for too long."

"You are right." He looked disgusted now. "Jayr—"

"Your guests are waiting. Excuse me, my lord." She made her bow and ran.

Chapter 14

Rainer saw Viviana slip out of the keep, and followed her, as he had been ordered to. She wandered aimlessly, now and then pressing a handkerchief to her eyes, until she stood at the edge of the lake and stared across it.

He thought he might leave her there, until he saw the dark gleam of a copper dagger in her hand. She rolled the hilt between her fingers in a compulsive manner, as if steeling herself to grip it and put it to use.

The sight of the seamstress choosing death over dishonor destroyed something in him and made something else grow in its place.

"It is a beautiful night," he said from behind her. She didn't move, although her hand tightened on the blade. "The moon smiles down like that smug cat from the child's story."

Viviana sounded calm when she replied, "So it does. Would you excuse me, Rain? I should like some privacy."

"One often does when one is contemplating one's mortality." He came to stand beside her. "Do you mean to pierce your heart, or cut through the cord at the back of your neck?"

"I don't know what you mean."

Oh, how cool she was. "When I leave. When you kill yourself with that dagger." He cradled his throbbing arm, which Nottingham had broken again during his latest interrogation. "I am only curious, as I am pondering how I will go about it. Surely I will bungle it unless I have some example to follow." He glanced sideways at her. "You will permit me to stay and watch, won't you?"

"You don't know what you are saying." Viviana's wet eyes closed. "Go back to the keep."

"He ordered me to shadow you," Rain said conversationally. "I am supposed to prevent you from harming yourself."

"He knows me well." She shuddered.

"As he does all of his victims," Rain agreed. "How did you come to be under his power?"

"Famine ravaged my village when I was sixteen," she said softly. "There was no work, and when the crops failed, the youngest and the oldest began dying. Then the Lady of Sherwood sent her men to collect the youngest and prettiest girls and bring them to the castle. When she chose me to serve as her maid, I thought I had saved my family. I did not know what she was, or what she meant to do with me."

"I remember you." He smiled when she stared at him. "I served the lady as her fool."

"That was you?" She took a step back and looked all over him. "Oh, my God. It was."

"The last time I saw you in your human life was the morning you were taken down into the dungeons. Like the other girls, you never came back." He hung his head. "When my turn came, do you know I fought him? Valiantly, I might add. Three days later I dug myself out of the ground. I went at once to the lady, to warn her that she had imprisoned a monster in her dungeons. I was a consummate fool, you see."

Her face turned wooden. "How did you escape Sherwood?"

"Farlae," Rainer said. "He came to make a gown for the lady, and he took a fancy to me. She agreed to let him have me in exchange for a new wardrobe. The bitch traded me for a handful of gowns and petticoats. How did you attain your freedom?"

"I helped him escape her." Viviana raised the dagger, and then offered it to him. Her hand shook so much it appeared as if she were waving it at him. "Will you do it?"

He looked down at her steadily. "Let me fetch another one, and we can kill each other." He lowered his voice to a whisper. "Imagine the fun. Harlech and Farlae will go mad, thinking that we were secret lovers who chose death over them. They would never recover from it."

The dagger slipped from Viviana's hand, and she fell against him, sobbing. He held her with his one good arm, and let his own tears run from his cheeks to her hair.

The sound of wings drew his gaze upward, and he watched a flock of birds flying across the lake as they made their way south. There, he knew, they would stay until the ice and snow in the northern country melted and it was safe for them to return.

"Viviana." He drew back and took her hand in his. "I think I know another way."

Alex's chills subsided as soon Michael made Nottingham leave the ball, although it took a few minutes for the numbness to recede from her hands and feet.

"That feels better," she told him as he chafed her hands between his. "Nothing quite like vampire-induced hypothermia." She smiled up at Phillipe, who offered her a mug of steaming mulled bloodwine. "This won't make me puke, I hope. I'm wearing white. You'll never get the stains out."

"Try a sip first," he suggested.

Alex did, and the hot, spiced wine covered the taste of the blood that had been mixed in with it. When her stomach didn't reject it, she sighed. "Better. Thanks, Phil."

"I looked for an electric blanket," the seneschal told her, "but all I could borrow was this." He held up a small heating pad covered with short, tawny hairs. "Lady Harris brought her favorite terrier with her, and it seems that Sookie dislikes sleeping on stone floors."

Alex almost choked. "Sookie? Who names something they like *Sookie*? Isn't that the word you use to call pigs?"

Michael leaned close. "Would you like to know what Lady Harris calls Lord Harris in private?"

"How would you know that?" When he only gave her an enigmatic smirk, she shook her head. "Never mind. So what turned on Nottingham's ice machine? Robin breathe on him?"

"I gather he did not care for Scarlet's ballad," Michael guessed. "No doubt he has listened to gossip and discovered that Locksley was once an outlaw. Robin has had a difficult time gaining acceptance among the European Kyn."

"Ex-cons are hard to trust," Alex said, nodding. "Was the song true? Did Rob break up his girlfriend's marriage?"

"Some say Marian did come to Robin to beg him help her flee before she was made to marry Guisbourne," Michael said. "Others claim that he kidnapped her."

"The king wasn't too thrilled about all this, I take it."

"Marian's father paid the king a handsome amount of gold to approve the match," Michael said. "Robin had titles and land, but no money. There was no contest."

"So you had lobbyists screwing up your government, too. Interesting." Alex finished the mulled wine and set the mug on the table. "Robin got Marian to the convent, right? How did she die?"

"Guisbourne killed her."

Alex looked over her shoulder at Scarlet. "Well, that wasn't in the song."

"He didn't run her through with his sword, my lady. He used other, more brutal means to end her life." Scarlet knelt down beside her. "Guisbourne forced himself on her. He wished to disgrace her and shame her into marrying him."

"It was common practice in our time, I fear," Michael said. "Marriages that had not been consummated were easier to prevent or annul. Few women went to the altar virgins."

"Possession being nine-tenths of the law, I suppose." Alex glanced at Scarlet. "It gets worse, right?"

"When Lord Robin delivered Lady Marian to the convent, she was with child." Scarlet ducked his head. "She never told him or anyone; perhaps she had hoped to conceal it. As soon as my lord returned from the Holy Land, he went to the convent to retrieve her. The nuns could offer him only dreadful news: Both Lady Marian and her baby died during the birthing."

"Poor girl." Alex recalled all the happy endings she had seen for different movies about the star-crossed lovers. "Robin must have felt like everything he'd done was for nothing."

"He gave her freedom from Guisbourne, who would have made her life a living hell," Scarlet said softly. "It did not matter what it cost him. My master would have moved heaven and earth for Lady Marian." He rose, bowed, and retreated.

"I hate unrequited love stories. They always sound like something Nicholas Sparks would write." Alex got up and sat on Michael's lap. "How about you cheer me up?"

Amber sparkled around the edges of Michael's turquoise eyes. "Is that a personal proposition, my lady?"

"I could do a little lap dance for you," she mused, "but Mom told me that kind of thing was unladylike."

"You have often said that you are not a lady." Michael kissed her temple. "So you have not grown weary of my attentions?"

She knew what he wasn't saying. Since they'd come to the Realm they hadn't had sex. It wasn't exactly unusual for them—being seigneur often kept Michael too busy to have time for fun—but after the almost continuous sex they'd been having since she'd gotten back from Ireland, it seemed off.

No, Alex thought. *I haven't had sex with him since the dreams started.* In fact, she had gone out of her way once or twice to *avoid* having sex with Michael.

Avoiding having sex with the best lover she had ever known. She was losing her mind.

"Alex?" He turned her face toward him. "You do look tired. Shall we go?"

"Yeah." She looked over his shoulder and saw Jayr practically running across the room. The seneschal's face looked hot, and her sleeve had been ripped at the shoulder. "Ah, no. I'll be right back." She stood and went to intercept Jayr.

Nottingham's seneschal stepped into her path. "My lady, may I have the pleasure?" He held out his hand and gave her a modest smile. "I should warn you that I am the finest dancer in all of Florence."

"Maybe another time." Alex went around him and ran.

As soon as the seneschal saw Alex coming after her, she turned around and went to her. "Doctor, something is wrong." She grabbed Alex's arm and pulled her to a secluded corner. "This potion you put into my veins . . . I fear it is poisoning me. Or perhaps driving me mad. I must have an antidote."

"There's a big difference between being poisoned and having a psychotic break," Alex said, feeling a small, ugly stab of pain behind her eyes. "Calm down and tell me what happened."

"I do not know." She propped her hands against the walls. "I am hot, and then I am cold. My skin wants to peel itself from my body. I cannot even bathe without . . . I feel strange things."

"I did warn you that your feelings might change," Alex had to point out.

. . . burn . . .

"My *feelings?*" Jayr echoed incredulously. "My body has developed a mind of its own. I scarcely know what I will do from one moment to the next. I gave him leave to do anything to me. I kissed him, as if it were nothing. I cannot stop sweating. My hands tremble so that I cannot grasp a weapon. What has any of that to do with my feelings?"

. . . burn the . . .

"Back up." Alex took hold of her wrist, focusing on the girl instead of the pain hammering on the inside of her skull. "You kissed who as if it were nothing?"

"My lord Byrne." Jayr squeezed her eyes shut for a moment. "It was utterly humiliating."

. . . no, not here . . .

"I don't see why," Alex said, gasping a little as the pain switched off and the disjointed thoughts ended. "He's the one you're doing this for, isn't he?" She closed Jayr's open mouth with one finger to the chin. "You've been very cagey, kid, but yesterday was not my birthday."

"I am my lord's servant," Jayr said. "It is wrong of me to feel as I do. To act as I did."

"Oh, bullshit." Alex lowered her voice. "Honey, I'm sure it was no hardship for him to be kissed by you. All you have to do is see you two together. It's pretty obvious."

Fear joined the anger in her eyes. "You know nothing about me or him."

"So I know nothing." Alex had embraced denial often enough to give Jayr time to cling to hers. "Anything else you want to bitch about?"

"Only that I asked you to help me change my body," Jayr said through gritted teeth. "Not destroy my life."

"Let's see if I've got this straight," Alex said, ticking off what she said next on her fingers. "You're experiencing unreasonable irritability, body temperature fluctuations, impulsivity, and unusual sensory reactions, and all that is resulting in unfamiliar behavior. Plus you got to kiss your boss. That cover all the bases?"

"Yes," Jayr all but shouted. She pressed her hand to her

mouth, dropped it, and murmured, "You see? This drug is poison."

Alex shook her head. "No. The anger and confusion, the weird urges, the boss kissing, all classic signs of late-stage puberty. You're not dying, sweetheart, and you're not poisoned. You're becoming a teenager."

Jayr's fingers curled into fists. "I am seven hundred and ten years old, Doctor."

"Chronologically speaking, yes, you are. But physically?" She lifted her shoulders. "Your body has just found out that it's seventeen, and it's throwing a party."

Jayr looked at her boots. "What more will happen to me?"

"The physical changes are the next stage," she assured the seneschal. "Judging by how fast you're metabolizing and responding to the synthetic gonadotropin, it won't take long for the hormone fairy to drop the main shipment. Expect incoming breasts, hips, and curly hair growing in very inconvenient places."

"I meant my mind." Her eyes flashed up. "Will the drug affect my reasoning, my judgment? Would I wish to harm him? Would I try?"

"Jayr, oh, God, no. It isn't going to be like that." Alex tried to put an arm around her, but the seneschal backed away. "If anything you'll fuss more over him and want to be with him all the time. You'll be miserable when you're not, and you won't be able to stop thinking about him until you're together again. You'll dream about him and being with him." She saw Michael approaching, and reality dwindled for a moment as several things clicked into place. "The dreams will be really hot."

"That is all I can have," she heard Jayr say. "Dreams." The seneschal stalked off.

Michael took her hand in his when he reached her. "Why was Jayr shouting at you?"

"Because I deserved it." Alex reached up to give him a quick kiss. "Listen, handsome, I've got to head over to the infirmary and check something out. I'll meet you in the room later."

She hurried off before he could reply.

* * *

Byrne tracked Jayr as she made her way from the ball to her chambers, but kept enough distance between them so that she did not detect his presence. He would not frighten her again, but he would explain himself and make peace with her.

And he would, as soon as he worked out why he had kissed her.

Jayr's path ended at her rooms, and there Byrne hovered, unsure of what to do next. He knew he had shocked her by seizing her as if she were human and making free with her body. His apology had been as pathetic as taking advantage of her oath. No, he should go, forget what had happened and act as if it never had. As bruised as her dignity was, she would surely do the same. It could not happen again. He would keep his hands away from her. He would respect her value to him and his household. He would resist his desires.

He would not kick in her door and seize her so he could kiss her again.

Byrne listened for several minutes, but heard nothing from inside the room that indicated what Jayr was doing. She rarely took time for herself and never took her rest before attending to him. He tried the door and found that it was not latched, and opened it to a small gap to see inside.

Jayr stood in front of the rectangular looking glass on her wall, her back to him, her tunic gone. She turned slightly right, then left, tucking in her chin, studying her breasts.

Byrne's hand slipped from the latch as he looked at the reflection she made. Her breasts were not like most women's, as they had no weight or fullness to them, but they were no longer completely flat, as some assumed. Gentle swells, they rose slightly around her small, flat nipples. Her shirts and tunics completely covered them, and they were what made her seem fashioned like a man.

Above one nipple lay the blurred, raised birthmark he had once heard her call her heart scar. It was the color of blooming heather, the same color her eyes sometimes flashed. He sometimes caught tantalizing glimpses of it when her collar fell open.

He knew how Jayr despised how she was made, and wondered why he did not feel the same. During his human life he had always favored big, buxom women, mostly because they were built to take large, heavy men with relative ease. Thin, delicate women were more fragile, and the thought of accidentally hurting them unmanned him. Becoming Kyn made it only more necessary to avoid them.

Then, too, they reminded him too much of Jayr.

Byrne realized that he didn't care that Jayr's hips didn't flare out or that her breasts were barely noticeable. Compared to the other women he had known, Jayr seemed almost exotic, like a gazelle among bovines. His hands still itched to caress the long lines of her pale neck and back. Among other things.

Byrne's gaze followed the long, gentle curve of her spine down to her bottom. The new trousers she wore were not as loose as most she owned, and lovingly hugged the slim curves of her hips.

The imprint of the velvet whispered its memory against his palms. He had put his hands on her buttocks at some point during the kiss. He was almost sure he had squeezed them.

Her skin was very soft there, he knew from the only other time he had held her so. That day she had worn a full skirt, and he had reached under it to discover only a thin pair of drawers between him and her flesh. He had used the split in the crotch to tear them away from her.

Before he had lifted her up.

Before he had brought her sex to his mouth.

Before he had kissed her there.

A low, wounded sound dragged his attention back to Jayr. Both of her hands pressed over her chest, covering it now, and she was staring higher, at the reflection of the door.

She could see him watching her.

Byrne closed the door soundlessly and slumped back against the wall beside it, breathing in deeply to clear his head. He had taken her once, and had sworn never to force himself on her again. She trusted him to keep his word to her.

But nothing could drive him away from her chamber, not even the shame of knowing he would give up his last coin to go inside and lie with her again.

Byrne slid down, sitting at her threshold as she so often had his, feeling the chains of time tightening around him. If he could not tear himself away from her now, how was he to leave her behind?

He could take her with him, he reasoned. She was sworn to him, not the Realm. She would stay with him and keep him from dying of loneliness. If he was patient—if he took time to court her, prepare her—they could be more than master and seneschal. She had told him that she was his to do with as he willed. He had only to make her want such a thing.

And the day would come when something went wrong, when some impossible turn of luck smashed through the fortress of his control, and Jayr would be the only living thing near him. The only life upon which his affliction could feed.

Byrne closed his eyes. That was how he would let her go. By knowing what he would do to her if he did not.

Chapter 15

Veils of purple and white silk danced around Byrne, drawing him into the palace. From the mosaics and the archways he could see he had returned to the ancient lands, where dark men fought with enormous curved blades and kept their women locked up in seraglios.

Patchouli-scented smoke drifted around him as the intricately knotted carpet beneath his feet lifted him into the air. It flew him through corridors of golden stone and blackened woods until it gently landed in front of an arch in the shape of a woman's form.

Byrne stepped off the carpet and passed through the arch. Inside he saw a room of braziers and pillows, incense and fountains. Stately palms grew from enormous earthen pots to spread their arching green fronds against the sun, for there was no ceiling. He thought the room empty until he saw her in one corner, almost hidden by stacks of pearl-covered books.

Jayr?

She occupied a plain narrow bed, her long legs bare, only a soft old leine covering her body. The material was so thin he could see the dark circles of her nipples beneath it. Pearls glinted from the gores in her sleeves as she turned a page in one of the priceless books. Her hair, shadows spun with moonlight, spilled over her shoulders and trailed down to her hips.

If nothing else, the hair told Byrne he was in a dream. He moved forward until he stood beside the bed. "What are you reading?"

His seneschal spared him a glance. "Love poems." She drew her finger down the page, lingered on a line, and then closed the book and her eyes. "They speak the language I cannot."

Byrne bent and picked up one of the books, but the pages in it were blank, gold leaf polished to a mirror finish. "Is that all you do here? Read poetry books with no words in them?"

"I write the words with my eyes." She turned over on her stomach and rested her cheek against her pillow. "I read them with my heart." She smiled up at him. "You are not really here, either."

"I am not?" Byrne sat down beside her.

She turned onto her side, and the leine slipped down, exposing her breasts. "I am wishing you here." She looked down and grimaced, tugging the nightdress up to cover herself.

The front of her leine had also ridden up, revealing her bare legs. Byrne caressed the long line of her thigh, feeling the muscles tighten against his palm. "What am I to do in your dream?"

She shook her head. "You are the master here. You must tell me what I am to do."

That was a temptation he could not refuse.

"You told me that you pleasure yourself, lass." Byrne's gaze drifted down the length of her body. "Show me how you bring yourself."

Her eyes went wide. "I cannot do that."

"Since you told me, I've imagined it a hundred times. A thousand." He stretched out beside her. "I would like to see it this once."

Jayr's eyes closed. "It is shameful."

"Is it now." He chuckled. "All the times I have done it, I never thought so."

She sat up, going still when she saw him unfastening the front of his trousers. "What are you doing?"

"Showing you first. You see how hard you have made me?" He tugged the curving, erect organ out and fisted it. "It took but a glimpse of your pretty tits."

"I did that?" She swallowed and stared at the reddened, swollen head of his penis. "I should send for some women."

"I don't want them. I want to see you. You will lie back and show me what you do when you pleasure yourself," he said. When she didn't move, he added, "You are sworn to obey me, Jayr."

Her expression turned anguished. "Even in my dreams?"

"Especially in your dreams. Dinnae be afraid, lass. No one will ever know what we do here." He stroked his hand up and down. "You wouldnae leave me to do this alone, would you?"

Awkward now, she reclined and stared up at the erotic tapestry over their heads. "I have never been watched."

"One night, while you are sleeping, your lover will slip into your room. He will hide himself in the shadows when you wake with his name on your lips." He ducked his head so he could whisper the rest against her ear. "He will watch as you push away the blankets and caress yourself with your hands. Show me what he will see."

Her gaze locked with his. "You will laugh at me."

"No, lass," he said, his voice going deep. "Never will I do that to you."

She took a deep breath, as if to brace herself, and then clasped her hands on either side of her neck.

"Tell me what you are thinking," he urged.

"I think of you," she whispered, stroking her thumbs across the narrow bridge of her collarbones. Slowly she brought her fingers down, raking her nails over her skin. "I pretend my hands are yours, and that you are touching me so. I feel your teeth piercing me, your tongue licking me."

Byrne's cock twitched as he watched her gently cup her breasts. "My bite arouses you."

"As much as a kiss," she murmured, spreading her fingers over the small mounds and palming her nipples. "More so when I touch myself here. I think of your mouth on my breasts." She pinched her puckered nipples. "Suckling on me, taking my blood and soothing the aching and longing. You make them twine inside me."

Heat surged through him. Her hands moved like shivering flowers. "Go on, lass."

She seemed mesmerized by the motion of his hand as he worked it up and down, her own hand unconsciously echoing his rhythm as she cupped and massaged her breast. Her left hand moved away from the ruddy peak it was tugging to inch down her side, until it lay just above the soft, bare petals of her mound.

"Sometimes I think of that day when you were under me,

holding my hips and bringing me to your mouth," she said, her voice uneven. "When I do, I throb as if it were happening again. As if you were kissing me in truth." She parted her thighs and covered herself with her hand. "Here."

"Wider," he said, his voice growing hoarse. "Bend your knees. Let me see again where I kissed you."

Her breasts rose and fell on ragged breaths as her legs shifted. Her heels indented the sheets beneath her as she drew her feet up and separated her legs, so slowly Byrne thought he might go over just watching her long, tight muscles quiver. Then she pulled her hand back, tracing over the plump, slick gateway to her cunt. It had flowered open, displaying her treasures, the sheen of her need, the tip of her jewel of pleasure at the top of her sex. It swelled with tiny pulses, with her heartbeat, a sight so erotic his mouth went dry.

"I kissed you," he said, bending forward until his breath touched the soft flesh framing the jewel. "How? Where?"

"Your lips moved across me." She touched her folds, rubbing them with a gliding touch. "You pressed your tongue against me. Inside me."

He remembered, dimly, her struggles in the pit. "Did you like how it felt?"

"It frightened me. I have never felt such a thing. Then it took me over and possessed me." Her fingertips grazed the narrow slit, making it open for an instant. "You rubbed your tongue here, against this." She edged her thumb closer to the pearl protruding from her folds. "It felt like satin brocade."

Byrne wanted nothing more than to put his mouth to her again, to fuck her with his tongue until she screamed with pleasure. "Show me how it was. Play with it for me."

Her fingers moved, faltered. "I cannot do any more. It is too—"

"You can for me." He jerked his fist, feeling his balls drawing up tight between his own legs. "Show me."

Her eyelids fell, but only for a moment. As soon as her fingertips stroked over her jewel, a moan escaped her lips, and the muscles of her legs turned to cords. She touched herself lightly, with a circling, pressing motion that became shorter and more urgent with every passing moment. Her sex went from damp to wet, reddening and puffing as she tormented herself.

Something like a spring coiled in Byrne's groin. He straightened, using the longest, hardest strokes he could on the straining length of his cock.

"I am going to spill myself on your pretty tits," he told her, the words bursting from him. "Now you bring yourself for me. *Now.*"

Jayr's back arched as she pressed the heel of her hand against her slit, her long body shaking with the force of coming, her hands falling limp and motionless to her sides. Byrne uttered a deep groan as his cock jerked, almost recoiling with the force of the stream jetting from it. His ejaculate painted her breasts with long, thick ribbons of cream that seemed as if they would never end, until he felt the last surge coming through him.

"So warm." Jayr's hand stroked across her breasts, rubbing his semen into her skin.

He changed the angle of his penis, spilling himself onto her cunt. As the last of his seed jetted against her jewel, her hips jerked and she cried out, shaking as he brought her again.

Byrne flung his head back, his skull slamming into cold stone. Black velvet enfolded Jayr and the seraglio, pushing him back, past the archway and the white and purple veils into the silence of the hall and the place where he sat outside Jayr's rooms.

Byrne saw the wetness spread over the front of his trousers. The dream had made him spill himself in his smalls like a boy. He pushed himself to his feet. One of his hands reached for the door latch; the other became a fist. It had been his dream, not hers. Even if she had somehow shared it with him, he had no right to trespass on her rest. Not in this state.

He would wait until she awoke, and then it would be his turn. He would show her. He would show her everything.

After waking from a long and terribly erotic dream, Jayr found that rest eluded her. She gave up chasing it shortly after noon and rose to bathe, then sat and sifted restlessly through her poetry diary. One long and solemn verse she had thought nearly perfect now seemed contrived and hollow. After several attempts to inject life into the lines, she ripped out the pages, crumpled them, and threw them at the fireplace.

The paper ball bounced off the hearthstones and rolled out of sight.

Irritated with herself, Jayr went to retrieve it when her mobile rang. It was Harlech, sounding cool and distant as he related a problem with the supplier in town.

Jayr couldn't leave the Realm during a tournament, and she wouldn't trust herself until Alexandra Keller reversed the effects of the treatment. God only knew if it had been responsible for making her dream like a wanton. "Send Rain to deal with it."

"Rain is gone," her second told her. "So is Viviana."

"What?"

"From the looks of things they ran off together last night," Harlech said flatly.

"Damn." She pressed her fingers against her eyelids. "Harlech, Rain would not do this. He is devoted to . . . another. Viviana loves you. There has to be an explanation."

"Farlae has gone to track them." Harlech sounded as if he didn't care if they were found. "These matters in town must be attended to, Jayr."

"Send someone else. Anyone."

"I fear I am needed at the stables. Which reminds me—the stable master says the rye and oats that were delivered are inferior. The feed order for next month will have to be adjusted and the delivery moved up two weeks."

Something Jayr would have to do in person, as she had opened the account. She would have to go or they would run out of grain for the horses. She could also check to see if Rain and Viviana had been seen by any of their human friends. "What else do we need from town?"

Harlech gave her a list of errands that would keep her out for hours.

"Have the truck brought out to the front drive," she told him. "Someone will have to attend to our lord while I am in the city. Is Dr. Keller in the infirmary now?"

Harlech confirmed that she was, so Jayr went to see her

before leaving for the city. She found Alexandra sitting and peering into a microscope.

"Doctor."

Alexandra lifted a finger without raising her head from the scope. "Give me a sec."

The time drew out to several minutes before it became apparent to Jayr that she was being ignored. "I will return another time."

"Hold your palfreys, kid; I'm almost finished." She groped for a pencil and began jotting down figures on a pad filled with them. "Forty-two, twenty-three, and eighty-seven, and I'm done." She straightened and smiled at Jayr. "I didn't want to count them all over again because I'm lazy. Ready for the next injection?"

Jayr's eyes widened. "After what happened to me last night? You must be jesting."

"What happened?"

"My lord and I . . . and then I dreamed—" She stopped. She couldn't tell Alexandra these things; they were too private. "It matters not. I have to go into the city. I need you to reverse the treatment. Will you do it now?"

"Sure, not a problem. I whipped up a batch of Jema Shaw special last night." She switched off the microscope's light and went to retrieve a syringe.

Jay felt taken aback by her reaction to her demand. "You do not object?"

"You want to play Peter Pan forever, that's your business." She plunged the needle into a vial of liquid. "No skin off my nose."

"I cannot serve my lord in this state," Jayr told her. "I do not even trust myself to be among humans." *Or go to sleep, for that matter.*

"Hey, I understand. Things like tits and a sex life and being a normal woman aren't as important as looking like a guy and waiting hand and foot on Byrne." She patted the exam table. "Come on. I don't have all day. Night. Whatever."

Suspicion made her eyes narrow. "You are trying to shame me."

"You think?" Alexandra set down the needle and folded her

arms. "Quit worrying about his lordship for two seconds. What do *you* want, Jayr?"

Last night Byrne had come to her, had seen her looking at herself. Jayr had not been ashamed that he had seen her. Catching him watching her in the mirror had thrilled her.

And dismayed her, for there had been nothing for him to see.

"I want to be like other women," she admitted. "But—"

Alexandra's hand whipped up. "No buts. Be a kid or a woman. Decide. Now."

"Very well." She scowled as she went over to the exam table. "Can you speed up the process?"

Alexandra laughed. "Oh, now it's not fast enough?"

"Give me two injections. You said there was nothing in the formula that could hurt me. Doubling the dose should double the effect, should it not?" She would simply keep busy and have someone else attend to Byrne for the day.

"It might." The doctor hesitated. "But that much hormone in your system could really throw your body into overdrive."

"I must go into town tonight. Two of our people have left the Realm and . . . It is complicated. In any event, I will be too busy to do anything foolish." She held out her arm.

"I want you to come back here before dawn so I can check you over," Alexandra said as she administered the shot. When Jayr stood, she added, "Wait; I need to talk you about something else. You told me that Byrne was the one who changed you from human to Darkyn, right?"

"He was."

"I don't think so." She discarded the syringe. "Last night I ran a test to compare your blood sample with one I took from Byrne. They don't match. As a matter of fact, your blood doesn't match any other sample that I have in the database."

"Why would my blood match anyone's?" Jayr shifted her weight. "I am an orphan. My parents abandoned me. I had no blood kin among our kind."

"That's not what I mean. If Byrne infected you, the pathogen in your blood should be identical to his. It isn't." Alexandra picked up some small strips of glass and brought them to the microscope, then arranged them beneath the lenses before she stood back. "Come here and look."

Jayr peered into the lenses of the device and saw two squares filled with moving dots. "This is what our blood really looks like?"

"Yep. The red things with the black centers are your blood cells," she told her. "The red things with no centers are the human blood you ingest."

Jayr watched the dots collide with one another. "My blood cells are attacking the human cells." Ferociously, in fact.

"They're absorbing them. It's their food." Alexandra touched something on the scope, and the lenses switched, making the images grow larger. "See those three little dots in the center of the black nuclei?"

"Barely."

"They're the troublemakers," Alex said. "They're present in every cell of your body: blood, bones, tissues, nerves, everything. They've mutated them. They're what make you, me, and all the other people at the party Kyn."

Jayr saw the differences between the two images. "They are not the same."

"No. Which means your mutation is different from Byrne's. Which means he didn't infect you."

"He must have," Jayr said, lifted her head to look at the doctor, "for he was the only one there that day. I gave myself to him. There was no one else."

Alexandra thrust her hands into her jacket pockets. "Are you sure about that?"

"Yes. Perhaps." Jayr felt confused. "My memories of that day stop at the moment my human life did. I lay dreaming until I woke up, changed to Kyn."

Alexandra nodded. "Who was with you when you regained consciousness?"

"My lord Byrne. He had brought me back to his encampment and cared for me until I awoke. I took so long to change he thought I might die of it." Jayr recalled how confusing that time had been, and how gentle Byrne had been with her. "He explained that it had been an accident, that he had not meant to change me."

"Yeah, I bet." Alex tapped her finger against her lips. "When he took your blood, did he share you with anyone else?" When

Jayr shook her head, Alex added, "So he drained you dry himself?"

"I think he must have. It was the only way to change a human to Kyn." She saw Alex's expression. "You know what it was like. The seigneur did the same to you."

"My change took a lot longer and was way more complicated," the doctor said wryly. "There's just one big fat problem with how Byrne changed you. He couldn't have done it."

"I am Kyn, Doctor," Jayr said.

"Are you sure that you were unconscious for more than three days?" Alex asked.

"I cannot say." Jayr frowned. "That is what my lord told me at the time. We were both unconscious for some days. Then he awoke and called out until his men found us in the pit."

"Even if Byrne and you were unconscious for a couple of days, he couldn't have woken up first, taken you back to his encampment, or cared for you while you were changing," Alex stated emphatically. "Draining you dry would have put you in rapture and him in thrall. According to what I've been told, thrall would have kept him unconscious for three to seven days. He'd have been out cold for at least as long as you were."

"If what you say is true, then another did make me Kyn." Jayr said. "But if it was not Byrne, then who did?"

Alexandra gave her a sympathetic smile. "I think we need to ask your boss that question."

After the humiliation of spending himself in his pants while he slept outside Jayr's door, Byrne had returned to his bed to lie alone and watch a shaft of sunlight crawl across the ceiling. Sometime near sunset he fell asleep, only to be awakened by Beaumaris's attempts to start the fire.

Byrne put a hand to his head. "Where is Jayr?"

"She is attending to the guests, I believe, my lord." He rose and stepped back, beaming as the kindling flared, and then frowning as the small flame extinguished. "Are there birds nesting in your chimney, my lord?"

Byrne sat on the edge of the bed, trying to shake off the sluggishness left from his wretched night. "What?"

"The fire does not breathe, my lord. I should summon the sweep—"

"Forget the fire," Byrne said. "Summon my seneschal." She never let the fire smoke.

"Jayr is greatly busy, but I am happy to attend you, my lord." Beaumaris's eyes darted to the wine rack. "May I prepare some refreshment for you? I think the new merlot from California is exceptionally good. Farlae says—"

"Beau."

"My lord?"

"Get out."

"Yes, my lord." The man bowed quickly and backed out of the room.

Byrne rubbed his pounding temples before starting the fire himself. Thirty minutes later he was still alone, the room hazy with smoke. He tossed a bucket of water on the wood to put out the fire, which only resulted in more smoke. At last he went to the intercom at his bedside and smacked it with his fist. "Jayr?"

Harlech answered. "She is not available, my lord. May I be of service?"

Not available? She was his seneschal, not a parking spot. "Find Jayr and send her to me."

"Yes, my lord."

As he waited, Byrne prepared and drank two goblets of bloodwine, one after the other, to clear his head. When Jayr did not arrive, he washed and dressed. He would show her how little he needed her or anyone to dance attendance on him. What he needed her for—what he wanted her for—would be far more pleasant. For both of them. If nothing else, last night's interlude had proven that.

Still she did not come to him.

By God, would he have to go and track her himself?

A knock on the door made Byrne look up. Finally she had come. When she didn't enter, he crossed the room and yanked it open.

"Why do you not—" He stopped and looked down. It was not Jayr, but Nottingham's seneschal. "What do you want?"

Skald bobbed a bow and addressed the turned-up tips of his

lurid green court shoes. "I am to deliver a message to you, my lord."

"Well?"

"Lord Cyprien expressed a wish to ride with you. He has taken his mount to the grove of trees on the north side of the lake. He asks that you meet him there." Skald tucked his hands behind his back and gave him a timid glance. "Shall I accompany you as your groom, my lord? You know I am the finest horseman in Florence."

"No. You can go tell the stable master to saddle my horse." Byrne slammed the door in his face and went to the intercom. "Harlech."

"My lord?"

"Have you found my seneschal?"

"I regret to say that I have not, my lord."

Byrne did not issue any further orders. The intercom lay in pieces, thanks to his fist.

As Byrne made his way to the stables, he stopped every man of the Realm who crossed his path and demanded to know if they had seen Jayr. All of them claimed they had not and offered to look for her. The innocence of their expressions aroused Byrne's suspicions, and he made a detour to stop at the wardrobe keeper's chambers.

Farlae came to the door in his shirtsleeves, an open bottle of bloodwine in his hand. "May I be of service, my lord?"

"You can tell me where Jayr is," Byrne said. "Dinnae bother to deny that you know. Nothing happens under my roof that you or your spies cannae see or hear."

"I know that Jayr went into the city early this afternoon. Just as I know that you spent most of the morning sitting outside her bedchamber door." Farlae propped himself against the door frame, his one black eye glinting. "As does, I daresay, the entire *jardin*. Doesn't seem like a very comfortable spot. Is there something amiss with your own bed?"

Byrne's lips peeled back from his teeth. "What business is it of yours what I do? I am master here. I will take my rest naked, on the battlements, among a herd of goats if it pleases me."

Farlae shrugged. "Goats are overrated, or so I have heard.

Sheep, now, they are said to be quite another matter. I may have to investigate that myself." He drank from the bottle.

Killing his wardrobe keeper, Byrne decided, would not take a great deal of effort. The hall held at least twenty objects with which he could end the man's existence. Only the prospect of Rainer's weeping held him back. "Why did Jayr go to town?"

"Deliveries held up, damaged goods, paperwork to be signed, feed deliveries rescheduled, the usual," the wardrobe keeper said casually. "I hope she remembers to pick up the parts that came in at the Singer center for my serger." He thought for a moment. "I believe a week ago Rain requested that Jayr order four gallons of latex paint from the hardware shop. It seems he tired of the colors in his rooms. Too bad he won't be here to repair them."

"These errands could be handled by anyone. These are the last days of the tournament; Jayr knows she is needed here—" Byrne stopped and gave Farlae an incredulous look. "You did this deliberately."

"The serger failed on its own," Farlae drawled. "I will need it repaired if I am to tailor all that Lycra the humans must have for their spring season costumes. I had nothing to do with the paint order. Rain is gone off with Viviana. Good riddance." He took a drink from the bottle.

Byrne stabbed a finger in his face. "This nonsense was but an excuse to send her into the city. You did this to keep her away from me."

Farlae lowered the bottle and smiled. "Perhaps we did this to keep *you* away from *her*."

"You've gone mad," Byrne said blankly. "Every one of you. My own men, rebelling and conspiring against me. In my own keep."

"Doubtless we are." Unimpressed, Farlae studied the condition of his nails. "Will there be anything else, my lord?"

"Get stuffed." Byrne walked away. "No." He stopped and turned around. "Call Jayr on the contraption she hangs on her ear. Tell her I command her to return to the Realm and report to me at once."

"Oh, dear." Farlae held up a familiar-looking device. "Do you mean this contraption? I fear in her haste to go it fell out of her pocket and into mine. Well, Harlech may have helped it get there."

Byrne grabbed it and threw it against the wall, where it exploded into a hundred fragments.

"That," he said, staring into Farlae's black eye, "is what happens to a man's head when I lose my temper."

"Indeed." Farlae folded his arms and looked interested. "What happens to a woman's?"

For a long time Byrne stood and said nothing, saw nothing. For his insolent wardrobe keeper's questions explained everything. He had lived with these men, trained with them, fought beside them. They were loyal to him because he was suzerain, and they lived by Kyn rule. Some of them admired him. Most of them feared him.

They were loyal to Jayr because they loved her.

"I would never hurt the lass," Byrne said.

Farlae's mouth took on a faint sneer. "That is not what I saw last night outside the ballroom."

"I kissed her," he roared.

"You terrified her," Farlae shouted back, smashing the bottle of bloodwine against his doorway. "You see, my lord, you were not the only one tracking last night. So tell me, when did your seneschal become your prey?"

"I love her."

The three words rang between them, echoing down the hall until the shocking sound of them died away. Farlae crouched and began picking up pieces of the broken bottle.

"Christ." He knelt to help him. "This is a wretched bloody mess."

"It need not be." Something like kindness softened Farlae's craggy face. "Aedan, if you love Jayr, do not force her into something for which she is not ready. Give her leave to come to you, if that is what she wishes. Give her time." Sorrow filled his eyes. "God knows, you cannot hold someone you love if they do not feel the same for you."

There was no more time for this. "I'm riding out to the north side of the lake to meet with Cyprien. Tell anyone who is still interested that I will return in an hour."

Farlae took the shards of glass from him. "Yes, my lord."

"And, Farlae," he said, staring into his hellish eye. "Rain has as much interest in Viviana as I do in a herd of goats."

The wardrobe keeper inclined his head. "Thank you, my lord."

Byrne left for the stables. His favorite palfrey, a big, good-natured stock mare who had more stamina than pedigree, stood saddled and waiting for him. He refused the stable master's offer of a groom and rode out to round the lake.

Byrne took his time making his way to Cyprien's appointed meeting place. The night air cooled the heat in his blood and restored some order to his thoughts. Farlae, he realized, had provoked him only in order to accomplish the same. When Jayr returned from the city, he would settle this thing between them.

How he would do that, Byrne didn't know.

He reached the north side of the lake but saw no sign of Cyprien at the edge of the groves. Large black beetles flew out of the grass as his mare rode through it, whizzing past Byrne's face as they made their startled escape. Then something longer and more lethal passed by his head and struck the ground in front of the mare. She skittered back a moment before something struck Byrne's neck, sinking in like a heated poker.

He reached back to pull the thing from his neck when another struck his left shoulder. The shafts told him they were arrows; the pain told him they were copper tipped. He kicked his heels into the nervous mare's sides and headed for the cover of the groves.

The mare plunged down, falling away from him, screaming as the ground beneath them vanished.

Chapter 16

"You cannot begin the archery contest until Lord Byrne returns," Jayr heard Harlech say as she carried in the last of the feed sacks and dropped them on the stable master's pallet.

"Very well, where is he? Gone off with your wife, too, Harlech?" There was a heavy thud, and the speaker grunted before gasping, "'Twas a jest."

"'Tis not funny, Reg," Beaumaris advised.

She came around the corner and found Harlech and several of the men standing in a loose group. "What is amiss here?"

"Lord Byrne has been gone for hours." Beaumaris glared at one of the trainers, who was holding a hand to his belly. "The archers are growing restless, as are the guests."

"He should be in his chambers," Jayr told them. "If not there, the guards' hall. Someone should be with him." She turned to Harlech. "Who did you send to attend him in my place?"

"That would be me," Beaumaris said. "I lasted but two minutes before he ordered me out. I could not help it that the fire smokes."

"His chimney always funnels the worst of the wind during the day," Jayr said. "I close the flue every morning to keep the backdraft from blowing ash into the room. You have to open it or the fire smokes."

Beau looked up at the roof beams. "*Now* she says something."

"Our lord has not been in the best of moods since you left," Harlech said to her. "We have searched the keep from one end to the other, and checked the guest rooms as well. He is not here. Did he say to you where he might go tonight?"

"I did not speak to him about his plans. He would not leave during a tournament." Jayr turned and spotted an empty stall. "There. His palfrey is missing. He must be out riding."

At that moment a horse came trotting into the barn. The palfrey's empty saddle sat on her back, and her ears flicked as she whickered to the other horses.

"Or not," Beaumaris said.

Jayr caught her and checked her for injuries, but found none. She handed the reins over to one of the grooms. "Perhaps he went for a walk instead. Ask Lord Locksley if he would preside over the archery contest." She went to saddle her horse and then called Harlech over.

"I will go with you," he offered.

"I thank you, but no." She thought of the excuses she could make and then abandoned them. "I would have this time alone with him. We have much to discuss."

He nodded. "I will see you tomorrow night, then."

"It shouldn't take that long," she said.

Harlech gave her an enigmatic look. "Only remember that the joust begins at moonrise."

Few Kyn could ride horseback while tracking, as the air and the movements of the animal dispersed Kyn scent. Jayr had never been particularly adept at the skill, but she knew Byrne's scent better than any other save her own, and under most conditions could detect even the slightest trace of it. She always smelled heather around the stables, for Byrne spent a great deal of time with the animals, but rarely did it lead far from the stalls. Tonight she caught a trace of him outside the barn, and trailed it to the water's edge, where it took a turn to the north.

"Why would he come out there?" Jayr murmured as she scanned the north embankment.

No riding paths went through that part of their land, much of which was covered by long diagonal rows of orange and grapefruit trees. As she wheeled her horse around, the skin on her arms and legs came alive with nerves, and the pit of her stomach clenched.

Danger. He is in danger.

She urged her mount into a gallop and bent low over his neck as they rounded the lake. She reined him in to look carefully, but saw no one. Then, barely registering in her ears, the distant sound of a familiar voice.

"Down here."

Jayr dismounted and ran toward the sound. A large, irregular hole stretched out in the clearing just before the groves. She ran over and stopped short of the edge of it. The scent of heather, strong and burning hot, wafted up from the pit. Her head spun for a moment as she looked down and felt as if she had been thrust back in time.

"My lord? Is that you?" She felt the ground loosening under her feet and staggered back as a two-foot section of ground crumbled.

A thready ghost of Byrne's voice drifted up to her. "Stay back."

The hell she would.

Jayr rounded the sinkhole, looking for a stable edge, and then dropped down onto her belly to peer inside. She couldn't see him. "Are you injured?" When he didn't answer she called, "Aedan?"

She crawled over to see past an outcropping of stone, and spotted Byrne. He lay ten feet below her, his big body motionless and spread-eagled on a rock. Blood covered his face and stained the front of his tunic.

He was not dead. This could not kill him. She would run back to the stables and fetch men, rope, and horses. They would pull him out. Jayr took in a deep breath and tasted a vile tinge in the air.

Copper from open wounds.

"I am coming, my lord." She could not risk leaving him to go for help; even as fast as she was, the poisonous copper might kill him before she returned. She kept a coil of rope on her saddle; she would fetch that and use it to lower herself to him. She thrust herself up on her hands and knees and went still as the earth rumbled beneath her.

The hole spread wide, pulling in more of its sides and Jayr.

It happened too fast for her to react; the earth took her and flung her into its depths. She screamed when she landed on her shoulder and felt bones crack. Rocks pelted her, soil choked her, and then the dark pit swallowed her alive.

Some time later, how long she didn't know, she opened her eyes. Her heart kicked in her chest and she coughed violently, clearing the dirt from her nose and mouth. Rocks shifted and fell away from her as she tried to prop herself up with the hand she could feel, then bit her lip as more pain stabbed through her left side. Her left arm wouldn't work, and her shoulder had become a ball of agony.

"Lass." A big hand groped and pulled more of the rocks away from her. Byrne's battered face appeared before her eyes. She tried to help him and gasped. "You're hurt; be still."

He uncovered her and pulled her up against him, propping them both against the side of a rock. The movements jarred her arm and forced a groan from her.

"Let me see." When she did, he felt the top of her arm and shoulder. "It's come out of place. Be brave; this will hurt like the devil."

He turned her arm and jerked on it at the same time, and Jayr stiffened as her bones shifted and ten thousand daggers stabbed into her shoulder.

"Good lass." He held her close, panting. "It's back now." He started to say something, then groaned and slumped over, rolling away from her.

"Aedan." Jayr ignored the pain and crawled over to him. The gash on his head was already healing, but blood soaked the back of his tunic. With effort she dragged him into the dim light coming from the top of the hole. Seven broken arrow shafts protruded from his back and shoulders, their barbs deeply embedded in his flesh. The smell and the blood coming from the wounds told her that the barbs were copper.

Jayr shoved her hand into her pocket and took out her knife. She would have to do this quickly or the copper would taint his blood and stop his heart, and then nothing might bring him back.

"You can't do this the night before my joust, my lord," she muttered as she tore his shirt away. Although he was unconscious, she thought on some level that he might be able to hear her. "You have to be there to award the trophy to me, for I intend to win." She gripped the knife tightly. "Aedan, if you can hear me, I am taking out the copper now. I will be as quick as I can."

It sickened her to stab the blade into his body and root with it until she felt the barb and could pry it free of his flesh. But he lay unconscious, and if she were swift she could have them out of him before he awoke.

"There." The arrowhead she plucked out looked familiar, but the copper burned her hand and she threw it away from her in disgust. "Six more and we will be done."

One by one she removed the arrowheads, their curved points rending his flesh and making the wounds bleed faster. When she had taken out the last, she tore at her own uninjured arm with her fangs, carving deep gouges into her own flesh. She then held her arm over each gash, letting the blood from her wounds drip into his.

Slowly Byrne's wounds stopped bleeding and the edges began to pull together.

At last it was done, and she fell back, staring up. Above them she saw dirt, rocks, and, distantly, the night sky. Her fall had caused the sinkhole to expand; her best guess was that they were at least forty feet down in the earth.

The immediate danger was past now that Byrne's wounds were free of copper, she thought. Soon the men would come and rescue them—and then she remembered what she had said to Harlech back at the stables.

I would have this time alone with him.

Jayr rolled her head against the rock under her, laughing helplessly. No one would come looking for them tonight. Harlech wouldn't let them. They probably wouldn't be missed until the joust tomorrow night.

"This amuses you?" Byrne rasped.

"My lord." She turned and saw him propping himself up on his elbows. "How do you feel?"

"Like a pincushion." He rolled his shoulders and looked up. "Can we climb out?"

She tried to lift her left arm, but could barely move it. "Not without help. Who shot you in the back?"

"I dinnae see, and then the horse threw me in here." He

paused, turning from side to side before he eyed her. "What did you do?"

"I cut out the barbs," she said. "They were copper."

"What else did you do?" He seized her right arm and turned it up, exposing the slowly healing gashes from her fangs. "For the love of God, lass."

"I couldn't leave them in you, and it was the only way to stop the bleeding and close the wounds once they were out." Tears welled in her eyes. "Aedan, who would do this? What if they come back?"

"Shhh. We are alive; we will get out of here." His arms came around her and he pulled her against him. "But you must stop jumping into holes after me. It never turns out well for you."

She choked back her tears. "That is your opinion."

Byrne brought her onto his lap and held her, rocking a little as she pressed her cheek against his heart. They sat that way together until the moon passed over, and Jayr eased away from him to check her arm.

He watched her carefully rotate her shoulder. "How is it?"

"The pain is gone, but the arm stiff." She flexed her fingers. "Fortunately I carry a lance on the right side, or I would have to forfeit my place tomorrow night."

"The men will find us, and then you can see Cyprien's leech."

She had to tell him. "The men won't be looking for us tonight. I had thought you were walking, and before I rode out after you I asked Harlech to give us some time alone together. He will not send anyone to search. If we wish to get out of here, we must do it ourselves." She stood and reached up, testing the stability of shelves of coral rock above them. "If you can give me a boost, my lord . . ."

His hands spanned her waist and turned her around. "You cannae climb with that arm. We are staying put for now. Why did you wish to be alone with me?"

Jayr reached up to dislodge a root tangled in his hair. "Ever since the full moon, things have been different between us. More intimate than perhaps they should. I had thought we should talk about it."

His fingers brushed at something on her cheek. "Only talk?

You could think of nothing else to do with me once you had me at your mercy?"

Jayr felt relieved that he was not angry with her, and angry that he found it amusing. "I am serious, my lord."

"So am I. The men told you that I spent most of the morning sitting outside your bedchamber." His brows rose as he studied her face. "Ah. The men *didnae* tell you." He ran his thumb along the line of her jaw and traced the curve of her ear. "I dreamed of you there, and I think you knew it. Do you remember being in the seraglio with me? You were reading books covered in pearls."

Her throat tightened, and she thought shame might finish her off then and there. "It was not real. It did not happen."

"That I know." He tangled his hand in her hair. "For if it had been real, I would have done much more than watch you."

She didn't know what to think. He had been with her in her most private moment. He knew.

"In the dream, you said that you thought of me when you pleasure yourself," he murmured, lifting her face. "Did you mean it? Do you think of me?"

He spoke as if he were unsure of her, and then Jayr understood: He didn't know. Not her thoughts or her heart. He would not put faith in a shared dream. He needed her to tell him, to show him.

"How could I not? You made me a woman. You taught me what pleasure is. I have never forgotten that day." On impulse Jayr turned her face into his hand and kissed his palm. "There has been no one else for me but you, Aedan. I am yours."

"There is this matter of the debt between us. I made you my seneschal the last time you saved my life." His hand stroked gently over her shoulder. "How can I repay you?"

"You can make it turn out well for me." With every ounce of courage she possessed, she slid her hand up and cupped his neck. "You can make me your lover."

Byrne brought his mouth down to hers. Before he kissed her he said, "You're sure, lass? If you change your mind, you cannae run away from me down here."

Jayr smiled. "I am through running, my lord."

The world fell away again, silent and unimportant as his

mouth touched hers. Such a simple thing, a kiss, but when Jayr opened for him and met his tongue with hers, she felt a thousand different sensations. No dream could have equaled the taste of him, or the liquefying heat that spread from their lips down the length of her body. Distantly she wondered if she could survive just this, for it made every other feeling dwindle to nothingness.

He brought her wounded forearm to his mouth, soothing the healed but still-tender skin with a dozen kisses. His hands turned her, tugging at her shirt, pulling it over her head. As the cool air touched her inadequate breasts, Jayr automatically brought her hands up, and then stopped as she remembered him looking at her in the mirror.

"I am not like the women you choose," she said, aching with regret.

"I never wanted a woman like you," Byrne told her, trailing his fingers from one flat nipple to the other. "I wanted you. I settled for them."

He put his mouth on her, sucking at the areola until her nipple hardened, and then turning his head to kiss and suck at the other.

Jayr shifted under him, cradling his big body with her arms and thighs, shivering as he nipped at the faint curves. He pushed his hips, fitting their sexes together, his key to her lock. The thought of having him opening her, stealing inside her and learning all of the secrets hidden within her body, made her fangs spring out, long and eager.

He knew the hunger was on her before she did. "Yes." He caught the back of her head and pressed her face to his throat. "Taste me again."

Shamelessly she bit him, arching as her teeth punched through and his blood soothed her dry mouth. His hands hooked on the waist of her trousers and ripped them apart, baring her to his fingers. As she sucked, he tugged and shredded, destroying everything keeping their skin apart. She lifted her mouth to look down and see his arm bulging, his erect penis in his fist as he worked it against her. The tip of her clit protruded from her folds, and when he grazed it the sensation proved so intense that all of the breath rushed out of her.

Byrne's eyes glowed, and his tattoos curled as his mouth moved into a slow smile. He repeated the motion, deliberately teasing the small, stiffening protrusion.

"It feels like a faerie's tongue," he told her, slowly rubbing the helmet of his cock all around the rosy tip.

Jayr groaned as her fluids made them both slick, and then felt something close over her clit and tug at it. Not his fingers, but something narrow and tight.

Byrne went still, his face drawn and hard with excitement. "Look, lass," he whispered. "Your jewel is kissing my cock."

Her eyes went wide as she saw that her clit had penetrated the slit in his crown. She was inside him. When she tried to draw back, he held her still.

"Let them have their kiss," he said hoarsely, holding his shaft and gently pumping. His slit worked over her, tightening as the head around it and her clit swelled.

Jayr's head snapped back as the friction and the clasping pull tossed her body into a bonfire of fear and delight, consuming her in its relentless inferno. Byrne caught her scream before it left her mouth and shifted, plunging his cock into her convulsing slit as she exploded.

"Now, my lady," he said, panting into her mouth, "it is my turn to fuck *you*."

He gathered her hips with his hands and lifted her, pistoning his shaft into her body with deep, soul-shaking power. Jayr's hands anchored onto his arms, her eyes fixed on his as he plowed into her, holding nothing back, forcing the slick tightness to give way to his need. He felt too big; he would surely split her in half. And then another heat began to grow, one devouring both of them, clawing and dragging until it seemed they became one thing, all motion and fire, and the agony of being so near became too much. Byrne rammed himself into her, grunting with the effort of holding her down as she answered, her body molten fire under the hammering, inescapable weight of him.

Byrne's arms locked, and then his big body began to shake as if it might fall apart under the strain. He slowed, almost unmoving, and then stabbed deep, holding himself in the quivering clasp of her body as his semen pumped into her.

"Christ Jesus." He fell on her, pulling her to him as he rolled to his side. "So that's what it's like to fuck your way to heaven and back. I've always wondered."

"Aedan." Jayr realized she had scored both of his arms with her nails and reached up to touch his mouth, her fingers bright with his blood. "I didn't know it would be so . . ." There weren't words for it. "Unusual."

"Lass," he said, and laughed a little. "Let me say this now, so that there's no confusion later. Anytime you want to feel *unusual* again"—he kissed her mouth—"you come to me."

Alex hadn't planned on dozing off during the archery contest. But one minute she was sitting with Michael and watching men shooting very long arrows from enormous bows, and the next she was walking through Dundellan.

During her abduction Alex had become very familiar with the layout of the castle, first during her escape attempts and later while trying to find a cure for Richard Tremayne's condition.

Everything looked just as it had when she had been held hostage, Alex thought. Torches burning in iron wall holders, cats wandering all over the place, the smell of dust, leather, and silent despair. She didn't remember the cold stone halls being filled with purple-blue dragonflies, but maybe Gabriel Seran was visiting, too. She certainly remembered the swarms of bugs Gabriel could summon and control with his talent. He'd used them like a weapon when trying to get to Nick, the woman he loved.

Dreaming of Dundellan seemed a little pointless, though. Gabriel and Nick were off somewhere being happy, Richard was undergoing successful therapy that was changing him from cat-man to vampire-man, and all the bad guys were dead or locked up where they couldn't hurt anyone anymore.

Alex stopped and looked around. "Why am I here?"

The dragonflies all flew down the hall and landed on a door marked with a glittering golden apple. If that hadn't been clear enough, a shaft of purple-blue light poured out of the keyhole.

"Gotcha." Alex walked to the door, stepping over a few fat cats sprawled on the floor along the way. It was nice to see that the felines were so healthy. Until she had come up with a treatment, Richard had been living on their blood.

She knocked and politely waited. When no one answered the door, she reached to check the knob and watched her hand move through the wooden door panel. All it took was a breath and a push, and she was on the other side.

"Alex." The blond giant sat holding an oiled rag to the blade of a long broadsword. He dropped both as he rose and came to her. "You came."

"You called me. I heard you." At least, she was pretty sure she had. She looked up the muscled wall of his chest at his face. "I know you." She glanced around them. "You brought me here when I was hurt."

"I did." He went down on one knee. "But I am the one in need of healing now, my lady. Will you come back to me now?"

"I hated Ireland," she said, walking around him to avoid his hands. The walls of the room faded from stone to canvas, and Alex tripped over a pillow as she turned and found herself back in the desert tent. "I'm not too crazy about this place, either."

The blond man, who was now lying on a pile of furs and silks at her feet, reached up and pulled her down to him.

"Stop thinking, love. We have all night." His scent poured over her, bathing her in larkspur as he rolled over her. "I am at your service."

It may have been his words, or the absence of the dragonflies, or the way he ripped open her blouse. Whatever it was, it brought everything back to her: the attack by Richard, the wounds she had suffered, and waking up alone with the captain of the guard in his room. At first Korvel had tended to her injuries, but then he had used his talent on her to make her imagine being with him, just like this.

"You son of a bitch." Alex grabbed a handful of his hair and yanked his mouth from her neck. "What did you do to me? Did Richard put you up to this?"

Korvel's eyes, the irises gone almost entirely purple-blue, darkened. "I did nothing. Richard knows nothing. Kiss me." His head snapped sideways as she clouted him with a fist. "You came here of your own free will."

"The hell I did. Get off. *Off.*" Alex shoved at his chest until

he rolled away. She scrambled out of the tangle of furs and pillows and moved until she had half the tent between them.
"Where are we? Oh, tell me you did *not* kidnap me again." He
said nothing. "Unless you'd like your head hanging from the
nearest pole, Captain, you'd better start talking."

Korvel gestured around him. "It is as you see." He picked up
a gauntlet and tossed it at one wall of the tent. It didn't bounce
away but slid through it, leaving gentle ripples in its wake.
"Nothing but a dream. If you do not care for this place, we can
return to the castle. You have only to say."

"Are you telling me that I'm asleep?"

"We both are."

"Okay." Alex had a feeling that part was true. "And you just
happened to stumble into the same dream I'm having?" She
held up a hand before he could reply. "Wait, I remember what
you said the last time. You told me that I sent smoke signals for
you or something. And you came, and decided to . . . pick up
where we didn't leave off. I'll bet you did something to my
memories so I wouldn't fight you, too."

He shrugged. "It was not permanent."

"How nice." Alex folded her arms. "Did you forget whom I
belong to, and how consummately he's going to kick your ass
for doing this to me?"

"I cannot enter your dreams without an invitation," Korvel
said softly. "You were correct. This is no real place, and we are
not here. You are in America; I am still in Ireland. Only our
minds have come together. But you initiated the contact. You
reached out to me. And you came when I called for you."

"Across the Atlantic Ocean." She planted her hands on her
hips. "Telepathically."

"Our minds are one. No distance can separate us now." His
eyes, hot and dilated, moved over her. "You can be with me
here, Alex. Anytime you wish. We have but to sleep. He cannot
read your mind. He will never know."

Incredibly, part of her wanted to jump him and finish what
they'd started. A mindless, slut-eager part that, as soon as she
woke up, she was amputating. "*I'll* know."

He shrugged. "You knew in Ireland."

"I know that your talent makes human females want to

screw you." She needed three hours, a tub of hot soapy water, and a hard-bristled scrub brush. "It affects me the same way, and you knew it. I stayed away from you because of it. *That's* what I know."

Korvel's mouth flattened. "Then why have you been summoning me all these weeks? You can call Cyprien just as easily. More so, for you are bonded to him by blood. His *sygkenis*, his woman, his life companion. He created you. He commands you. If he is, as you say, your love, why is he not here in your dreams, Alexandra?"

She knew where he was going with this. "Nice try, Captain, but I'm only going dutch on this little guilt trip. You knew this was wrong. You could have stopped it from your end."

"I had no choice."

"Right. Well, dream's over. Go home." She went for the tent flap.

"Please, Alexandra, don't leave me again." His voice wound around her, a warm and unbreakable rope of velvet. "I came because I could not help myself. I fell in love with you in Ireland. I am still in love with you."

She glanced back. "To repeat for the thousandth time, I'm in a committed relationship. I do not bed-hop, even in my head. I'm *taken*."

"I don't care." The proudest and most reserved Kyn Alex had ever met now looked prepared to grovel. "I will take whatever you give me."

"If you're telling me the truth, all you can have is my sympathy. Good-bye, Captain." Alex stepped through the tent wall.

The tent, however, wouldn't let her through. Alex hung, trapped in the cold, stinging gel of the stuff, dead dragonflies floating in front of her eyes. She opened her mouth, but no sound came out, and behind her the purple-blue light blazed, scorching her back, until she felt the skin start to shrivel and blacken, and knew she was going to die.

The tent wall shook, and then it dissolved as two long, beautiful hands caught her as she fell through the light and the darkness.

Open your eyes.
Alexandra, I am here.

Come to me, chérie.

Alex heard Michael in her head, felt him in her blood. He was holding her, kissing her, and if she didn't wake up he would die with her.

Alexandra.

"Michael."

Alex opened her eyes. She was back in the infirmary, on the floor this time, and Michael hovered over her, pinning her shoulders down, his eyes a solid amber and his mouth white.

He looked awful. She'd never been so glad to see him.

"Hey." She wriggled her shoulders and winced. "Don't I rate a bed?"

"*Mon Dieu.* You are awake." He lifted her gently into his arms. "You were in the bed," he told her as he carried her back to it. "You had a seizure and went into convulsions. After you fell I was afraid to move you."

"Don't you sound all medical." That explained the sensation of falling. "How long have I been here?"

"Three hours. You fell asleep at the archery contest. When I couldn't wake you I brought you here." He tried to smile. "I would call a doctor, but the only one in the house is on vacation."

He thought she was sick, physically sick. She had to tell him now.

"Michael, I know this is going to sound a little weird, but I had a bad dream. I've been having a lot of them." As he laid her down, she caught his hand. "I need to tell you this before I forget, or he makes me forget, or whatever happens to me when I wake up."

Alex told him everything, starting with what had happened at Dundellan after Richard's attack, how Korvel had tended to her, and the bizarre attraction she had felt for him, thanks to being exposed to his talent, which made every woman desire him.

She didn't make any excuses for herself or the captain, but gave Michael the facts as she remembered them. She described the dreams that she could remember, and repeated what Korvel had told her.

"That's all I've got," she said at last. "Whatever he's been doing to me—and I think my subconscious might have helped—it's over. If it happens again, I'll tell you."

Michael sat holding her hand and looked at her without saying a word. His eyes had faded from amber to turquoise, but she couldn't read any expression in them.

"You can yell at me if you want," she told him, his silence making her nervous. "I was practically cheating on you in my dreams."

"It is not your fault, *chérie*." He stood and moved away from the bed. "Korvel bonded you to him while you were being held by Richard. Possibly after the attack, as you suspected."

"How could he do that? I hardly knew the guy."

"He likely used his blood to help heal your wounds. At that time the bond you and I share was weakened because we were kept apart. He created a new bond before ours was severed." He shook his head. "All this time you have been caught between the two of us. That is what has been making you suffer since your return. You cannot belong to two masters."

She didn't think the Darkyn could hard-wire monogamy into a relationship, but there was still a lot about them and their condition that she didn't know. "I love you. You're not my master, but I love you. I may have been influenced by his talent, but I don't love Korvel. I don't even like him anymore."

"It has nothing to do with your emotions. The blood bond between a Kyn lord and his *sygkenis* is exclusive, unless he dies. Many times the *sygkenis* dies soon after, but some can bond with another lord. You are not like us in many ways; perhaps that is why you bonded with both of us at once." He took a deep breath. "Do you still want to go to him?"

"I don't know." Alex didn't like the way this conversation was heading. "Am I in trouble for this? Are you kicking me out?"

He hunched his shoulders. "I will let you go. If that is your wish. I will . . . I will try."

"I wish," she said carefully, "that you'd come over here. You have a gorgeous ass, but I'm tired of talking to it."

Michael came to her. The torment in his eyes made her heart wrench. "Will you stay with me?"

"Baby, I'm not going anywhere."

"Alexandra." He took her in his arms and held her close, tucking her head under his chin. "What have I done to you?"

"This wasn't your fault. Richard grabbed me. Korvel was nice to me. And then somehow he messed with my head, but not at my request. I just waited for you to come and get me." She snuggled against him and felt a deep, abiding joy spreading through her. "I was afraid that the only reason we were together was because of the bond thing. That it was making us love each other. But it wasn't. It isn't."

"The bond is very strong," he admitted, kissing the top of her head, "but it cannot create love where there is none."

"Yeah, I just found that out. Korvel fell in love with me, but the feelings were not reciprocal." She sighed. "So it looks like you're stuck with me, seigneur. Unless you're tired of this yo-yo we have for a relationship. In that case, I guess I could call the airport and see when the next flight to Chicago—"

He tilted her head back and smothered the rest of what she meant to say with his lips.

Chapter 17

The exile stood in the guard tower and looked out over the land. Now that Aedan mac Byrne was dead, it would be his: the bloodright denied him ever since his father had learned of his existence and sent him away so that no one would know he was his true heir.

He had had a bad moment when he had seen the girl ride out to the grove. She had already ruined everything for him once; he could not permit her to do so again. But then, to his delight, she had fallen into the trap. This time he had ensured that it was deep enough to prevent any escape. It would keep her where she belonged—in the ground.

It would be foolish to ride out again to gloat over the lord's dead body. It would be foolhardy to go only to assure that the girl could not escape. Of course, if he were caught, he could easily shift the blame.

He looked out over the land. Whatever he did, it would be his by next moonrise. By bloodright.

Robin of Locksley left the keep and walked over to the stables. At the entry to the barns, Nottingham's seneschal, looking comically small atop one of the largest of Byrne's chargers, nearly ran him over.

"Pardon, my lord," he shouted, trying to control the steed and nearly losing his seat. The big animal snorted and bucked once before leaping into a gallop.

"Damned fool," Harlech muttered as he strode out. "I told him that horse is too much for him."

Rob looked up at the sky; dawn was only an hour away. "Where goes the finest horseman in all of Florence?"

"Back to Italy, I hope." Harlech spit on the ground. "If he does not first fall in the lake and sink like a stone."

Rob saw Skald's mount change direction and grew thoughtful. "Harlech, saddle that ivory gelding Byrne refuses to sell to me."

Even in the dark, the destrier's tracks were plainly visible, so Rob simply followed the trail. Skald had rounded the lake and disdained the riding paths for the north shore of the lake. Rob caught sight of him just after the small man had dismounted and was struggling to loop his mount's lead around the lower branch of an orange tree.

Rob tugged the gelding to a stop and surveyed the area. At first he saw nothing of curiosity, only the lake's edge, the citrus grove, and the taller black oaks and scrub pines behind it. Then Skald hurried over to a patch of cleared land beside the grove, and Rob spotted the dark scar in the center of it.

He secured his mount and walked over to stand behind Skald at the edge of the yawning gap.

"It's a sinkhole," he said, making the seneschal jump and whirl around.

"My lord Locksley." He sheathed the ornate dagger in his hand. "You alarmed me." He gestured toward the hole. "My master bade me ride out to find Lord Byrne. I heard a voice call to me, and saw this."

"The land here has loose pockets and sometimes collapses in on itself," Rob told him. "The 'voice' you heard was likely some rocks striking one another."

"Forgive me, but I am sure it was a man." Skald gingerly approached the edge. "Hallo? Is there anyone down there? Do you require assistance?"

"What do you think, you daft prick?" Rob heard Byrne's voice call back.

"Aedan." Rob went to crouch at the edge. Forty feet below, a bare-chested Byrne stood holding Jayr, wrapped in a tattered shirt, in his arms. His heart clenched. "How badly is she hurt?"

"She must have tried to climb out while I slept, and fell," Byrne told him. "She's banged her head, her shoulder's wrenched, and she's lost too much blood for me to replace. I've got to get her back to the keep."

Rob looked at Skald. "Ride back to the stables and tell Harlech what has happened. Have him send rope and men to help me pull them out."

"At once, my lord." Skald started for his horse, and then hesitated and faced him. "I found this near the edge." He handed him an arrow.

"Fine." Rob tossed it aside. "Go quickly."

While he waited for help to arrive, Rob walked the perimeter of the sinkhole. Fissures and depressions on the surface formed a complete web two to three feet around the edges.

Byrne watched him. "How bad does it look?"

"Wretched. This damned ground is unstable; any sort of pressure on the walls could cause another collapse." He measured the gap. "If we can set up a frame rig of some sort over it—"

"There's another way," Byrne told him. "You've got your phone with you?"

He checked his pocket. "I do."

"Call Scarlet. Have him send Nottingham down here."

"I will be happy to throw him into the pit," Rob said. "But first let me get the two of you out."

"The soil near the lake is always saturated," Byrne reminded him.

Rob saw his reasoning, took out his phone, and called his seneschal. To his credit Will didn't question his orders, and grimly promised to drag Nottingham by his testicles to the sinkhole if he refused to come voluntarily.

Harlech and his men came within a few minutes, as did Cyprien and Alexandra. The doctor had brought a folding stretcher, and spoke to Byrne about Jayr's condition. She also tossed down a bag of blood for him to give to her. Nottingham, followed by Will Scarlet, was the last to arrive.

"Seigneur." Nottingham bowed to Cyprien, and then pointed to Scarlet. "This man insisted I come here. I understand that Suzerain mac Byrne has fallen into a hole, but I fail to see what I can do about it."

Rob came to stand beside Michael. "Use your talent on the ground."

Nottingham looked down his nose. "Are you addressing me?"

"Unless there is some other idiot here who can turn things to ice with his touch," Rob said through his teeth, "I am."

Cyprien stepped between them. "Ganelon, he is right. If you can freeze the water in the soil, it will keep the walls from caving in while we pull them out."

"Very well, I will do it. For you, seigneur." Nottingham stripped the black gloves from his large white hands. He gave the men around him a contemptuous look. "Unless you wish to become statues, I suggest you move back to the trees."

"Freeze the ground," Rob told him before he retreated, "Nothing else."

Nottingham waited until they were clear and then crouched down, sinking his fingers into the earth.

At first nothing happened, and then Rob heard the sound of ice cracking. Narrow rings of white frost encompassed the ground around the Italian's hands, and the scent of aniseed grew thick. The rings expanded, sending out fingers of ice that crystallized everything in their path. The gentle sound of lapping water stilled as ice formed on the edge of the lake.

Small thuds made Rob turn around to see oranges, coated with thick, spiny frost, dropping from the trees.

Cyprien's breath painted the air white as he murmured, "Incredible. He's as powerful as Lucan."

Nottingham stood and drew a lace-edged handkerchief from his vest, daintily wiping the dirt from his hands on it. "The surface frost will begin to melt as soon as the sun rises, but unless the temperature changes, the ground will remain frozen for twelve hours."

"That is more than enough time," Cyprien said. "Thank you."

Nottingham turned and strode away.

Rob went to the edge of the sinkhole, where Alexandra joined him.

"Aedan?" she called down. "You two okay?"

"'Tis cold," the suzerain called back, "but we are not frozen."

Cyprien tested a patch of soil near the edge. "It feels like concrete."

"Bring the ropes," Rob called to Harlech.

They first lifted out Jayr on the stretcher by lowering it to Byrne, who tied her to it and secured the ends with two separate ropes. Robin grabbed the edge of the stretcher as soon as it was within reach and lifted Jayr up and out.

The knot in Rob's chest eased as he looked down on her, until the scent of heather filled his nose and he saw that the only garment she wore was Byrne's shirt.

Alexandra knelt down beside the unconscious seneschal and carefully checked her head. "No skull fracture that I can feel, but I'll feel better with an X-ray. Let's get her back to the infirmary." She gestured to two of the men, who picked up the ends of the litter and carried it to a waiting Land Rover.

Rob didn't have time to pull Byrne out of the pit; as soon as the rope was tossed to him he used it to climb out hand over hand.

"Jayr." Byrne hoisted himself over the edge. He smelled more of tansy than heather. "Where is she?"

Rob gave him his hand and helped him up, and then punched him in the face. Feeling his knuckles split as they slammed into the Scot's jaw gave him vicious pleasure.

Cyprien grabbed Byrne before he fell back into the sinkhole. "Locksley."

Robin ignored Michael and glared at the man who had been his best friend. "I can smell her all over you. She was hurt, but you still couldn't leave her alone, you coldhearted bastard."

Byrne rubbed his jaw. "That is between me and Jayr."

"I think not." Rob turned to Cyprien. "I want this *jardin*. I will do whatever you say to have it. If you do not think me capable of ruling two suzerainties, I will turn over Atlanta to whomever you choose. You have but to say the word."

"You can have the Realm," Byrne said softly from behind him. "But she belongs to me."

Rob turned to lunge at him, but the seigneur put himself between them and pushed Locksley back.

"I will take what you have said into consideration," Cyprien said, his expression shuttered as he looked from Rob to Byrne. "Enough harm has been done on this night. Return to the keep."

"Seigneur." Skald came and held out a handful of arrows. "I found more of these."

"You." Byrne grabbed him by the front of his florid tunic and lifted him off his feet, shaking him like a dog would a rat. "You played a part in this." He looked at Cyprien. "He brought me a message from you. He told me that you summoned me here."

"I sent no such message," the seigneur said.

"I am innocent, my lords!" Skald protested. "I did not know the message was false."

"Who bade you to do this?" Rob demanded. "Your master, perhaps?"

"No, my lord." The seneschal swallowed. "I received the instructions from Jayr. Your seneschal gave me the message."

Byrne's eyes flared red. "You lie."

"I swear by the Virgin, 'twas she who bade me come to you." Skald gestured wildly toward the keep. "It was just as I had risen to attend to my duties. I always rise early. She was leaving the keep and said she had no time to deliver it herself."

"Put him down, Aedan," Cyprien said, and bent to pick up the arrows Skald had dropped. "I've seen these before, but I cannot recall where."

The scrolled mark on the arrowheads made Rob seize one and examine it. "These were stolen from the ranges."

"How do you know?"

"Because I made them myself last summer," Rob said, and pointed to the star he had etched into the arrowhead. "That is my mark."

"But these do not look like your arrows, my lord," Skald put in anxiously. When everyone stared at him, he added, "I was admiring Lord Locksley's quiver during the competition. All of your arrows have brown feathers, my lord. Not white."

"They're not mine." The arrow snapped in half as he closed his fist. "They were stolen, Michael. Someone wishes to blame this attack on another."

"Perhaps." Cyprien frowned. "For whom did you make these arrows, Robin?"

Byrne answered for him. "Jayr."

*   *   *

The hum of a machine dragged Jayr back to consciousness. She looked up to see one of the machines Alexandra Keller had ordered hanging over her face.

"Don't move," the doctor said as Jayr lifted a hand to push it away. "I'm taking some pictures of your head."

Jayr wanted to ask why, and then she remembered what had happened in the sinkhole. Aedan had fallen asleep, but she had been too happy to do the same. She had looked up and spotted a series of stones that looked as if they could bear her weight. She had started climbing as fast as she could, and had been halfway to the top when something struck her in the face.

"You are supposed to be on vacation," Jayr said as Alexandra moved the machine's arm away from her face.

"Yeah, that worked out real well, didn't it?"

She touched her scalp where it throbbed, and winced. "I fell."

"You sure did," she said briskly. "Twice. Byrne did a nice job of fixing your dislocated shoulder, by the way. Let me put this film in the developer, and then we'll reminisce. Stay put."

Jayr probed the sore spot on the side of her head. The flesh had healed, and the bone felt intact. She sat up and was looking for her clothes when Alexandra returned.

"I'm sorry, what did you not understand?" the doctor asked, planting her hands on her hips. "The *stay* or the *put*?"

"I must go to my lord," Jayr said, winding the sheet around her. "He is in danger."

"And yet you're here, all banged up. Maybe *you* need a seneschal." The doctor shook her head and handed her some folded garments. "These are my scrubs. The pants will be way too short, but they'll do until we can get some of your stuff."

"Where *are* my clothes?"

"All you had on when we got you out of that hole was Byrne's shirt, which was in pieces. You looked extremely sexy in it, too." She grinned. "So? In between getting beat up all to hell, did you have a little fun?"

Jayr didn't know what to say, and then she did. "I think I have a new hobby."

As Alex laughed, Jayr dressed in the scrubs. A timer chimed, and Alex left again to return with a sheet of film, which she placed on the light box on the wall.

"You really do have a nice, thick skull," the doctor said as she studied the film. "No fractures, no bone chips, no internal bleeding. Congratulations, kid. You have a headache."

"That much I could have told you myself." Jayr turned as Byrne came in. She began to smile, and then remembered they were not alone. "My lord." After the night they had shared, it seemed ludicrous to bow. "I am glad to see you."

Byrne said nothing, but came to her, took her in his arms, and kissed her breathless. When he lifted his mouth, he looked at Alexandra. "Her head?"

"She's fine. The shoulder and arm will be stiff for a couple of days. I'd recommend bed rest, but under the circumstances I don't see that happening for a while." Amusement twinkled in her eyes. "Excuse me; I have to go do something pointless in the next room." She left them alone.

Byrne checked Jayr's head and shoulder with his hands. "What were you thinking, trying to climb out on your own? You could have broken your neck."

"The attacker could have returned at any time," she pointed out. "It is my duty to protect you." She looked over his shoulder as Harlech and Beaumaris came in. "Harlech, has there been any word from Viviana?"

"None yet." Her second avoided her gaze. "My lord, if Jayr is well enough, the seigneur wishes to speak with her in the guards' hall."

Byrne stepped in front of her. "She stays here."

"I must change, but I can go," Jayr told him. "Harlech, what is this about? The attack on our lord?"

He looked miserable. "Yes."

"Lord Locksley says the Italian is behind it," Beaumaris said, looking hopeful. "'Twas his seneschal who sent our lord into the ambush. Nottingham must have been lying in wait for him there. But Nottingham denies it, and says the evidence clearly points to . . ." Beau caught Byrne's eye and fell silent.

Harlech uttered a vile curse and stalked out.

"Well?" Jayr felt impatient. "Whom does Nottingham accuse of trying to kill our lord?"

Byrne put his hand over hers. "He accuses you."

Michael put two guards on Locksley, and had Nottingham and his entourage move to the opposite side of the guards' hall. The rest of the Kyn he ordered out of the room so that he could conduct the necessary interviews.

Nottingham's guards spoke only Italian and Arabic, but Michael had learned both during his years as a warrior priest. Each testified that their master had never left the compound until summoned to the sinkhole to help with the rescue. Three of Byrne's guards reluctantly supported their statements.

"It means nothing, seigneur," Locksley said after the men were heard. "He could have sent an assassin to do the work for him."

"All of my men were here with me," Nottingham said smoothly. "Unless you have assassins for hire here at the tournament, I could not have sent anyone to kill the suzerain. Have you asked Lord Byrne's seneschal where she was? For she was not here."

"The men have already said she was in the city," Locksley said.

"She told them she was going to the city, and they saw her leave the Realm alone. That is all." Nottingham sat back in his chair. "No one can say for certain where she went."

"I find it highly unlikely that Jayr would try to kill her master," Michael said, "and then nearly die trying to save him."

"Why do you assume that she went into the sinkhole to *save* him?" Nottingham asked. "She must have heard him call out, and knew her first attack had failed."

Locksley gave him a filthy look. "You are pathetic."

"You have been very friendly with the girl," Nottingham observed sourly. "You made the arrows she used to shoot Lord Byrne. Does she serve as your assassin?"

Robin's eyes turned black, and the guards flanking him grabbed his arms. "I will cut your tongue out of your head for that."

Michael saw Jayr and Byrne enter the hall with two of their men. "Enough."

"Seigneur, I demand an apology." Nottingham shoved Skald forward. "My man has testified that the girl was the one who gave him the false message. We have the arrows she used to shoot the suzerain in the back. The outlaw has admitted that he made them for her. She was found in the pit with Lord Byrne. What other proof do you need?"

Jayr strode quickly forward. "I did not attack my lord, and I gave no message to your seneschal. If he claims that I did, he lies."

"You see, master?" Skald shook his head sadly. "I told you she would put the blame on my head. She thinks me a fool."

"You *are* a fool," Locksley said.

"No, my lord, I was made one. By her." The small man straightened his shoulders and assumed an air of dignity. "Do you know, when we came here, she did not even tell me that she was a woman? Small wonder everyone laughed when I called her brother. My lord, she used me because she knew no one would believe me."

"Stop this." Jayr looked stricken and furious. "You are lying. I never gave you any message. Tell them the truth."

Skald cringed and retreated behind Nottingham. "Protect me, my lord. Either she will kill me to silence me or the outlaw will. He followed me from the stables when I rode out to find the seigneur." The seneschal's eyes widened dramatically. "Why, I think he meant to do me harm."

Locksley began to clap his hands and laugh. "An inspired performance. Bravo."

"Was there another reason you rode out there tonight?" Nottingham asked Locksley. "To see that she had finished the job, perhaps? With the suzerain dead, and me framed for the murder, you would could have her and the Realm all to yourself." Nottingham's black eyes drifted over him. "Or did you mean to kill her *before* she could bare your sins to the world?"

Locksley wrenched his arms in, smashing together the heads of the guards holding on to him and shoving them away. He snatched the sword from the wall and started across the hall for Nottingham.

"Locksley."

Byrne got to the furious suzerain before Cyprien could, and locked an arm through his from behind. Michael knocked the sword out of his hand, caught it, and tossed it to Phillipe.

"Aedan," Locksley said, his voice a growl, his gaze fixed on Nottingham. "He is mine."

"Not yet, Rob." Byrne held on and looked over his head at Michael. "Lord Nottingham is no longer welcome in my territory, seigneur. If you wish him to live much longer, send him back to Italy."

Michael looked over at the Italian, who had drawn his sword, as had every one of his guards. "All of you will stand down now. I have promised to find out the truth behind this attack. Until I do, no one will be held responsible or made accountable for imagined crimes. Anyone who disobeys my orders will be immediately exiled from this country."

"I will not leave," Nottingham said. "My honor has been questioned, and I have the right to challenge the one responsible. Let this matter of guilt be decided in the old way, on the jousting field, with copper lances. Tonight."

"Yes. A fight to the death. Oh, sweet Christ, yes." Locksley gave him a beautiful, terrible smile. "I accept."

"I would not soil my lance with you." The Italian walked past him and stopped in front of Jayr. "I challenge you, seneschal."

Chapter 18

Byrne answered Nottingham before anyone could speak. "Your challenge is refused," he said flatly. "Pack your bags, take your heathens, and get off my land."

"I have done nothing wrong," the dark lord said, "and until honor is satisfied, I am not leaving."

"Now will you let me deal with him?" Locksley demanded as Byrne released him.

"Shut up, Rob," Byrne said. He saw the Saracens subtly re-arranging themselves around their master and knew his own men were doing the same around him and Jayr. "I rule here, Nottingham, and she belongs to me. I say that she is not fighting you."

"Seigneur." Nottingham turned to Michael. "Under Kyn law the suzerain cannot interfere, and the girl cannot refuse."

"Challenges are fought by men," Michael said calmly. "Jayr is a woman. According to Kyn custom, you cannot fight her."

"Challenge me, you fucking coward," Locksley taunted. "I'll teach you how men fight."

"Law is superior to custom," Nottingham insisted, ignoring Locksley. "Men of rank are obligated to accept any challenge. She calls herself seneschal, does she not? That is a man's rank. She has a man's form and muscle, wears a man's clothing, and carries a man's weapons. She trains and fights with men. She holds rank over every man in the Realm save one." He gave Jayr a smug look. "In what way is she a woman?"

"If you need that explained to you, pal," Alexandra drawled, "you're dumber than your jacket." She came around the table to stand beside Michael. To him she said, "Jayr's shoulder was dislocated and is still healing. She's in no condition to fight anyone."

"He knows that," Locksley said, "or he wouldn't have challenged her."

"Jayr only needs one arm," Harlech said suddenly. "She's better with a lance than any man in the Realm. She'd skewer him on the first pass."

"I'll skewer him now," Locksley promised, "if someone will give me back my bloody damn sword."

Everyone began speaking at the same time, with Michael trying to sort out the different arguments. Byrne felt indifferent to the squabbling. Laws and customs didn't matter. The Italian would not touch a hair on Jayr's head, and if he tried Byrne would relieve him of his limbs.

As more of his men joined in the arguments and the noise swelled to a roar, Byrne decided to take Jayr back to his chambers. They were both exhausted, and he wanted to go to sleep as he had last night, with her in his arms. As he reached for her hand, he discovered that she had moved away from him and now stood before the Italian.

Byrne swore and went after her.

"Lord Nottingham," Jayr said quietly just as Byrne came up behind her. "I accept your challenge."

"No."

Byrne's voice silenced every other one in the hall.

"No, lass," he said, turning her around with gentle hands. She gave him a look so solemn it almost relieved him, until he saw the wounded pride in her eyes. Of course, she was accepting to save face. He could help her. "You heard what Lady Alexandra said. You're not fit. You cannae be jousting with that arm."

"I carry on the right, not the left," she said. "The challenge was made to me, my lord. It is my honor being tested, not yours. I will fight him."

She had the courage of a hundred men, his Jayr. "I know how you feel—"

"No, my lord, you don't. You cannot decide this for me." She looked at Cyprien. "What Lord Nottingham says is true. I am a seneschal. I know my duty to my lord and my place among the

Kyn. I have never relied on my sex to excuse me from what must be done by someone of my rank, no matter how dangerous it was. I will not start now."

"Jayr," Cyprien said kindly, "think carefully on what you say."

"I understand how Lord Nottingham feels better than anyone," she explained. "I have also been accused of terrible things. Like him, my honor as seneschal demands that I answer those accusations. Like him, I have only my word to offer as proof. That is not enough, obviously, so I will answer with my lance."

"If that is how you feel," Cyprien said, "then no one will interfere. The challenge has been made and accepted. The Kyn will bear witness when you meet Lord Nottingham on the field of honor."

Byrne stared at him in amazement. "You name yourself my friend? He will kill her."

"Aedan." Jayr's hand curled around his. "This is how it must be done. Trust me. Have faith in me."

"So I may sit and watch as you are slain?" He flung her hand away from him. "You cannae do this. I forbid it. *I forbid you.*"

Misery darkened her eyes. "Forgive me, my lord, but I must."

Jayr had never defied him, Byrne realized. She had always bent herself to his will and had carried out his plans and wishes without question. She had been an extension of himself, one he had relied on without thinking. She had always put his needs before her own. Even now she apologized to him, as if defending her honor might inconvenience him.

He knew, suddenly, how to make her obey. "I am your master, and you are sworn to me above all others. I order you to refuse this challenge."

No harder gauntlet could have been thrown. Their love, still new and untried, might not sway her, but the blood bond between them, of lord and seneschal, could not be broken.

And then, so quietly that he almost didn't hear the words, she shattered it. "I will not, my lord."

"So be it." His heart as heavy as a stone, Byrne turned to address his men. "Before the tournament began, I asked the seigneur to choose a new suzerain for the Realm. As of the new year, I will rule here no longer. Until that day, I am still suzerain. Vows made to me will be kept."

Harlech took a step forward. "No, my lord. For God's sake, do not—"

"You vowed by bond of blood to serve me and my house, and to obey me in all things," Byrne said to Jayr. "By refusing to follow my orders, you've broken that vow, and so you've released me from my obligations to you."

She took a step back, and Nottingham swore under his breath.

He shifted his gaze to Cyprien. "Seigneur, I call on you as witness, and declare that this female has broken faith with me. She no longer holds position in my household or rank among the Kyn. Her weapons and possessions will be confiscated, her privileges revoked."

"No," Jayr whispered, horrified.

To her, Byrne said, "Jayr of Bannock, I discharge you from my household. From this day forth, you no longer serve me as seneschal."

"Byrne can't really do that to Jayr, can he?" Alex asked Michael as he accompanied her from the hall to the infirmary. "I mean, just for saying no to him?"

"He is determined to keep her from fighting Nottingham," Michael said sadly. "Unfortunately, he saw discharging her as the only way."

"I don't get the rules here. Jayr could fight the Iceman as long as she was a seneschal. What difference does it make now that she's unemployed?"

"She has no rank, and only men—or persons—of rank may be challenged," Michael told her.

Phillipe chimed in. "Being a seneschal is not merely a job, Alexandra. It is much like entering into a marriage or having a child. One makes a lifetime commitment to one's master."

"Okay." A thought occurred to her. "But now that she's a free agent, can't someone else pick her and make her a seneschal again? I mean, if all she needs is the job title . . ." The men stopped walking and stared at her. "What did I say?"

"Locksley would not discharge Will," Phillipe said to Cyprien. "He wishes too much to fight Nottingham himself."

Michael nodded. "Who else among us has no seneschal?"

"Halkirk," Phillipe said. "His man was killed two months ago during a skirmish with the Brethren in Marseilles. He came here to choose a replacement." He grimaced. "And he asked Jayr to make some recommendations."

"Find Jayr." Michael turned to her. "Alexandra, I must go and speak to Lord Halkirk."

"No problem." She waved them away. "I'm going to go clean up the infirmary. See you guys later."

Alex finished an hour later in the infirmary, and packed up her medical case before she left for their rooms. It had been a long night, and for once the prospect of going to sleep didn't scare the daylights out of her. She felt tired but happy. She'd have to set an alarm; she had a feeling she was going to crash hard the minute her head touched a pillow.

Something banged behind a closed door as she passed it, and she heard someone shouting inside.

"You idiot."

At first she thought the door was made of white wood, until she looked closer and saw the frost-covered surface. Some of the tiny crystals fell as a heavy weight slammed into the door from the other side.

"Master, please!"

Alex put her hand in her pocket and used her jacket to force the latch. The door groaned and swung in, dislodging a row of icicles that rained down on her head and shoulders.

Inside the chamber Nottingham held Skald by the throat suspended above the floor, and was using the seneschal's battered face as a punching bag. Blood gushed from the small man's nose and mouth.

"Someone need a house call?" Alex asked as she set down her medical case and took out her tranquilizer gun.

The Italian barely glanced at her. "This is not your concern, my lady," he said through clenched teeth. "Please remove yourself."

"Stop hitting the little guy or I'll sedate your ass." When Nottingham ignored her and continued pounding Skald, she loaded a cartridge of nickel sulfate hexhydrate solution, and aimed for the back of the Italian's neck. "Last chance. *Nottingham.* Put him down."

Nottingham threw Skald against the wall, waited for him to land, and then strode over and began kicking him.

Alex fired. The tranquilizer dart sank into the base of Nottingham's skull. He stopped, reached back to claw at it, and then gave her an incredulous look.

"What is this?"

"Time for you to take a nap," she said, watching as he fell sideways over a chair, crushing it as he went down.

Skald pushed himself up on his hands and knees and vomited blood all over the frozen floor before collapsing on it and going still.

"Terrific." Alex put the gun back in her case and went to the seneschal, rolling him over. "Skald, can you hear me? Look at me."

He could only open one eye. "My thanks, my lady." He turned his head and coughed to clear the blood from his mouth.

Alex wiped his face clean and quickly realigned his nose before the cartilage healed crooked. He gasped.

"Sorry, I know that hurt. I've got to check you for internal injuries." She opened his tunic and gently palpated his neck, chest, and belly. Other than extensive bruising, which was already beginning to fade, she found no broken bones. "He didn't mess you up too much. You're going to be okay."

"What did you do to my lord?" Skald asked, eyeing Nottingham's motionless body.

"I shot him with a tranquilizer dart. He'll be asleep for a couple of hours." She stood up. "Let's get you over to the infirmary. Can you walk?"

"I cannot leave my lord like this," Skald said. "Someone might harm him. I must stay with him until he wakes. My lady, please, could you bring me a wet cloth for my face?"

Alex went into the bathroom and soaked a washcloth before bringing it out to him. "You sure you don't want to come with me? He might decide to give you another beating when he wakes up."

"No, thank you, my lady." Skald scrubbed his face with the

cloth. "I am certain that when my lord wakes he will regret taking out his temper on me. His rage came from being unable to avenge himself on Lord Locksley."

"What's his deal with Robin?" Alex asked. When Skald hesitated to reply, she added, "You can tell me. I'm probably the only unbiased person here, and I might be able to help straighten things out."

"I begged my lord to let the truth be known." Skald looked miserable. " 'Tis why he was beating me." He swallowed. "My lord is English, not Italian. Before he took the name of Ganelon of Florence, he was known as Guy of Guisbourne."

Alex's jaw dropped. "Maybe you got hit in the head harder than I thought."

" 'Tis true, my lady, although as Lord Guisbourne he never committed the crimes attributed to him. His half brother, a nameless bastard, replaced him as the master of Sherwood after the Lady Marian died."

Skald told her a different version of the story of Guy, Marian, and Robin, explaining how learning of Marian's death in childbirth had driven Guy out of his head with grief.

"My lord's mother long wished to take control of Sherwood. She seized the chance brought on by my lord's derangement and had him locked in the dungeons. From that day his bastard half brother Ganelon, who was much beloved by his mother, became Lord Sherwood."

Alex looked at Nottingham. "If he's really Guy of Guisbourne, why didn't anyone—why didn't *Robin*—recognize him?"

"During his human life my lord feared assassination, and so always used his half brother to take his place in public," Skald admitted. "In fact, my master and Lord Locksley never actually met in person. My lord's mother dared not kill him, lest his men find out and expose her bastard son as an impostor, but she intended to keep him imprisoned for the rest of his life."

"Like *The Man in the Iron Mask*." When Skald gave her a blank look, she shook her head. "Doesn't matter. Go on."

"There is not much more to tell," the seneschal admitted. "When my lord escaped the dungeons, the hateful crimes his brother had committed in his name forced him to flee England and never return."

"So it was this half brother, the real Ganelon, who started the *jardin* wars, and killed all the women and old folks, and got himself and everyone in Sherwood executed?" Skald nodded, and Alex rubbed her head. "This is giving me a migraine. Okay. If all this is true, then why didn't your master come clean after his brother was killed?"

"I cannot say, my lady. I think my lord felt partially responsible for his half brother's evil. It is why we lived such a reclusive life in Florence. When we were forced to flee he chose America because he hoped few here would know of or remember his family." Skald's expression tightened. "So many things we did not know before we came. Had I known he still lived . . ."

"Who lived?"

He blinked. "Lord Locksley, of course. My master was enraged to discover that he was given a *jardin* here. He will never know peace until he avenges Lady Marian's death."

"Robin didn't kill her," Alex stated. "Guy raping her and getting pregnant did. Or did his brother do that, too?"

"My lord worshiped Lady Marian. He would never have forced himself on her." Skald met her gaze. "'Twas Lord Locksley who got her with child."

Alex started to argue with him, but stopped as she remembered how Nottingham had looked at Locksley in the hall. "So that's why he challenged Jayr. He thinks Locksley's in love with her, and killing her would be the perfect payback for Marian. Boy, does he need an update." She gave Skald a wry look and added, "Byrne and Jayr are the ones who are in love. Locksley is just a friend."

"I see." The seneschal frowned. "That does change things."

"What's Guy the Disguised going to say when he finds out you told me all this stuff?" Alex asked.

"I think it will take a great burden off his shoulders, my lady," Skald replied absently.

"Michael does need to know about this before these guys kill each other." She picked up her medical case. "I'll tell him exactly what you told me."

"You cannot go yet, my lady." Skald took something out of his tunic and pointed it at her. "For I need more time now. This land is my bloodright, and I will have it."

Alex's eyes widened. "Hey, that's not a toy—" The gun fired, and she looked down at the dart in her chest. "You little bastard."

As she fell, Alex heard him say, "Not after tonight, my lady."

Michael discovered that he was too late to stop Halkirk from interfering.

"Of course I took Jayr as my seneschal the moment she offered to pledge herself to me," the suzerain said lazily. "She's tireless, faithful, and damned handy with a blade. She's kept the Realm running smoothly for centuries. She gets along with the men. She'll be a great asset to my household."

Michael held on to his patience. "She is interested in reacquiring rank only so she can accept Nottingham's challenge."

"I gave her leave to accept it," Halkirk said, shrugging. "I've seen her ride before, and she's never been beaten. You needn't worry, seigneur. After tonight that cold bastard can spend eternity making blizzards for Beelzebub."

Michael left Halkirk and met Phillipe in the corridor.

"Jayr has gone to rest in her chambers," Phillipe said. "She intends to ride against Nottingham tonight."

"Where is Byrne?"

"I could not find him." His seneschal looked as frustrated and tired as Michael felt. "Alexandra has not returned from the infirmary. Should I fetch her?"

"No, she is probably caught up in something. I will go and pry her away from her instruments." Michael looked at the sunshine pouring through the windows. "You should rest, my friend. We have a few hours before the joust. I will think of something."

Michael walked down to the infirmary, which he found empty. He tracked Alexandra's scent out of the room and followed it to the guest quarters. It ended at Nottingham's chamber door, which had not been secured.

"Alexandra?"

The scent of aniseed flooded his nose as soon as he entered

the dark room. Beneath it he smelled lavender, blood, and death.

A man lay on the floor, a sword buried in his neck.

"Nottingham?" Michael went to kneel beside him. A pool of blood surrounded the Italian, whose head had been severed from his neck by the blade. Propped up against the wall near him sat Alexandra, unconscious, a tranquilizer dart in her chest.

"She is very kind, your lady," a voice said from behind him. "I will remember that."

Michael drew his dagger and turned, but not in time to avoid the dart that pierced his side. He fell on top of Nottingham's body.

"Rest now, my lord," Skald said, smiling as he took hold of Michael's limp arm. "All will be well."

Chapter 19

B yrne locked himself in the Realm's business office, the last
place anyone would think to look for him, and spent most
of the morning making the necessary arrangements. As soon as
the sun set he would collect Jayr and leave the Realm in
Cyprien's capable hands. Once they arrived at the remote cabin
he had purchased for himself in the Carolina mountains, Byrne
would settle things between them.

Jayr knew him better than anyone; she would understand.

He completed his work and left the office, but felt no desire
to seek his empty bed. After what he had said to Jayr he
doubted that she would be sleeping either. No, her wounded
pride would probably have her clearing out her chamber and
packing up her belongings. He would go to her and explain so
that she would not be tempted to do something foolish, like
leave the Realm on her own.

Byrne found her door locked against him this time, but he
had expected that. He opened it with the key he had found in
the office and let himself inside.

The curtains blocked the sun from the room, but Jayr had
left her computer monitor on, and its glow shed thin light over
her desk. Byrne could see her curled up in her narrow bed in the
corner and went to switch off the machine. She had left something written on the screen, and out of idle curiosity he read it.

> *How truthful may I write of this,*
> *The want of love, the love I hide?*
> *My passion drowned by cowardice*
> *Yet evermore by hope revived.*
> *You do not want me*

However much I need.
You will not see me
However much I bleed.
Thus I dwell in silence, for
I have made well my prison
loving you, evermore.

The poem continued, and as Byrne read on he felt his chest
grow hollow. She wrote of longing as if it tormented her, an
agony she believed she had inflicted on herself as punishment
for daring to love. The last verse seemed to shriek her despair:

How are we to live, my lord,
ever together, forever apart?
The night between us poised, a sword,
forged and edged in my cinder heart.
I cannot have you,
however much I long.
I cannot leave you,
this bond too strong.
Thus I go on as I have before,
burning in Eden, with you,
evermore.

A bound journal lay next to the computer, and Byrne opened
it, knowing he was likely intruding on her most private thoughts
but hoping to find some happier sentiment. Inside he found it
dated by the year, and filled with a series of sketches. Jayr had
drawn him again and again, and had rendered his face from
every angle, detailed with startling accuracy. Somehow she had
transformed his barbaric visage into the face of a proud, handsome warrior. This was how she saw him, this noble savage.

He flipped through the pages, and where there were not
sketches his name appeared repeatedly written with flourishes
and scrolls, as if it were precious to her. He looked up on the
shelf above the computer, where a long row of other journals
stood. He took one down at random and found more sketches,
all of him. Aedan mac Byrne sitting before a fire. In the guards'
hall. Standing on the battlements. He took down another, and

then another. His face and form filled every page, his name the only words recorded. The journals spanned the last twenty-five years.

Slowly he put back everything as she had left it. She loved him, of that he had no doubt, but she had loved him for far longer than he had ever suspected. No one could pay such a tribute out of liking or admiration. No, Jayr had suffered with her love, had endured it in silence, aching and burning with it, hiding all when she was with him, then returning to her lonely chamber to draw his face over and over, year after year, as if he were the only thing of importance in her world.

How could he ever be worthy of her? Love her as she deserved to be loved?

Byrne went to stand over her bed. The long, loose tunic in which she slept looked worn. It had been made for a man much larger than her, and that puzzled him until he recognized it as one of his own that he had discarded.

Even in her sleep she wrapped herself up in him. Bitterly he regretted that he had no poetry, no soft words to give to her. All he knew was the need to be one with her, to fill her as she filled his heart.

As he watched her he began absently unfastening his own tunic. The soft sounds of his clothes dropping to the floor stirred her to turn over.

"Aedan," she murmured, still asleep.

Byrne knew he should wake her, talk to her, explain what he had done and ask why she had never told him. Instead he pulled back the covers and slipped into her bed, taking her into his arms. His old tunic slid up, baring her from the waist down, and the need to be inside her surged through him, trampling his guilt and turning his cock into a rigid spike. Before he could think he had eased her left thigh over his right leg. His hand cupped her, and some part of him felt with wonder the soft, downy new hair that abraded his palm. He stroked her, coaxing silky fluid from her tight slit.

"Aedan," she murmured again, pushing against his hand, seeking relief.

Byrne felt an unfamiliar weight against his chest and tugged up his old tunic. Two small, full breasts pushed out from Jayr's body, begging for his mouth.

The skin of his cock's head stretched, tight and painful, as blood and need engorged him. He guided it to her with a shaking hand, hissing as they touched and her cool, sweet honey spread over him.

Jayr's eyes opened, first to slits, then wide. "Aedan." She braced her hands against his chest as if to push him away, and then as her breasts jiggled she looked down, aghast. "What has happened to me?"

"I cannae say, lass." He bent and brushed his mouth over her nipple. "But 'tis beautiful."

"Alexandra's potion worked. She's made me into a woman." Jayr met his gaze. "Why are you here? You don't want me."

Suddenly, inexplicably, rage boiled inside him. All of the lonely years. All of the women, meaningless, pointless. All of the longing and denying and watching and wishing and never knowing, never suspecting for a moment that she loved him, and had kept that love from him.

"I dinnae want you?" Byrne shoved himself into her, forcing her to take every inch in that single stroke. "I dinnae love you? You meant nothing to me? This is what you thought all this time?"

Her nails sank into his flesh. "My lord—"

He clamped his hand over her mouth. "I read your sweet words. I know what you have done. You say you are mine but you have kept yourself from me." He drew back and forced himself into her again. "I wanted you. I love you. By God, I could kill you."

Tears spilled over his fingers, scalding him like liquid copper. He slid his hand to twine in her hair, and touched his forehead to hers.

"Lass." What was he doing to her?

"Kill me, then," she whispered. "It would be a mercy, for I cannot leave you."

"Never." He looked into her wet eyes. "I will never let you go."

Her sorrow dissolved his rage, gentling his hands and melting their bodies together. He pushed past her resistance and into her, taking her mouth with his tongue as he worked his penis inside her, possessing all of her spaces, filling her with the dance of flesh to the symphony of hunger. She wept and struck at him and buried her fangs in his shoulder and pleaded for her release. He forced her to his will, punishing her and wooing her with his body, keeping her from coming until she was mindless and thrashing beneath him.

He wrenched out of her, sliding down her body, and brought her, sopping wet and swollen, to his mouth. A single stroke of his tongue over her jewel and she came, her body locked, her hands twisted in his hair, words of love mixed with sobs pouring from her.

Byrne came up beside her, turning her to him, holding her as he slid into her. He pressed her face against his chest, and groaned as she tightened over him, milking the pleasure and the seed from him in long, slow pulls.

He kept her there, joined to him, and held her until sleep claimed them both, unaware of the door opening, or the man who came to stand over them.

Robin of Locksley looked down at the lovers in silence, his hands becoming fists and then hands again.

"So be it."

He reached down, pulled the coverlet over them, and left as silently as he had entered.

The sign that dangled from the doorknob of room 413 of the EconoMotel in Dothan, Alabama, read, DO NOT DISTURB. It had hung there ever since the couple staying in the room had checked in.

The floor maid saw it when she pushed her heavy cart down from room 412, and considered reporting the problem to the desk manager. She hadn't been able to get into the room to clean or change the linens for days. She put an ear to the door, heard voices and the television, and sighed. If they wanted to use old towels and sleep on old sheets over and over, that was their business.

Inside room 413, Viviana put down the telephone and spoke to the man reclined on one of the twin beds. "Beaumaris says that Nottingham is to fight Jayr. Lord Byrne ordered her to refuse his challenge, and when she did not, he discharged her from his service. She is sworn to Lord Halkirk now so that she may fight."

"You see? The minute you and I leave the Realm, the place falls to pieces." Rain muted the television set, but watched as the latest episode of *Top Design* continued. "We could wait to see if she kills him. That would be rather convenient."

"We could." She sat down on the bed next to him. "I do not wish to. Jayr is my friend. I miss Harlech." She took the remote from his hand and switched off the set. "You know that you miss Farlae more than you lust after Todd Oldham."

"I am only infatuated with Todd's overbite." He regarded her gravely. "Vivi, if we return Guy could very well expose us both. The seigneur would be within his rights to demand our heads."

She nodded and stared at the hands she held folded tightly in her lap. "I miss Harlech," she said, unable to offer any other reasonable argument.

"Farlae will have moved into my rooms," Rain said, fiddling with the remote. "By now he's probably contemplating painting the walls black and covering my furnishings with navy linen." He gave her an indignant look. "He would do it, too, just to spite me."

"Some things are worth risking a beheading," she said softly. "Should I call the lobby, then, and tell them we will need a cab?"

"Immediately."

Jayr checked her mount before strapping cushioning pads to the horse's front and hindquarters. For this final practice she decided to use the leather trappers, which were lighter than the heavy metal peytral, flanchards, and cruppers she would use to protect her mount during the joust.

Her movements echoed in the barn, which, aside from the stabled horses, was deserted. Harlech likely had ordered the men to clear out to give her time alone to prepare and think. Lord Halkirk had already told her he did not expect her to begin her duties until after the tournament. Somehow she would have to explain her change of circumstances to him. He would understand. He had probably accepted her as his seneschal only out of pity, or only because he thought she would not live long enough to serve him.

She had everything to live for now. Aedan loved her.

Aedan had also discharged her over the challenge, and had kept from her his plans to give up the Realm. She still felt the sting of betrayal over his actions, but she would not allow herself to regret giving her heart and body to him. He had done what he had out of love for her, to protect her.

She shouldn't have left him alone in her bed, but she had needed time to think. Being with him had been lusty and primitive and shocking; it had also been tender and powerful and comforting. Through every moment, every touch, every whisper, she had felt the strength of their bond. Not as master and seneschal, but as man and woman, key and lock, seed and field.

Loved and beloved.

"How fares the arm?" Robin of Locksley asked as he came into the barn.

"It is not as loose as I would like," Jayr said, fitting the horse's head with a brown leather shaffron and buckling it to the crinet covering the mane. "But I can hold my shield and the reins, and that is enough."

Locksley picked up her practice shield, a rectangular square of metal save for the bouche, the channel on the top right side where her lance would rest. He traced some of the scars in its surface.

"You are almost as tall as I am, and we have a similar build," he said casually. "In the saddle, with helm and armor, no one could tell the difference between us."

"Probably not," she agreed, tightening a strap.

"I can ride against Nottingham in your place."

Jayr's fingers stilled as she stared at the fringe of black mane under the edge of the crinet. "You think I will lose, too?"

"I think he will cheat." He turned her to face him. "Let me do this— No," he said, pressing his finger to her mouth when she would have spoken. "I was there. I listened to all the arguments, all the proud words being tossed back and forth. They mean nothing when you ride onto that field. There, the only thing that counts is ability. He has deceit and cunning, and two good arms."

"I have truth and honor," Jayr said. "And one good arm. Although I am in need of a practice opponent." She checked the sky, now purple with twilight, and took down one of the wooden lances from the practice racks. "Will you ride against me, my lord?" She tossed the lance to him.

Locksley caught it. "I should knock you over the head, lock you up, and take your place anyway."

"You could try." She took down another lance and flashed across the barn to stand behind him. "But you will have to catch me first."

He looked over his shoulder, his exasperation plain. "You cannot do that on a horse."

She tapped his lance with her own. "Let me show you what I *can* do."

The sound of voices shouting in Arabic woke Harlech, who stumbled out of bed and pulled on his trousers before staggering out into the hall to see the source of the commotion.

Three of Nottingham's Saracens ran past him, followed by Farlae and Beaumaris. He trotted after them, catching up with his men outside the hall to the guests' quarters, where a crowd of drowsy Kyn milled about in confusion.

"What the devil is happening?" Harlech demanded.

"Someone has done us a favor," Farlae told him, "and cut off Nottingham's head."

"They've killed the seigneur and his lady, too," someone called out.

Harlech waded through the guests to Nottingham's quarters. There he saw Skald and the Saracen guards standing in a circle around three bodies. The seneschal pried a bloodied sword out of his master's throat and examined it.

"I have seen someone using this," Skald said, turning it over and wiping the blood from the hilt. " 'Twas in the lists, I think." He frowned and thought for a moment before turning and seeing Harlech. "You, there." He held up the blade. "Whose sword is this?"

Harlech recognized it at once, but he had no intentions of telling the little man that. "I cannot say."

"The lord's girl bested me two days ago with that blade," one of the guests' men said.

"Does this weapon belong to Jayr?" Skald asked Harlech politely.

"It does, but obviously it was stolen by another," Harlech said quickly. "Jayr would never do this."

"Just as her arrows were stolen and used to shoot Lord Byrne," Skald said. "What an unfortunate coincidence. I will relate this to my men." He rattled off something to the guards in rapid Italian.

The Saracens muttered among themselves, and their captain gave Harlech an ugly look.

"We will find Lord Byrne and get to the bottom of this." He waved Beaumaris and Farlae inside. "Take the bodies to the infirmary and store them in the chill room."

Skald looked at the crowd of Kyn outside. "My lords and ladies, did any of you see someone enter my master's chambers earlier?"

No one said anything, and then one of the women spoke. "I saw Lord Byrne's seneschal leave this hall as I came back to my rooms this morning. She looked . . . well, angry."

"Thank you, my lady," Skald said. "Was anyone else seen near these chambers?"

No one replied.

Skald turned to Harlech. "Where is Jayr?"

"You cannot condemn her for walking down a hall," Harlech protested. "It proves nothing."

"My master was murdered in his sleep, with a sword that belongs to her," the seneschal said calmly. "She was the only one seen near here at the time. She lost her place in this household over my master's challenge. Who else had more cause to hate him or wish him dead?"

"This is wrong," Harlech said. "I know Jayr. I know she would not do this. She is being framed."

"By whom? Who would do such a terrible thing to her?" When Harlech didn't answer, Skald nodded. "I ask you again: Where is Jayr?"

"I saw her walk out to the stables, but half an hour ago," one of the guests said.

Skald issued orders in Italian to the guard and pushed past Harlech. The Saracens followed.

"Wait. *Wait.*" When they ignored him, Harlech swore. "Beaumaris, assemble the men. Farlae, find Lord Byrne."

Chapter 20

Alexandra woke up with a dry mouth, a throbbing head, and a sheet covering her face. She shoved it away and sat up to find herself on a gurney next to a shelf unit stacked with bagged blood. Next to her were two other bodies draped with sheets: one white, the other soaked on one end with dark red blood.

The memory of Skald shooting her came rushing back, and she rolled to her feet, hurrying over to yank back the blood-stained sheet. Nottingham, his decapitated head placed neatly on his severed neck, stared up at the ceiling.

"*Chérie.*"

She turned and gaped at Michael as he pulled the sheet away and sat up. "Are you hurt?" She went to him and looked all over for wounds.

"No, I am well. Skald shot me with one of your darts when I came to find you; I think that is all." He looked over her shoulder. "Where are we?"

"In the refrigerated room. He must have killed Nottingham and brought us all in here." She strode over to the door, saw there was no inside handle, and pushed at it. It didn't move. "We're locked in. Why would they lock us in? Didn't anyone bother to check for a pulse?"

"I cannot say, *chérie.*" Michael came and tried the door, and then looked around the room. "There must be something we can use to force it open."

Alex went over to cover Nottingham's body. Whoever had decapitated it had done it with one blow. She closed his eyes, and felt something touch her arm. When she saw it was a hand trying to grab her, and Nottingham's eyes opened, she screamed.

"Alexandra?"

"Jesus, Michael, he's not dead." She slid her hand under Nottingham's neck. "Skald didn't cut all the way through his neck. His spinal cord is intact. I can't believe it. He's still alive."

Michael came to stand beside her. "His head is almost completely severed from his body. He cannot live like this."

"With a little luck he won't have to." She scanned the room. "Get me five of those suture kits over there while I look for a knife."

Michael gave Nottingham a doubtful look. "Even you cannot repair such a wound."

"I can try. He's lost so much blood that nothing has healed over." She ripped open a cardboard box, looked inside, and dropped it before reaching for another. "Hurry up, and put on some gloves from that box over there."

He brought the kits over and set them on the gurney he had vacated. "Why do I need gloves?"

"Because they help you grip better." She found a small box of copper-coated scalpels and an intravenous kit. "You're going to be my nurse."

Alexandra gloved, took out her penlight, and carefully probed the massive neck wound to assess the damage.

"Point of impact was the larynx, part of which is gone, and the rest is smashed all to hell. The sword severed the neck muscles, the trachea, the esophagus, and all the major blood vessels." She shifted the light and peered. "Skald doesn't have much of a swing. The blade bounced off one of the cervical vertebra. The axis, I bet. That's the one that forms the pivot so the head can turn." She straightened and saw that Nottingham's eyes had shifted. "Oh, God, Michael. He's staring at me."

"He can still see and hear you."

"Did they bring my case in here?" She looked around. "I've got to knock him out for this."

Michael searched through the room. "I do not see it." He went to the gurney. "Lord Nottingham, my *sygkenis* will operate on you to try to repair the wound in your neck. You must go into the dreamlands. I will call you back when it is done."

Nottingham closed his eyes and didn't reopen them.

"He's doing that trance thing you did when I operated on you," Alex said. "You call it going to dreamland?"

"Dreamlands," he corrected. He watched her rig the IV and prepare an impromptu instrument tray. "How will you do this?"

"I'll start with repairing the blood vessels, and then the trachea and the esophagus," she said, tugging off her jacket. "I'll work my way out from there, and once I get to the muscles we'll start the IV. You're going to assist me."

He eyed the horrific wound. "Alexandra, I do not know the first thing about surgery."

"Think of this as a crash course. Now listen." As she rolled up her sleeves she went through the instrument tray with him, naming everything on it. "When I ask for something, put it in the hand I hold out. If I tell you to do something, no matter what it is, do it." She glanced at him. "This is going to be ugly, messy, and fast. You ready?"

He nodded.

She held out her hand. "Clamp."

If anyone in medical school had ever suggested to Alex that she might someday attempt to reattach someone's head to his body, she would have laughed herself into an appendectomy. A wound as ghastly as Nottingham's would have killed any human being instantly.

But as she reconnected the severed ends of the blood vessels, Alex realized that the Kyn pathogen did more than mutate human beings; it preserved them under the worst possible circumstances. Kyn could live without oxygen, nourishment, or comfort for months, even years. No microorganism, bacteria, or virus could survive in their bloodstream; the pathogen killed everything foreign to the body. All it wanted was human blood, which passed undigested through the Kyn's drastically altered digestive systems and sustained it.

Vampirism for virtual immortality.

Alex couldn't follow a single procedure to repair Nottingham's neck wound; she had to lump together ten different and separate reconstructive surgeries. She was working with the barest, most basic supplies, which didn't help. But as she slowly progressed outward her work held, giving her more confidence. By the time she reached the neck muscles, she felt sure Nottingham had a fighting chance of recovery.

"Start the IV," she told Michael, "and keep your fingers crossed."

"I cannot start the IV if my fingers are crossed," he said, offering her a charming smile when she glared. "You did say to do whatever you told me to, no matter what it was."

"I can still kick you while I'm operating," she told him. "Remember that."

Michael removed the clamp on the IV tube, and blood fed down into Nottingham's arm. As Alex rejoined the neck muscles the interior repairs she had made began to seal over. She had to work at top speed to suture the epidermis together before it, too, healed. Feeling a little dizzy, she stepped back to survey her patient.

"Holy shit," she breathed. "I think I did it."

A half-inch channel of new, pink skin enveloped the outer sutures and formed a ring around the outside of Nottingham's throat. At the same time, he inhaled, his chest lifting as his lungs filled. Alex listened for any wheezing or whistling that would indicate blockage of the trachea, but his breathing sounds were normal.

She wouldn't break out the champagne just yet. "Okay, let's wake him up."

Michael put a hand on Nottingham's chest. "Ganelon of Florence. Lord Nottingham. It is over. Come back to us."

Nothing happened.

Michael called his name several times more, with the same disheartening results. "Sometimes Kyn retreat to the dreamlands and for reasons of their own never return. I do not think he is coming back, Alexandra."

"Bullshit. I didn't just spend three hours stitching him back together for nothing." She remembered what Skald had told her, and although the idea made her cringe inside, it explained why he wasn't responding to Michael. "Let me try. And don't get pissed off about this." She leaned over her patient. "Guy of Guisbourne, rise and shine."

Nottingham opened his eyes, blinked, and stared at her.

"*What* did you call him?" Michael asked, his anger flooding the room with the scent of burning roses.

"He's not the same Guy," Alex said. "The Guisbourne you all hate was his half brother. He took his place, had him locked up, and then ran him out of England. This Guy never fought in the *jardin* wars. He was hiding out in Italy. Skald told me the whole story."

"Before or after he shot you?" Michael's eyes, half amber now, pinned her with a glance. "Very well. Let him speak for himself."

"He can't." Alex faced her patient. "Your larynx was completely crushed, Guy. What little the sword left wasn't enough for me to rebuild. I'm sorry."

Nottingham put a hand to his throat, feeling the new skin, and then stared at the ceiling.

"What difference does that make?" Michael demanded.

"A lot. No larynx, no voice," Alex said flatly. "He'll never speak again."

Byrne woke near sunset and reached for Jayr, only to find himself alone in her bed. On her pillow lay a sketch of a stalk of heather entwined with a tansy flower. He rolled onto his back and looked at it for several minutes before he rose and dressed.

Beneath the flowers she had written his name and hers. *Aedan and Jayr.* She had also written another word. *Evermore.*

Byrne went up to the battlements to look out one last time at his lands. Although central Florida was nothing like his birthplace in the Scottish Highlands, the two shared a nameless, untamed quality about them that even the cement and steel of the modern era could not completely mask. He would miss the sweet smell of the orange blossoms in the air when the groves bloomed, and the quiet lapping of the lake's water against its pebbled banks.

Two riders drew his attention as they rode out to the practice field. From this distance they almost looked like twins. Then Byrne recognized one of the horses as Jayr's favorite mount and began to swear slowly and viciously.

Byrne did not have his lover's speed, but he reached the practice field just as the two completed their initial pass.

Amusement colored Jayr's voice as she called out to her opponent, "You do know that you are to *strike* me with your lance, my lord. Not use it to fan me."

The man removed his helm, and Byrne saw it was Locksley.

"Strike you?" Rob echoed. "Do you mean give your shoulder as tender a caress as you did mine?"

Their laughter stopped Byrne as nothing else might have. He had already humiliated her before the Kyn, stripping her of her rank and casting her out of his service. He had come to her bed without an invitation, and had exercised his dominance over her there. Now here she was practicing as if she still meant to ride against Nottingham tonight. Perhaps it was not what it seemed. Perhaps she had come simply to ride with a man she trusted and whom they both called friend.

Byrne stepped back behind the cover of a root-bound ficus tree to watch the next pass, and saw Jayr shift at the last possible moment, avoiding Locksley's lance as her own dipped sharply, catching him under the elbow and tilting up to unseat him. Locksley crashed to the ground, knocking off his helm in the process. His mount rode on, leaving Rob to drag himself up from the ground and slap at the dirt and grass covering him.

She could have beaten Nottingham, Byrne thought.

"Unfair," Locksley shouted, moving to retrieve his helm. He kicked the remnants of his wooden lance, which had snapped in half. "That nag has been trained to throw her rider at the sight of an uncertain lance."

"If that were true," Jayr called back, "she would have bucked you off back at the stables."

Locksley jerked upright, his laughter abruptly cut off. His hands became hooks at his throat, and Byrne saw them tear at a bright streak coiled there. Locksley's body soared straight up into the air and then dangled, twisting and kicking.

The copper noose around his neck tugged him ever higher into the rambling branches of the black oak.

Jayr wheeled her mount around and jumped the tilt barrier, hurtling toward Locksley with reckless speed.

Byrne saw a blur slice through the air. "Jayr! To the right!"

Jayr veered, but not in time. A gleaming lance rammed through her and knocked her backward over the horse's hindquarters. She landed directly under Locksley, pinned to the ground by the lance, the end of it gleaming as it bobbed.

Byrne ran until he reached her, and then dropped to his knees. The lance, made of copper, impaled her on the right side. Was she dead? Someone had surely killed her.

"My lord." Jayr looked up at him. She was not dead; she lived, she breathed. "Robin."

Byrne looked up. Locksley had been lynched with a copper-bound cable, and still writhed furiously as he tried to free himself. "I will cut him down." He put his arm across her abdomen and wrapped his other hand around the lance. "I must take this out of you first."

Fire exploded in Byrne's back, knocking him away from her. A small, hard boot drove into his ribs, flipping him over to roll down the incline. He grabbed handfuls of the grass to stop his fall and tried to rise, collapsing again when the blade in his back twisted. His chin scraped the ground as he saw them coming.

Saracens, led by Skald, advanced onto the field, their weapons drawn and their faces dark with killing rage. They surrounded Jayr in a loose circle as the seneschal went to stand beside her.

Skald looked down at her with an expression of pity. "My master is dead, and my men think you killed him."

Jayr answered him, her voice low and clear: "I did not do it."

"I know. I did. He would not let me claim my bloodright, you see. After I slay you and this fool hanging above us, I will finish your master. My younger brother, in fact." Skald cocked his head. "You can tell the men that I am the murderer, not you. Do you speak Italian, or Arabic?"

"Kill me." Jayr looked past the seneschal, and for an instant her eyes met Byrne's. "Blame me for all of it. Only spare my lord." She cried out as Skald leaned his weight against the lance, driving it deeper into her body. "Please."

"Aedan took everything that belonged to me in Scotland. I was born first, but because my mother was a villein and unmarried, the laird named him heir. When I went to him and told him I was his son, my father sent me away." Skald looked down at her. "I tried to kill my brother at Bannock, to regain my bloodright, but you spoiled that. I had to go away. I tried to forget. I went to Italy. The mac Byrnes died out and I thought . . ." He shook his head.

"My lord does not know you are his brother." Jayr gasped. "Tell him. He will welcome you in his house."

Skald laughed. "He would not wipe his boots on me." He held out his hand, and one of the Saracens gave him another lance. "They will say it took two lances to kill you. You will become a legend among the seneschal." He lifted the weapon above his shoulder, aligning it with her heart.

Madness devoured pain as Byrne rose from the ground.

Jayr refused to close her eyes. Her time here had come to an end, and although she ached with the thought of dying now, she would not cower from it. She turned her face away from Skald, determined that the very last thing she would ever see would be of her choosing.

She chose to look upon Aedan mac Byrne, her lord and master, the one she loved above all others.

Somehow Byrne had risen from the ground, the long knife Skald had thrown still buried in his back. He came forward, his steps silent, his face more like a terrible mask than the visage of a living man. His eyes had changed from deep, melancholy twilight blue to a glowing garnet red that spread over the whites and made it seem as if his eye sockets were filled with blood.

The eyes of a warrior gone berserker.

"What do you stare at, girl?" Skald asked.

She answered him honestly. "Death."

The Saracens had sharper ears, and one of them turned just as Byrne was upon him. One huge hand crushed the guard's throat as the other took his ax. The guards around him began to shout, and then fell silent as the ax flashed through the air around them. Their bodies stood rigid as their heads began tumbling from their shoulders, bouncing around their feet.

Byrne began chopping his way through the Saracens, cutting them down as if they were little more than deadwood. Some were able to raise their crescent-curved blades, but the ax severed their arms before they could land a blow.

Nothing stopped a warrior in berserker, the battle rage.

Byrne had told Jayr that men with his affliction did not recognize friend, foe, or innocent on the battlefield. Taken by berserker rage, the warriors knew only that what lived had to die by their hand. Byrne would butcher everyone in his path until there was no one left to kill.

Skald reacted to the hail of limbs and heads by turning back to her, shifting his weight as he brought down the lance. Jayr kicked out with her leg, smashing her boot into the seneschal's ankle. The lance scored the top of her shoulder but landed in the ground, pelting her face with dirt.

"You worthless piss catcher," Skald shouted, reaching for the lance. His head snapped back as his right eye sprouted an arrow, and he screamed.

Jayr took hold of the first lance and with a wrenching cry pulled it out of her shoulder. She saw the seigneur lowering Locksley to the ground, and beyond him Nottingham fitting an arrow to the bow he held.

Skald tried to do the same with the arrow in his face, cursing and weeping as he grasped the long shaft. "'Tis my birthright, not his. It'll be mine now, all of it, and I'll burn it down before I let them take it away." He looked up into Byrne's bloodred eyes. "I am the eldest son, the mac Byrne; it is all to be mine, not yours."

The ax came down, splitting Skald's head and cleaving through him until his body fell apart, the two halves spilling his blood and insides across the ground.

Jayr saw Byrne walk over Skald's remains as he stalked toward Nottingham. Alexandra shouted for Michael, and the men of the Realm hauled back what Saracens still lived. No one could stop Byrne, however, and anyone who tried would be slain.

Jayr pressed her hand over the wound in her shoulder and took a deep breath before she flashed across the field, stopping in front of Nottingham.

"Aedan," she said, holding herself up by force of will alone. "The battle is over now. You have won."

Blood and gore dripped from the ax Byrne held and spattered Jayr's face as he raised it. She did not flinch, but kept her

gaze steady as she looked into the violence in his eyes and held
out her hands.

"I know you can hear me," she told him. "I am here, my lord.
I need you with me. I love you. Come back to me now."

The ax froze in place before the hands gripping it slowly
lowered it to the ground. The bloodied shaft slipped free of
Byrne's fingers as he stared at her as though mesmerized.

"Here," he muttered. "Alive."

"Yes, my love." She smiled, moving in to grasp the hands
lifting toward her. "You saved my life."

"Life. Saved." At her touch the blood rage in his eyes faded,
and Aedan mac Byrne emerged from his personal hell to pull
his woman into his arms. "Jayr."

Chapter 21

Michael Cyprien supervised the removal of the dead and the wounded from the field while Alexandra converted the infirmary and four other rooms next to it to a temporary hospital. She inspected Jayr's lance wound first, but found that lingering inflammation from the earlier dislocation had actually protected the bones of her shoulder from being broken by the lance.

"You won't be arm wrestling anyone for a few days," Alexandra told her as she strapped her into a sling, "but leave it alone and rest, and it should heal without complications."

Byrne assured her that he would personally supervise Jayr's recuperation before he carried his seneschal out of the infirmary.

The few surviving Saracens refused to let Alexandra touch them until Michael explained in Italian what had happened. The sight of Nottingham terrified the men, and Michael had to send him out of the infirmary before they would rest.

Michael instructed Harlech to move the bodies of Skald and seventeen dead Saracens to an outbuilding for later burial.

Alexandra worked tirelessly through the night, and Michael stayed with her, helping her treat the wounded and doing what he could to make them comfortable. When the last patient had been seen, he took her back to their rooms and coaxed her into bed, where she fell asleep as soon as her eyes closed.

For two hours Michael lay beside his woman, holding her and breathing in her scent as he thought of nothing in particular. After the day of betrayals, carnage, and destruction, simply being with her felt like a miracle. Skald could have easily killed either or both of them while they were drugged. He suspected the kindness Alex had shown to the deranged seneschal had saved their lives.

The next evening Michael summoned his suzerains to the guard hall to decide what was to be done about Nottingham. Alexandra insisted on attending.

"If there's going to be a trial, I want to be there," she told him. "And Nottingham should have an attorney."

Michael chuckled. "The Kyn do not have attorneys, Alexandra. Nor do we want them. Attorneys are like the plague. No, they are like *two* plagues."

"Nottingham can't speak up to defend himself," she told him as she changed. "If you want this to be fair, he needs someone to represent him and tell his story."

"If Skald did not invent his story," Michael pointed out.

"I don't think he did." She turned so he could zip up the back of her dress. "This is going to sound weird, but I think Skald really felt sorry for Nottingham."

Michael sighed. "Alexandra, he tried to cut off his head."

"Yeah, but before that he seemed really sympathetic." She clipped her curls back from her face. "Do I look okay?"

He caught a stray curl near her ear and tugged it gently. "You are beautiful."

"You won't kill him, will you?" she entreated him. "I didn't perform the world's first successful head reattachment on Nottingham just so some pissed-off Kyn could cut it off again."

"I think his near-beheading was close enough." Michael kissed her. "Don't worry, *chérie*. Even the Kyn can be reasonable and open-minded on occasion." He held out his arm.

Alex shook her head. "You go ahead. I need to stop by the infirmary and check on my patients. I'll meet you there."

Michael went to the guards' hall, where every suzerain at the Realm was present, along with Byrne, Jayr, and Locksley. Byrne looked calm and, for the first time since Michael had known him, completely at peace. Beside him Jayr sat, silently watchful and curiously radiant.

Michael took the time to greet each of his lords before standing up and addressing the room. "Much has happened since yesterday, and to dispel the rumors that are doubtless running rampant, I will tell you what I know is fact."

He began with the attack on Byrne, and how Skald had framed Jayr for it, and then progressed to the challenge and the second attack on Nottingham, finishing with the brief, bloody battle on the practice field.

"What we do not know is whether Skald acted alone, of his own volition, or if he was doing so with the knowledge and consent of Lord Nottingham," Michael said, and paused before adding, "Before Skald drugged my *sygkenis* and attempted to behead his master, he told Alexandra that Ganelon of Florence was once known as Guy of Guisbourne."

Locksley choked on the wine he was sipping.

The suzerains muttered among themselves; they were not men prone to shouting in outrage, but their anger was clear. Michael held up his hand and, when silence fell over the room, continued.

"Most of us were at court the day Richard passed judgment on the traitors of Sherwood. We witnessed many executions, including Guisbourne's." He glanced at Locksley, who sat rigid with disbelief. "Robin, if there is some possibility that your kinsman did survive—"

"I buried his parts in five different graves," Locksley said, his damaged voice rasping out the words. "The dwarf lied. Guisbourne is dead."

"Well, whoever this Italian is, he is behind the attacks," Adolfo put in. "That much is plain."

"I agree. That fool seneschal couldn't have acted alone," Halkirk said. "Even if he was, as he told Jayr, Lord Byrne's brother, he didn't have the wits to plan his revenge. Nottingham came here seeking power, new territory, and men. He could have easily encouraged his seneschal's madness to serve his own purposes."

"Nice theory," Alexandra said as she came into the hall with Nottingham. "Problem is, it's totally wrong."

Michael gave her an exasperated look. "I know you wish to defend this man, Alexandra, but you cannot know what he thought or did."

"Sure I can." She held up a pad of paper. "He wrote down the whole story." She offered it to Michael. "You can read it later. I'll give you the short version. It's a real eye-opener."

Alexandra repeated the story Skald had told her, detailing how after Marian's death Guisbourne had been replaced by his bastard half brother, and ultimately driven from England long before the *jardin* wars had taken place.

"No one can substantiate this tale," Halkirk objected when she finished. "Skald is dead. The Saracens know nothing of Nottingham's life before he came to Italy. What proof can he offer that what he has written is truth?"

"I will testify that it is," Viviana said as she entered the guards' hall with Rainer and Farlae. "So will Rainer." She glanced at Nottingham before she faced Michael. "Seigneur, we are the last survivors of Sherwood *jardin.*"

Alex felt better after Viviana and Rainer supported Nottingham's story, even when they diplomatically left out some important details. Although she suspected the details weren't important, she thought Nottingham deserved to have the entire truth known.

"Is there any more to be said before I decide Lord Nottingham's fate?" Cyprien asked after he gave Viviana and Rainer a full pardon.

"I have a question." Alex turned to Locksley. "Why have you been telling everyone for years that Lady Marian came to you for help?"

Locksley glowered. "Because she did."

"She asked you to kidnap her the night before her wedding?" Alex asked. "I'm thinking *no* here, Robin."

Locksley shoved away from the table and tried to stalk out. Phillipe and Will Scarlet barred the door.

"Master," Will said gently. "They will understand."

Locksley stared at his seneschal. "Lady Alexandra, you are meddling in matters that will only cause pain to those who do not deserve it."

"No pain, no gain," she replied. "Robin, you need to set things straight. For you and the other people here who were involved."

"If that is the sad song you would have me sing, my lady, so be it." Locksley strode to the center of the room and faced Nottingham. "You know the stories that have been told about

Lady Marian and me and Guy of Guisbourne. We both loved her, that much is true. But the real Marian never loved either of us. She had been sent away to the convent when she was but ten to be educated, and that gentle, reverent life captivated her. She chose to devote her life to God. She was . . ." He stopped, and covered his face with his hand.

Byrne picked up the story from there. "Marian's father refused to let her take vows. She was his only child, and a wealthy heiress in her own right. He betrothed her instead to Guy of Guisbourne, that he might find favor with the king. When she pleaded with Guisbourne to release her, he forced her into his bed." He watched Locksley walk over to the window.

"What the boys aren't saying is that all this was too much for her," Alexandra said. "Marian went crazy. She had to be locked up."

Everyone looked at Locksley, who stood with his back to the room.

"We played together as children, Marian and I," he said softly, unexpectedly. "I loved her more than my life. When I saw what Guy had done to her, I took her away to Scotland. My old friend Aedan arranged for her to live at a convent in the Highlands, where the sisters could care for her." He turned around. "Alexandra, how did you know that she had gone mad? Only Byrne and I knew the truth."

"Guy knew." She picked up the pad. "He wrote it all down."

Locksley shook his head. "After I became an outlaw, Byrne sent word that Marian had died in childbirth. The baby, a daughter, survived. To protect her from her father, Byrne and I sent the child to be raised in another convent in the south of England. I joined the Templars and did not come back to England until I had become Kyn. I went to find Marian's daughter, to see that she was well, but found that she had run away to Scotland. She had not wished to become a nun, you see. She went looking for her parents."

Jayr turned and stared in horror at Nottingham.

"I did not meet her until the last battle of Bannockburn," Robin said. "I found her in a pit trap with my old friend. She had saved his life by giving him her blood, but the vein continued to bleed after he had fed. I found her dying in his arms." He walked up to Byrne and Jayr. "'Twas I who took you from the pit that day, Jayr. I gave you my blood to change you. I cursed you to become Kyn."

Michael broke the silence that followed. "Lord Nottingham, the testimony offered by others forces me to accept your claims. However, you concealed your identity from us. Your seneschal caused many, unnecessary deaths as he sought his revenge, and there is no way for us to know whether you were privy to his plans. For these reasons, I will not accept your oath or your presence among us. As soon as your men are well enough to travel, you will go. You are banished from this country."

Nottingham rose from the table, bowed to Cyprien, and then faced Jayr. He tore open his tunic, baring the left side of his chest. He then bowed to Alexandra and left the hall.

Jayr held Byrne's hand tightly as she tried to digest all she had heard. That someone as dark and cold as Nottingham could be her father seemed unbelievable to her. So, too, the thought of Lady-Marian, the heroine of a thousand tales, being her mother.

"Aedan mac Byrne," Cyprien said. "Do you still wish to step down as suzerain of the Realm?"

Byrne met her gaze for a moment and nodded.

"I have made my decision on the one who will take your place." Michael drew his sword. "Jayr, come forward."

Jayr frowned. Why would the seigneur need her assistance in appointing a suzerain? Shrugging, she rose and went to stand beside him.

"No," he said as he guided her around to face him. "Here. Kneel, Jayr of the Realm."

Utterly confused, Jayr went down on one knee.

"For your continual courage and devotion to the men and women of this *jardin*," Michael said, raising his sword over her head to touch the flat of the blade to the top of one shoulder, then the other, "I name you lady paramount, suzeraina of the Realm." He held out his hand to her. "Rise, Lady Jayr."

Jayr took his hand with hers and stood. It had to be a mistake. A jest, that was it. The seigneur was making merry with her. But if he was, then why were the other lords in the room on their feet, applauding? Why would Alexandra be smiling at her so? And Byrne . . .

Byrne came to stand before her, his eyes glowing. "I fear I must cancel our travel plans, my lady."

"Aedan," she whispered. "This cannot be happening."

"Come." He drew her away and led her to the alcove where he had first kissed her. "I am so proud of you."

"What? Why?" She tried to shrug off the numbness of her shock. "I did nothing to merit this."

He shook his head. "You saved me. You stood up to Nottingham. You showed the Kyn what truth and honor mean."

"But Aedan, no female has ever ruled the Kyn," she argued. "I have no training for this. Who am I? An unwanted bastard child whose black-hearted father raped her mother and drove her insane."

"You are my lady," he said, and kissed her.

When he lifted his head she said, "You will not leave now, will you? I do not want the Realm if I cannot have you with it."

"I know now there is one Kyn who can stop me from killing and bring me back from hell. So before you take oaths of loyalty from your men, I would offer you mine," he said, dropping to one knee in front of her. "I willingly undergo everything for you, my lady, and will serve as your seneschal for all the days of my life. Will you accept my service?"

Jayr covered her mouth with her hand to hold back a semi-hysterical laugh. Her lord, kneeling before her. Pledging himself to her. Never could she have dreamed such a thing. Then his scent drifted over her, and the calm he always brought to her heart made it all so simple and clear.

"I accept you as my seneschal, Aedan mac Byrne," she said softly. "I give you service, honor, and the protection of my house." She bent over to kiss him. "And I give you my heart, and my love, for all the days of our life together. Evermore."

Alexandra began carrying Michael's mobile phone around in her pocket, hoping it would ring before they left the Realm for the airport. As she was tidying up the infirmary, it did.

"Alex Keller. This had better be my brother, the idiot who should have called long before now."

"I'm happy to hear your voice, too," John said. "How are you, little sister? Did you have fun at the tournament?"

She looked at the mound of bloody, used dressings in her hands. "Like you wouldn't believe. Where are you, Johnny?"

"Sacramento. I got a call from one of my ex-Brethren friends in North Carolina." His voice chilled. "Seems the order has set up breeding facilities, using runaways and homeless kids, all over the U.S."

"What are they breeding?"

"Future Brethren."

"That's just peachy." Alex tossed away the bandages. "What are you doing? Why are you involved in this at all? Why not call the police?"

"I'm looking for the central breeding facility, which is out here in California somewhere." Now he sounded tired. "I know how the Brethren work, and I'm human; they're expecting vampires to attack them. The police would never believe any of this; you know that."

It seemed her brother had found another hopeless cause. "So what can you do about it?"

"Find it and gather all the information I can about it to bring back to Cyprien."

"*My* Cyprien?" she echoed.

"He has enough influence and power to expose this and put a stop to it," John said.

Alex rubbed her forehead. "Big brother, the last time Michael went after the Brethren, they used copper pipes to beat off his face."

"It will be different this time, Alexandra. I don't have time to explain, but"—the sound of a distant car horn came over the line—"I have to go; that's my ride. I'll be in touch."

"Johnny—" Alex heard the line click, and then disconnect. She stared at the phone for several seconds, then swore and began beating it against one of the metal-topped exam tables. "Stupid, stubborn, suicidal son of a bitch."

"You called?" Robin of Locksley said from the doorway.

"Not anymore." Alex dropped what was left of the battered mobile phone into the trash bin before beckoning Locksley inside. "Before you take off for Atlanta I'd like to get a blood sample from you."

"Have I not spilled enough at this tourney?" he quipped.

"I need it for the database. It'll only take a minute, and it'll help me calm down." She smiled. "You aren't afraid of needles, are you?"

"You must make haste," he told her as he followed her inside. "Scarlet says we must reach the highway before morning rush hour. He becomes very irate if we do not."

"Men—always trying to beat the gridlock. That's what creates it, you know." She took out a syringe and gestured toward an empty chair. "I meant to ask you something earlier. When you got to Bannockburn, how did you know that Jayr was Marian's daughter? Will told me she doesn't look anything like her mother."

"She wore Marian's ring on a chain around her neck," he said, the amusement fading from his expression. "I left it with the child when I took her to the south of England."

"It's a plain gold ring," Alex pointed out.

"Engraved with the words 'Joy always, your Maryan,'" he replied evenly. "I checked."

"Maryan with a y?"

"'Twas the old way she wrote it." Robin shrugged. "Are we finished now?"

"Scarlet will wait. Let me take one more look at that neck." Alex pushed up his chin and released the first three buttons of his shirt. The ligature wounds left by the copper cable had closed but had not vanished; a thin, raw-looking scar encircled his throat.

"Pretty, isn't it?" he asked the light fixture.

"I've seen better," she told him as she palpated the healing tissues. "Korvel, Richard's seneschal, has a much more macho ring around the collar. He told me he'd been hanged for a couple of weeks."

He grimaced. "I believe I will be satisfied with my scars as they are."

"Good plan." She tilted his head to one side to check beneath his ears. "Yours will eventually harden and turn green as the copper deposits in your skin oxidize, but they shouldn't be too noticeable. Why would Marian have a ring engraved to herself?"

"Perhaps she meant to give it as a parting gift to someone, and never had the chance." He plucked the penlight out of her pocket and played with it. "So where do you and Michael travel next? Chicago, or New Orleans?"

"I think we have to go to Europe for some big seigneur to-do. Should be nonstop laughs." She sighed and patted his chest, then frowned as she felt a depression in the pectoral muscle. "What's this? Someone get you here, too?"

"No." He reached as if to stop her from unfastening more buttons, and then let his hand drop to his thigh. " 'Tis nothing, Alexandra. An old scratch."

"A scratch, huh?" She pulled his shirt aside and inspected the faint depression below his left clavicle. "More like a missing chunk of manly chest. Who did this to you?"

"A fool."

"Before you grew fangs, or after?"

"After."

Alex's fingers told her that the unnamed fool had gouged out a plum-size section of skin and most of the underlying tissue, yet there was no evidence of any sort of penetrating wound.

Locksley scowled down at her fingers. "Must you poke like that?"

"Considering that the only weapon that could have caused this wound would have had to have been made of copper, and this is right over your heart, yeah, I do." Alex stepped back and tilted her head as she studied his chest. "You know, if I were going to stab you in the chest, I wouldn't do it sideways."

The side of his mouth curled. "Fortunately for me, few assassins have your skill with a blade." He stood and went to work on the buttons.

Alex covered his hand with hers and made him trace the outline of the depression. "Look how it's shaped. Like a heart with a dent in the side. Whaddaya know? Now where have I seen that before?"

"It matters not, I assure you. Now I must be off." Quickly he turned her hand over and raised it to his lips. "It has been a delight, my lady."

"Port-wine birthmarks are hereditary," she said bluntly, pulling her hand away before he could kiss it. "Passed from parent to child. They commonly show up in the same area on the body."

"As you say." He walked toward the door.

She beat him to it and braced her arm across the threshold. "And without laser treatments, the only way to get rid of them is by skin graft or excision." She saw his eyes darken. "We already know the Iceman doesn't have one. That's why he left out the part about raping Marian when he wrote up his statement. He didn't do that to her, and he tore open his shirt and flashed Jayr to prove it. No birthmark, no rape."

His lips turned white. "Marian had such a mark. She passed it to Jayr."

"Unless you saw Marian naked to the waist down," she countered, "how would you know that?" She waited, but he said nothing. "You didn't recognize Jayr by the ring she wore, and you didn't turn her from human to Kyn just because she was Marian's daughter. You knew the minute you saw that birthmark whose daughter she was." When Locksley didn't reply, she added, "Fine. But I am right about Guy, aren't I? He told the truth when he said that he never touched Marian, didn't he?"

"What a man covets drives him to do desperate things." Locksley unsheathed his dagger and made it dance across his fingers. "Byrne, Nottingham, even poor Skald, all victims of their secret desires. Wouldn't you agree, Alex?"

"Robin."

"I cannot give you the answers you seek." The blade began to spin faster. "I will wager that if the parent who shares Jayr's birthmark ever had discovered her existence, he would never have claimed her as daughter."

"And why the hell not?"

"Marian went mad, but she remained a maiden. At least she did, it was said, until a fool in love tried to bring her back to sanity." His eyes lost their focus as his vision turned inward. "I cannot defend him, but perhaps he thought that by showing her all of the ways that men and woman love, she would come back to him."

Alex swore under her breath.

"Instead, his act of love only made her retreat into a different sort of madness. A silent stillness so profound that she seemed to be sleeping with her eyes open. The sort of madness from which one never awakes." Robin closed his eyes, took in a quick breath, and then looked at her. "Guisbourne did not kill Marian. Neither did the child. The fool who forced his love upon her did."

She groped for something to say. "So he made up for what he did to Marian by looking out for her kid."

"His child. Marian never wished to be a mother, only a nun." Locksley spun the blade so fast that air whistled around the metal. "If the fool did do as you say, I think he must have done so in secret."

"Secrets catch up with you, if you haven't noticed." Alex shook her head. "I have a feeling this one will come back and bite that fool in the ass someday."

The blade snapped into his fist. "Lucky, then, that we will never know who he was." The charm returned in full force as he slid the dagger back into its sheath. He took her hand and kissed the back of it. "Until we meet again, my lady."

"Robin, you have to tell Jayr."

"Tell Jayr what, Alexandra?" he asked as he straightened. "That her father was an unfeeling, selfish bastard so obsessed with having the one woman he had ever loved that he killed her? She already knows that." He ducked under her arm, going out into the corridor, but stopped and turned to give her one last, bleak look. "By God, so does he."

Turn the page for a special preview
of Lynn Viehl's next Novel of the Darkyn,

TWILIGHT FALL

Coming in July 2008 from Onyx

"I've learned to cultivate many heirloom flowers over the years," Liling said. "But I still miss Mrs. Chen's gardens, and that ugly, cranky, suicidal apricot rosebush of hers."

A sudden bump of turbulence made Valentin frown, and Liling wrapped both hands in a protective gesture around her teacup.

She peered through the window. "The clouds out there look very dark." Lightning flashed, and she drew back and shuddered.

"I had thought the weather would be clear for the flight." Valentin pressed the intercom button on the console. "Is there a problem?"

"We've encountered an unexpected storm, sir," the pilot replied through the cabin speaker. "We're ascending to avoid the worst of it. You should keep your seat belts fastened until we're clear."

"Thank you." He didn't care for how the pilot's voice had wavered; the man sounded as if he were as nervous as Liling. He looked across to her and noted how her color had changed and her lips were pressed together. "It should be over in a few minutes."

Liling nodded, but her eyes stayed fixed on the window.

The turbulence increased until the jet bounced as though it were on springs. Liling lost her grip on her teacup, which flew across to smash against Valentin's chest.

"Mr. Jaus." She fumbled with her seat belt before she knelt in the space between their seats. She brushed away the broken bits of porcelain and pressed her linen napkin against the quickly spreading stain. "Did it cut you? Are you hurt?"

"I'm only a little wet." Seeing her like this, on her knees in front of him, made his fangs ache.

"That tea was so hot." She pressed her full lips together as she lifted the napkin to look beneath it before her anxious gaze moved up to his face. "It must have scalded you."

Oh, he was burning, but the tea was nothing compared to her touch, her scent, the midnight delights beckoning to him from the darkness in her eyes. The tantalizing perfume of her skin, like sun-warmed peaches, filled his head, his thoughts, his blood. He bent, wondering if her lips would feel as soft and sweet as her breath against his skin.

"Valentin?" Liling's lips parted on his name.

If you kiss her, you will take her.

"It's nothing, Miss Harper." As Valentin rose, he reached down and gently lifted her, placing her back in her seat. "I keep a change of clothing in the back cabin," he told her as he fastened her seat belt over her lap. "Please excuse me for a moment."

Valentin focused on regaining control as he walked into the back cabin. He felt nothing for Liling, just as she felt nothing for him. The turbulence must have triggered his defensive instincts; shedding so much scent in such a confined space would have bespelled any human. By the time he changed and calmed himself, the effects of *l'attrait* would wear off. Liling would never realize how close she had come to being ravaged by his endless, cursed hunger.

He didn't bother with the lights; like all Darkyn, he didn't need them to see. Shrugging out of his jacket, he pulled off his tie and reached for the top button. As always, it resisted his one-handed efforts to unfasten it. It infuriated him to be so clumsy, even though he knew there was nothing to be done about it. He might be a cripple, but he would be damned if he would be reduced to having someone else dress him.

The shirt was new, the fabric around the buttons stiff and unyielding. Viciously he tore at the front of it, sending buttons flying as he ripped it from his body.

"Mr. Jaus? I found a towel and a first-aid kit in the restroom." The door to the cabin opened, and a small shadow blocked out the light shining in from the center cabin. "Do you need some help? There's some burn cream here."

"I am not burned." He didn't want her to see the flash of his fangs, which had sprung into his mouth the moment he had heard her voice. "Thank you, Miss Harper. Please go back to your seat before the turbulence begins again."

"This was my fault." Liling looked down at the buttons on the carpet around his feet and stepped inside, closing the door behind her. "Please, let me help you." She put her hand on his useless arm. "It's the least . . . I can . . ." She went silent as her fingertips brushed over the long, narrow recess in his flesh. The place where Thierry Durand had brought down his blade and severed Valentin's arm from his body.

The towel fell from Liling's other hand as she gently traced the length of his scar, following it all around his arm. "What happened to you?"

"It was an unfortunate accident." He turned his head so he would not see the pity on her face. "There was only so much the physician was able to do to repair it."

"When did you have the reattachment surgery?" Her voice sounded thin and strained.

"Some time ago." He hated her seeing him like this, only half a man. He did not want to face her sympathy or her revulsion. "I am partially paralyzed, Miss Harper, not helpless. You may leave me to deal with this."

Instead of hurrying away, Liling stepped closer, bringing her other hand up to the scar. She bent forward and brushed her lips against the recess of flesh.

Valentin went still. "What are you doing?"

Her lips moved against his scar, but whatever she said was lost in the accompanying rush of sensation. Human warmth, effortless and beautiful, wrapped around his cool flesh and sank into him, until he thought he could feel it seeping into his very bones.

No lover had ever touched him like this.

The delicate curve of Liling's cheek brushed his shoulder as her small hands slid down to become the gentlest of bracelets. She looked up at him, tears making her black eyes wet. "I'm sorry. I'm so sorry."

Sympathy had always angered him, but hers only made him wish she had been there the night he had lost the duel with Thierry. Her touch might have saved him then.

It was too late now.

Valentin tried to move away from her but discovered that he didn't want the moment to end. Before she could speak of her pity again, he brought his good arm up around her narrow waist, curling it around to pull her closer.

"No," he murmured when she stiffened. "Stay."

He closed his eyes as Liling relaxed and rested her hands on his chest, where the warmth followed and lingered, surrounding the cold stone of his heart.

He held her for as long as he dared, until the need to taste her became a beast, clawing and writhing inside him. Then, very carefully, he took her hand and brought it to his lips.

That her compassion aroused him as much as her beauty made him even more disgusted with himself. "You should be careful. You don't know what you do to me, *mein mädchen.*"

"I'm touching you," she said, her voice low and shy. "I wish I could do more."

Valentin despised himself for using his talent, but it didn't stop him from asking her, "What more do you want?"

"I'd like to kiss your mouth." Her fingers turned in his, pressing against his lips. "And put my hands on you, and move them all over you. I want to be naked with you. I've thought about how it would be. How you would make me feel. I've dreamed of you with me, in my bed, and then I wake up all alone and shaking."

"You cannot desire me." He could not believe her words. *L'attrait* compelled her to make such claims, not her heart. "Tell me the truth, Liling. Now."

"I've wanted you since the first time I saw you," she answered, the words leaving her lips with halting reluctance, as if she fought saying them. It was the same with every human he compelled to tell him something they considered a shameful secret. "It was when you brought Luisa the camellias for the first time. I saw you and thought you were a prince out of a fairy tale. Then you spoke to her, and I knew that you were better than a prince. You treated Luisa with such kindness and respect." She swallowed. "I envied her your friendship."

Valentin's hand trembled as he slid it into her hair to cradle the back of her head. "Why did you never say anything to me?"

"You're an important man," she whispered. "I'm only a gardener. I knew I could never be with you."

"Liling." He kissed her forehead, the bridge of her nose, the curl of her upper lip, the curve of her jaw, and breathed in the luscious scent of her. "You were wrong."

SEDUCTIVE VAMPIRE ROMANCE FROM

LYNN VIEHL

The Novels of the Darkyn

A *USA TODAY* BESTSELLING SERIES!

If Angels Burn

Private Demon

Dark Need

Night Lost

"Darker than sin, erotic as hell, and better than good chocolate...Viehl opens a rich and tasty vein and treats the vampire universe to a sharp new set of fangs."
—Holly Lisle

Available wherever books are sold or at penguin.com

J.R. WARD

DARK LOVER

THE DEBUT NOVEL IN THE *NEW YORK TIMES* BESTSELLING BLACK DAGGER BROTHERHOOD SERIES

"Deliciously edgy, erotic and thrilling."
—*New York Times* bestseller Nicole Jordan

In the shadows of the night in Caldwell, New York, there's a deadly turf war going on between vampires and their slayers. There exists a secret band of brothers like no other—six vampire warriors, defenders of their race. Yet none of them relishes killing more than Wrath, the leader of The Black Dagger Brotherhood.

The only purebred vampire left on earth, Wrath has a score to settle with the slayers who murdered his parents centuries ago. But, when one of his most trusted fighters is killed—leaving his half-breed daughter unaware of his existence or her fate—Wrath must usher her into the world of the undead—a world of sensuality beyond her wildest dreams.

Available wherever books are sold or at penguin.com